M000218558

BASED ON A STRANGE BUT TRUE EVENT

THE CIRCUS PIG

AND THE

KAISER

A NOVEL

CAROLYN KAY BRANCATO

STATION
SQUARE
═ MEDIA ═
NEW YORK, NEW YORK

THE CIRCUS PIG AND THE KAISER: A Novel Based on a Strange But True Event
Copyright © 2019 by Carolyn Kay Brancato
Published by Station Square Media
115 East 23rd Street, 3rd Floor
New York, NY 10010

All rights reserved. No part of this book may be reproduced, stored in a retrieval system, or transmitted in any form or by any means, electronic, mechanical, or otherwise, without the prior written permission of the author, except for brief quotations in articles and reviews.

Disclaimer:
This novel is a satirical tale based on one historically accurate incident. Although the author conducted extensive research into the period, both for Germany and Russia, all characters in the novel are entirely made up and bear no resemblance to actual people. To this day, there continues to operate a circus in Moscow run by the descendants of Vladimir Leonidovich Durov, who, according to their website, train small circus animals without cruelty.

Editorial Production: Diane O'Connell, Write to Sell Your Book, LLC
Copyeditor: Linda H. Dolan
Cover and Layout Design: Steven Plummer/SP Book Design
Production Management: Janet Spencer King, Book Development Group

Printed in the United States of America for Worldwide Distribution

ISBN: 978-1-7336380-0-5

Electronic editions:
      Mobi ISBN: 978-1-7336380-1-2
      EPUB ISBN978-1-7336380-2-9

First Edition

DEDICATION

To Howard

And to all those artists and journalists who dedicate their
lives to preserving freedom of expression

CHAPTER ONE

June 1907, Eastern Germany on the Border with Russia

SLIVERS OF LIGHT streak through the flaps of the circus tent. They refract into a rainbow as the setting sun melds into the reds, yellows, and blues of the big top, which isn't very big at all—though it makes up in color for what it lacks in stature. Vladimir Leonidovich Durov chuckles as he admires the benches he's directed the stagehands to arrange in neat rows. Perfectly suitable for their new audience in Germany, which he's certain will be much more orderly than the slovenly Russian crowds back home. Soft calliope music wafts from the peanut stand, which doubles as the ticket booth, proudly welcoming customers. Soon it will be show time and Durov experiences a rush, a thrill. But he also feels the familiar stab of fear he can't escape before every performance, even after all these years. And tonight, that fear claws at his gut as never before. So much is riding on this performance, which will determine not only his future but the destiny of their entire impoverished little circus as well.

In his midthirties, Durov has an honorable square jaw and an earnest but weathered face. Despite his bulky frame, he is always buoyant, dancing on his flat feet—rather like Lyudmila, the trained brown bear. Backstage, he kneels and, with great reverence, opens his heavy leather trunk that's covered with faded travel stickers. Pawing with his powerful, calloused hands, he grins as he picks up the dainty and elaborate costume his younger brother, Anatoly Mikhailovich Durov, has lovingly sewn for his Sasha. Delicate gold braid catches the light, refracting back into his proud, sparkling eyes. Suddenly, the light from a red stripe on the tent casts a deep scarlet glow over the bosom of the costume, blossoming like spilled blood onto the rest of the material.

He sucks in a deep breath and crosses himself in the Russian Orthodox manner. *Otbrosit' d'yavola (I cast out the devil)!* He whisks the costume from the light and tries to quell the terror rising in him by bringing his index and middle two fingers together, kissing them and solemnly laying them on the polished bronze icon that glows inside the trunk—one of dozens he's placed backstage to expel the demons.

Just then, he notices something else. He wrinkles his broad, craggy forehead. A crease in the fabric! *Nyet! Nyet!* This will not do. Tonight, Sasha must be an unqualified success. The whole town is coming, and what a triumph she will be. He swears, "I will uphold the Durov family honor, no matter what the kaiser's dragoons have threatened."

He hurries to smooth the costume and looks down at her, his eyes misting with love. In the radiance of the sunset, Sasha gazes up at him with her soft, deep brown eyes, expectantly waiting for him to dress her. Durov draws in a long, proud breath, infused with the smell of sawdust. Still picturing the kaiser's troops descending upon them, his hands shake and panic wells up. Fighting to get control, he resolves that no matter what befalls them, he will protect his Sasha. He'll defend his family's right to artistic freedom, even in the face of the terrifying authoritarian repression bearing down upon them.

He reaches down to her. "*Da, da, moya devushka.* Yes, my little girl." As he strokes her snout, she snorts and wriggles her dark pink corkscrew tail. "Yes, my little piggala." His eyes twinkle, coaxing her. "Just let me finish straightening out this costume for you." She snorts some more, and he notices, with unabashed pride, that she does not slobber onto the costume.

CHAPTER TWO

Three Months Prior, The Countryside Outside Moscow

STANDS OF WHITE birch, glistening in the brilliant spring sunlight, stretch to the horizon on both sides of the old post road some thirty kilometers from Moscow. A river swirls by, and blindingly bright yellow daffodils push through the rich, snow-encrusted earth. Durov gently urges on his mules, as his wagon rolls steadily along.

"Look at that one! And see that one over there!" He marvels at the fetching elegance of the dachas that the wealthy Muscovites have built on land given them by the tsar. Would that the tsar had given him even a tiny plot, he might have been tempted to settle down. But no, as the wagon lulls him with its sways and bumps, he is content that the traveling circus is in his blood. He leans back and savors the scenery.

Passing by one especially elaborate dacha with numerous porches—front, side, and back—he slaps his younger brother on the back. "Look, Anatoly," he motions with his thick hands. "That one is the most expensive of all." Anatoly, in his early twenties, is taller than Durov, slender as a reed, and quite comely with his boyish mop of curly blonde hair. While Durov has long since resigned himself to his ordinary looks, he's proud that his younger brother is a handsome fellow. Anatoly clearly inherited their mother's striking features.

Anatoly stammers a pleasant reply: "Imagine h-having enough m-money to build such h-homes and only use them p-part of the year."

"Right you are. Lucky we have our very own caravan for the whole year."

"L-lucky we have it at all, after l-last two y-years."

A weakening in his knees causes Durov to shift the reins to one hand and grab onto the sides of the bench with the other. They barely survived the past two years, filled as they were with civil unrest, strikes, and economic downturn. It's only been since the beginning of this year that the tsar has permitted any kind of entertainment to take place, including the wildly popular folk circuses. And much as he and the circus performers and crew despise Nikolai Mikhailovich Kologrivov—the self-important oaf, circus owner, and ringmaster—they're grateful he's called them back together. The small band of performers and crew of the optimistically named *Great Fedorovitch Circus* have agreed to come, despite their unvarnished hatred of Nikolai. This hatred stems not only from his general meanness but also from the knowledge that he's drunk their profits away for years. But having no other form of income, they are now assembling once again; for Durov, this is not only a resurrection from certain starvation, but also a chance to regain his family's honor.

"Anatoly, look back." Durov slaps his thigh. "They're really coming."

The circus people pull their traveling wagons, with huge wooden wheels and colorfully painted sides, then settle them around a large pond where wild ducks wildly quack at the disturbance. When the first stagehands arrive, Durov embraces them, pounding them affectionately on the back. Then they set about erecting a large makeshift tent in a nearby field.

After the tent is erected, the performers make theatrical entrances to remind the others they are great entertainers: the fire-eater arrives in a blaze, clowns on unicycles juggle myriad plates between them, two young ladies contort themselves as they backbend into the tent in perfect synchronicity, the sword-swallower gulps down a flash of steel, four dwarf brothers climb onto each other to form a walking pyramid, and so on. As each act enters, Durov and the others applaud wildly.

"Wonderful to see everyone. At least we have work!" Durov proclaims, a wide grin broadening his already broad features. They twitter and laugh with obvious relief to be assembled once again.

Then Boris, a small man in his forties with a trim goatee, arrives. Durov immediately swoops him up into a bear hug and twirls him around.

Struggling to maintain his composure, Boris says, through smiling but clenched teeth, "Nice to see you too. Now put me down."

Durov booms with laughter and sets the little man down on several boxes piled high. In the circus hierarchy, Boris is relegated to being only a clown, although he's always wanted to be a magician like his late father. He just could never get the hang of all those magic tricks. Nevertheless, Boris always wears his father's magician's top hat (which is much too large) and his father's robe (which is much too long). Even so, Boris has a commanding, precise, and deep Shakespearean voice that belies his pint-sized stature.

"Bloody Sunday," Boris moans. "Outrageous that the tsar's palace guards opened fire on all those peaceful protesters."

Before he can agree with Boris, Durov spies Lottie, pulling her many lavender shawls around her. As the circus fortune-teller, she is a diminutive lady of indeterminate middle age, with a shocking blast of bright red hair. "It's even more unfortunate that we've had to endure all these protests and strikes throughout Mother Russia," she says, taking her place next to Boris. She adds, "Although I could have predicted it."

Durov puts his arms around the two, elated to have things back to normal between them. Lottie the fortune-teller and Boris the would-be magician haven't stopped feuding. Boris insists that magicians are not part of an occult cult, rather they rely on earthly, entirely explainable, sleight-of-hand. Lottie insists her fortune-telling expertise is based on a miasma of the spiritual and otherworldly.

Boris sneers and says, "Of course you would think you predicted it." Then he smiles and adds, "My dear Lottie."

Despite Boris's disparaging remarks, Lottie twitters and adjusts one of her many shawls, reveling in any attention he pays her.

Durov turns to welcome the rest as they make their entrances, his spirits lifting higher and higher with each new arrival. He does not concern himself much about politics, preferring to channel his energies into raising and training his beloved pigs. Still, he had hoped that the tsar, who had a reputation for generosity and fairness, might have been genuinely upset about the violence. But no, the tsar's advisers had vehemently counseled him to refrain from extending any form of civil liberty—the right to freedom of assembly and a free press—that would erode the monarchy.

As a performer in a revered circus family, Durov was taught by his father to explore new ideas, to push the boundaries of entertainment. Fortunately, with his family's horses, this approach never collided with the political issues of that day. And while Durov speaks his mind and believes everyone should have the freedom to do so as a matter of general principle, he's relieved that the tsar has never seen fit to restrict what he now puts into his pig act—counting cards, climbing ladders, sliding down chutes, and so on. Certain now more than ever that his pigs are easier to understand than any of this political stuff, Durov says, "After all we've been through, it's wonderful to see you all." Everyone applauds and cheers.

Just then, Ivan Ivanovich Zubov, the older brother in the Zubov Trapeze Family, barges into the tent. In his late twenties, Ivan is tall, dark, and very handsome, except for a large nose—which, in his perpetual state of arrogance, seems to stick out well beyond the rest of his face. Anna Tatianna Ivanova Zubov, his petite teenage sister, gracefully waltzes in behind.

"What's the meaning of this confab?" Ivan protests.

Durov steps up. "Ivan Ivanovich, we're just getting reacquainted, that's all. No need to start off so bullheaded."

"You mean pigheaded, don't you, pig trainer?" Ivan sneers. "How are those filthy beasts? How many of them did you have to eat to survive?"

Boris jumps up and inserts himself between the two taller men. "Ivan Ivanovich, I wouldn't be so quick to insult Durov here. He's been quite instrumental in organizing the circus for our performance tomorrow evening." Ivan frowns and looks down at Boris, but before Ivan can level an insult, Boris says to Anna, "My dear Anna Tatianna. How you've grown."

Durov turns to look at Anna, who is dark like her brother, with long, raven-black hair and beautiful porcelain skin.

"Why thank you, Boris. I wish I could say that I'd grown here." She giggles and modestly puts her hands on her nonexistent bosom.

Lottie rushes over. "But you look even more beautiful than ever. Doesn't she, Anatoly?"

Durov blanches, recalling how he was responsible for his younger brother growing up with no parents. And now, despite all that, he beams with pride that his dear friends Boris and Lottie think so highly of Anatoly that they want to pair him with the lovely Anna. He wishes Anatoly were not so pitifully shy that his stammer magnified whenever he tried to talk around her.

"W-w-why y-y-yes." Anatoly twists away from her, hiding his face under his curly hair.

Ivan breaks in: "Don't forget, Durov—everyone—the Zubovs are first in the circus parade. We are the highest class of anyone here."

Boris whispers none too softly, "How could we?"

Ivan ignores him. "So whatever you're talking about, we need to know before you talk about it."

Durov smirks. "You'll be the first to know whatever we don't know."

Resisting the urge to punch Ivan on his large nose, Durov steadies himself for the sake of his newly reunited circus family. Ivan is always categorizing people by class, looking down on the various types of circus performers gathered together to make a show. With his ferocious arrogance, he has publicly and unabashedly made fun of what Durov considers the glorious essence of the circus itself—an egalitarian place that attracts performers of every shape and size, from every province of Russia. Durov's thick chest swells with pride to know that the circus awakens in these assorted performers the impulse to create a spectacle that is a unified whole—in a space where magic and dazzle come together. Even better, the circus is democratic—not only for the performers, but also for the audience. A diverse group of aristocrats and workers from every sphere of society sit together, as one, to enjoy the show.

Just then the circus owner, Nikolai Mikhailovich Kologrivov, strides in, snapping his bullwhip and chewing some stray hairs in his grizzled black mustache. "So I see you've all agreed to come back."

Durov sighs. So much for reverie.

Nikolai is a towering lanky man in his late thirties who wears his black tunic cinched at the waist, Cossack style, which gives him an even meaner demeanor. He whips around to Boris, stroking the handle of his whip. "Anytime you want to climb back into your father's magician's trunk and disappear for good, it'll be fine with us."

Durov steps between Nikolai and the smaller man. "Look, Nikolai. We're all here and ready to go to work. Why don't we leave it at that?"

Nikolai cocks an inebriated, bloodshot eye, underneath a bristled, bushy eyebrow. "And I see we have our very own Vladimir Leonidovich Durov with us today to help us set up for tomorrow's performance." He bellows, "We're very happy to have you work for us." He snaps the whip for emphasis.

Durov balls his fists, his weathered face turning crimson. *I should run him out of here right now.* If only the circus were still owned by Durov's family, he could put a stop to Nikolai's incessant and gratuitous cruelty. He thinks back to how the circus came to Nikolai. Nikolai's grandfather had—in the longest-running dice game anyone could remember, during which more barrels of vodka were consumed than anyone could remember—lost the title to the circus to Durov's grandfather. Legend has it that, years later,

Nikolai's father used a trick deck of cards that belonged to Boris's father, the circus magician, to swindle the title back from Durov's father. Notorious for his cruelty to animals, Nikolai's father was mauled to death by an otherwise completely docile brown bear, who had just learned to waltz. Thus, the circus passed to Nikolai, who has systematically attempted to outdo his father's reputation for meanness to any creature he can get his whip on.

Before Durov can rage against Nikolai for swindling the circus away from his family, Ivan intercedes. "Look, Nikolai, pay no attention to this serf." Ivan turns to Durov, sneering. "You'll get things in order for our performance? As always?"

Anatoly tugs at Durov's sleeve, shaking his head vigorously, clearly worried his brother will do something rash.

Durov puts his arm around his brother, nods, and simmers down. "Ivan Ivanovich, of course. All these good people here are depending on it."

Ivan pounds Durov on the back, mocking him in an overt, excessive gesture of goodwill. "Wonderful! Great to see you all." He turns to Nikolai. "Time to seek out the ladies of the countryside? Quite a few dachas are already occupied by those wealthy Muscovites."

Wincing, Durov watches Ivan and Nikolai march off arm in arm, howling with laughter.

Boris looks after them. "At least they'll leave us in peace to set things up."

Lottie sidles up to Boris. "If you need any help, just ask. And I'll get my brother." Lottie's brother Bronzy doubles as the circus strongman and cook.

Boris bows and tips his magician's hat. Out flies a bird. He runs off to catch the bird, calling over his shoulder, "Does your brother have any birdseed in the circus larder?"

The others laugh, collect their things, and under Durov's direction, set up the circus for the next evening's show.

⚜

During the first few performances, Durov paces backstage, ready to spring into action should someone need his help. But the seasoned performers—who have been keeping in shape, as circus people do when they're not traveling—immediately get back into the swing of things. Everything goes remarkably well. Five nights into their run, however, Durov's optimism is shattered as Nikolai returns from a night of womanizing with disastrous news. They must move immediately and get as far away from Moscow as possible. Rumors fly, even as the circus people rush about pulling up stakes.

Boris, in his clown costume, hurries past Anatoly. "I heard Nikolai got himself into quite a pickle."

Durov shouts at the stagehands, "Hurry up with those benches." Then he mutters to Boris, "I heard he picked the wrong woman to seduce. Some highborn lady from Moscow."

"That idiot," Ivan shrieks, as he hauls a wad of netting. "I told him she was above his station. No one listens when I tell them how important class distinctions are."

"Our l-little ones are q-quite upset," simpers Anatoly. "O-oinking terribly, having to p-pick up and r-rush off."

Scurrying past Anatoly, Lottie pulls her shawls closer. "How could he do this to us?"

Durov sighs and crosses himself. He musters his strength to gather them all together for their next journey.

CHAPTER THREE

THE CIRCUS'S MEAGER collection of mules and caravans slowly makes its mournful trek through wide steppes and expansive barley fields toward Western Russia. Durov bemoans the loss of their profitable venue outside Moscow. And while Anatoly sees to their pigs, Durov constantly checks the animals pulling the wagons, making sure they have enough water and food. As they get farther away from Moscow, however, Durov's step lightens. He feels an intense spiritual uplifting as he surveys the verdant ground, where young spikes struggle to burst through the earth and fulfill the spring's promise of renewal.

They approach a border of steep woodlands, backed up against a range of tall, luxuriant mountain firs. Nikolai chooses a field for them to make camp, but Durov is irate. "This field is right in the path of that forest runoff. With any amount of rain, it will turn to mud."

Nikolai's gravelly voice booms, "Vladimir Leonidovich Durov, you are wrong, as always." He zeroes in on Durov with his dark, malignant eyes. "But even if you are right, your pigs will surely feel at home in the mud."

Despite Durov's admonition, Nikolai orders the circus laborers to position their two dozen mules and equal number of rough-hewn circus wagons into a semicircle. Sure enough as Durov warned, a spring rain soon dumps waterfalls onto the circus and turns the ground to mud. The large, wooden wagon wheels, swollen and waterlogged, straightaway soak into the soft ground, making deep ruts.

Durov sighs. *By St. Gregory, why do the fates always rain down upon me?* He genuflects and, resigned, once again organizes the circus stage-hands: "Let's get to work men." They put down a network of planks, laid out in spokes across the deep spring mud. These planks will enable them to walk between the wagons, the practice tents, and the animal corral.

When the planks are laid, Durov and his brother, Anatoly, see to their animals, each bringing two pails of leftovers from the canteen to feed them. Durov dances his solid frame along the planks, whistling happily at the prospect of feeding his dear pigs.

"How are you doing, dear brother?" Durov looks back as Anatoly trots behind, shouldering a wooden pole with a bucket of leftovers balanced on each end. A stab of guilt jolts Durov. His gentle and loving brother has never once blamed him for their family's misfortune with their stallions. In fact, Anatoly seems to love their pigs almost as much as he does—except for Sasha, whom no one could love more than Durov.

Passing Nikolai's wagon, painted with the circus acts from years gone by, creates a searing, painful reminder to Durov of how his own youthful pride caused his family's downfall. This disgrace causes Durov, to this day, to labor under a perpetual state of penance, carrying heavier pails and doing harder work than his younger brother.

Calling over his shoulder, Durov asks, "Are you sure those pails aren't too heavy?"

Anatoly is cheerful as always. "N-not at all. Any more in your b-buckets and they would overflow."

"Well, if you need my help, just say so."

As they come alongside Nikolai's wagon, there is a scream from within, then a slap. Durov abruptly halts and turns back to his brother. Anatoly neatly steps aside on the narrow plank, dodging his brother's large and muscular back. Another scream. Durov's square face reddens, and he squeezes his powerful hands, tightly gripping the handles of the pails.

"I ought to teach that fellow a lesson."

"We-we don't want any t-trouble."

"No trouble to stop a man from beating a woman."

"From b-beating his w-wife, you mean." Anatoly nudges Durov along. "If y-you tried to stop every Russian who b-beat his wife…"

Durov chews his lip in resigned disgust. Damping down his fury, he resolves one day to dish out to Nikolai what Nikolai dishes out to his new wife, Natasha—a fine woman like that, highbred from Moscow. Although he's been a lifelong bachelor, Durov is sure he would know how to treat a woman, based on his vast experience with training animals.

The taller Anatoly looks down at his older brother. "I know you t-think Nikolai Mikhailovich is a c-cad, but we c-can't afford any more t-trouble."

Durov clenches his fists. Nikolai is a cad and a brute, but Anatoly is right. Things have been terribly hard for them lately. First just getting back to work after all those strikes. Then having to pull up stakes after only five performances in the countryside outside Moscow—after Nikolai made a huge blunder by choosing the wrong woman to seduce.

"Why is he allowed to treat such a highborn woman that way? Any woman that way?"

"Be-because no one in Russia comes between a man and his w-wife."

Deftly balancing on the planks, Durov shakes his head in disgust as the noises continue from Nikolai's circus wagon—a lot of scuffling and yet another slap. The noises sharply ricochet off the tall firs, magnifying in the open clearing, where the wagons continue to descend into the mud. Durov is torn: on the one hand, he wants to deliver the food in his pails to his hungry pigs; on the other hand, he wants to tramp directly over to Nikolai's wagon and put an end to the brutality he hears from within.

He hesitates, his normally bright eyes clouding over. "This really isn't my affair." Still, Durov is furious that Nikolai would abuse Natasha. Durov would never be so cruel to any animal, or any human either.

Anatoly sags under the weight of the pails dangling from the ends of his pole. "Durov, c-could we please go. These are h-heavy and the little ones are h-hungry."

Durov sighs deeply as he looks at his younger brother, pale and blonde and pure of heart.

Anatoly puts his pole and the pails down. He musters the courage to speak frankly to his brother. "Madame N-Natasha...she would have been better of-off m-marrying you."

Durov jerks his head back. "It's that obvious? How I feel about her?"

Anatoly scratches his curly head and looks away, ostensibly to check on the leftovers in the bucket. "Pigs are very smart animals," Anatoly hesitates, then continues, "Most-most pe-people don't realize how smart they are. S-see how easy it is to t-train them to count. And pick up each c-card in their mouths and lay it at your feet—so people think they're c-clairvoyant. And climb all the l-ladders. Speaking of l-ladders, I need to reinforce—"

"Is it really that obvious?" Durov's normally deep voice is hushed and an octave lower. "How I feel about Madame Natasha?"

Anatoly says, with a boyish grin, "Well...our dear p-pig Sasha...she is, she's jealous whenever Madame N-Natasha comes over to t-talk to you. Tha-that should tell all you need to kn-know."

"Never really thought of it like that."

Anatoly offers, "There are other w-women in the circus."

"You mean Svetlana, the bearded lady?"

Anatoly smiles weakly. "Or maybe V-Valeria, the fat lady?"

"For Christ's sake. Why not the Siamese twins?"

"Well, t-two are better than one—or none, which seems to be the c-case right now."

"You should talk."

Anatoly shyly kicks one leg back and forth on the plank. "Anna Tatianna

Ivanova w-would never look at a pig trainer like me. She's a t-trapeze artist. They're first in the c-circus parade."

"But she's a lovely girl. A little on the slender side. I prefer a woman with a bit of meat on her bones." Durov chuckles as he traces the lines of a voluptuous woman. "But you're right about Natasha. I can't help being in love with her." Durov lets out a long breath. "Another reason Nikolai hates me."

"He hates you because everyone in the, in the c-circus admires you. They look to you to m-make things right. Besides, even th-though he's married now, all he does is g-go out whoring with Ivan and d-drinking away the box office take."

"My dear brother. You are so right, but what can we do?"

The bright afternoon sunlight slants through the tall firs to the west and onto the muddy clearing. The light glints off the lacquered wagons in the circle, each advertising the skill of the performers within. As Durov bends to pick up his pails, he admires the wagons with rainbows of painted colors on their sides, displaying the decorative artistry of his fellow performers—people he also feels a responsibility to protect from Nikolai. A riot of painted hues. Floating, fanciful bearded ladies, contortionists bent into extreme physical positions, trapeze artists defying gravity without benefit of net, and dwarfs shot from cannons and landing on trampolines.

Even though he loves the whimsical art on the circus wagons, Durov will usually walk out of his way to avoid Nikolai's wagon. But today, he cannot dodge it, the way the planks are laid out in the mud. He comes square up against the paintings of his parents and his family's fine white horses, still showing through the thin wash of paint covering them. Choking back a sob, he makes out the elegance of his mother, glowing in an aura of white tulle as she balances on his father's prized white stallion. Durov struggles to move, emotionally and physically, beyond the bitter past. He thinks how far their little family has fallen in the circus hierarchy—reduced to training pigs, not horses. Even so, he knows Anatoly is right—they must bring Sasha and the little pigs their food. As he passes

Nikolai's wagon, Durov zeros in on the images of Nikolai—the brute him-self—as ringmaster. Much as he would like to, Durov cannot ignore the shrill noises wafting from within.

CHAPTER FOUR

Natasha Sergeyevna Kologrivovana sits in front of an abacus that rests on the small desk in the corner of Nikolai's dreary circus wagon—now hers as well, by marriage. Imprisoned in this nightmarish new world she can hardly believe she now inhabits, she desperately wants to upend the desk and throw the abacus out the small window. She shudders to recall how completely surprised everyone in the circus was when Nikolai appeared with her as his new bride. Pounding her large hand on the desk, she rages to think she's lost everything—her wealthy, refined Moscow family and her comfortable place in society. Begrudgingly she has to admit that, being so tall and euphemistically regarded as "solid," she's never even remotely been considered a beauty. Still, even though she'd been pushing hard against the spinster-confirming age of thirty-five, and even though she'd had few desirable marriage options, she can't believe she'd succumbed to a rakish fellow like Nikolai. She slams her eyes shut and pictures him—tall in his fancy ringmaster's uniform, seducing her after a performance in the countryside outside Moscow. They were caught, and on pain of prison, he was obliged to marry her.

A sob bursts up and lodges in Natasha's throat as she recalls how her dear father, immediately following the ceremony, unceremoniously disowned her. If that were not enough, the circus was immediately ordered out of the region. Having no other choice that horrible day, she left her home and arrived at the circus with a fashionable Paris umbrella and a single trunk of Moscow finery. Aghast at the uncouth manners of the circus people, she nevertheless did her best to hide her reaction, and graciously greeted everyone as the owner's new wife.

The early afternoon sun now barely penetrates the small windows of the dark wagon. Natasha wipes away a tear as she lights a beeswax candle, then returns to her stack of bills. Her nimble and long fingers whir, left to right, over the abacus beads and through the metal rods. She tries to make sense of the hopelessly confused finances of the circus. She winces, thinking back to how her father taught her the mysteries of simple mathematics and keeping records—how proud he had been of her mathematical acumen. Clearly chagrined that she was no beauty, he was still prepared to raise a large dowry to marry her off, as their station in life befitted them.

As Natasha plows through the stack of bills, her temples throb. She feels the heat of her anger rise as she nervously twists the tip of her long chestnut-brown braid. She desperately wants to throw the bills into Nikolai's face and make a run for it. As a lump of acid collects in her throat, however, she's forced to confront the truth—she has nowhere else to go.

Suddenly, she sweeps the abacus beads to one side, wiping out her calculations. She smashes the bills onto the desk, rips off her spectacles, and furiously rubs the bridge of her nose. Her olive skin reddens and blotches. This cannot be happening to her. She's worked fiendishly to clean up the accounts—and to wash away the disgusting smell of spilled beer and vodka that perpetually permeates their wagon. At each stopover to rest the animals in their journey west, she's spent the days of rest earnestly trying to manage the books and scrub years of accumulated filth from the walls, barely making a dent. Then Nikolai would inevitably return early in the mornings, reeking from a night of debauchery. Buried alive in grime.

No chambermaid, no lady's maid, no footman. Her father's stables were cleaner, better furnished, and more welcoming than this hovel. The wagon is more like a prison than a home.

Natasha's voice is ordinarily deep and somewhat manly, even more so when she's angry. She booms, "Nikolai, *chert voz'mi* (damn it). These accounts—we're going bankrupt."

Enraged that there is no response, she darts her eyes around the grim wagon. She looks over to their small bed where the gigantic Nikolai lies crosswise, sleeping off the night before. His shoulder-length, carbon-black hair, grimy with sweat, splays over the bed. His forest of a beard is covered with drool that drips in gobs onto the floorboard. Natasha flattens her large hands onto the table, torn between pure hatred of him and hatred of herself for ending up like this. Just one injudicious night. But oh, it had been bliss to be told she was beautiful, even if she knew the bastard was lying through his long black beard. She swallows hard, trying to accept that she has no alternative but to make the best of it and accept this as penance for her sins.

She crosses herself, kisses three fingers, and lays them on her cherished icon, which she's fastened onto the wall overlooking the desk. Her only comfort in her wretched circus wagon, the icon is bronze with a painted face of the Virgin in the center. It glows in the candlelight. Hurriedly leaving her home, she'd stuffed her travelling case with her icon and as many silk skirts, lace handkerchiefs, cloisonné hair combs, and precious mementos as she could manage. Her chest tightens as she visualizes her dear brother slip a jeweled dagger into her satchel, holding back his tears and muttering that she might find it useful. She couldn't tell whether he meant she should sell it or use it against Nikolai. The louder her husband snores, the more tempted she is to do the latter. But no, this is now her lot in life, so she will make the best of it. She must make the best of it, by St. Basil. But...she does not have to tolerate the obscene noises that oaf makes as he sleeps off his drink.

She straightens up in her wobbly chair, rises, then stomps to the side of the bed, where Nikolai's stockinged feet hang way over—at least she managed to get his boots off when he stumbled in last night. She gives his feet a short, swift jab with the heel of her boot. Nikolai responds with a slobber, silence, then a sharp intake of air, followed by a booming sputter. Exasperated, Natasha shakes her head, retrieves a pitcher of water from the bureau, and walks over to Nikolai, waiting for his mouth to crater open again. At the last minute, she reluctantly decides she can't very well drown him in their wagon, so she dumps the water onto his head.

Nikolai bolts upright, frenetically whacking at his matted hair, as if batting away a swarm of bees. "*Chto*?" He cocks open one bloodshot eye. Nostrils flaring, he attempts to rise from the bed. Still horrifically hung over, Nikolai bellows, "N-Natasha. *Kak ty smeyest*?"

Not to be cowed, Natasha shrieks, "What do you mean, 'How dare you?' How dare *you* come home drunk! Once more. You took up the whole bed. I had to sleep on the floor again."

Through his haze, Nikolai adopts his most charming, womanizing demeanor. "It's good for your back, my dear wife." He staggers up, arms outstretched, intending to hug her.

Fueled by his flattery, despite her best instincts, Natasha feels a brief pang of lust. Then her olive skin purples with rage. That is precisely what got her into this horrific mess in the first place. She backs several paces away—all she can manage in the cramped space within the cheerless wagon. She threatens to smash the pitcher over his head.

Not successful in appeasing her, Nikolai suddenly angers, zigzags to the closet, and starts pawing through the pile of clothes. "Where are my boots?"

"Get out of there!" shouts Natasha, painfully aware that when she's this furious, her deep voice sounds more foghorn than human.

Nikolai yells, "Who do you think you are?"

"You'll ruin my silks."

"I will?" He takes one of her skirts and staggers backward, his huge frame immediately bashing against the side of the wagon. He rips her skirt in two. "Here. Twice as many silks for you." Then he adds, in a mock bow, "My queen."

Natasha's wretched sense of loss comes to a head, and she heaves the pitcher at Nikolai, just missing him as he ducks to pick up his boots. Hopping on one foot, then the other, he bounces between the walls of the wagon while trying to pull his boots on—an obviously familiar and well-practiced maneuver. He smiles gingerly at her, tobacco-stained teeth poking through his thick black beard. "*Oy*, now I see you're really mad. Time to vacate the premises." He grabs a bottle of vodka and weaves toward the door.

Natasha is overwhelmed by all the hurt and anger of her failed attempts to make a go of this marriage. She's in despair at what one night of indiscretion has cost her—her family and her posh life. She runs the few short steps it takes to bar Nikolai's way, and she slaps him hard across the face. The slap makes a noise she knows must surely be heard outside their wagon, but she doesn't care. Clearly not wanting to engage with her, Nikolai bends down and butts his head into her stomach. As he knocks her back onto the bed, she screams. She would kill him right now if she could get her hands on him. Meanwhile, vodka bottle in hand, Nikolai turns to leave the wagon, groping for the door in his vastly hungover state.

CHAPTER FIVE

A S DUROV AND Anatoly pass by Nikolai's wagon, Durov is startled to see a small, rounded door pop open. The colossally tall Nikolai bends nearly in half to get through. He clutches his vodka bottle in one hand. With the other hand, he holds onto the door as he lurches down the wooden steps, trying to right himself as he lists farther and farther to the left with each step.

Nikolai pauses mid-descent, sees people milling about, and growls back into the wagon, "So high and mighty." He teeters onto the next step shouting, "By St. Nicholas, you'll be the ruin of me, Natasha." He takes a swig of vodka as he holds onto the door handle that creaks horrifically in his sinewy and hairy fist.

Watching all this unfold, Durov blinks his bright eyes, fascinated that the door is holding at all. He chuckles as he regards Nikolai's extreme hirsuteness, which, he thinks, might well qualify the brute for a "Wolfman" attraction in any circus sideshow.

The little door, dwarfed by the gargantuan man, finally comes unhinged. Durov is overjoyed to see Nikolai careening down. The vodka bottle soars high and then lands neck-down in the mud. Nikolai plops his butt hard onto the bottom step, plunging his boots deep into the muck to keep from falling headfirst. Although Durov knows he should have more sympathy for the unfortunate drunken man before him, memories of Nikolai's stubbornness and meanness thwart any such charitable feelings. Durov may not know people as well as he knows his pigs, but he's certain that brutality can never be condoned for either animals or people.

Nikolai pushes aside a mass of grizzled hair. Licking his lips, he fixes his stare at the vodka bottle in the mud, clearly trying to decide if any of the vodka is salvageable. Then, looking farther down into the mud, he roars, "My boots! My brand new boots!"

As Nikolai struggles to pull his boots out of the mud, Durov and Anatoly stifle their laughter with little success. Peering from under a forest of bushy black eyebrows, Nikolai looks between the brothers; Durov fears he's trying to decide which one of them to go after first.

Anatoly says, aside to Durov, "His b-boots are new. We-we can a-always tell when his b-boots are brand new b-because they squeak."

Nikolai, having overheard, rages, "Yes, they squeak when they're brand new. But look at them now!"

Just then, Ivan barges out of his practice tent on the perimeter of the circle of wagons. Durov notices with some envy that Ivan is using a practice towel to wipe sweat from his bare and extraordinarily well-muscled shoulders.

Ivan confronts the bellowing Nikolai, shouting, "*Chto za huy*, Nikolai? I'm in the middle of my training routine."

Although Ivan and Nikolai are drinking and womanizing partners, Nikolai scrunches up his face in pure, venomous anger that anyone would actually yell at him, the circus owner. Nikolai opens his mouth to scream at Ivan. But Durov, anxious to calm Nikolai so he won't take his anger out on Natasha, interrupts him.

"Surely such good friends as our estimable circus owner Nikolai Mikhailovich Kologrivov and our great trapeze artist Ivan Ivanovich Zubov wouldn't be arguing with each other, would they?"

Dumbfounded, Nikolai stares at Durov, trying to decipher the implications of Durov's last comment through the fog of his hangover.

Durov quickly jumps in, "Well, that's settled. Now why don't we all run along and finish our—"

"Why don't you finish feeding your filthy pigs?" Ivan sneers. "Quite a fall from grace compared with those white horses your family used to own." Ivan's long, fine fingers whip the practice towel from around his neck. Flinging it at Durov, he says, "Here, you might need this to clean yourself off, pig trainer."

Durov grins, his forced smile playing across his broad, square face. "Why thank you, Ivan Ivanovich." But suddenly, Durov grabs the end of the towel and pulls Ivan off balance, sending him—and his silky trapeze slippers—into the mud.

Seeing Ivan's feet also stuck in the mud, Nikolai booms with gravelly, uncontrolled laughter. Durov has never liked Ivan because of his flagrant womanizing—especially in the company of Nikolai's blatant womanizing. So Durov is delighted to see this handsome, muscled man sink into the mire. Durov smirks at the flash of crimson spreading over Ivan's good-looking face, then he quickly picks up his pails and signals to Anatoly to move away from the impending brawl.

Ivan shouts at Durov, "You think you're such a man of the people, like that's a good thing."

Durov comes to a dead halt at Ivan's taunts, meant to attack him for his egalitarian beliefs that everyone should be treated with respect. He angrily whips back around, ready to do battle. But then he guffaws as he watches Ivan—cut down to the same size as the "lowliest" performer he routinely disparages—pull each slipper out of the sludge.

Ivan's voice is normally as melodious as his face is handsome, but now he shrieks like a fishmonger's wife: "They're ruined, you idiots. I'll have to hose them off." Hyperventilating, Ivan is barely able to get the words out. "They'll shrink, and I'll never get the same traction on the wire."

Putting down his pails, Durov calmly leans over and squints to get a good look at Ivan's slippers. His mouth curls into a wry smile. "I could take them off your hands, Ivan. I'll teach Sasha how to waltz, and she could wear them."

Ivan's eyes widen. At first, he seems confused, then slowly, a rich, deep red floods his comely face.

Durov taunts, "Would you have another pair? My pig has four hooves, you see."

Grunting, Ivan hauls off, ready to slug Durov.

"A kopeck for each? But only if you have four, that is."

Ivan swings. Durov ducks. Then Durov and Anatoly rush off as Ivan's delicate hand collides with Nikolai's heavily forested beard and both sink deeper into the mud.

CHAPTER SIX

DUROV AND ANATOLY bring their pails into the pigpen at the far end of the animal corral. The late afternoon is fast upon them, and a cool breeze rustles the trees at the edge of the clearing. Durov calls his pigs over as if they were his children. He fondly watches them squirm for the most advantageous feeding spot. A dozen in all, they are variations on the colors of pink and white, and most are small to medium-sized. There is one large, gray-and-white male. And finally, there is his prized Sasha, pink and proud with an elaborate corkscrew tail that Durov is certain must be the envy of every other pig.

As Anatoly tosses the food from the buckets, Durov bends his solid frame to stroke each pig in turn. "Always pet them when they're eating, Anatoly. So they trust you."

Durov chortles as the pigs snort and slobber. He nods and hums to himself, delighting in the thought that every circus act is a sacred tradition. Every animal is a gift from God, to be treated with love and care—never cruelty. *We are not animal tamers; we are animal trainers. And we must come to know and understand each precious creature in our charge.* He pets the pigs, looking into their eyes to determine what motivates each one, then tailors his training accordingly. That way all the animals under his charge feel valued. "Yes, yes. Isn't that right?" he says, as he kneels and scratches them behind the ears. This is what makes them perform such that both animal and trainer can bask in the warmth of the audience's applause.

Imagining this applause in his head, Durov jumps up and struts back and forth. He's immensely proud that his family pioneered a revolutionary way to train animals, with carrots, not sticks. *Wouldn't it be wonderful if everyone knew about my methods? That would put an end to the endless cruelty visited upon most animals under the control of most humans.* This is how he'll venerate the sacred circus tradition that his father, with every fiber of his being, instilled in him and his younger brother.

A frown crosses Anatoly's soft, pale face. "Nikolai thinks the way to train animals is to b-beat them."

"Someone should beat him the way he beats his mule and—"

"N-Natasha?" Anatoly looks away, embarrassed.

Durov forms his square jaw into a broad smile. "A woman you can grab onto." He squints and shakes his head. "I'll never know what she saw in him." He strokes Sasha, holding her head and scratching behind her soft, hairy ears. "Sasha, my little piggala. You'd never be so stupid, would you?" Sasha's pointy ears curl, and she grunts with delight. Durov is all too aware that people say he's much too fond of his animals—they think he's crazy for treating them like children—but he doesn't care.

He misses the horses, of course. But he accepts that God has seen fit to deal him this hand—to punish him for his past transgressions. In the waning sunlight, a sharp wind picks up and Durov gets some blankets to fasten against the pen as a windbreaker. As he leans back on his haunches, he recalls that day, so long ago when he was just a teenager, determined to make his father proud that he could train their new colt. Their circus camp was carefully hidden, because the Old Tsar didn't like gypsies, circus people, and other "degenerates" to roam freely in the countryside. Durov sneaked the colt out and quietly led him to the far end of the adjoining pasture. His training was going very well, until the Cossacks spotted them.

He was terrified as they swooped down and tied him to a tree, ready to whip him into telling them where he'd gotten such a fine colt. He's sure he never would have betrayed his family, but just then, his father appeared at the edge of the pasture, looking for Durov. It didn't take long for the riders to follow his father's tracks back to their camp and steal all their horses. Most of the circus people had gone into town to provision, but Durov's beautiful mother was still in camp. Somehow, she just managed to hide young Anatoly in a costume trunk before their captain set upon her; Durov and his father howled in agony as the others made them watch. After that, she never spoke and hardly ate. All that was left of the animals were some pigs the circus had brought along to feed the performers. So Durov began to train one of them, while his parents, stunned into mute terror, silently watched. A few months later, both his mother and his father just gave up heart and died, leaving him to raise his sweet brother.

Shuddering, Durov returns to the present. As he secures the blankets around the fence, he looks over to his little, eager pigs and his eyes well up. The tragedy was so many years ago, but its memory is as razor-sharp as yesterday. Durov slumps, his bulky torso folding onto itself. He thinks how impossible it would be for any woman to love such a pitiful man. He can never be trusted to protect anyone he loves. Only the oinking of the little ones rouses him to feed the pigs in the remaining shades of pale orange light before twilight descends.

Durov's throat closes up as he becomes increasingly enraged, considering how vulnerable and impoverished they've become under Nikolai. So many people depend on the success of the circus—this little band of ragtag wagons, tents, and costumes. It's ironic that the country folk who pay a kopeck for a seat on the benches think their lives are so glamorous. The circus plays one night, maybe two at most. Then everyone with money has already come, so they pull up stakes and move on. True, the glamor and sequins can be smoke and mirrors, and backstage is actually very hard work. But the hard work is worthwhile because it reflects the honor of his circus family. Despite his tragic blunder as a teenager, he fervently believes every performance brings him closer to salvation. His life is deemed worthwhile when he can, for even just one performance, direct the animals under his sacred charge to make the children in the audience believe in the divine goodness of man.

Looking to the west, Durov sees a sign—the sun hanging motionless on the top of the ridge of mountains. He crosses himself and says a prayer that he'll be allowed to continue his penance and keep the circus family running, despite Nikolai's best efforts to the contrary. Durov sighs deeply, pats the pigs, and brushes straw from his worn corduroy trousers. Despite his bulk, he gracefully rises to his feet and holds his hands up, as if conducting an orchestra. The pigs stop eating. All their crunching and grinding noises come to an immediate halt as, in unison, they thrust their right front hooves into the air and curl them up and down.

Anatoly sadly shakes his curly head. "You'll n-never get the little ones to behave like h-horses. They're just too heavy to s-stand on their h-hind legs."

Durov lowers his hands, and the pigs grunt back down, snouts up, waiting for the bits of corn husks he tosses them as part of their training. "I know. I know." He rubs the mist from his eyes. "Someday, the Durovs will return to their former fame as trainers of the finest horses with the most beautiful ballerina on…" He stops, his voice trailing off. Durov swallows down tears as he straightens up the already straightened-up blankets around the corral fence. When Durov finishes, Anatoly puts his slender arm around his brother's massive shoulder.

"I'm s-sorry that I don't remember our m-mother like you do."

Durov pinches his eyes shut, and then he opens them and fondly gazes at Anatoly. "At least you got her good looks and that ridiculous curly blonde hair from her side of the family, you little *govno* (shit head)." Durov wrestles with Anatoly, gets him in a playful headlock, and kisses the top of his head. "Let's get some rest, while the little ones nap after their supper." Glancing at the pigs, Durov smiles, his bright eyes shining with optimism. "We need something new in the act to keep us on our toes."

CHAPTER SEVEN

SOFT SPRING RAIN beats lightly on the rounded top of Anna Tatianna Ivanova Zubov's circus wagon. Inside, Anna gaily twirls around her wagon, every inch of which is decorated with bright red-and-cream swirls of paint. Her bright red dressing gown flies apart, revealing her black tunic and flesh-colored tights underneath. Even with her porcelain skin, lustrous raven-black hair, and heart-shaped face, she still considers her best feature her long, swan-like neck, which seems even longer on such a petite—some might even say scrawny—girl.

Singing to herself, Anna leaps and twists, picking up each worn silk pillow and kissing it before she arranges it just so. She places each exactly as her mother always did, on the small trundle bed that doubles as a couch. She proudly adjusts each cherished picture covering the walls— gilt frames with sepia photographs of the Zubov Family Trapeze Act in various gymnastic positions. There is her father, Sergey Ivanovich Zubov, a robust man. There is her handsome brother, Ivan Ivanovich. And Anna's late mother, a voluptuous and dark beauty, is in almost every photo, hugging her fragile daughter, who smiles lovingly up at her.

Anna stops her straightening up and listens for a moment to the soothing patter on the roof. She kisses the icon above her bed. For her, the gentle rain is a blessing. It washes away her sadness with the promise of new and fresh beginnings. She sighs with contentment, as the rain makes her feel protected inside the wagon she shared with her mother. Anna has come to understand that her father's extreme jealousy drove her mother to insist on having her own wagon, while her father and brother lived apart in theirs. She's not certain how her mother managed this strength of will, perhaps arguing that their premiere status as the trapeze act justified a second wagon. That would have been the kind of ego-satisfying argument her father might have accepted. Whatever the rationale, Anna treasures the wagon with all her mother's memorabilia.

As she returns to the photographs, however, Anna catches sight of her profile under the glass. *I've hardly filled out since these photos were taken.* She's well aware that she has the boyish physique of a gymnast and that her diminutive size enables her to be exceptionally talented on the trapeze, every movement a graceful arc of fluid motion. But she's exasperated that people continue to treat her like a child because of her size. And because men in Russia clearly appreciate more *zaftig* and full-bodied women, she's increasingly panicked about her prospects for marriage.

How wonderful it was, a few towns back, when that slender, well-dressed youth approached her after their act. He was about to present her with a lovely bunch of roses. Anna posed from side to side, twisting her long neck this way and that, thrilled to have that kind of attention. But her father, Sergey, clenched his fists and stomped over to the fellow. Her father isn't a tall man, but as the catcher in the act, his shoulders are like a bull's. And with the black tape wrapping his wrists, he certainly did appear threatening to that poor boy. How terrible it was that the boy dropped the roses and ran from the tent. All she had left of him were the flowers, so she scooped them up and brought them to her wagon. She wistfully hung them upside down to dry, and she's cherished them ever since. She stomps her tiny foot. Sergey and Ivan have recently become even more controlling. They don't want to diminish the act by losing her to a husband, so now they won't even let her talk to a marriageable young man.

Anna crosses herself and prays that the gentle shower outside will wash away all the tears she's shed since her mother died and left her under the ironclad control of her father. She returns to her sylph-like figure in the glass of the photos. She bites a fingernail to the quick and curves her back, trying to plump out her breasts to make herself more attractive. Her father and brother hate it when she bites her nails. They say it makes her fingers softer—so that it's harder for her brother to transfer her to the second trapeze and for her father to catch her on the way back. *Let them drop me. I don't care anymore.*

Wiping away a tear that has settled in her dark lashes, Anna turns her attention to entertaining Madame Natasha, the new and recently arrived wife of the circus owner. She plans to ask Natasha to intervene with her father to let her have a greater a role in the family act. Of course, she's always loved the act of flying—soaring, defying gravity, making graceful arcs and daring summersaults with her body. Secretly, however, she figures if she does more, she'll be noticed as an attractive and suitable wife. Then she can realize her dream of escaping the bossiness of her father and Ivan. She can quit the circus and settle down as mistress of her own grand, stationary home with no wagon wheels. She dreams of having a large, glassed-in gazebo on the summer side of their house. She can sit there and hear the delicate and nourishing rain as she plays dominos with her children. She doesn't suppose Natasha will want her to leave the circus, as it won't be good for business—the trapeze act definitely needs a woman. But Natasha doesn't have to know her ulterior motive in wanting to do more in the act. So...first things first.

As she looks in the glass, she stretches up her lovely neck and pinches her alabaster cheeks to bring color to them. She tries to pat back the tip of her large nose, the only blemish on her otherwise lovely heart-shaped face. How horrible that her brother and she seemed to have inherited this most unwanted feature. She giggles—on Ivan, it fits with his perpetual arrogance. But on her, it's totally out of place and fashion. Didn't she try wearing scarves to distract from her nose? But she only ended up looking more like a bandit or an Egyptian belly dancer. She sighs, then pouches out her flat stomach, imagining a baby forming within. Her round eyes widen as she imagines her baby's father, a handsome and respectable gentleman, promenading with her as she pushes a child in an ornate pram. *My husband will cherish me. He'll be strong and stand up to my father and Ivan. Then I'll be the one to order everyone around.*

Anna picks up a cloth to polish her most precious item, her mother's porcelain, claw-foot tub. A plank on top serves as a makeshift dresser. She centers the round mirror in its mahogany frame. She lovingly caresses her mother's hairbrush and old pots of cream—she never opens them, but she moves them about on the dresser to play-act using them. Everything must be in its place for Madame Natasha. She checks the water in the ancient, dented, silver samovar she's polished to a high gleam. Anna takes down a box of sweets and smells them, swooning as she places them, piece by treasured piece, on a china plate, strategically hiding its cracks and chips.

There's a gentle rap on the wagon door. Anna lifts up in a small, light jump, ties her dressing-gown shut, and rushes to the door. If she plays her cards right, this could be the most important conversation of her life.

She opens the door and looks around to make sure no one's watching. Anna's voice is lilting and bright with youthful energy. "Come in quickly, Madame Natasha. We don't want my father or brother to see." Her translucent skin glows against the flash of her long black hair. "Tea will be ready in a minute."

Natasha huffs up the last of the wooden steps and heaves herself into the wagon. Anna slams the door shut. Natasha shakes the rain from her kerchief, pats her thick braid back in place over her shoulder, and bends down to hug the diminutive girl, crushing Anna to her ample bosom. "No need to go to such trouble, my darling Anna Tatianna."

With the breath nearly knocked from her, feeling nervous in Natasha's presence, Anna whispers, "I'm so happy to see you."

Natasha's voice is deep and raw. "By St. Basil, it's wet out there."

Fluttering about, Anna assumes Natasha is frustrated at having to propel herself up the wagon stairs in the rain. She quickly gives the older woman a small, embroidered towel to dry off.

"Oh, thank you. I appreciate your invitation." Natasha's voice changes to a calmer, almost sweet tone. "I've no one to talk to around here, and you're such a lovely girl."

Anna beams. She is desperate for Natasha to like her—to help her get out of this wretched circus. She quickly says, "It's my honor, Madame." Anna takes Natasha's kerchief and the towel. She motions Natasha toward the heavily pillowed sofa bed. Anna sits down on a dainty stool.

As Natasha sinks her large rear down, the pile of neatly plumped pillows goes flying. "Oh, dear Anna...let me make this awful mess into something nice. You don't mind, do you?"

Horrified that Natasha has found fault in how her mother always arranged the pillows, Anna bites her tongue rather than object. She grits her teeth and motions to her little stool. "You can sit here, if it's more comfortable."

Natasha jolts her chin back and squawks, "Me? On that little thing? I'd splinter it in a moment, my dear." Then she adds in her deep but kind voice, "But thank you anyway." Natasha folds her voluminous silk skirt beneath her voluminous bottom and settles down.

They sit in silence for an awkward moment, listening to the rain drumming harder on the roof. Natasha looks around at the circus memorabilia covering the walls. Following Natasha's gaze around the photos, Anna catches her breath and is filled with the horrible memory of the night her mother died. Her father insisted they not use a net. Did he drop her on purpose? Ivan always swore it was an accident, but the circus people whispered that her father was jealous of Grisha, the strongman. And Petri, the rigging man. And Vronksy, the elephant trainer. *Everyone in the circus*

41

loved my mother. My mother loved everyone too, except not in that way. But no one could tell my father anything. They still can't...

The samovar hisses and bubbles, and Anna jumps up, putting these horrific thoughts aside. "The tea. Oh, and I have some sweets too."

"No, thank you." Natasha pats her waist, thinks a moment, and then shrugs. "Well, maybe just one." Natasha studies the dilapidated samovar and sighs wistfully. "You can't imagine what my family's tea service was like." A look of shame comes over her and she quickly adds, "Not that I don't appreciate your tea, my dear."

The rain bombards the small panes on the windows of the wagon. Anna nervously draws her dressing gown tighter and decides to ignore the older woman's offensive words. She changes the subject to something she never tires hearing about—the grand things in Natasha's former life. "Tell me, once again, how elegant everything was."

Natasha waves a large hand. "Oh, my dear, I've told you ten times."

"Tell me eleven times," Anna pleads, dreaming of a wealthy life. "We'll have our tea, and then I have to go practice before my father and Ivan yell at me." Anna bites a nail. She truly loves the feeling of flying in the air, but she hates how they control her every move. She rubs her wrists. Ivan will soon be wrapping her wrists tightly to make sure her tiny hands have a sturdy base for him to swing her—and for her father to catch her, so he doesn't drop her like...

"Anna, are you all right? You're trembling."

"It's just the torrent of rain. I really want to hear. Just one more time, *obeshchayu* (I promise)." She forces a smile, whisks over to the small cupboard, and gets two small glasses with silver handles. She proudly places them next to the samovar, turns to Natasha, and stamps her petite foot. "I'm not going to pour unless you tell me how you used to go skating and then how everyone went for tea."

Shifting on the couch, Natasha's long skirt dislodges more silk pillows. She smiles weakly and shoves them back under her, bouncing as if adrift in a small boat. As she starts to describe her former life in Moscow, Anna hears a lovely cadence in her deep voice. Anna settles in to listen to the story, once again.

"Well…all right. The last time I went, our troika was drawn by three horses in silver harnesses. We glided up the frozen slopes to Petrovsky Park to skate on Priesnienskie Pond, near the Zoological Garden. In the twilight mist, you could hear the orchestra playing waltzes for the skaters." Natasha's face brightens, and her olive skin takes on a pink flush.

Anna, intent on currying favor with Natasha, ignores the torrent of rain, hums a cheerful tune, pours the tea, and waltzes over to Natasha. "And you were under your fur wrap. Sugar cube?"

"Oh no! Well…maybe just one." Natasha takes the cube between her teeth and sips the tea through it. "You know, my dear, I never used to drink tea this way. But everyone in the circus does." Natasha shrugs. "I don't want to be thought of as a snob."

Pursing her lips, Anna is flatly annoyed at the insult to her way of life, but she catches herself and nods enthusiastically. "No one would ever think that of you! Please, do go on."

"The orchestra at the edge of the pond was sheltered by this huge plaster shell—"

"And the rink was surrounded by lighted globes. A sweet?"

"Oh no, my dear! Well…maybe just one." Natasha pops one into her mouth and talks as she chews. "My hands were buried in my fur muff. Military gentlemen swirled around me." Natasha's deep voice is lilting now. "Their grand handlebar mustaches stiff with frost."

"And then you went to—"

"The Café Philippov. At the corner of Tverskaya and Glinichevsky Streets. Oh, my dear, it was so warm inside, and the place smelled of perfume. We had our tea. And pies with meat, eggs, mushrooms, cream cheese, and jam. Then there were succulent tarts and all kinds of bread. Black, brown and—"

"Even white."

"There now, you've heard it all again."

Anna's eyes well up. Try as she will to suppress her sadness at her lot in life, a tear slides down her cheek.

"I'm afraid I'm just making you miserable. Giving you a taste of what you'll never experience yourself."

Anna flushes. *That's what you think.* She smiles sweetly. "At least I can hear about it." She pauses, then can't resist an impish dig. "I can't imagine why you gave it all up for—" Anna stops short, feigning a blush. "Oh, I'm sorry. I didn't mean..."

Natasha fights back a sob, then blurts out, "I don't know myself. How stupid could I have been?"

Anna tries to regroup. "But Nikolai was...was imposing." Anna rips through another fingernail as she searches for the right words. "And quite the charmer." She's mortified to have spoken so frankly and risked Natasha's support. "Another sweet?" Anna holds them out for her to help herself.

Natasha eyes the girl with suspicion. "You don't have to pretend." Then Natasha adds, with a girlish giggle, "Well...just one more. Only to finish this tea, mind you. To have the tea and the sweets to come out all even, you know."

Anna offers Natasha the sweet. Then, thinking how the driving rain is unsettling her and how much she hates her overbearing father, Anna takes one for herself and ravenously demolishes it. As the flood of sugar surges through her, she resolves, *I'm going to eat so much and get so fat that I can't be in the act anymore. Then I'll be plump enough to attract a real gentleman.* Suddenly, she's horrified, remembering her skimpy costume. Anna turns her back, contracts her stomach and spits the offending sweet up and into her hand.

"Are you all right, Anna?"

"Ahhh...yes," she says, hiding her hand behind her. "Sometimes I get so excited hearing about your grand life in Moscow, I just sneeze. Silly me."

Anna looks at the older woman and feels a pang of guilt that she's just cozying up to her in order to use her. She hates that she's become so adept at burying her feelings—she can hardly feel what they are anymore. She despises herself for carrying on like nothing's wrong when she's really ready to scream how much she hates her father. How she'd like to kill him for insisting so long ago that the riggers take the net down for what he claimed would be the highlight of the act. She remembers his words: "It's the danger that brings in the crowds." If only her mother hadn't given in that time. If only she'd held her ground, like she did insisting on having this wagon, which is Anna's only refuge.

The downpour outside begins to abate, replaced by a light rain. Once again, Anna rallies. "Would you care for some more tea?"

Pouring more of the steeping brew, Anna again longs for the warmth of her mother's reassuring caress. She closes her eyes and remembers her mother's glamorous face, the sequins in her costume dazzling and reflecting in her onyx-black eyes. Lately, that face has begun to blur, its lines becoming less distinct, less etched in her mind. She looks longingly at Natasha, who is about the age her mother would have been. *Maybe I'm not just playing her. Maybe I am sincere in having feelings for this woman.*

Anna is comforted by what has turned into a light drizzle on the window pane—which she's sure will wash away all her troubles. She shakes off her fears and turns to Natasha. "More sugar, Madame?"

CHAPTER EIGHT

THE MORNING'S HEAVY rain finally tapers off to a light drizzle, and the midday sun bursts through the dense clouds. Durov enters the canteen tent, still fuming over how that drunken lout Nikolai treats Natasha. Nikolai threatens the livelihood of their entire circus family and denigrates the noble, egalitarian essence of the circus itself.

Durov always feels a measure of relief that the canteen is located at the edge of the semicircle of circus wagons, set as far away as possible from the other wagons to reduce the hazard of fire breaking out and spreading to destroy the wagons. He recalls, years ago, when his father loaned him out to another regional circus to help an elderly animal trainer and friend of their family. Durov saw how a fire laid waste to that circus. The horror of people and animals trapped in the roaring blaze impressed upon Durov the tenuousness of life. It made him want to succeed that much more, which ironically led to his own downfall and that of his family.

It is engrained in the Russian spirit to drown one's sorrows in that which is made from grain—vodka. But Durov searches for redemption and penance without the mind-numbing comfort of those kinds of spirits. Not that the little circus has sufficient funds to supply vodka in the mess anyway. Durov snatches his tin bowl and wooden spoon from the service table and motions for Anatoly to follow. They queue up and wait for the gong to summon them for their one meal of the day.

Muttering to himself, Durov nods his usual greeting to the cook—the tall and massively dome-headed Bronzy who doubles as the strongman. The cook's helper is Bronzy's petite sister Lottie—the circus's psychic and fortune-teller. At last, Bronzy brandishes his mallet with a great flourish. His massive arms and chest are completely covered with vibrant tattoos of interlocked hearts and intermingled women. He strikes a round brass gong that can be heard for miles—the signal that supper is served.

Every time Durov enters the canteen, he cringes, his thick neck blotching red, because the seating is arranged according to the circus hierarchy. The owners, Nikolai and Natasha, and the high class acts like the trapeze are seated at the first table. This is where his family's act used to sit. Now the animal acts and the clowns are assigned the second table, while the riggers and stagehands, laborers and mule skinners make up the third and last table. Every meal is a humiliation. Durov gets his food as quickly as he can and motions for Anatoly and Boris to join him at the second table. After she finishes helping Bronzy, Lottie scoots in next to Boris. Durov chuckles to see her still flirting with him, seductively adjusting the several fringed shawls she wears crisscrossed diagonally, in opposite directions, across her tiny shoulders. The rest of the circus clowns, the four dwarf brothers, Pasha, Masha, Vasha and Max, scramble onto the benches. Durov is amused to see them gesturing and making faces as they vie for Lottie's attentions, even as she only has eyes for Boris.

Once he's seated among his brother and friends, Durov typically enjoys his food. He generally feels quite exuberant and affable at supper, especially when the weather is fresh and the sun is shining, as it is now. But today, despite the noon hour's repast before him, he's uncharacteristically sullen. He stares intently at the first table where Natasha lays out silverware for Nikolai and herself, presumably in an attempt to civilize the brutish dunderhead.

Durov remembers back to the time when, as a boy, he sat with his parents and his smiling, blonde baby brother at that same hallowed head table. Nikolai's father was the circus owner then. And Nikolai, an impossibly tall and perpetually nasty teenager, kept kicking Durov under the table and then denying it when Durov called him out. Durov soon learned it was best to take matters into his own hands. He started playing tricks on Nikolai, rigging trip wires so pails of water would fall on him, and such. Kid stuff. Nikolai would generally respond in kind, although never anything dangerous. Until one day Nikolai escalated things by hanging a chicken upside down in a nearby field and torturing it. Then Durov was horrified to find that Nikolai secretly stuffed burrs and bits of broken glass under the saddle of his family's prized white stallion. When Durov privately confronted him, Nikolai insisted that this was the way to tame animals—make them hurt until they obeyed. Durov backed off, sensing there was probably no way to alter the depth and direction of Nikolai's sadistic bent.

Thinking back to those childhood days, Durov can only imagine how Nikolai must now be attempting to *tame* Natasha into becoming a loving and devoted wife. How was it possible that she was taken in by him in the first place? *Women...my pigs are easier to understand.*

Hearing laughter at his own table, he drifts back to the conversation. He looks over at Boris who reaches into the pocket of his baggy clown pants and announces to the table, "I'll trade anyone my goulash for your black bread, if I can't produce a canary."

Durov shakes his head. "I'm not falling for your old canary in your pants-pocket trick."

Pasha, the eldest dwarf sitting on the end of their bench, nudges Masha, the second eldest dwarf. Pasha smiles, revealing several missing teeth, and whispers to his brother, "He's never gotten that bird out of the right pocket yet."

"Boris, p-please stop p-performing that trick. You're m-mistreating that poor bird," Anatoly softly adds.

"You just want our bread because this goulash tastes worse than what we feed our pigs," Durov interjects. Remembering that Lottie is the cook's sister, he winces. "Sorry, Lottie. But you must admit, your brother is a better strongman than a cook."

Boris adds, "You can say that again, Durov. No offense, Lottie."

"Gentlemen, please." Lottie primly straightens her shawls. Pasha and Masha exaggeratedly sit up straight to get her attention, but she ignores them. Vasha and Max strain to sit even straighter than their brothers, but Lottie continues to ignore all of them. She keeps her attentions glued to Boris.

Durov gets up and hugs Lottie. "We mean it, Lottie. No offense."

She smiles at Durov and pats his hand, which makes him regret even more that he took his anger at Nikolai out on her, especially since she's had a very hard life. Nikolai hired her and her brother Bronzy, figuring he could make a bundle on them, since they could do double duty as circus acts and cooks. They had been with one sideshow or another pretty much their whole lives. They'd run away from their orphanage after the unscrupulous nuns were about to sell Lottie to a St. Petersburg brothel and Bronzy to the Siberian mines. Their current life certainly saved them from unthinkable misery. Durov considers this another reason to view the circus as a conduit for salvation—if not for his own, then at least for them.

As he sits down again, Durov watches Lottie sidle up to Boris, with whom she has clearly been enamored since she arrived at the circus. Durov laughs out loud and claps as Boris, with a theatrical flourish, produces a fake flower and gives it to Lottie, who twitters and shyly accepts it. Boris seems satisfied at his act of kindness—he strokes his neatly trimmed goatee, which gives him the look of a petite but kindly devil. He produces a gigantic napkin from another pocket and fastidiously tucks it under his chin, preparing to eat. He turns to Durov, clears his throat, and in his deep and erudite voice, says, "You're unusually quiet this afternoon."

Durov barely hears Boris, as his attention has drifted back to what's going on at the head table. Nikolai, Natasha, and the Zubov Trapeze Family are having their supper. Nikolai wears his usual long, black, Siberian-style tunic that accentuates his imposing height and massive physique. Durov taps the table nervously, then angrily. He wishes he were more formidable as a fighter. He knows he could never take on the bearish Nikolai, but he can't stop obsessing over how to get Nikolai to treat Natasha better. Tapping harder and faster, Durov turns his attention to Ivan and bristles. Ivan, in his dressing robe so obviously left open to reveal his sculpted chest, plays up to Natasha. Ivan flaunts his escapades with Nikolai and flirts with her at the same time. How annoying that Ivan is smoothly pulling this off, in contrast to Durov's own conversations with females, which are always awkward—except, of course, when he's talking to his pigs.

It sounds to Durov like Nikolai and Ivan are joking about one of their vulgar womanizing sprees. Ivan laughs much too heartily as he leans in, trying to get Natasha to smile. Durov is pleased to see that she moves her plate around, ignoring them both. Anna sits quietly, chewing more of her fingernails than her goulash. Anna's father, Sergey Ivanovich Zubov, is a massively muscled and balding man. Sergey slurps his goulash and then exchanges his bowl with Anna's half-eaten supper, wolfing hers down as well.

Anatoly whispers, "Durov, you're n-not still angry about N-Nikolai and N-Natasha, are you?"

"Never get between a man and his bride," Boris says, holding his nose as he goes to take a bite of goulash. "Especially if the man is a crazy, violent, Siberian cad."

Nodding, Anatoly says, "Yes, e-especially if the man is a crazy, violent...huh? Don't call him a cad, Boris. You'll only in-incite my-my brother."

"No matter, Boris." Durov tries to change the subject. "*Ya khochu yest.*"

"Yes, I'm hungry t-too," Anatoly quickly adds.

Durov scarfs down a lump of food. His craggy features scrunch as he chews and chews and chews. He swallows with a gulp. "What they do in their wagon is their...well...but why must he disrespect her in public?" Durov doesn't know what he hates more: Nikolai abusing Natasha in private or in public. Either way, his father taught him that this behavior is wrong; you must revere the woman you've linked your life with through the sacred act of marriage. And next to Durov's feelings about how sacred his animals are, wives come in a close second. He sets his jaw and shakes his head, thinking maybe if he had a wife of his own, she might even come first. He sighs, reluctantly shifts his focus back to his food, and takes another bite.

Everyone at the table follows Durov's example and digs into the goulash, chewing and chewing and chewing. Pasha tries to compliment Lottie. "The goulash may be a bit tough, but the spices are...well...spicy. Aren't they, Masha?" Masha nods vigorously, which is followed by even more forceful nodding by Vasha and then by Max. Masha chews with his mouth open, exposing even fewer teeth than Pasha. Max elbows him, motioning for him to close his mouth and mind his manners in front of Lottie.

Boris takes a swig of wine. "*Oy*, watered down again. Those bastards."

Lottie offers, "I'd settle for some nice *kvas* with honey."

"Better yet, some real vodka." Boris turns to Lottie with a deferential tilt of his head. "I don't mean to demean the cook. We're all well aware how stingy Nikolai is." Boris finishes his meal with a dainty touch of his oversized napkin to his goatee, adding, "Durov, I'd be more worried about Nikolai and Ivan wrecking the circus with their exploits. Either we get run out of town, or there's only half pay because they imbibe the box office take. And, you'll notice, they knock back the vodka and leave us this watered-down slop that isn't fit for pigs. No offense."

Durov rips off a piece of bread and turns it over in his thick hands. His mind swirls with conflicting thoughts. He's furious at Nikolai but worries a confrontation will only serve to inflame him and make things worse for Natasha. He knows that the continued decline of the circus will destroy not only his treasured extended family but also the animals he holds so dear. Something must be done. At times, a rabid animal must be put down, and doesn't Nikolai qualify? But that's doing what Nikolai would do, and Durov cannot violate his family's cherished values. What else? As he ponders how to rid the circus of Nikolai, he sees the Zubov family get up from the head table to leave for their practice session. As the patriarch of the family and the catcher in the act, Sergey's custom is to raise his arm; then he, Ivan, and Anna jump up at exactly the same moment, bow, and prance out, pretending to wave at the audience—even though there's no audience and no one's applauding. Anna hangs back, solemnly kisses Natasha on both cheeks, and sighs deeply as she catches up with her high-stepping father and brother.

As Nikolai stumbles over to Durov's table, wielding a bottle of vodka, Durov swiftly chews the bread, as if fortifying himself for battle. The four dwarf brothers see Nikolai coming, jump up, run around the benches, and pantomime his drunken stumble. They keep well below Nikolai's line of sight, which isn't at all hard for the small men.

Nikolai plops down on the bench next to Durov, drunkenly slurring, "I've got good newsh for you, pig trainer. We're going to taksh a trip to where they really don't like your filthy swine."

Anatoly meekly objects, "Our p-pigs aren't d-dirty. They j-just like r-rolling in the m-mud to c-cool themselves."

Nikolai slouches menacingly toward Anatoly, but Durov, with a sharp intake of air, extends his arm to block him. Nikolai looks under his bushy black eyebrows that nearly obscure his vision, making it virtually impossible for him to look Durov in the eye. Behind and on either side of Nikolai, the dwarfs weave and bob their pantomime of the drunken Nikolai. Durov tries, albeit not very hard, to suppress his laughter at the spectacle.

Durov asks, "Where are we going, Nikolai Mikhailovich?"

"To Prussia, thatsh where. We're going to take advantagesh of the booming economy."

"Germany?" Boris lets his napkin fall. "That's where the kaiser's preparing for war. And proclaiming all those nasty, strict, and repressive edicts he says are reforms."

Lottie blurts out, "We're going to Germany? Strange coincidence. I had a vision just last night." She leans into Boris, lowering her voice conspiratorially, "The trip to Germany's not going to work out well."

Ignoring her, Nikolai raises his towering frame and leans across the table toward the diminutive Boris. He blasts, "You want to be serf-shssh your whole lives? Peasants?" He whips around unsteadily, trying to focus on where Durov sits. "And you...you like all thesh weird people from everywhere in Russia coming into our circus?" He mocks Durov: "The universality of the cir-suh. They're only provincial degenerates. You think thatsh such a big draw?"

Incensed at Nikolai's ridicule, Durov balls his fists, ready to strike. But before he can, Boris puffs himself up, and he, too, leans across the table, until he's nose to nose with Nikolai. "My grandfather came from the provinces. He was a grand illusionist and a big draw for this circus. As was my father."

Nikolai yells, "But you're only a clown now, aren't you?"

Behind Nikolai's back, Pasha whispers to Masha, "And what's wrong with being a clown?" Then Masha whispers to Vasha, "And what's wrong with being a clown?" Then Vasha whispers to Max the same thing. They stick their tongues out, grab the sides of their mouths, and make clown faces. They laugh at Nikolai, slapping their knees and silently pantomime laughing uproariously.

Chuckling at this merriment, Durov nevertheless waves to caution them, least Nikolai see them and direct his anger their way.

Boris, leaning across the table up against Nikolai, continues to stand his ground. He rolls his eyes as he waves away the fumes from Nikolai's rancid garlic breath.

Durov instinctively knows that Boris's refusal to back down puts him in imminent danger from the violent, drunken, and abusive Nikolai. So Durov jumps up and inserts himself between them. "Nikolai, leave Boris alone."

Anatoly adds urgently, his voice cracking, "Yes, l-leave him b-be. He's a g-good clown." Anatoly starts to stand to offer his support, but Durov nudges him back down and out of the way. He also surreptitiously motions to the dwarfs to take their seats and not make trouble.

But Nikolai won't let it go as he booms to the table at large. "But he's not funny." He hunches his colossal shoulders and looks directly into Boris's eyes. "You have to be funny to be a clown, little man."

Boris's face turns as red as the beets missing from their supper.

Despite his bravado, Nikolai is so inebriated that it only takes a small push from the tips of Durov's fingers to set him back down on the bench.

Seeing he's now a safe distance away, Boris screws up his courage and berates Nikolai: "I'll have you know, there's a good reason why I'm so short. My father, the great magician Spasinsky—Boris Vladimir Spasinsky, if you recall—was the very first to perform his famous saw-the-lady-in-half trick. But then, you see, when he sawed my mother in half, well…she was pregnant with me at the time. That's the reason I came out so short, I'll have you know."

To support Boris's story, the four dwarf brothers together say "hup" and clap, as they do at the beginning of one of their acrobatic stunts. Then Pasha stands on Masha's shoulders to pantomime Boris's father, the great magician. Vasha grabs Lottie's shawl and wraps it around his shoulders to mimic Boris's mother. With a grand magician-like flourish, Pasha starts "sawing" Vasha (the mother) in half. Then Max somersaults and comes out of Vasha's legs—"short" like Boris. They all take a bow, Vasha gallantly returns Lottie's shawl, and everyone at the table wildly applauds—except for Nikolai, who shakes his head, obviously trying to get his inebriated brain around the gist of the action.

Smiling weakly, Boris turns to Lottie for understanding, which, Durov is pleased to see, she readily provides.

Nikolai, in his drunken haze, next turns to Anatoly. "Anatoly Mikhailovishhh, why ish-ishn't this guy funny? We pay him to be a clown and he's shusposed to make the children laugh."

Anatoly tries his best. "Well, I guess it's…it's because he really doesn't c-care that mu-much for children."

Boris scrunches up his face and booms in his deepest, most articulate, Shakespearean voice, "That's absolutely ridiculous. Of course I like children." Then, stroking his goatee apologetically, he adds under his breath, "The little brats. Should be seen not heard." He turns back to the table with a forced lightness. "Well, I don't generally mind them, but on very rare occasions, you could say they ruin…just a teensy bit—" He booms, "They ruin my concentration."

Puzzled, Anatoly shakes his curly head. "B-Boris, what kind of con-concentration does it t-take to be a clown?"

At this remark, all four dwarfs start objecting, but Durov quiets them down.

As Nikolai's head thuds down onto the table, Boris swipes his vodka bottle and takes a long, satisfied swig. "I'll have you know, it takes a lot of concentration and timing. Counting how many circles to run around that stupid little cart that all four of our dwarfs climb into and, I might add, pile on top of me. Making sure there's confetti and not water in the pail I throw into the audience."

Honest to a fault—in the true Durov tradition—Anatoly adds, "But Boris, I don't think that w-woman two towns back a-appreciated getting her dr-dress soaked."

Lottie bats her false eyelashes at Boris. "It was rather hot that night, so I thought you cooled her off quite nicely."

Pasha laughs and nudges Masha, obviously knowing who was responsible for the switch.

Eyes flashing in a combination of anger and hurt, Boris says, "Someone must have put real water into my pail."

Vasha and Max smile a "who us?" smile, while fiercely shaking their heads no.

Boris looks askance at them and shrugs. "Or perhaps my aim was slightly off. If only her bosom hadn't taken up two seats—" Boris stops and motions to Nikolai, now snoring in Durov's goulash. "Durov, bet you'd want to bet your goulash now."

Durov reaches out his muscled hand and grabs the comatose Nikolai by his unruly mane of greasy black hair. As he lifts up Nikolai's head, strands of noodles cling to Nikolai's beard. "He's a drunken lout, but he might have a good idea. A new place will mean new customers." He lets Nikolai's head go, and it plops back down, splashing goulash all over the table.

Lottie jumps up to wipe away the mess. All four dwarf brothers immediately rise up to assist her by mopping up everything on the table—dislodging tin bowls, wooden spoons, and the like. Finally, she motions to them to sit back down, turns to Durov, and softly presses her case: "I'm not certain it's a wise idea to go to Germany. Truly, I saw it last night…a vision in the cards." She shudders and wraps two of her shawls tighter around her. "A tall, gangly German dragoon and—"

Raising up his small frame, Boris interrupts, "Lottie, you will pardon me, but I don't believe in psychic phenomenon. Everything can be explained by earthly sleight-of-hand—it's what we magicians do."

Lottie raises up her even smaller frame. "Boris, you will pardon me, but I can assure you that there are vibrations from the spirit world. And I communicate with them. I'm telling you there's going to be trouble in Germany."

He eyes Lottie for a moment, and then he nods and turns to Durov. "Perhaps she's right. Why not hedge our bets and not go? Besides, there are huge mountains between us and these so-called, potential, not-yet-in-the-bag, new customers. How would we get across?"

Before Durov can answer, Natasha, who has been talking to the others at the head table, comes over to Durov's table with a cloth. She lifts Nikolai's head and wipes his beard. Her deep voice is filled with remorse: "Excuse me, Nikolai must have eaten something that didn't agree with him."

Durov hates to see Natasha debasing herself to cater to Nikolai. *Why doesn't she fight back? Stand up to that beast?*

Boris, Lottie, Anatoly, and the four dwarf brothers simultaneously reassure Natasha: "*Da, da.* Of course. *My ponimayem.* We understand." Behind her back, they cross their eyes, roll them around, and try to suppress their laughter.

For Natasha's sake, Durov feels shame rising up. His craggy, weather-beaten face flushes crimson. He is determined to show her the kind of respect any wife deserves—especially such a cultured woman. Durov gets up to assist Natasha. Meanwhile, Boris neatly corks the vodka bottle with a plug of black bread, wraps it in his napkin, and slips it into one of his baggy pants pockets. Anatoly's eyes bulge as he starts to protest, but Boris puts an emphatic finger to his lips. Lottie continues to wipe up the mess on the table, while Durov helps Natasha lift Nikolai to a somewhat standing position. The dwarf brothers rush around on either side of Natasha to assist her, but she looks at them, obviously noting their small size in contrast to the towering, albeit slumping, Nikolai. She smiles graciously, but firmly waves them off. As Durov and Natasha stand the drunken Nikolai on his feet, Durov says, "I understand, Madame Natasha, that we're heading west to Germany."

Natasha struggles with her husband's stray arms and sagging legs. She groans, "That's what I'm told. I only hope the journey will be worth the risk. It's either going to make our fortune or break us altogether."

Certain she is correct in her assessment, Durov admires her forthrightness and her business acumen. *She should be running the circus, not this sagging lout. In fact, we should be running things together but—*

He stops himself, chagrined at the dishonorable implication of coveting another man's wife—even if she is most likely an astute businesswoman and could very possibly lift them out of their downward spiral. Durov narrows his eyes and forces himself to concentrate on working with Natasha to steer Nikolai to their wagon.

When they reach the steps, Nikolai slips from their grasp and crumbles onto the bottom step. Natasha winces, embarrassed for the two of them. "I think he just needs a moment to recover."

Embarrassed for her, Durov nods. He stares at the side of the wagon at the faint painting of his own father's glorious horse act. He feels acutely ashamed of the family's defeat. Just then, some distant memory pushes through; he stands tall as he recalls that his great grandfather's wife was actually the first to have the knack for training horses. Nadezhda Andreyvena Durova was a stubborn girl, born in an army camp in Kiev, the daughter of a Russian major. By all accounts, she was headstrong—their family's most notable trait.

Durov pictures his father sitting him down and telling him how Nadezhda tamed a stallion everyone considered unbreakable. During the Napoleonic wars, at the age of twenty-four, she disguised herself as a man using the name of Alexander Sokolov and enlisted in the Russian army. She brought her horse Alkid with her to the barracks. Durov stands even taller as he is filled with pride remembering that she thoroughly distinguished herself on the field of battle. Despite being a woman, or perhaps because of it, she was summoned to the palace at St. Petersburg by Tsar Alexander I, who awarded her the Cross of St. George.

A drunken snort from Nikolai, still crumbled on the bottom step of his wagon, startles Durov.

Natasha bends down to Nikolai and pries open one eye with her finger. Bloodshot. She lets it go and it slams shut. "*Oy*, he's not going to wake up for some time. We can't leave him here."

Durov takes the brunt of Nikolai's weight while Natasha opens the door. Then Durov jettisons Nikolai headlong into the wagon. Nikolai lands facedown on the wooden floor.

Natasha is flustered. "Help me get him to the bed, will you?"

Although Durov is perfectly inclined to leave him right there on the floor, he obliges. They get him up to the bed just as Nikolai starts to snore full blast. Durov detects a strange vulnerability to Natasha's expression, as if she were not only angry at her husband's behavior but also deeply saddened about her lot in life.

She seems to rally, saying, "He's out cold now. Thank goodness we got him here." Natasha smooths her long skirt and nervously straightens herself up. "I appreciate it, Durov." She looks around the dark and cheerless inside of their wagon. "I'm sorry things are such a mess. I've been trying to straighten up but…well…keeping the books and all—"

He senses she doesn't want him to go, but he feels awkward being, in essence, entirely alone with her.

As he turns to leave, she stammers, "*Zakhoditye na chaj*?"

"Why, yes. I'd love some tea."

"To thank you for your trouble, that is."

"That way, I can help if he falls out of bed."

She smiles weakly. "I'm afraid he's down for the rest of the day."

They stand for a moment, nervously watching Nikolai and listening to his basso concerto snoring. Durov looks around the wagon and notices that Natasha has pinned up a series of sepia photographs of her time in Moscow, presumably to make it seem more like a home. She rapidly cleans off the clutter from a small table and motions for him to sit. He watches, keenly admiring how she makes a dark infusion of tea in a teapot and then adds water from the samovar, the way high-class Russians make tea. She gets out saucers and porcelain cups and—again a mark of the wealthier class—puts a lump of sugar into his cup instead of obliging him to suck on the sugar in his teeth as he drinks.

He moves his bulky frame around, settling on the chair and preparing to drink the tea. "This is very nice. Ah…thank you, Madame Natasha."

She sighs, looks directly at him, and cautiously adds, "You mean this…is how I used to live and that was very nice, don't you?"

Durov flushes. "I wouldn't presume."

Natasha absent-mindedly twists the end of her thick, chestnut-brown braid. It catches golden in the slanted light from the small wagon window, and Durov catches himself wondering how that long, thick mass of hair might look on a muslin pillow next to him. Then he thinks, *Of course she's probably used to silk pillows, and I've never had anything of the sort. But…*

He realizes he's been looking away while deep in his thoughts, and he now looks back at her. He leans into her, distressed to see her eyes brimming as she tries to hold back tears.

"I'm sure you wouldn't presume anything of the sort, but you might as well ask. How it is I came to fall so low?"

He jumps to reassure her. "We've all had our ups and downs." He crosses himself. "It's not for me to judge."

"No, I gather." She takes a sip of tea. "I like that about you. And it seems you often say exactly what you think."

"My father taught me. The hard way."

"He was a legend, I hear."

"But my family's fallen on hard times."

"I heard. I'm sorry." There's a long pause as she obviously debates whether to continue in this vein. Then she blurts out, "I know something about hard times." There is an awkward silence as Natasha finishes her tea and sighs heavily.

Although he's deliriously happy to be alone with her, Durov's eyes dart around the wagon, concerned about her reputation and the propriety of taking tea while her husband is passed out not two meters from where they sit. He wriggles in his chair as he starts to feel claustrophobic in the dark, closed-in wagon. Much as he relishes this time with her, he knows the gentlemanly thing to do is depart. Looking for an excuse to leave, he stutters, "Ah, M-Madame N-Natasha—"

"Do you think it's a good idea to go to Germany?" Natasha looks over at Nikolai's sleeping bulk, then turns back to Durov. "I ask you in complete confidence."

Durov preens a bit, pleasantly surprised and genuinely pleased she would seek his opinion. He decides to stay after all. He knows that the circus people consider him to be their manager, even if he lacks the formal title because Nikolai is jealous that he's far more capable. Nevertheless, he's surprised to learn that his reputation has likely reached Natasha. He leans back and gently puffs his thick chest. "Since you ask, it could be very good for business. But frankly, I don't think we're equipped for such an arduous journey. The wagon wheels are too flimsy. It's one thing to travel the relatively flat steppes, but quite another to scale mountains."

"I see. But what if we've no money and he'd be sent to…ah…to debtors' prison if we didn't leave?"

"It's that bad, is it?" Durov shifts uncomfortably, distressed both at the overall situation and at what Natasha must be suffering on behalf of her debauched husband. He keenly watches as she, with great effort and a trembling in her large hands, gracefully sets down her tea. What a fine woman she is, well-bred with strong flanks and a thick mane of chestnut hair, even wrapped up in the modest braid she wears. His lips curl into a slight smile. He feels honored she's asked his opinion. Seems to value his advice. Needs his support. She's not completely lost her spirit, and he vows to help her renew it. The same kind of spirit he once had, before he fell from grace and ruined his family. His smile broadens as he considers that helping her regain her sense of self-worth might also help him along the path to his own salvation.

Durov nods several times. "You can count on me, Madame Natasha."

As she places her hand on his sleeve, he sees that it is large and strong, surprisingly so for an aristocratic woman. He admires her strength and warms to her touch. He glances furtively at Nikolai, passed out on the bed. Could he be mistaken, or do Natasha's brown eyes have a warmth in them, possibly inviting him to stay? Or is he just wishing they would? His usual self-doubts immediately rush in. *What could she want with a pig trainer? And a not very handsome pig trainer at that.* But still, she seems quite genuine in her respect for him. *Is it just professional respect, because I'm good at managing things around the circus? Or could it be something even more?*

A knock at the wagon door interrupts them. Ivan's voice calls out. "Is everything all right, Madame Natasha?"

They both fluster as if caught in some improper act. Natasha defensively whips on a fringed shawl and adjusts her thick braid over it. Durov chews his lower lip as he sees Ivan's comely features fill the door. Ivan's smile is broad and his movements light and graceful as he bounds into the wagon. Durov keenly watches Natasha's response, relieved to sense that she is also not happy with this interruption.

She says, in a restrained and formal voice, "Ivan Ivanovich, thank you for coming. Nikolai is resting now. We got him back just fine."

Ivan casts a quizzical glance at Durov. "I see. I'd heard he'd taken ill."

Natasha's deep voice turns frosty. "Well, not really. But you'd know more about his general condition, I expect."

Ivan strides over to Nikolai, picks up one arm, and lets it fall freely. "Yes, I see he'll be fine when he...ah...has a bit of sleep."

Durov exhales sharply, annoyed that, as Ivan checks on Nikolai, his flowing silk dressing gown flies open, exposing his skintight practice clothes that show off his prime physique.

"You must let me see to you while he is...ah...indisposed." Ivan turns on all his good-looking charm and focuses his ingratiating manner on Natasha, who—Durov notices, to his distress—starts to melt.

In what Durov can see is false modesty, Ivan closes his dressing gown and puts his arm around Natasha's shoulder, speaking softly, confidentially, "Nikolai and I are like brothers, you know. I'm sure he's told you how close we are, Madame Natasha. You, being the most important person in his life."

Natasha hesitates. "Well, I don't know about that."

"Oh yes. Nikolai and I...we may have our less admirable moments. And we may like our vodka a bit too much for our own good—"

"For everybody's good," Durov says, not entirely under his breath.

Ivan, ignoring the interruption, continues, "But whenever he's soused, he does nothing but tell me how much he loves you." Natasha looks askance, but Ivan perseveres, quickening his pace. "How fortunate that a woman of your city-bred aristocratic class saw fit to even look at him. I can tell you, he regards you as a goddess. Worships the very hem of your skirt."

"Really? I hadn't realized he'd spoken about me that way."

Durov quickly adds, "Ivan, that's not entirely tr—"

"Oh yes. By St. Nicholas, I swear it, Madame."

"Frankly, I never figured…well…this is nice to know, Ivan Ivanovich." Natasha's face beams as she allows Ivan to escort her back over to the little tea table. "Makes it all a bit more worthwhile, if you know what I mean."

"Indeed I do, Madame. It's only fortunate I can provide you with some small measure of comfort." Ivan smiles broadly, revealing a shining, complete set of real teeth. Out of the corner of his mouth, he sneers and says, "Thank you, Durov, for helping us out." Ivan sprightly moves to usher Durov out. "I think we can manage from here."

Suddenly, Durov is as tongue-tied as his brother. "But…M-Madame N-Natasha and I haven't f-finished our discussions." He casts a plaintive glance at Natasha, willing her to take his part. He's relieved to see her open her mouth to object, but he's crest-fallen when Ivan jumps in.

"Of course Madame Natasha is thankful for your time, but she realizes how much work you have to do around here. Don't you?" Ivan turns and smiles seductively at her. "Natasha?"

Before anything further can be said, Ivan nudges Durov out of the wagon. As Ivan slams the door, Durov hears him say, "Oh, the samovar's bubbling. Tea? May I get you some tea, Natasha? Let me tell you more about how much Nikolai values you. I expect you've had quite the shock this afternoon."

Durov seethes as he clomps down the steps. Boris and Anatoly walk by, arguing about whether they should go to Germany.

Anatoly asks, "What's the m-matter, Durov? Didn't you get N-Nikolai settled?"

Boris winks at Durov. "I expect Natasha appreciates your assistance. Nikolai will drink himself to death soon enough and helping her out…that's the best way to win her heart."

Disgusted, Durov tramps after them. "*Oy.* Women. I prefer pigs. They're less fickle—smarter too."

CHAPTER NINE

Following Durov's departure, Natasha is left alone with Ivan, while Nikolai relentlessly snores in the background. As Ivan turns to see to the samovar, she looks him up and down, very taken by his striking good looks, even if he has the Zubov family's slightly outsized nose. *Very manly... wouldn't want him too pretty.*

Natasha settles back to await being served more tea, enjoying Ivan's aura of majestic, aristocratic gracefulness. His every movement is exaggerated with a delicate, yet masculine flourish. She watches as he slicks back his shiny black, pomaded hair and pours the tea. She closes her eyes, but can't recall any more handsome and sexy officer amidst the swirl of waltzing couples in the grand ballroom of the tsar's palace. She grabs her shawl and pulls it tight, chiding herself for being so stupid as to allow herself to be seduced by that oaf on the bed behind her instead of this handsome man before her.

As she sips her tea, what happened that night flashes through her mind. True, Nikolai was a passionate, if somewhat crass, lover. And it was the first time any man had paid her anything like that kind of thrilling attention. She knows she must have been mad. Actually, she was mad. Mad at her father for pressuring her to make a match while belittling her for her lack of marriageable prospects. She seethes as she recalls her father nodding at her ample rear and joking, "All your best years are behind you." She remembers the sour look on his face as he chided her that she would end up a spinster if she didn't do something...and fast.

Natasha's broad shoulders slump as the shame of it courses through her. She attempts a small, polite laugh, in the deep voice that her father also ridiculed. She winces, as her father's reproaches flood back: "You and your brother should have traded voices...and physiques too, while you were at it." Why did she have to grow so tall and have hands so large, when her delicate brother could easily have inherited them instead? And what good did it do her, to be the better horseman, longing to play polo, whereas he was so impossibly timid that horses always sensed they had their own lead?

Ivan looks over to her cup and asks, "Shall I pour some more?" As he pours, Ivan poses this way and that, flirting outrageously with her.

She pretends to be eyeing him, even as she remembers the time she and her brother planned to disguise her so she could enter the tsar's grand horse match instead of him; but they were discovered, she was locked in her room, and her sweet, gentle brother was humiliated on the field. And how the society girls giggled when she split her corset during her debut in St. Petersburg. She knew she shouldn't have eaten so much the week following that last fitting. But she was nervous—terrified really. And ultimately furious at everyone for judging her so harshly—although no one has ever judged her as ruthlessly as she's judged herself. Natasha's olive skin turns purple with the horror and shame of it all. Ivan, however, appears to be interpreting her reaction differently.

He edges closer. "Madame Natasha...Natasha?"

She nods as demurely as she can, demure being a most unnatural state for her. "It's just that the tea is so warm, Ivan Ivanovich."

"Please, call me Ivan." He narrows his dark eyes, and Natasha notices, with astonishment, that his eyebrows are as pomaded as his hair.

Ivan whispers, "You know, the aristocrats in this country must stay together. These peasants won't ever be satisfied even though the Old Tsar freed them so they're no longer serfs. They're going to insist on more and more." He nods. "I'm afraid we are in for more and more uprisings."

Natasha exhales sharply, remembering what it was like to be an aristocrat in Russian society. But even as she'd reveled in her high station in life, she'd never wished ill on the peasant class. "The so-called attempted revolution two years ago? I don't think they meant to incite the riot that ensued."

Ivan lifts his chin to talk down his nose to her, in an "aristocratic" manner. "I'm sure they did, don't you think?"

Natasha lifts her chin in response. "No, I don't think so. It was just unfortunate that they managed to converge on the White Palace from all directions at once. It rather caught the guards off guard, if you take my meaning."

Ivan shrugs and pulls a tiny box from the pocket in his dressing robe. He pinches some snuff into his nose. "Yes, well..." He tries to avoid sneezing until he can finish his dissertation. "But, it's just the beginning with these low-life peasants. I'm sure you see that we must be prepared for the worst." He sneezes just as Nikolai snorts and turns over. "And we must stick together to protect our aristocratic heritage." Ivan leans in with a conspiratorial lifting of one of his pomaded eyebrows.

Natasha studies Ivan's handsome features. She must confess she likes being wooed by him, but she doesn't like the judgmental words emanating from his finely shaped mouth. She reaches toward a nearby cabinet to grab a fan, intending to flourish it like a lady at court to give herself some breathing space. Ivan, however, intercepts her hand and places it high up on his thigh. For a moment, she smiles at the feel of how well muscled it is, then jerks away. She tries to keep her tremulous voice level. "Pardon me, Ivan Ivanovich...I mean Ivan." She casts an anxious glance toward Nikolai.

Ivan says, "I recognize that pitch in his snore. He's only halfway through sleeping it off. We have lots of time, *moya dorogoy*, my dear Natasha."

Natasha, distressed and flattered all at once, says, "Ivan, I-I don't know what you mean."

"Surely such a handsome woman as yourself has been pursued by many men. Just because you're married—"

"To your closest friend."

"Let's just say to my friend. Nikolai doesn't really allow anyone to get close."

"I've noticed." She plans to give him a slight push back, but, not realizing how her anxiety has contributed to and magnified her own strength, she shoves him quite hard. Flustered and not wanting to offend, she blurts out, "You must excuse me. Everything is still rather new for me here, and I don't want to—"

"Make him angry? Of course not," he whispers. "I promise you, he's really out cold." Ivan grabs her hand and kisses it, up along her arm. She breathes deeply, meaning to stop him at every kiss, until she realizes he's advanced to her shoulder.

"Ivan, I really—" *His skin is so smooth.*

He kisses her neck.

"I really do think—" *How nice to be embraced by someone who's not as hairy as a bear.*

He kisses her ear.

"Ah...what was I saying...I do think—" *If only Nikolai were so gentle...so thrilling. I could let Ivan do this all day.*

Ivan moves to kiss her on the lips, and she leans into him. But at the last moment, she swoops out from underneath his embrace and stands. "I'm sorry, but you need to go."

Ivan's lips are kissing the air before he realizes she's not within range.

She says with as much firmness as she can muster, "Ivan, I'm quite serious." *Damn my convent upbringing.*

Ivan straightens up and bows slowly and deeply from the waist, as a good aristocrat would. "Of course, Madame. I did not mean to overstay my welcome. We can certainly continue our political discussions another time." He rolls his head around, cracking his neck, as if to begin his warm up. "Besides, I must get to my practice session. I will do something special to get your attention at our next performance."

Natasha's olive skin flushes as, despite herself, she feels the warmth of attraction. "You already have my attention, Ivan."

He smiles seductively, then kisses her chastely—but lingers a bit too long for pure chasteness—on both cheeks. "*Bonjour,* Madame."

She hasn't heard French spoken since being at the tsar's court. She's conflicted—it is so very comforting, but now so very foreign in her banished state. But she gives him an overly cheerful, gentle-but-dismissive tap on his muscular chest with her fan. "Good day, Ivan." Watching him go, she stares lustfully at his tight rear end and bites down on her knuckle—hard.

CHAPTER TEN

ORDINARILY, WHEN THE caravan is on the move, Anna Tatianna Ivanova Zubov preens on the front of her wagon. She loves to model her mother's traveling cape, with its swooping neckline that flatters her own long, swan-like neck. She also adjusts herself to show off her mother's long woolen skirt, although she has to fold the top over and over so it fits her much shorter frame. Despite enjoying being dressed up like her mother, however, she hates to ride next to her brother, Ivan Ivanovich. He won't let her drive her very own caravan. And he has no patience for allowing her to stop and give small clumps of wildflowers to Daisy, their mule.

Now, as the circus trudges from Russia to Germany over the mountainous terrain, it's gotten very rough. At first, it was sunny in the countryside below, and Anna was excited to pass great stretches of fields, bountiful and full of budding spring crops of hay, barley, corn, and beans. As they climb, however, the farmland gives way to a forest so dense the sun is barely able to penetrate. Patches of late spring snow melt during the day, then freeze up again at night, causing yawning ruts in the dirt road and making the increasingly narrow path a treacherous mess of slippery patches.

Mist rises through a light drizzle, which Anna would typically find comforting because rain always washes away her sadness. But Anna pulls her traveling cloak tighter as she realizes that the combination of drizzle and mist is not only distressing but treacherous. It obscures the severely rutted path ahead. Anna feels a tightness of fear enveloping her like a second cloak as she surveys that the road is so narrow there is barely enough room for one mule, much less the double rig that the larger and heavier wagons require. Anna's voice is normally as clear and light as a tinkling bell, but she strains it shouting, "Ivan, you must slow down! You must!" She pounds her tiny fist on his knee. "Daisy will lose her footing."

Miraculously though, Daisy and the other mules fight on, and even though the air is thinner, the animals don't yet seem to be affected by the altitude.

Anna grabs the side of the jolting wagon and takes a deep breath. She cranes her long neck out to check up and down the wagon train. She squints, trying to see through the mist to determine whether other wagons are having similar difficulty. She and Ivan are about a third of the way from the front of the train of wagons, and she looks up and back to see rolls of canvas and brightly colored fabric sticking out of the small square windows of the performers' wagons. Lorries are covered with iron and steel poles. Rolling cages hold the smaller animals, such as the dogs, the pelicans, and the falcons. She's grateful that the two brown bears ride in closed-in boxes on wheels, not only for their own comfort against the elements but also to avoid frightening fellow travelers they might encounter along the road. Way at the end, the circus elephant, Zoya—their small pachyderm, which is all the circus can afford—drags a kind of sledge behind her, piled high with circus trunks that she will lift, one by one, with her own trunk when they camp. A variety of performers, looking remarkably like ordinary folk when they are out of costume and makeup, are dispersed throughout the two-seat buggy-fronts of the wagons. Like Anna, they are all encountering a series of molar-dislodging bumps as they rein in the harnessed mules to keep them on the narrow and precarious path.

The caravan pulls to a stop to rest the animals. Ivan gets down from the wagon to grudgingly feed Daisy. He sneers at his sister. "Daisy is just as dumb and even more stubborn than you are."

In addition to treating her mule with wildflowers, Anna likes to give Daisy a piece of sugar to keep up her energy and spirits. She jumps down, reaches into her pocket for a cube, and wraps her tiny hand around it. She closes her eyes, remembering how her late mother used to tell her how graceful she was and how important it is to have a woman to add appeal to the act. Normally Anna can't bring herself to eat sugar, lest her father chide her for being too heavy to catch. But she takes vicarious pleasure in giving the sugar to her mule. Now, however, with her anger boiling over at the increasing oppressiveness of her brother, she's more and more tempted to eat some herself. *Just plop it in my mouth and swoon over a flood of sweet sensations. Float buoyantly in a sea of mounds and mounds of sugar.*

Anna bites a nail as she tries to resist the sugar meant for Daisy.

"Stop biting your nails, Anna Tatianna Ivanova," Ivan barks. "You'll jeopardize your grip."

"Ivan Ivanovich, you're worried about my well-being now?"

"If your cuticles bleed, I don't want to be the one to drop you."

"Like Papa dropped—"

"*Zatknis!* It was an accident."

"After she tried to run away?"

Ivan leans menacingly over Anna, whispering through his perfectly white, clenched teeth. "Why would she leave her children? Tell me that."

Anna cowers. "I . . . I don't know. I've never known, and I wish she hadn't left us—I mean, I wish she hadn't died." Tears stream down Anna's heart-shaped face.

Through her tears, she sees Ivan look around, clearly afraid the others will notice them fighting. As everyone mounts their wagons again, she slips Daisy the sugar and takes her place in the buggy, as far away from Ivan as she can manage.

Ivan snaps the reins to get their mule started. He growls, "You've got our mother's wagon. And her precious porcelain tub, which weighs a thousand kilos. We drag it everywhere just for you. So stop your sniveling or that tub and this wagon, with all her worn-out pillows, goes over that cliff. And you get to live with us in our wagon."

Anna bites her lip. While she misses her mother, she's begun to think fondly of her visits with Madame Natasha, who reclines on her mother's soft silken pillows even if they are shabby. She was enthralled to hear Natasha say, on her last visit, "My dear, it is totally unfair that women have to obey the men in their lives, especially when the women are, as often happens, infinitely more capable."

Anna had nodded her head in silent agreement, bitterly remembering the many times she'd suggested improvements to the act. Never taken seriously, she'd been appalled when Ivan suggested something she already came up with and their father heaped praise on him for *his* innovation. Even as she wholeheartedly agreed with Natasha, did she feel true affection for the older woman, or was she just cozying up to her to get an act of her own? So she could be noticed by a gentleman who would propose to her and take her away from the circus altogether?

Daisy strains to pull the wagon up the steep incline. Anna sighs as she feels even more protective of the mule, but she knows she can't do anything about the situation. Anna can hear Nikolai's drunken serenade up ahead, as he and Natasha ride in their wagon, leading the woeful little caravan.

Anna turns to her brother. "How can he drink so much?"

"He's built up quite a tolerance."

"So have you."

"Listen, Annala, my drinking liberates me from gravity. I can fly higher when—"

"You're drunk. That's what you always say. But you need to keep your timing straight or both of us could get hurt."

"You should keep *your* timing straight—when you open and close your not-so-pretty little mouth or—"

"Papa wouldn't like you threatening me."

He snarls. "Threaten? This is just friendly, brotherly advice. My dear sister, you're stuck in the act. No man wants to marry your ugly little pile of bones."

"Maybe not in Russia, but I hear there are gentlemen—with refined tastes—in Germany."

"Keep dreaming, Annala." Ivan laughs maliciously and slaps Daisy with the reins, while Anna fumes.

The caravan moves slowly on. A steep mountain is on their left, and a sharp cliff falls directly off the road on their right. The increasing drizzle makes the footing even less secure, and some of the circus people take out tarpaulins to shield themselves. Anna hates when Ivan puts up their tarp, because he feels freer to heap verbal and sometimes even physical abuse onto her.

Up ahead, however, the mist appears to be clearing. Anna can more clearly see Nikolai's tall form drunkenly swaying outwards from his wagon, his long black hair flying loose in the spirited wind. His singing ranges from slurred Russian folk song to operatic screech. Anna shifts uncomfortably on the bench. "I hate to see Madame Natasha subjected to that."

"*Da...da...*he never could carry a tune."

"That's not what I meant."

"*Oy.* She's in a rough spot. I won't say anything against *moy tovarishch* Nikolai but—"

"Everyone says it for you. We have to go to Germany because he—and you—drank away all our money." Anna's alabaster skin reddens in anger as she brushes a few wet raindrops from her skirt.

"Who says that? Natasha?" Ivan shifts the reins to one hand and, with his other, surreptitiously and viciously squeezes Anna's pale, slender arm.

"Ouch. *Prekrati eto!*"

"I want to know what Natasha told you. If you don't say, I'll wrap your wrists so tight—"

"It's no secret. She thinks we'll make more money in Germany. Especially since we aren't welcome in so many villages in Russia. I expect you and Nikolai know why."

"She's a bit of a cow. But she's got a good head on her shoulders—I'll say that for her." He clucks his tongue and snaps the reins to make Daisy go faster and keep up with the caravan. Then he clearly has an idea and leans back. "Come to think of it, if anything ever happens to Nikolai, she will need someone to help her run the circus."

Anna swiftly turns toward Ivan. She knows how malicious her brother can be, but it's hard to imagine he'd actually do something criminal. And against his bosom friend and drinking companion, Nikolai. "You're not suggesting—"

"You said yourself how much she doesn't deserve a lout like Nikolai."

"That's not what I meant." Anna knows Natasha isn't fond of Nikolai, as she's confessed privately many times. But the man is her husband after all. "You aren't planning anything—"

"Don't worry. I've seen him drunker than that skunk Durov tried to tame a while back."

As the wagon crosses a rough series of bumps, Anna wraps her traveling cape closer and sighs, "That skunk certainly was an unfortunate mistake."

CHAPTER ELEVEN

DUROV JOSTLES IN his wagon and adjusts the reins to direct his mules this way and that, as he tries to keep them steady on the rut-filled mountain road. He and Anatoly are pulling behind their wagon a separate cage full of pigs, which squeal horrifically at all the bumping. Durov keeps checking behind them, as he hates to put his animals through needless stress. "They don't care for this terrain."

He looks out at the thick, dense forest on the left, mountain side of the road. The right side of the road benefits from a view of the sunny foot-hills they've left behind, although there is a sharp and precipitous drop-off over the side of the cliff. Durov shifts uncomfortably as he notes that the road, sheltered by the tall fir trees, does not sit in the sun long enough to melt the ice, which makes the switchbacks in the narrow road all the more death-defying. The brief drizzle doesn't help, as it freezes in patches. But fortunately, the sun comes out again. Even so, Durov knows that his vigorously oinking pigs are smart enough to sense the danger.

"I k-keep putting a lot of extra hay to...p-pad their cage," Anatoly volunteers. "But they keep eating it."

"When we stop, let's find something else to dampen the shock. Even so,

I'm worried this road is too steep. The switchbacks put us much too close to the edge for our mules to safely manage."

"They don't see very well, do they?"

"That's what I'm most worried about."

Durov takes it upon himself to look out not just for their own animals but for all the circus people, the clowns, the laborers, the trick dogs and their trainers, and the bears. The only animal who seems to be taking the trip in her stride is Zoya, the elephant, who plants every step with care and doesn't seem to notice if she's going up or down the steep gradient. The dwarf brothers need two of them up front on their wagon at any one time to keep their mule on track—one to sit on the top of the bench and work the reins, and the other to sit in the boot of the buggy to steer. As the one steering is too short to see the road, the one up top has to scream directions. Durov finds their whole noisy situation quite unnerving, although he admires their ingenuity.

Some of the other sideshow acts have also learned to work together. The lady with no arms sits next to the man with no legs, and between the two of them, they actually manage quite well. And the Siamese twins have choreographed who will pull which rein and who will push which lever, so their routine is as smooth as anyone's.

Up ahead, Nikolai whips his mule as he goes into an operatic trill. Durov clenches his teeth, trying to control his fury. "He shouldn't be driving drunk like that. He's endangering Natasha, not to mention his mule. Someone should whip him like he whips that poor creature."

Anatoly adds, "It's a g-good th-thing mules can't hear very well either. That aria is real a-animal cruelty."

"I don't know how Natasha stands it." Durov leans out and strains to catch a glimpse of her, to make sure she's all right. Anatoly is capable enough to steer the wagon himself—even if he doesn't think he is. Durov considers whether he should jump off their buggy, run up ahead, and dislodge Nikolai. But that would create a scene, and Nikolai, already drunk, would likely take it out on Natasha when they made camp that night. So Durov settles in for the long haul.

Suddenly, he hears screeching up ahead. Nikolai screams at his mule and whips her harder. "You stupid beast. Get back on the road."

Natasha yells, "Nikolai, *Zadirzhat*. Stop it right now. You'll kill that mule and us too."

Durov winces in horror as the wagon tilts over the edge of the sheer cliff. The drop is so steep and long that the valley below is barely visible. As the wagon begins to turn over, Natasha jumps clear. Durov runs to help right the wagon, with Ivan close on his heels. Durov can see that Nikolai, in his drunken state, has fallen upside down into the crevice in the buggy, between the bench and the front end. Durov is mesmerized at how such a large man can fit into such a small space.

Natasha, lying on the ground, looks up at the wagon and shrieks, "Nikolai, watch out. Pull up. Pull up."

Durov gasps to see that Nikolai, thinking he's right side up, is actually pulling the reins in the wrong direction. Ivan helps Natasha up from the dirt. He hesitates for a moment and then, with a malicious sneer, turns to the hitch that connects the buggy seat from the bigger wagon. Durov recoils to see Ivan start to pull up on the iron bar to unhinge the buggy.

"Don't! Stop!" Durov yells as he tries to right the buggy with Nikolai in it. The mule's front hooves scramble over the edge, and, terrified, she brays horrifically as she tries to maintain her footing. Durov shouts at Ivan, "Stop. You're going to kill that mule." As a quick afterthought, he adds, "Nikolai too."

Paralyzed with disbelief, Durov watches Ivan strain to uncouple the buggy—then it separates from the wagon. The buggy crashes over the cliff as the mule shrieks and Nikolai screams, "Noooo!" on the same note as the end of his aria. Down they go, tumbling, mule over buggy, buggy over Nikolai, Nikolai over mule, and so on. Falling and crashing against the craggy mountain cliff.

Durov stands, as if in a trance, watching this slow motion avalanche.

Down, down, down they go. Bronzy, the strongman, runs over and jumps onto a tree, hanging out as he leans over the cliff to get a better view. He winces and jerks his head back just as two relatively equal splattering sounds—one for Nikolai and one for the mule—are heard from below. Bronzy slowly shakes his massive, domed head and crosses himself.

Almost in shock, Durov hesitates, considering what to do. He looks over at Ivan, who shrugs and breaks into a weak smile as he holds the iron bar in his hand. Durov thinks back. It all happened so fast. Is it right to accuse Ivan? Even if he did it intentionally, how could Durov tell Natasha that Ivan, rather than helping, just pushed Nikolai—and that poor mule—to death. Mightn't the buggy have gone over anyway, given Nikolai's reckless drunken driving? Besides, didn't he also want Nikolai dead? And if he accuses Ivan, someone might just as easily accuse him, since he was standing right there. He decides it's better to carry on and keep the circus together. And...might Natasha, now a widow even become interested in him? *That's too ungentlemanly a thought to even consider right now.*

He shrugs and nods to Ivan, communicating that he won't say anything. Ivan smirks in return. Then they both turn to help Natasha. Anna races over, joined by their entire circus family. Svetlana, the bearded lady, sobs, tears running down her hairy chin. The fat lady, Alesha, screams over and over, layers of blubber jiggling beneath the tent she wears as a dress. Grigori, the fire eater, burps hot ashes. The four dwarf brothers rush about, pantomiming their distress, as they dart from the edge of the cliff and back to the wagon in perfect Chinese fire drill formation. Everyone else reaches out to comfort Natasha: "Are you all right? What happened? Nikolai was drunk, but...how horrible for Nikolai...how horrible for you, dear Natasha."

Durov can only think, *How horrible for the mule.*

When the commotion dies down, Durov is both shocked and distressed to see that Ivan has taken complete control of the situation—and Natasha. Ivan offers to escort her to the next outcropping, where they can make camp and decide what to do about Nikolai's death.

Durov attempts to intervene. "Madame Natasha, might I help—"

"No need," Ivan quips as he takes Natasha's arm and leads her away.

Watching them go, Durov bitterly reflects on how, with his weathered and craggy features, he was never the kind of fellow to attract the girls. No one except his mother ever appreciated how sincere he was and how good he could be to his animals. She used to stroke his broad forehead and tell him that any woman would be happy to be treated as well as he treated their horses. Durov fights back the lump about to take over his throat and turns to see to the mules in the caravan; he goes along the line to quiet them down, then returns to his wagon, where Anatoly is adding pine boughs for extra padding to the pig cage.

He wraps his arm around Anatoly's slender shoulder and whispers into his ear, "Don't tell anyone, but I think Ivan pushed Nikolai off the cliff on purpose."

Anatoly's soft eyes widen as he brushes a lock of curly hair off his forehead. "I wouldn't put it p-past him. You should look after Natasha b-before he gets his h-hooks into her."

"The woman just lost her husband, for Christ's sake."

"All the more r-reason she needs s-someone like you, not some h-handsome, m-muscled g-gigolo like Ivan."

Durov rolls his eyes. "Handsome, muscled…that makes it easier to compete for her affections."

"You've got to. Not just for N-Natasha's sake, but for everyone in the circus. We need you—not Ivan. He'll just r-run things even d-deeper into the ground."

"If she's so blind, he can have her."

Anatoly sighs. "Durov, don't go getting all p-pigheaded on us now."

CHAPTER TWELVE

Since Ivan has changed wagons to escort Natasha, Anna Tatianna luxuriously spreads across her whole buggy. But she deeply mistrusts her brother's intentions toward the newly widowed Natasha. The circus caravan pulls up at the next clearing, which is sheltered against the mountain from an increasingly strong wind. Durov directs them to make camp on the relatively flat ground, although it is still frozen in patches. Anna shivers against the cold; she is relieved that she chose to wear her mother's high boots, having stuffed them with rags to fit her tiny feet.

Since the accident, Anna has cried big, overblown tears. Not for Nikolai, but to convince Madame Natasha she has a bond with her, especially now that she is a widow and in total command of the circus. Anna sees an unexpectedly fortuitous opportunity to argue at least for a more featured role in her family's trapeze act, if not for an act of her very own. She decides to take charge of Nikolai's funeral arrangements. Through her blubbering, Anna urges Natasha to sequester herself in her wagon while Anna makes arrangements. She rushes to the canteen where she implores Boris, the most articulate person around, to perform Nikolai's last rites.

At first, Boris, who is violently adverse to anything faintly resembling anything faintly religious, vehemently declines. And when the diminutive Lottie walks right up to the pint-sized Boris and offers to add a spiritual note to the proceedings, Boris is even more aghast. "What? In front of everyone, you want to spout your psychic mumbo jumbo over a dead man?"

Lottie grabs her topmost shawl and pulls it tight around her. "Boris, we don't have a dead man. He went over the cliff, remember?"

"All the more reason I should conjure up his image in my inimitable, magician-like way."

Anna steps back out of their way, amused at how Boris and Lottie always fight, despite their obviously genuine attraction to each other—which neither will admit. Their esoteric arguments over magic and psychic phenomena are well beyond Anna, but she enjoys hearing them anyway. Boris insists that his magic is purely in the earthly, practical realm of illusion and sleight-of-hand, while Lottie argues that her trances represent real psychic ethereal communications with the netherworld.

Boris turns to Anna and whispers, loud enough for Lottie to hear, "I'm sorry Lottie can't contribute to the service. We can't have anything sacrilegious." He strokes his goatee for emphasis. "I will do the service by myself, my dear Anna."

Lottie rises up on her tiptoes and angrily looks Boris in the eye. "Have it your way, but I'm going to meditate for his poor departed soul."

It's time, Anna thinks, *to break them up before there's a fight, which might upset Natasha.* She reaches across the top layer of Lottie's shawls and gently swings her around. "Dearest Lottie, I'm sure Madame Natasha would be very happy to have a private session with you to contact her beloved, dearly departed Nikolai—"

Boris interjects, "I rather doubt that. I'm sure she's glad he's gone, the drunken lout."

Anna ignores him, continuing to lead Lottie away from the fray. She looks back over her shoulder and says, in her most gentle and convincing voice, "Boris, why don't you go and prepare. It's getting late, and we should conclude everything by sunset. Please, we all want this to go smoothly." She turns to Lottie. "Perhaps we can get your brother to help us set up."

Lottie casts a haughty glance back at Boris. "Of course. We don't want this to be more of a fiasco than necessary."

Anna, Bronzy, and Lottie march solemnly to the side of the cliff nearest to where Nikolai and the mule went over. They enlist the help of the workers to assemble the benches from the canteen wagon into a makeshift altar with church pews. It's the first time Anna has had the chance to assert herself in front of the whole circus. She twitters about, excited to be directing everyone. The circus people bring tall bronze candlesticks, beeswax, and icons, and heap them onto the front bench, which serves as the altar. The four dwarf brothers decide to give Nikolai the kind of one-gun salute they use in their act. This occurs when they wheel in their cannon and Pasha, Masha and Max stuff Vasha into its mouth. Then, despite Vasha's overblown wailing and crying, they shoot him out, into a net, to great applause. Now, for the funeral ceremony and their one-gun salute, they run around the cannon, checking the fuse and the mixture of gunpowder, trying to decide where to aim it so no one will get hurt.

As the sun starts to plunge west behind the mountain, the late-afternoon light begins to dim into the gray-green of forest twilight. Anna hurries everyone along, and as they start to assemble, Boris appears in his father's long magician's cloak—which, as usual, he keeps tripping over.

Anna feels panic rising in her gut, as she's horrified to think that Boris will ruin her plans to impress Natasha with a flawless funeral performance. She rushes over and whispers, "Boris, what are you wearing?"

Anatoly races over and takes Anna's side. "Boris, you can't w-wear a magician's r-robe to officiate at a fu-funeral."

Anna turns to Anatoly and gives him a radiant smile. How strange it is, how rare, and how nice, to have someone fervently support her.

Boris quips, "Why not? We don't have a body. And we're consigning his spirit to the unknown."

Anna says through gritted teeth, "Some people…perhaps his widow, Natasha, might not appreciate your approach." She looks to Anatoly for further reinforcement, which he gladly provides by vehemently shaking his curly, fair-haired head.

Boris is crestfallen. "I had hoped she'd view me as the great magician I strive to be. Like my father." Boris reaches into his sleeve. "Here's my rabbit!" He produces a white dove, which he stuffs into another pocket, then pats his cloak all around. "Oh, wait." He smiles broadly. "Here's my rabbit." He pulls out a black silk top hat, looks inside, and shakes his head. No rabbit.

Anna's porcelain complexion reddens as her exasperation mounts. She rolls her eyes at Anatoly and gently elbows him, encouraging him to restrain Boris.

"B-Boris, this isn't an au-audition," Anatoly snaps.

She nods, encouraging Anatoly to get bolder.

"Boris, I-I insist you t-take that cloak off and p-put your birds b-back in their cages. Your rabbit, Rabbit, too."

Anna raises an eyebrow.

Anatoly turns to her. "His rabbit is named—"

"Rabbit. All my rabbits are named rabbit."

Anna asks, "How can you tell them apart?"

Boris, all too happy to oblige, says, "Well, you see, my dear, you pick them up and turn them over—"

Anatoly, horrified, jumps in: "Boris! That's not w-what she m-means."

"Oh, all right." Boris slips the robe from his shoulders, and three doves and two rabbits scramble out. Anatoly and Boris run to catch them, scooping them up into Boris's top hat.

Despite her anxiety over the funeral arrangements, Anna giggles at the spectacle. Her lustrous black hair streaks auburn in the sunset.

Deep into the chase, Boris calls over his shoulder, "We'll be right back, Anna Tatianna." In a few minutes, Boris returns, having exchanged his magician's robe for his Sunday finest—a corduroy suit with a vest and watch chain. Anatoly has straightened himself up as well, and the two of them walk arm in arm. Anna, much relieved, goes to Natasha's wagon and retrieves her, solicitously ministering to her as she directs her to the front of the benches arranged for the ceremony. Natasha has fashioned a thin, black veil to cover her long chestnut-brown braid, which she's wrapped around and around on the crown of her head. Anna thinks she appears to be more in shock than grief. But she's relieved that the veil hides Natasha's face, affording some privacy from the curious and peering eyes of the circus folk.

Anatoly slips in beside Anna on the front bench. His mop of curly hair shines golden in the last of the sunlight. She stays where she is, so he will have to sit close. *I am so happy he's being so kind and paying attention to me. But of course, he's just a pig trainer, and I couldn't possibly be interested in him.*

Anna smiles at Anatoly, and he shyly smiles back. They both take a deep breath as Boris starts the service.

"We all knew Nikolai to be—" Boris looks to Anatoly for encouragement. Anatoly mimes a large man, wearing a costume.

"Oh yes, he was a big man who filled out his ringmaster's costume very... well... very full."

Anna winces, squinting her large black eyes down into almond-shaped slits, hoping Boris will get through it without offending anyone—too much. She looks around to see Lottie, buried in a mound of shawls topped with a black one for mourning. Lottie sits on the other side of Natasha, in rapt attention and hanging on every word Boris utters. Given their miniature statures, the four dwarf brothers have also claimed places in the first row. Several of the sideshow attractions also sit there, including the Siamese twins, who only take up one spot between them, and the petite bearded lady, Svetlana. She is so small that she can afford to give half of her allotted space to the fat lady, Valeria, who needs all the room she can get.

Anna notices Durov standing off to the side, his hands clasped respectfully in front of him. She's not sure why he does not participate. She knows her brother Ivan has been kind to Natasha, something quite uncharacter-istic for him. And there seems to be some tension between Durov and Ivan, but Anna puts it from her mind. She wills everything to go smoothly so she can be credited with organizing things properly and thereby rise in Natasha's esteem.

She turns back to listen to Boris.

"*Da, da.* Nikolai always made quite a splash, whenever he went out at night—" Anatoly waves his hands no. Boris nods. "*Nyet*...I mean he made quite a splash whenever he went into the ring." Anatoly nods. Boris says, "Yes, and in the ring, he was very commanding. And everyone knew he had new boots because they always squeaked. God rest his soul." Boris waves his hand, making a vague motion that the others interpret as genu-flecting in the Russian Orthodox manner.

The four dwarf brothers cross themselves and mutter, "Amen," in unison. Lottie uses the edge of her topmost shawl to wipe away a tear.

Anna is thankful the service finishes without a hitch. She's also very touched that the huddled group is trying, as she is, to muster as many tears as they can for Natasha's benefit. No one is actually grieving for Nikolai, but Natasha has been good to the circus folk and hasn't flaunted her former high-class status. While the circus people will always consider Natasha an outsider, they're generous people, and all the family any of them has. So they feel compelled to demonstrate the trappings of a family funeral—complete with vodka, dancing, sibling rivalry, and lots of arguments.

Later that evening, the moon rises and illuminates the caravan, clinging alongside the mountain. Nikolai's wake is in full force, and Natasha sits on a bench alongside Anna, watching the dancing. Because she wants to be the person to most comfort Natasha, Anna is annoyed to see Ivan, swilling vodka, approach Natasha.

"Poor fellow." Ivan sits and tries to put his arm around Natasha. "At least he didn't feel a thing."

Anna cringes at her brother's forward, obnoxious manner, and she's delighted to see Natasha slide away from him. "Thank you, Ivan Ivanovich. I appreciate your concern, but—"

"I don't think she wants to be rushed, Ivan," Anna interjects, angry that her brother could be so callous. *He thinks that because he's so good-looking, every woman will fall at his feet. But Madame Natasha won't. Now she's out from under Nikolai—in more ways than one.* Anna giggles to herself at her salacious joke.

The muscles in Ivan's jaw twitch. "What's so funny Annala? Why don't you find some of the riffraff to dance with and let the high-class grownups talk?"

Natasha turns red. "Please, Ivan. This isn't the time for family quarrels."

Anna wants to be alone with Natasha, so she is perturbed at Anatoly, who is approaching. In his nervousness, his stutter becomes even more pronounced. "Anna, i-is there anything I-I ca-can d-do? Get you so-some vodka? Something more t-to eat, perhaps?"

While Anna has always been fond of Anatoly and his gentle ways, and while she's grateful to him for standing up to Boris before the funeral service, she is resolute; he simply isn't the kind of gentleman she'd like to have the opportunity to become interested in. "That's very sweet of you, Anatoly. No, thank you. We just want to be left alone, don't we, Madame Natasha?"

Natasha nods. "Gentlemen, I appreciate your concern, but Anna's right. This is a solemn night for me...and for all of us."

Ivan, however, will not take no lightly. He stands and grabs Natasha's hand, pulling her up. "Oh, come on, Natasha. We all know that you know you're better off without Nikolai. No one would blame you for dancing on his grave—although we don't have a grave, but you know what I mean." He brings her close to him, in a dancing position.

Natasha struggles to disengage from Ivan. Durov, who's also been keeping an eye on Natasha, rushes over.

"The lady says she doesn't want to dance, Ivan. You'd better go and find another partner."

Anna watches intently as Durov glances at Natasha, obviously hoping that she will back him up. In any case, Anna doesn't want trouble between Durov, whom she respects, and Ivan, who is, after all, her brother. A broken arm would put their entire act out of commission for months. On the other hand, it would sideline Ivan so she could take a bigger role and be more noticed. But no, she can't wish her brother physical harm, so she stands up and, in a neat gymnastic feat, inserts herself between Ivan and Durov.

Ivan steps back, takes a swig of vodka, raising the bottle high and almost clipping Durov on the chin. "All right. I can take a hint." He staggers off.

Natasha says, "Thank you all for being so kind to me. I need to retire. This has been a very stressful day, and I've got to think about where we go from here. Do we return to Russia or go on to Germany?"

Durov gently takes her by the elbow, leading her toward her wagon. "Of course we understand. We can talk about this in the morning. There are big decisions to be made, and we want you to know we support you, no matter what you decide."

Anna looks after them and then turns to Anatoly with a smile. "Durov is an admirable man, isn't he?"

"I think s-so. But he's my brother, s-so I would have t-to think so, wouldn't I?"

"Not necessarily." She bites a nail and says, more to herself than to Anatoly, "Ivan is my brother, but sometimes I really hate him." She shyly looks up at Anatoly. "Oh, it's just that he's so bossy. I'd like to do lots of things in the act, but they won't even let me try."

Anatoly's voice becomes clearer and more forceful. "Wha-what kind of things?"

Anna takes a deep breath and decides to confide in him. She leans over and lets her long black hair brush against Anatoly's shoulder. She whispers, "I could do some high-wire tricks of my own, if only I had the rigging."

Anatoly's boyish face breaks into a huge grin. "I'm good with ropes. I know how to tie the pigs up when we have to brush their teeth."

"You'd help me?"

"Of c-course. Just tell me when you want to p-practice. I could s-string something up from a tree br-branch, fix up a pulley like Durov showed me, and pull you up." He takes a deep breath. "I can tell by l-looking, you are much l-lighter than our b-biggest pig, Sasha."

Anna blushes. "That's quite a compliment." *He's a bit odd, but really sweet.*

Anatoly is emboldened. "W-would you care to d-dance, Anna Tatianna Ivanova?"

"You can call me Anna, if you like." She smiles as she takes his soft but strong hand. She's amused that he's not immediately sure where to go, so she leads them to the circle of dancing.

The party remains in full force as long as the vodka flows, the balalaika music plays, and there are people sober enough to dance—even if they land on their asses trying to squat and kick their legs out. Boris, in his deep voice, has donned his magician's robe and articulates an entertaining string of patter as he tries out some new card tricks. Anna is delighted that people wildly applaud, even though they're so drunk they clearly aren't really following.

Long about two o'clock in the morning, someone decides to take the traditional *dance with the bear* a bit too seriously and lets Lyudmila, one of the brown bears, out of her cage. Fortunately, she has, as tradition would have it in their little circus, learned to do the two-step. So the dancing continues until dawn.

CHAPTER THIRTEEN

THE SUN RISES on the circus camp, huddled between the mountainside and the rocky cliffs. A pale golden light illuminates the cluster of wagons with their lacquered and fanciful painted sides, still muddy from yesterday's climb. Natasha walks just beyond the camp in the wet morning dew, her long, black skirt edging the tips of the damp grass in the clearing by the side of the cliff where Nikolai went over. Her boots are soaked through, but she doesn't feel the wet. She casts her mind back to that first night with Nikolai, remembering how charismatic he was in his ringmaster's uniform. So in command of all those people. She was flattered that he zeroed in on her and her cousin, Georgiana.

Georgiana had convinced her to sneak out of her father's dacha that evening. Georgiana had pleaded, "Your father's gone back to Moscow, and the circus will only play a night or two at most." So, while the groom was having supper in the downstairs kitchen, the girls took the horse and buggy and slipped out of the stables. Georgiana was slender and pretty and reckless; Natasha had always been in awe of her ability to attract every man within a fifty-meter radius. Even as she now trembles in the morning dampness outside the circus camp, Natasha remembers trembling as she put on her cloak, sure that someone would notice Georgiana and that perhaps he'd have a friend to notice her. Maybe some well-bred officers from the nearby regiment.

Natasha picks up a small stone in the field and angrily flings it over the edge of the rocky cliff. *I was a sucker for a uniform. The wrong uniform.* In a fog of despair as thick as the morning mist, she ponders her situation. Not only is she disowned by her family, with no prospect of returning to her former comfortable life, but she did it all for a man who turned out to be an abusive oaf. *How could I have allowed him to intimidate me? Be so disrespectful…God rest his soul.* Natasha shivers in the chilly, thin air, thinking that not only is she alone again, but she's surrounded by all these…these circus people. *This band of freaks and slovenly laborers.* Since Nikolai had no brothers or sons, the circus is now her responsibility. If they go bankrupt and she can't pay the wages due, she could be forced to trade Nikolai's prison of a circus wagon for the very same debtors' prison Nikolai had been headed for.

Irate at the situation and at herself, Natasha snaps off a branch from a white birch that glows golden in the sunrise. She violently swishes the branch in the tall grass. She looks up to the mountain road with its switchbacks and steep cliffs, streaked with sunlight deepening the craggy hollows and making the path all the more foreboding. She tries to think of something to lift her spirits. Well, these circus folk may be low class, but she has to admit, they have treated her like a queen—even though most of them clearly hated Nikolai. Curious, how these outcasts are more sincere than everyone in Moscow, who had tittered behind her back at her awkwardness and big hands. At how she didn't glide on the dance floor. At how her gloves kept wrinkling up because her palms were so large and sweaty.

A deep, gentle voice breaks through her thoughts. "Madame, are you all right?"

She turns to see this square, not very tall, and not at all elegant man, emerge from the morning mist. His footing sure, he charges through the tall grass. There's something about him that seems quite honest and reassuring.

"Durov! I was just getting some fresh air. To clear my head."

"That was quite a wake last night, Madame Natasha. You must be exhausted."

Natasha finds herself smiling as she discovers, much to her surprise, that she enjoys having him near. Someone with whom she can be totally frank and who won't judge her for her past transgressions. Her voice is hoarse and even deeper than usual. "I might be exhausted if only I could feel anything—my head is throbbing so."

Durov shyly smiles, but then doffs his cap, his voice growing serious. "I came to find out what you wish to do. Some of the men are beginning to sober up. We have to pack up differently if we're climbing the ridge or going back down."

Natasha's throat closes up in panic. She's never had this kind of responsibility. Summing accounts for practice on the abacus like her father taught her is nothing compared with managing an enterprise by herself—even a small ragtag circus.

Durov adds, "We've got to weight the wagons for either an ascent or a descent." He waits, respectfully, patiently, for her reply.

Natasha realizes that ever since she married Nikolai, she's not been used to being treated so deferentially. And by a craggy-faced, robust, and square-jawed man who's obviously quite capable—someone all the others look up to. "What do you think, Durov? I trust your opinion—"

Just then, Ivan bounds up. "Good morning, Natasha." He rakes his long fingers through his pomaded mass of dark hair. "You're looking rather well considering...I mean...isn't it a fine morning?"

Natasha's cheeks burn. "I hadn't really noticed, Ivan Ivanovich." *My, even after such a rough night, he's as handsome as ever.*

As Natasha stares tongue-tied at Ivan, Durov interjects, "I'm sorry, but—"

"It'll be good to get back to Mother Russia and rebuild our circus," Ivan jumps in. "I'm sure we'll be welcome in more villages now that Nikolai is...well, you know what I mean."

Natasha turns away from Ivan, suddenly afraid to disagree. She weakly acquiesces. "I suppose you're right." The next instant, however, she feels a flash of anger that she's allowed herself to be conditioned by Nikolai these last few months to not counter a man's advice.

Durov quickly adds, "If you'll pardon me for saying—and it really is your decision, Madame Natasha—but I think Ivan Ivanovich is wrong. We're almost at the summit, so the worst is nearly over. I never agreed much with Nikolai, God rest his soul. But I, too, have heard there are lots of wealthy people in Germany."

Ivan's voice is sharp. "Nonsense." He turns to Natasha and adds, with reproach, "The Zubov Family is the main attraction, so we must have the primary say. Certainly over the opinion of this...this pig trainer."

Natasha senses their fight is as much over her as over how to lead the circus; she has to confess that she rather enjoys the attention they're paying her. *Not that they would ever have a duel over me, as I might have dreamed about in Moscow.* She looks between them: Ivan, who seems quite belligerent; and Durov, who is firm in his opinion but exceedingly respectful.

Ivan leans into her and whispers, "Those of our class need to stick together."

She turns to face him. *True, he has high-class bearing, but that's probably more because of his arrogance than any claim to rank.*

He adds, "I'm sure Nikolai would have wanted me to take over, make this important decision—so you don't have to fret a moment longer."

His solicitous tone comes across as a sneer. She takes a step back, the hem of her skirt swishing in the moist dew. She bristles as she realizes Ivan sounds more and more like Nikolai. *Being told what to do...those days are over.* She looks into Durov's earnest, weathered face, then back at the glamorously handsome Ivan, and considers whom to trust. She finally concludes: *I've lost everything in Russia. I might as well start over in Germany.*

Natasha glances over her shoulder to see the sun now fully above the eastern horizon, gleaming in the thin mountain air and warming the day. She imagines cleaning out their filthy wagon, giving away Nikolai's clothes—still reeking with vodka and beer—and opening her prison up to the light. She smooths her skirt with her large hands and straightens her back. "I think Durov is right. What have we got to lose?"

Ivan huffs and sniffs, then wheels around and half-stomps, half-prances off, calling over his shoulder, "*Da, da.* You both think so now. But I am telling you, you're making a big mistake."

Natasha calls after him, "Maybe so, but it's my mistake to make."

She nods with satisfaction as Durov respectfully bows, giving her courage in the face of the terrifying anxiety she feels as they face the road ahead.

"Madame Natasha, I promise that my pigs and I will work hard to make it all come out right."

"*Bol'shoye spasibo* (thank you very much), Durov. Let's hope the Germans aren't too fond of their bacon."

CHAPTER FOURTEEN

DUROV HASN'T FELT such pride in ages, as he tells the circus folk that Natasha has given him her confidence to take charge. Fueled by the optimism of being able to start afresh in a new country, he joyously dances his bulky frame around the wagons, making sure all is secure. Then he leads the performers and laborers as they set off for the summit. While Anatoly takes care of their rig, he drives Natasha's wagon, his chest heaving proudly as he sits next to her. Despite some rough-going near the top, they crest it and descend the other side of the mountain into Prussia. They make that night's camp along the road in a flat space. And by midafternoon the next day, Durov grins broadly as the caravan emerges from the dense forest onto a dazzling bright landscape.

They pass rows and rows of newly planted spring potato and bean fields, as well as groves of stately chestnut trees that edge the pastures. Durov marvels at how immaculate the houses are, with their thatched roofs neatly topping off whitewashed, half-timbered walls. There are flower boxes in every window. *Everything is absolutely spotless and orderly. I've never seen anything like it.*

As is their custom, the circus makes camp outside the town, so the ringmaster can go into the village and confer with the elders. These meetings determine how welcome the circus will be and what percentage of the box office the mayor will require for himself and for the town's coffers. Durov paces around the camp, anxiously awaiting word from Natasha about who she will choose for this important duty. Things must be settled right away before the townsfolk have a chance to solidify and possibly increase their demands.

He can't wait any longer, so he knocks and is invited to enter Natasha's wagon. He's startled to find the wagon cleared of much of its former clutter. The heavy curtains on the wagon windows have been thrown aside and cheery sunlight streams in. Anna is already hard at work pinning up Nikolai's ringmaster's costume to fit Natasha.

Natasha, standing for her fitting, calls to him in a coarse voice through gritted teeth, "Durov, do come in. Don't mind us."

He watches, amused, as she shifts her feet, obviously trying to stand still. Anna, exasperated, scoots on the floor around Natasha, gathering up the fabric to hem it at the arms and legs. Durov regards Natasha. *What a beauty she is, so stately even in that ridiculous costume.*

Anna implores Natasha, "Madame, you must hold still."

Natasha grunts. "What's taking so long, Anna Tatianna?" She squirms and turns to Durov. "I always hated to stand for my fittings. I wasn't as slim as the other girls, but really, when my last dressmaker whipped out an entirely new bolt of fabric—"

Anna whimpers, "Madame, there's too much cloth in some places and"—she measures across Natasha's rear end—"barely enough in others."

Durov, cap in hand, shifts uncomfortably from one foot to another. Although he would prefer to stay and admire Natasha, he doesn't think he should be there as the ladies continue their fitting. He starts to back out of the wagon. "Perhaps I-I should come back another time."

Natasha flings her arm out, pumping it up and down for emphasis. "Nonsense, we won't be long." As Anna grabs wildly at the flapping sleeve,

Natasha adds, "Besides, I need you to tell me what to say when we get into town."

Anna catches the fabric, flattens it, and sticks in a pin.

Natasha jumps, snarling. "*Oy!*" Then she manages a weak smile directed toward the girl. "Do be careful, dear Anna Tatianna."

Anna sighs and mutters through the pins in her mouth, "Maybe we should get Karenska. She's much more experienced."

"I don't want anyone to know until I'm all decked out and ready to go."

Durov twists his cap around and around, fervently wishing he'd waited a bit longer before entering Natasha's wagon. *Anatoly's costume fittings for our little pigs are never this hair-raising.*

Anna hands Nikolai's top hat to Natasha. With a flourish, Natasha grandly places it on her head. The hat promptly falls down Natasha's forehead, stopping only at her nose.

Natasha screeches, "*Nyet*, what a fat head he had." Sheepishly, she looks around, adds, "God rest his soul," and crosses herself, which causes the other sleeve to come loose.

Durov can feel his blood rising, both because he's embarrassed to be attending a lady's fitting and because he finds Natasha attractive—even with Nikolai's costume hanging off her and his top hat covering half her face. "I'd be ever so pleased to accompany you, Madame—"

"Natasha. Just call me Natasha." She tosses the hat to Anna, gruffly adding, "Get some fabric to stuff this thing." Anna flushes at Natasha's abrupt order. Then Natasha realizes that Durov is watching and adds, as sweetly as her deep voice will allow, "Will you, my dear Anna?"

Durov's weathered face flushes with anxiety. He really doesn't want the responsibility of negotiating with the villagers. Yet he feels he must shoulder the burden to help Natasha and the circus make a go of it in Germany. He shuffles his feet some more. "Ah...Natasha. I never actually went with Nikolai on his trips into town, and I'm not very good at bargaining."

"Don't you worry, Durov. I love to haggle."

"These Germans may not like to wrangle like they do back home. Everything seems so orderly here."

"Trust me. Everyone likes a good deal. We just have to make it worth their while."

"P-pardon me, Madame—ah, Natasha," Durov stammers. "May I ask if you intend to perform the other ringmaster duties as well?"

Anna stops, pins midair, waiting for Natasha's answer.

"I hadn't thought of it. But...why not? My father always made fun of my low—he used to say, manly—voice. It might just come in handy now. What could go wrong?"

Beads of perspiration appear on Durov's broad forehead. He is torn between his attraction for Natasha and his concern over the smooth running of the circus. "So long as you don't announce the bears too close to the trick dogs. And keep Zoya in her right place."

"Zoya? The pachyderm?"

Durov nods. "She's not very smart, but she knows precisely when she's supposed to go on—she's got a very good memory, you see."

Anna adds, "And don't forget, the Zubov trapeze act is first in the circus parade—"

At that moment, almost as if he'd been waiting outside the wagon door and listening, Ivan barges in, pompously declaring, "You must remember that we are first in the circus parade. But when it comes to the show itself, we're always the last to go on. The climax, if you will." Ivan eyes Natasha seductively.

Durov's face falls as he sees Natasha sneak a lusty glance at Ivan, even as she ostensibly ignores his remark. Natasha winces. "Such a lot to remember." She sighs. "But I'm sure you both will show me the ropes."

Trying to deflect Ivan's advances, Durov attempts to escort him out. "Thank you for stopping by, Ivan Ivanovich. It's getting a bit crowded in here, don't you think? We should leave the ladies—"

Ivan maneuvers in the small space and deftly slides past Durov. "*Da.*

Da. I'd be happy to show you the ropes, Natasha. We use lots of ropes in our act."

Trying not to explode, Durov manages a mere scowl. "Those aren't the kind of ropes she needs."

"Durov, don't you know a joke when you hear one?" Ivan glares. Then he turns to Natasha, adding lightly, "These pig trainers aren't very sophisticated, are they? By the way, Nikolai confided in me, so perhaps I can help you in town."

"More likely get us kicked out," Durov interjects.

Natasha shouts, "Listen, I need the two of you to stop fighting and work together. Everyone in the circus is depending on us. We should perform as soon as possible—tonight, if we can." She turns to check herself in the mirror. "How do I look?"

Durov raises his eyebrows, horrified to see one pant leg higher than the other and one sleeve lower.

Natasha slowly takes in her image in the mirror, then shrieks, "*Bozhe moy*! Anna, this won't do."

Ivan shrugs. "It's fine, believe me. We've got to go as soon as possible— can't keep them waiting. Natasha, just bend a little in one leg." Natasha bends her leg. "There, your trousers are even. Now slump your shoulder." Natasha slumps. "Perfect! The costume fits exactly!"

"They're going to think I'm some kind of cripple."

Ivan smiles. "But a very well-tailored cripple." Natasha glares at him as he adds, "Maybe having the circus owner be a cripple will play on their heartstrings."

Durov shakes his head, managing to suppress a laugh. But, as Anna helps Natasha hobble down the wagon steps, he thinks Ivan may have a point. *Once they see her bent up like that, maybe they will feel sorry for us and give us a good deal.*

Natasha reaches the bottom step and screeches, "*Oy*, these damn pins."

Durov frowns. *Maybe not.*

CHAPTER FIFTEEN

NATASHA SWALLOWS HARD as she screws up her courage for the forthcoming negotiations with the town leaders. Huffing her way down the wagon steps, she pauses for a moment to see that the morning mist has given way to a brilliant Prussian-blue sky; she crosses herself at this good omen. She coils up her long plait and jauntily plops her newly sized ringmaster's top hat on her head. The temperature is cool enough to be invigorating but warm enough to give heart to the circus people, who are already setting up for the performance they hope will begin in the early evening. She shudders, knowing they're all depending on her, and crosses herself once again to ward off any demons lurking about the circus camp.

Durov and Ivan follow behind her, arguing over the approach to take once they get into town. She passes by Bronzy, the strongman, who is setting out his hammer and rig. A neatly printed sign reads "Ring the Bell and Win a Prize."

Natasha steps proudly, feeling her new importance to the circus as its sole owner. She stops to examine Bronzy's sideshow act.

"See how I tie a string to the bell," he explains in his bottom-of-a-well, deep voice. "If the customer isn't strong enough to pound the lever and ring the bell, I momentarily distract him." He demonstrates. "Oh, look at that." Natasha turns to look. He laughs. "See. Then I ring the bell myself."

"That's very clever." Natasha smiles. "And compassionate. A man's honor is intact in front of the sweetheart he brought to the circus."

She pats her top hat for emphasis and starts to leave, but Bronzy adds, "So then I wager him he can't do it again, and of course, he wants to try. I let this go on until he finally has a pile of my money, then I don't ring the bell for him." Bronzy smiles broadly, showing all four of his front teeth. "I get all the money, and he goes away feeling good that he rang the bell nine times out of ten!"

Natasha pats him on the arm. "So it works out well in the end."

Bronzy produces a deep-throated snicker. "Especially for the circus, Madame."

As Natasha turns to go, Bronzy motions toward his sister Lottie, who is setting up the accouterments for her fortune-telling act under an awning in front of their wagon. Curious, Natasha goes over to see, feeling an increasing sense of importance as Lottie deferentially bows.

Lottie sports a deep pomegranate-colored turban and looks so wispy, she could easily be knocked over by one of the large ostrich feathers stuck in the back fold. She calls to Bronzy: "Brother dear, please come over and help me set the pedal."

Natasha steps closer, puzzled.

"Let me show you, Madame Natasha," Lottie says. "We're testing the equipment outside. But when I hold my séances, I take everyone inside our wagon into almost total darkness, except for a few beeswax candles. When I tap my turban three times, that's the sign I've made contact with the spirits from beyond. Then I step on the pedal, and in the dark, my brother raises the pulley and the table levitates!"

Bronzy gleefully demonstrates. The table goes soaring.

"*Nyet!*" Lottie shrieks to her brother. Then, weakly smiling at Natasha, she adds, "Sometimes he doesn't know his own strength."

Laughing, Natasha walks on, letting brother and sister squabble it out. She is heartened as all the circus people stop what they're doing to tip their hats or bow to her, wishing her success. She is fortified by their goodwill, but she feels increasingly uncomfortable as she limps along in Nikolai's sagging costume. So she decides to straighten up and to hell with how she looks. And while she's grateful for Durov's and Ivan's escort—and flattered by their attentions—she fervently wishes they'd stop quarreling, especially when they get to town.

As they start to leave the circus camp, Durov hesitates. "Does anyone speak any German?"

Ivan shrugs. "Never had the need."

Natasha groans, "My tutor covered some German, but my French is much better." She brushes off her costume as if preparing to introduce herself. "People in Moscow speak a great deal of French, especially when visitors come."

Durov adds, with a ring of hope in his voice, "Maybe here in Germany they speak Russian?"

In a tone intended to convince herself, Natasha says, "Sometimes—well, maybe just living across the border—people might learn each other's language, don't you think?" She quickly adds, "Enough to trade, that is."

Ivan flails his arms about. "I can try sign language." Loudly shouting, he makes some bold circles. "WE ARE FROM THE CIRCUS."

Natasha winces. "They're not deaf, Ivan." She takes a deep breath and adds, "Just be quiet you two, and follow my lead."

She notices that the dirt road into town is neatly laid out—what would have been deep ruts in Russia, have been filled in to form a surprisingly level surface. Each farmhouse they pass is tidy, with orderly piles of stacked wood. Natasha is charmed by the fragrant, blooming countryside. Freshly painted buildings from the town poke through the rustling chestnut trees. "Everything's so orderly here."

Ivan nods, whispering to Durov, "You've got to be orderly too, pig trainer."

Durov mutters, "That goes twice for you."

"Gentlemen, *pozhaluysta!*"

The town's main street, Kaiserwilhelmstrasse, forms a perfectly straight line, with the town hall at the far end. To their right, the brilliant white of a church with a tall spire shines against the pure and cloudless sky. Natasha frowns at the church's stark angles, bereft of the familiar brightly colored onion domes of the Russian Orthodox churches back home. She wonders how people can get up enough passion to be religious inside such a plain, unornamental building.

Natasha steps carefully up onto the sidewalk, avoiding the neat rows of geraniums planted along the kerb. Tall, blonde people are everywhere along the street. Shops burst with fresh breads, lace, linens, and the like: a bakery with rows of cheese and raspberry strudel; a butcher's shop with links of sausage draped over an iron bar behind the counter; a cobbler's shop with thick, high-buttoned shoes for women and tall, shiny black leather boots for men; a chemist's with rows of green and dark blue phials lining the shelves; and a kind of general produce store with wheelbarrow-loads of fruits, vegetables, and potatoes, carefully piled on the outside steps beside an iron bedstead with a featherbed for sale.

Breathing more deeply with every step, Natasha fights her growing anxiety. She longs to throw herself on that featherbed and fall deeply asleep, rather than negotiate with the town elders. *What if I fail? We will have crossed the mountains for nothing, and I'll end up in debtor's prison.* She can't bear the thought that having made such a mess of her marriage, she would fail again and plunge all these sincere people now in her charge into outright poverty. No, she steels herself in her poorly fitting ringmaster's costume, ignoring the occasional prick of an errant pin. She's capable of rising to the task. Everyone in the town will be thrilled to see their little circus. Glancing again at the spotless sidewalks, she makes a mental note

110

to ask the circus laborers to hose down the benches and clean up right away after the elephant's act. *By St. Nicholas, that pachyderm can poop!*

Dozens of pairs of curious, piercing, blue eyes are trained on the three-some. The townsfolk pause to watch them pass. The women have white, milkmaid skin and wear honey-blonde coils of braids, like crowns, encircling their heads.

Durov asks, "What are they using all those brooms for?"

"They're sweeping off the front steps to their shops," Natasha says.

Ivan quips, "But they're not even dirty."

"*Tishe*, Ivan, they like their exercise." Natasha waves at them. "*Oy.* Another pin." She forces a smile.

They walk the length of the street and come to the town hall, with its wide steps leading up to an imposing columned façade. Natasha is nearly hyperventilating now. She fights an almost overwhelming urge to turn and run, while trying to act nonchalant. She puts on a brave face as she whispers to Durov and Ivan, "At least it's not as impressive as some of the buildings I've been to in Moscow." She adjusts her ringmaster's top hat. "Let's go up and find the mayor."

Ivan steps in front of Durov to offer Natasha his arm. Durov immediately races around to her other side and offers his arm. Then the three ascend the steps in lockstep. Despite the tension of their current task, Natasha blushes at the attention Durov and Ivan show her. At her first debutante appearance, her father searched in vain for willing escorts and literally had to bribe two unwitting young men to accompany her. She couldn't have fallen any farther down the social ladder—until now. She tugs at her ringmaster's jacket. In her gut she knows that this venture is all the more important for her. She must prove she can make a success of her current dismal situation.

Above them, the town hall has a tall, ornately carved, double oak door, each side with a brass knocker in the profile of an eagle. They reach the top of the steps as Natasha winces from several more pinpricks.

Durov asks, "Which door should we use?"

Before they can decide, Natasha is startled to see the doors flung open by an extremely tall, cigar-chomping man in an elaborate German military uniform. His arms are so long that they stretch the full width of both doors. He clicks the heels of his shining, black, leather, over-the-knee boots, making a sound like a gunshot. This causes the already jittery Natasha to jump. Although she's familiar with a wide variety of Russian officers' dress uniforms, she's never seen such high gloss on any boots in Moscow. The German's face is long and lean, his watery blue eyes are set close together like a falcon's, and his wide handlebar mustache is thick and curled into tight corkscrew loops at the ends. And there are meters and meters of gold braid encircling his lean chest, while an iron cross hangs around his neck on an abundant gilt chain. Natasha looks up beyond the braid on his chest. There she spies his domed helmet, with its sharp, golden peak looking rather too much like a child's pinwheel top. She nearly bursts into laughter as she catches Durov's eye—and the trace of a smile at the corner of his mouth. She quicky coughs to hide her laugh.

Natasha clears her throat and asks, "Sprechen Sie russky?"

The soldier moves the chomped cigar to the other corner of his mouth and blasts them with a thin, high-pitched warble of a voice that belies his excessively tall figure: "*Russky? Ah ha! Ja, woher wusstest Du das.*" He switches to Russian: "How did you know?"

Natasha breathes a huge sigh of relief. "*Gute Vermutung*," she says, and then adds in Russian, "I mean, just a good guess."

Durov nods. "*Khorosho* (good). Impressive."

The soldier extracts the badly mashed cigar from his mouth. He bows as he says, "I am Sergeant Major Wolfgang Dunsendorfer." He cranes his long, thin neck down. He whispers to the three of them, "*Khorosho...Da...*Our glorious kaiser wants our military to be prepared."

Natasha takes a step back. "For what?"

Wolfgang smiles so broadly that the tips of his mustache graze the sides of his helmet. "Wouldn't want to let the cat out of the bag."

Durov becomes alarmed. "Sir, we are not fond of any sort of cruelty to animals."

Wolfgang's Adam's apple bobs up and down. "What?"

Natasha forces a smile. "Nothing. Please...you were saying?"

Wolfgang continues, "*Ja...Da...*We was waiting for you to come to register." This is apparently the signal for two other men to scurry out onto the portico. One is short and stout with a shaven head, built like the stump of a chestnut tree; the other is tall with longer limbs, built like the branches of that same chestnut tree.

The soldier turns to his right and booms in his reedy tones: "Our mayor, Herr Heinrich Fritz." And he turns to his left and booms, "Our registrar, Herr Fritz Heinrich."

Ivan whispers to Natasha, "Not hard to remember: Heinz and Fritz."

Natasha nudges him to be quiet.

She is not certain how seriously to take the spectacle before her—the overly elaborately dressed Wolfgang and his two odd sidekicks, Heinz and Fritz—but she decides to play it straight and starts to curtsy. She quickly remembers, however, that she's wearing the ringmaster's uniform. She decides instead to swish off her top hat and make a deep bow at the waist. As she replaces her hat, another pin jabs. She mutters to herself and then looks up and smiles weakly. "Yes, we came straightaway this morning. We arrived rather late last evening."

Heinz jumps in: "*Wir mögen es nicht.*"

Wolfgang translates, "He says, we don't much care for gypsies in our country."

"We're not gypsies. We are professional circus people," counters Durov.

Wolfgang relates this back to Fritz. Then Wolfgang frowns and mutters to Natasha, "They mostly understand Russian, but they want I should make sure their position is absolutely clear. Fritz says the Germans ain't going to welcome anyone who might…well…pollute…our pure Aryan blood."

As she looks back and forth between Heinz and Fritz, Natasha flushes, struggling to control her temper. She says to Wolfgang, "Would you please tell them, we have no intention of polluting anyone here. Most of our performers are members of traditional circus families."

The three of them confer, and then Wolfgang says, "They understand, but they heard about family inbreeding. That leads to deformities."

"Oh, *nyet*, sir," Natasha adds. "We don't tolerate any of that. All our deformed people are authentic circus acts."

Heinz and Fritz, clearly relieved, nod their heads in approval.

Durov adds, "And all your children will love our little circus."

Ivan is not to be outdone. "And all your adults will be absolutely, positively in awe of our trapeze act."

Wolfgang gleefully lifts his heels off the ground, bouncing his imposing, lanky frame up and down. In his high-pitched voice, he squeaks, "Our emperor, the glorious Kaiser Wilhelm II, when he was a boy, loved to watch gymnastics." He smiles shyly. "And I myself, absolutely *love* the circus."

Heinz and Fritz turn to Wolfgang—Heinz with his eyes popping, and Fritz with his mouth agape. Together, they say, "*Sie machen* (you do)?"

Natasha ignores them and concentrates on Wolfgang, her eyes widening in exaggerated mock-admiration. "Herr Sergeant Major, do you know the kaiser?"

Wolfgang hangs his head in feigned modesty. Natasha glances up at the peak of his helmet for signs that the top is about to lift off. Wolfgang says, "I got the pleasure of taking the boy under my wing, so to speak, when the old emperor ordered he should be exposed to the military. The prince got assigned to my regiment for almost a year. To his credit, the young fellow insisted on being treated as any soldier despite his—" Wolfgang motions awkwardly to his left arm.

Natasha recalls reading in the papers that the boy was born with a withered left arm and that, from a young age, he'd always tried to disguise his deformity. When he became kaiser, he tried to compensate by creating special, elaborate military uniforms. And he always had himself photographed holding various objects—a telescope, a sabre clamped hard against his left side. She adds, "You must have been greatly honored by having him in your charge."

Heinz and Fritz, clearly understanding the gist of the conversation, step on each other's lines. Heinz starts, "Yes, indeed—"

Fritz says, "Indeed, he was and our whole town is—"

"Honored to this day—"

"That's why Wolfgang's in charge of—"

"Registering foreigners who—"

"Want to work in Germany."

Durov jumps back: "Registering foreigners who want to work in—"

Natasha inwardly groans, as she finishes the thought, "Work in Germany? Ah...we didn't know we had to register our people in order to perform."

Wolfgang gleefully adds in his thin voice, "It ain't a bad thing. Necessary for our border safety, don't you know? We got to know the origin of all guest workers in our glorious Empire. We can't have any—"

Fritz says, "Riff—"

Heinz adds, "Raff."

Natasha is horrified that anyone might consider her riffraff. True, she's fallen very low in society's eyes, but really...riffraff? She's about to shout out her anger at these impudent idiots when Ivan interjects, pumping up his chest.

"Herr Wolfgang, are you suggesting that our famed trapeze act—the Zubov Family Trapeze artists—are...riff...raff?"

"Sure not, my good man," Wolfgang adds, sanctimoniously. "We just got to know there ain't gonna be any unfortunate issues with anyone what enters our country. What we care about is order, cleanliness, and the preservation of our Aryan race."

Durov whispers to Ivan, "No womanizing, hear?"

Natasha is miffed at the two of them and casts angry glances at Durov and Ivan. She offers a syrupy smile to the tall dunderhead. "Herr Sergeant Major, of course we are all of the same mind. And of course, our whole cultures are bound together by the fortunate relationship of the tsar and the kaiser. First cousins, don't you know?"

"Madame, I am aware of the *Blutbande*...how do you say..."

Ivan whispers to Natasha, "Did he say the tsar and the kaiser share blue balls?" Natasha shushes him.

Wolfgang continues, "But these *Blutbanden* (blood ties) ain't necessarily such that they mean we got a shared view of the orderly and proper—"

"There won't be any trouble. You have my guarantee," Natasha interjects.

"Well, in *diesem Fall* (in that case)—" says Heinz.

Fritz adds, "Wolfgang *er wird rauskommen*—"

Durov whispers to Natasha, "I agree, Wolfgang's certainly a weird rascal." Natasha ribs him with her elbow.

"Wolfgang will go out to your camp—" Fritz clarifies.

Wolfgang breaks in, "So you can register and pay your import head tax, *danke*." He grins as he shoves the remnants of his cigar back into his mouth and gleefully rubs his hands together. He turns to go. "*Auf Wiedersehen*."

Natasha rapidly calculates on the abacus in her head how much tax they can afford to pay and still make a profit. She feels faint and wobbly at the knees, but she sees there's nothing to be done except return to camp and await Wolfgang.

"*Do svidaniya*." She smiles weakly at Wolfgang, who bows and smartly clicks his heels, ejecting another disturbing gunshot sound.

CHAPTER SIXTEEN

Natasha, deep in thought, walks slowly and dejectedly back to the circus camp. She removes her ringmaster's top hat, allowing her long, thick braid to fall down onto her bosom. The farm houses that had seemed so neatly and charmingly arranged under a lovely, cloudless sky now look rigid, their uniform cleanliness a sign of stiff inflexibility. She knows full well how much more superior the Prussians consider themselves, compared with their Russian "cousins." She's devastated that she allowed herself to be talked into Nikolai's half-baked scheme to go to Germany, which has now obviously put the entire circus in even greater financial jeopardy. Worse still, their fate now depends on the whim of Wolfgang, an officious dragoon. Wolfgang may or may not register the circus people, and even if he does, he may or may not charge a reasonable head tax.

She angrily swishes the top hat back and forth against her side, thinking as she walks. She feels pinned under a crushing weight. She fears what will happen to them if they can't perform and have to turn around and head back over the mountains. With all the people and animals to feed—not to mention the wages the circus will owe the performers and laborers—Natasha feels closer and closer to the debtors' prison that she fears like nothing she's ever feared in her life. Damn, she should have refused to go to Germany in the first place. She should have let them arrest Nikolai and disband the circus while they were still in Russia. Swallowing her pride, she could have thrown herself on the mercy of her cousin Georgina to take her in.

Slowly, Natasha becomes aware that Ivan and Durov are still arguing fiercely as they walk behind her. As if she didn't have enough to worry about. She's exasperated at the two of them, although she must admit, she's still flattered.

Ivan shouts, "Wolfgang said he loves the circus. Just keep your dirty pigs away from him and—"

"My pigs? The children love my pigs. They're very smart and—"

"Filthy. Don't you see how clean everything is here?" Ivan motions around him. "Our biggest hope to be accepted here is the trapeze. Didn't you hear him say the kaiser loved gymnastics?"

Really, Natasha thinks, *why must they act like children?* The situation is dire; and here they are, shouting at each other. She tries to ignore them, searching her mind for clues to handle the situation. Her father was finance minister to the tsar. He would often deal with difficult, pompous people who tried to extract favors—often completely unreasonable ones at that. He also remained calm and told her that losing her temper was the best way to lose the upper hand in negotiations. Yet, with Wolfgang, she doesn't see much room for negotiation. He clearly has the upper hand and doesn't appear to be susceptible to the kind of flattery that always worked at the tsar's court. Suddenly, she has a bright idea—bribery always worked, her father said. But then, deflated, she realizes they hardly have any money. Her ability to bribe Wolfgang is severely limited. Despondent, she ignores Ivan and Durov and continues back toward the circus camp.

Ivan chases after her, whining, "Madame, you can't permit Durov to go on. It'll spoil everything for the rest of us."

Durov groans. "Pardon me, Madame. It would be a huge disservice to our customers not to show them my little ones. They're so intelligent and when they walk up those little ladders and then slide down—"

"Ha! Half the time, those beasts miss their footing on those damn ladders and end up falling on top of the ones sliding down—"

"Climbing up. They fall on top of the ones climbing up, you imbecile, not on the ones sliding down." Incensed, Durov stomps over to Ivan. "You've got it upside down."

Natasha is at her wit's end. "Stop it, you two. I want to talk to both of you."

Ivan says, "I'm telling you, Natasha, they don't like it—"

"Ivan, stop telling me what they like and what they don't like." Natasha feels on shaky ground, going against the star of their star trapeze act. But she can't stand it when Ivan treats her exactly as Nikolai did. "I'm not some kind of servant to order around." She takes a deep breath and, in an even deeper voice, blurts out, "I'm in charge now."

Ivan's handsome face falls into a heap on top of his elegantly muscular neck. "Well, of course. I-I was, I was only trying to help, Madame."

Durov backs up to let them argue. Natasha notices the corner of Durov's mouth curling into a smile.

Natasha tempers her voice. "I'm sure you were, Ivan. I just want you to know—"

"I can take a hint, Madame," Ivan huffs. "Just let me know if and when you want my opinion. I'm going to warm up for tonight. I only hope *you* can convince Wolfgang to let us perform."

Natasha sighs as, with a lusty eye, she watches Ivan prance away. Durov stifles a snicker as he watches Ivan leave. Then Durov offers her his arm. She turns to him, searches his craggy but earnest face. At least these two men, even if they are circus performers, are vying for her attentions. That buoys her spirits and gives her hope in her ability to work things out—and keep out of debtors' prison. With a burst of courage, she coils up her braid and stuffs it under her top hat, jauntily pats it onto her head, and takes Durov's arm.

CHAPTER SEVENTEEN

DUROV ESCORTS NATASHA to her wagon, then rushes to the animal corral to ready Anatoly and the pigs for their act tonight—in the hope that Natasha will successfully register the circus people with Wolfgang and that the head tax will not be prohibitive. Durov hates to see Natasha as ill-treated by Ivan as she was by Nikolai, and he wishes that she would finally put Ivan in his place. Still, he can't face the prospect of letting Natasha know how he feels about her. A fine high-born woman such as she could never be interested in the likes of him. And now that the circus might be in jeopardy again, any confidence he might have had has disappeared, haunted as he is by guilt that he was the reason the Cossacks found his parents' camp. *I'm a disgrace.*

Durov's square jaw quivers, and his robust chest constricts with despair. Even the bright sunshine, which sparkles on the lush green field beyond the corral, can't raise his spirits. As he approaches the pig enclosure, Anatoly greets him with a cautious look.

"W-were they very d-difficult?"

"They have to register everyone, and we have to pay a head tax to boot." Durov sighs. "This dragoon, Wolfgang, is all dressed up with heaps of gold braid on his chest. Even though he's just a common soldier, he's dressed exactly like photos you see of the kaiser himself. But the good news is that he loves the circus because the kaiser used to love gymnastics."

The pigs inside the corral spot Durov, and the little ones scramble to get close for him to pet them. They squeal like delighted children and try to raise up on their hind legs to please him.

"There, there, little ones." Durov's weathered face breaks into a broad smile as he bends down to caress them. Sasha, the biggest of them, holds back and waits her turn. At his whistle, the little ones separate, allowing her to barge though the line and bask in Durov's undivided affection. He presents her with a bunch of dandelions, one of several he picked and shoved into his belt on the way back to camp. She grunts and nudges him with her snout before delicately slobbering them down. As the others squeal, he laughs and gives them the rest of the wildflowers.

Brushing his hands off, he says, "Come now, Anatoly. We've got to rehearse the little ones on those parts of the act that will appeal most to these Germans. Let's get out the ladders and practice those."

At the mention of the word *ladders,* the pigs grunt and run to the far side of the corral. Anatoly frowns. "Oh dear. I reinforced the rungs on the ladders from when Sasha broke through last time—"

"Yes, that was unfortunate. She fell on top of Demetri, who fell on top of Petrova, who fell on top of—"

"D-don't remind me. But the r-rungs are stronger now, although I don't s-suppose they know that just yet. How do we c-convince them they're safe?"

"No matter. We'll start with some cards to build their trust. Later you can run up and down the ladders and slide down the slides, so they'll see everything's secure. For now, why don't you get the wooden cards out and lay them on the ground for the little ones to count and do their sums. But let's hurry. We've got to be at the top of our form in a few hours."

Anatoly rushes to open a trunk at the side of the corral. "Let's let Sasha do her card tricks first. Then the little ones can do their sums." He pulls out some pieces of wood that are painted as playing cards. Seeing these, the pigs return to the front of the corral and snort with anticipation. Anatoly turns to Durov, squealing with delight himself. "They want to show off how smart they are."

Durov laughs heartily, his eyes mellow with pride. "You're right. Sasha first, then the little ones. Unpack the playing cards and place them face down."

Anatoly spreads out three cards, face down.

Durov leads Sasha over to the cards and says, "Point, Sasha."

Sasha gently places her hoof onto the bottom of the middle card. Anatoly turns it over, announcing with a flourish, "The Queen of Hearts." Then Anatoly puts the card face down and mixes up the cards by rushing madly around, his blonde hair flying. Sasha calmly looks on.

Durov pats Sasha on the head. "Find the Queen, Sasha. Find the Queen." Sasha trots over to the third card and taps it with her hoof. When Anatoly turns it over, sure enough, it's the Queen of Hearts.

Durov applauds and shouts, "Brava, my dear Sasha. Brava." He dips into his trouser pocket for a piece of apple, which she slurps down in an instant. He feels a rush of pride that his method of training animals, with positive reinforcement and without cruelty, has paid off once again. He wishes he had the ability to publicize his techniques so that people everywhere would stop beating their poor animals—horses, mules, dogs, and any other animals under their charge. It would revolutionize behavior throughout Russia and even Europe—people could put away the awful whips they use on their unfortunate animals. Meanwhile, he's delighted to see Anatoly smiling at Sasha and clapping while the other pigs stamp their hooves in approval.

Boris happens by and quips, "*Chto proiskodit* (what's going on)?" He wears his father's top hat and long magician's robe; he's obviously been practicing his magician's act. As usual, he keeps tripping over the robe. In his deep and authoritarian voice, Boris says, "You are violating one of the most sacred principles of legerdemain. Teaching those pigs the kind of card tricks only a true magician should perform."

Durov smiles. "We thought you'd be happy that we borrowed one of your tricks. Think of it as warming up the audience for when you get your act together."

"You're right. I won't be a clown forever. But what you don't realize about being a magician—a true magician like my father was—is that you must have not only the sleight-of-hand technique—"

Anatoly interjects, "Can't we h-have a sleight-of-hoof t-technique?"

Boris ignores him, adding, "But you also have to project the drama of the story."

Durov adds, "Isn't it dramatic to see a pig perform such a feat?"

Boris raises up his short frame, his wizened but cherubic face reddening. "You can't do anything clunky. You must have lightning quick deception."

Lottie appears in a purple, triangular shawl, her abundant red hair flowing around her shoulders. "What kind of deception are you practicing now, Boris?"

Chuckling, Durov steps back to let the two diminutive people have a go at each other.

Boris eyes Lottie with some frustration. "Well, certainly not the kind of deception you practice with your so-called occult arts."

Lottie's pale skin flushes, exaggerating her red freckles. Clearly attempting to control her anger, she speaks slowly and softly: "My arts are not so-called. I have the privilege of being the recipient of many psychic gifts that allow me to see the vibrations of the discarnate."

"Huh?" Anatoly says.

"The dearly departed," Lottie adds.

Durov would give anything to get in touch with his dearly departed parents, to tell them how sorry he is, to this day.

Boris says, "I don't think anyone is ever dearly departed. I'm sure they all really wanted to hang around." He walks right up to Lottie, challenging her. "You think your séances provide people with solace, but I think you're just preying on people's vulnerabilities."

Anatoly deftly steps between Boris and Lottie. "But I've s-seen her powers. She took those f-flowers from the vase and floated them around the wagon. And then there was the h-harp. It was just sitting there across the r-room, and it started playing." He turns to Durov. "That gives me an i-idea. Maybe Sasha could l-learn to play the h-harp. Lottie, would you m-mind if we borrowed—"

"Thank you for the vote of confidence, Anatoly," Lottie says. "But that wouldn't be appropriate."

Boris quips, "No, we don't care for people borrowing things from our acts."

Durov is amused to see Lottie soften, as she flirts with Boris—who, as usual, seems oblivious to her not-so-subtle advances.

Lottie bats her eyelashes, which are so heavily made-up, she can barely lift them. "Surely, Boris, you must have some psychic ability yourself. I've seen you practice with the crew, asking them to pick something of value. Then you describe their families and some memorable incident."

"Look, Lottie, any magician claiming to have real supernatural powers would be ostracized. Magic is a craft of this world. The natural enemy of the occult."

Leaning in, Durov listens carefully, thinking about his parents. He can see this discussion is beginning to affect Anatoly—who is clutching the gold chain their mother gave him, which he wears around his neck.

"So how can you read people's minds?" Lottie asks.

Boris looks around, clearly not wanting anyone to overhear. "Well, I do pay attention—close attention—when the crew is slurring in their beers about their mothers and their wives. That's how I know enough about their families to describe specific incidents. I'm not a clairvoyant like you claim to be, just an observer of life. That's what a true magician is. Nothing occult about it."

It's clear to Durov that neither Lottie nor Boris is likely to be able to connect him with his parents after all. He turns to Boris. "But your father, in each town, used to call out into the audience and say the most remarkable true things about people's dead ancestors."

Boris leans in to whisper, and they all lean in to hear. "I'll tell you his secret if you promise never to breathe a word." They all shake their heads yes. "He used to go on ahead to each town and visit the cemetery. In so many of the villages we used to play, there were only about five family names in adjoining plots." Boris softens his voice, and they all lean farther in. "He had a remarkable memory. He'd gather information and then astound the audience with a few well-calculated guesses."

Durov is absolutely deflated. He had hoped there would be a way to ask his parents' forgiveness. Still hopeful, he asks Lottie, "But you have the ability to reach the afterlife?"

Anna, dressed in her practice clothes, comes skipping along and stops short at Durov's question. "Who's reaching the afterlife? Lottie, can you really do that? I really miss my mother and I'd love to talk to her."

Before Lottie can respond, Boris turns to her. "Lottie, it's cruel for someone to pretend they can reach our loved ones who've gone ahead."

Lottie's voice hardens: "But not if they can. Anna, death can be seen as an emigration. The spirit goes on a journey, and sometimes we can meet up with the departed at certain signposts. If you want, sometime I'll invite you to one of my private séances. Not the ones I do for the show."

"So you admit what you do is for show?" Boris defiantly swishes his robe for emphasis. "That's why your brother rigs up the pulley for your table. Don't deny it; I've seen him."

Lottie blushes. "Well, of course. In the short time we have for the sideshow before a performance, I have to make certain accommodations, shall we say. But Boris," Lottie bats her heavily laden eyelashes, "don't you do the same kind of thing?"

Durov gently shakes his head back and forth, amused that Lottie doesn't seem to want to give up her flirtation with Boris.

Lottie adds, "Why don't you show us one of your tricks. We can argue about prestidigitation and psychic powers another time. I know you're getting good enough. Very soon, I'm sure you'll be able to assume your father's role as the magician in our circus."

Boris seems truly touched by her attempt at détente. "Oh, if you insist."

Anna, Anatoly, and Durov vigorously shake their heads, relieved that the couple has come to some agreement.

Boris reaches deep into a pocket of his father's long magician's robe. "And here's a beautiful dove." Out comes a squawking chicken. Boris grabs it by its scrawny legs and looks around, confused.

Durov chuckles. "Boris, you'd better hide that chicken. Bronzy's been looking for it for tonight's soup."

Shoving the chicken behind his back, Boris says, "What chicken?" The bird squawks double time.

Anna giggles. "That chicken, Boris."

Boris whirls around, plops the bird into a back pocket. "Well, nice debating the spirit life with everyone. I've got to go practice." He adds, under his breath, "Bronzy's not getting my chicken for his pot."

Boris heads toward his wagon. Just then, a gust of wind takes his top hat. "My hat! Someone grab my hat!" His large, black top hat whirls up and around the pig corral. As Durov and Anatoly scramble for it, it floats over the fence and lands upside down in the corral, the satin lining gleaming red in the sunshine. Sasha wanders over, grunts, and smells it. She nudges it, and when she realizes it isn't something to eat, she raises her hoof, as if she's about to stomp on it.

Boris pleads. *"Ostanovit' yego* (stop, please)! Durov, don't let it squash my father's top hat."

Durov leaps over the fence and walks toward Sasha. He stops, quietly imploring her, *"Nyet, nyet.* Sasha, my darling piggala."

Sasha pricks up her large, pink and hairy ears and looks between Durov, Anatoly, and Boris. Lottie and Anna jump onto the rail of the corral fence for a better view. Sasha snorts, sniffs at the hat, and looks back at them as they all entreat her not to smash Boris's treasured hat. Her mouth opens up into a large and unmistakable smile as, hoof raised, she looks one last time at Durov, who frantically shakes his head. She snorts and then daintily puts her hoof down on the outside brim. The top hat swishes up, turning in the air. Sasha ducks, and the hat lands squarely on the top of her head, lodged neatly between her large, pink and hairy ears. Sasha snorts again, eyeing Durov for a sign of approval.

Durov is stunned into momentary silence. Anatoly steps back, amazed at the feat. Anna and Lottie hang frozen onto the fence. Boris leans forward on the fence, arms stretched toward his beloved hat.

Durov catches his breath and admires his prized pig. Like a proud father, he applauds, softly at first, then with greater fervor. "*Da, da.* Sasha. That's wonderful, my piggala."

Startled, Boris, Anatoly, Anna, and Lottie look at each other, then begin to applaud as well. Sasha snorts and wiggles her magnificent corkscrew tail.

Durov has a sudden idea. "You all weren't there, but the Sergeant Major, who apparently runs everything around here—"

Anatoly interrupts, "The one who's going to register us if he approves—"

Boris adds, "The one who determines the head tax and could throw us into bankruptcy if he wants—"

"Yes, yes, that's the one." Durov can barely contain his glee. "The kaiser loves his fancy uniforms, doesn't he? And Wolfgang obviously enjoys wearing those fancy uniforms with all that gold braid."

Sarcastic as ever, Boris adds, "The kaiser's preparing for war, emboldening his troops with all that gold braid and elaborate plumage. He's trying to drum up as much patriotic fervor as he can. So?"

"Don't you see how funny it would be if Anatoly were to make that kind of elaborate military uniform for Sasha, braid and everything?" Durov slaps his knee, then doubles over with deep, booming chortles. "And if she wears that fancy uniform and flips a helmet—just like she flipped the top hat—onto her head? And then I can say, like a ventriloquist, '*Ich will den Helm*.'"

Boris frowns. "*Ich will den Helm*? I want the helmet? What are you talking about?"

Durov is gleeful. "*Ich will den Helm* not only means 'I want the helmet' but—"

Boris gets it. Rolls his eyes. "It also means 'I am Wilhelm': Wilhelm, the Kaiser!"

"That's it, Boris." Durov's bulky frame shakes with laughter.

Anna, Lottie, and Anatoly look puzzled. Anatoly says, "But, Durov, I heard Ivan say—he was gloating, if you must know—that t-the kaiser doesn't like filthy pigs. So—and pardon me if I'm missing something here—how is he going to l-like a pig, even an intelligent and well-dressed pig such as our dear Sasha, f-flipping a h-helmet onto her h-head and l-looking like... well, not r-really... but k-kind of... like THE KAISER?"

Boris's eyes widen in fear. He starts out softly, in his articulate and commanding voice: "Durov, my good man. Have you lost your mind?" An increasing crescendo: "You want to have your pig flip a helmet onto her head, while you say, '*Ich will den Helm*' and—" A frantic climax: "And have people laugh at the pig as if it was THE KAISER??"

Anatoly adds blithely, "As if she was the k-kaiser; Sasha is a she." Then he throws an uncertain look at Durov.

"Yes, yes. Don't you see? People will love it." Durov feels a rush of confidence. The more he thinks about it, the more certain he is that this is the way to gain back his family's honor. What a triumph it will be to have his ability, as the foremost animal trainer in Russia, so prominently displayed before the German people—and the tsar, a cousin to the kaiser. What an international sensation it will be. And of course, Natasha. Won't she be pleased to have his act become a sensation in Germany and make enough money to bring the circus back from the brink?

Durov notices Anatoly, Boris, Lottie, and Anna looking back and forth, all of them wide-eyed and terrified. Suddenly, and in unison, they vehemently shake their heads no.

Boris says, "They may love it, but Wolfgang's not going to love it."

Lottie adds, "For once I totally agree with Boris. This Wolfgang person isn't going to love it, nor is the kaiser."

Anatoly pleads, "Durov, you c-could get arrested for tr-treason."

Boris raises his small hands, palms out. "Wait a minute. Not for treason. You'd have to be a German citizen to commit treason in Germany."

Anna adds, "Oh, I feel much better now."

Boris says, emphatically, "You'd be committing *sedition*. Since you're a Russian in Germany, what you'd be doing is called *sedition* not *treason*." Completely dejected, Boris plops down into his robe, making a headless conical shape. He calls to them from within his cone, "No matter what you call it, you'd be arrested. And I'm sure they'd arrest the whole circus with you." The cone starts to shake.

Lottie rushes over and looks down, inside the cone, pursing her lips in sympathy. Anna starts to cry, and Anatoly starts to whimper.

Durov calls to Boris, "Oh, all right, Boris. Stop shaking. Here, you'll feel better if I get your hat for you." He goes over to Sasha and tosses the hat toward Boris, who pops out of the cone to retrieve it. Durov kneels beside the pig and scratches behind one of her pointed ears, which flops over appreciatively as he strokes the long, soft hairs at the tip. From the side, her pink hairs shimmer in the sunlight. Sasha grunts, rooting her rounded, turned-up, pink snout against Durov's side.

Anatoly walks over to Durov. And Durov whispers, "Anatoly, don't you trust me?"

"Of course I t-trust you, Durov. I just don't t-think it's a good idea. M-making fun of the kaiser." Anatoly kneels on the other side of Sasha and scratches her other ear. "Besides, I don't see how I can make that kind of e-elaborate costume in such a short period of t-time."

Anna, straining to hear them, says, "Anatoly, did I hear you say you need help making a costume? I'm getting to be a pretty good seamstress. Just ask Madame Natasha."

Boris moans, "No, don't ask Madame Natasha. Don't make a fancy costume. Please, have you all gone mad?"

Anna offers, "Boris, while I'm at it, why don't I shorten your robe for you?"

Boris looks positively stunned. "What? And dispel the spells?"

Anatoly has a quizzical look. "Dispel the s-spells?"

Boris defensively gathers the robe in his hands. A faint squawking is heard from within. "If you ever shorten a magician's robe, it's no longer a magician's robe." He raises up his short frame, indignantly chiding Anna. "The spells are dispelled, if you know what I mean."

Anatoly comes to Anna's rescue. "I'm sure she didn't know that, Boris. No reason to be short with…ah…I didn't mean to say you were short…ah…"

"Never mind, Anatoly," Boris says. "I completely understand." The chicken squawks, gets loose from the robe, and flutters off across the pasture.

Lottie takes off after it. "Sorry, Boris. I'm sure my brother Bronzy would love to have that chicken for our supper."

Boris races after Lottie and the chicken, calling back, "Anatoly, I know you didn't mean to call me short. No harm done. But, Durov, there will be harm done if you perform that crazy pig act."

Durov shakes his head, indignant that everyone opposes his plan to save the circus. With a level of confidence he tries to make himself believe, he calls after Boris: "That's not going to happen. We're going to bring in the crowds, you'll see. Everyone will love the act. There isn't another circus anywhere in Germany or Russia with such a clever act."

Boris throws a scowl over his shoulder. "That's because all those other circuses with that kind of clever act have already been destroyed by the kaiser's dragoons." Boris hurries into the field after Lottie and the chicken, tripping over his robe.

Anna says, "Oh dear. This is all very unnerving. I'd better go finish sewing Madame Natasha's ringmaster costume." She scurries toward Natasha's wagon.

Anatoly fondly calls after her: "I'll h-help you with that r-rigging you wanted, Anna Tatianna. Just come and ask."

She turns and gives him a bright smile. "Thank you, Anatoly."

Durov frowns. "She's lovely, Anatoly. But I'm not sure you're going to have time to help her with her rigging and to sew Sasha's costume."

Anatoly sighs. "I sup-suppose you're right." He turns to Sasha and puts his arms around the pig's stout shoulders, measuring them. "How much b-braid do you think we're going to need?"

CHAPTER EIGHTEEN

B Y THE TIME Anna reaches Natasha's wagon, she is shaking and utterly confused. She has a duty to help Natasha adjust her ringmaster's costume, but she also fervently wants to take Anatoly up on his offer to help her with the rigging for her new act. She's only been able to mark it out on the floor of the practice tent after her father and brother have left, so she's desperate to practice her new solo full-out and high on the wire.

She pauses on the bottom step of Natasha's wagon, trembling with anticipation as she visualizes her act. She climbs up the ladder and walks with a balance bar along the thin wire, doing a somersault and rising again to her tiptoes. Hearing the applause, she takes a deep and graceful bow, like her mother always did. She continues to the other platform, deposits the balance bar, and takes hold of the rope, slipping her foot into a loop she's fashioned at the end. She dives off the platform and catches herself in the loop, then pirouettes, propelling herself around, spinning time and again to rousing applause. On one side of the audience, a fine gentleman's jaw drops, while on the other side, another gentleman tips his cane against his top hat in complete admiration. She smiles at one and then the other. Then she lifts her leg into a high kick and swings herself so that she's doing a back bend and placing her foot on the top of her head. Everyone is staring up at her, and both gentlemen simultaneously rise to start the standing ovation that ripples throughout the entire audience. Both are tall and smiling and have perfectly white teeth. As she glides down the ladder, both men wait below, fighting for her attention. The first hands her a bouquet of yellow roses, the second a bouquet of red roses. Anna's mother has coached her about taking curtain calls, so she takes a flower from each bouquet, kisses it, and gracefully curtsies as she presents each flower to each gentleman in turn. The one with the red roses, however, is even more handsome; so she lingers when passing him the flower, which encourages him just enough to take her into his arms, kissing her tenderly, lovingly, deeply—

"Anna, get me out of this wretched thing," Natasha bellows as she flings open the door of her wagon, her deep voice gravelly with exasperation.

Anna's romantic high is deflated like a pin pricking a balloon. As Natasha holds the door open, Anna bounds up the steps and into the wagon, her long black hair flying behind her. "Coming, Madame. I'm sure everyone was very impressed with you in town."

"I feel like a human pin cushion. Take this off right now...please, my dear."

"Of course, Madame. You must tell me all about it." Anna's pale skin flushes with excitement. "Will there be fine gentlemen, tonight?"

Anna pulls off one sleeve at a time, then the jacket, while Natasha gnashes her teeth at the pin pricks. Natasha flops down on her swivel desk chair, and Anna kneels, following her around in a circle, trying to pull down Natasha's ringmaster trousers.

"Ouch. You're stabbing me in my privates. Keep that up and I won't be able to have children."

Anna jumps back, blushing. "Oh dear."

"A joke. Don't stop. Just get it over with, will you."

Starting again, Anna swivels in the other direction. One last pull, a shriek from Natasha, and the costume is on the floor. Natasha is left in short pantaloons and a sleeveless blouse. As she rubs a dozen little red spots on her arms and legs, she starts to sob, "Damn that Nikolai, leaving me alone to handle everything."

"I take it things didn't go well in town?"

"I don't know, child. This dragoon's in charge of registering immigrants. Wants to see everyone's papers and approve them before they perform." Natasha sobs harder. "He's going to charge a head tax for everyone he approves."

Dejected, Anna starts to gather up the fabric, but then she feels a surge of optimism. "That's good news!"

"How do you figure?"

"Well, if he charges a head tax for everyone he approves, isn't it likely he'll approve everyone—so he can make more money?"

Natasha stares at the girl. "That makes a lot of sense." She stops crying, grabs a handkerchief, blows her nose, and gathers herself together. "You're very smart, aren't you?" she says, as she affectionately chucks Anna under her chin. "Now where are they?" Natasha flings open the drawers in the large wooden desk and rifles through piles and piles of papers, worn at the tops, bottoms, and all around the edges. She raises and lowers the roll top, jumps up, and looks behind and underneath the desk. "Where are all those files? These Germans are so precise, I've got to show him everything's in perfect order." She rummages some more. Anna stands back to avoid flying objects: quill pens, inkwells, and the like.

Anna softly says, "I take it you want me to make the final alterations on your ringmaster's costume?"

"What? Yes, yes, of course." Natasha opens the swivel chair seat and looks within.

Anna feels herself hesitating, then plows ahead: "And what about my new act, Madame? Do you think there will be gentlemen for me to impress?"

Natasha, flustered by all the papers flying about, slams down the seat. "Gentlemen? Your new act, did you say?"

Taking Natasha's reaction as a refusal, Anna is crushed. Her whole world is crumbling. As she starts to slink away, she rapidly blinks back tears. "Never mind. My father and Ivan would never have approved anyway."

Natasha swiftly turns to the girl. "Oh, no, don't go, my dear Anna. Now that I know, thanks to you, that we're almost certainly going to get past this head tax thing, I know we'll be sitting pretty. Of course you should perform your solo and be noticed." Natasha brings Anna over to the bed and sits her down, taking her delicate hands in her own large palms.

Anna's voice quivers: "Maybe I shouldn't be telling you this, Madame. But I can't help it. I just want to meet someone so badly. I dream of having a home of my own." Anna takes in a sharp breath. Now that she's spilled the beans on her true motive, she cringes because Natasha will be furious at her for wanting to leave the circus. Instead, she's shocked to hear Natasha's response.

"I had a home once, myself. But I was alone and tired of being made fun of, as a spinster, so I made a terrible decision. Don't you do the same, my darling girl."

Terrified of becoming a spinster herself—and thereby forever stuck under the control of her father and brother—Anna immediately sympathizes. "That must have been horrible for you, Madame."

Natasha squeezes Anna's hands. "Of course I would be sad to see you leave the circus. But you've become like a daughter to me, and I must confess that I only want what's best for you."

Anna throws her arms around Natasha and starts to cry. Natasha is also moved to tears. She hugs the girl, saying, "Anna, you must choose wisely. Don't be swept off your feet by your emotions. Make sure he's rich. I want for you what I never had: a good man who will take care of you...and who doesn't snore."

Reveling in the affection of the older woman, Anna is doubly happy to give Natasha good news. "Durov's planning a new act, which is going to bring in the crowds. I heard him and Anatoly talking about it, but Anatoly's not entirely certain they can pull it off in time for tonight."

Natasha springs to her feet. "What? A new act to bring in the crowds? That Durov's a clever fellow."

"Don't you want to hear about the new act?"

"I don't have time now. But whatever it is, if it's going to make us money, go tell them they've got to do it. And you're going to do your new high wire act as well. You should have seen how prosperous and clean the town was. People polishing boots that were already gleaming." Natasha leans down and grabs Anna by her shoulders. "These people have lots of money. Gold is just dripping off them."

Anna's dark, luxurious eyes grow round. "Really? Gold just drips off them?"

"Yes, my dear." Natasha motions to her ample chest. "You can't help but see it hanging all over them. Now run along and take my costume to fix. And tell Durov and Anatoly they've got to make up some posters for their new act." She rubs her large palms together. "Have the four dwarf brothers juggle them—I mean plaster them—all around town. We're going to bring in the crowds!"

Natasha goes back to rummaging through the desk. Anna, who can't believe the good news, bounds out of Natasha's wagon. She finds Anatoly and Durov standing at the bottom of the steps. "You'd better get Sasha ready for tonight," she says triumphantly.

Durov grins. "So she's on board?"

"Yes." Anna giggles. She throws her arms around Anatoly. "Oh, thank you for helping with my rigging." Her bright eyes shine. "She's agreed for me to perform my new act too."

As they hug, Anna suddenly pulls back. "Oh no. I forgot to take Madame's ringmaster costume to mend." As she rushes back into Natasha's wagon, she calls over her shoulder to Anatoly, "I'm so happy. It's going to be quite a night."

CHAPTER NINETEEN

A FTER PRACTICING THEIR new act, Durov ushers Sasha into the rear corner of the pen, where a litter of bright pink piglets lies sleeping, curled up hoof to snout. They rouse themselves with muffled snorts. Durov gently says to Sasha, "Now be a good girl and feed your babies. I'm going to look in our costume trunk for something we can make into a helmet. We're going to have such fun with your new trick." He lovingly strokes her head, "But you must practice to get it right—and on cue—every time." He tosses her half an apple. "Catch! Good girl!" As she grunts and chews, he bends down and scratches her between her ears, humming, *"Ich will den Helm...Ich will den Helm."* Meanwhile, the tiny piglets squeal and try to latch onto Sasha's teats. She shoves them away until she's finished chewing the apple. Then she settles down, lazily rolling on her side, and lets the piglets feed.

Durov scrunches up his ruddy face and coos, "That's right, my darling Sasha. You're such a good mother, aren't you? And so smart." As Durov starts to leave, four of the older pigs scurry toward him. He chuckles, saying, *"Da, da.* Demetri, Petrova, Gregory, Anton—you want to be part of the new act too, don't you?" He starts to throw them some apple slices, then stops. "Sit...sit now." They sit on their haunches, patiently waiting. Then he throws slices of apple just above them. They jump up slightly, as if they were dogs. *I could not be prouder of all my little ones than if I'd fathered them myself.* "Good...good...*Da*, you should have something to do in the new act too. I'll think of something, don't worry."

As Durov watches the four pigs settle down to eat their apples, he has another idea. *The royal family. They're all related aren't they? Queen Victoria, Kaiser Wilhelm, the Tsar, the Queen of Greece. How about having them all sit down at the table for a family dinner of corncobs?* Durov can't believe how smart he is. Satirizing the kaiser will be the first time he's employed political humor in his act—he's always preferred to focus on the nuanced aspects of intricate animal training that his father taught him. Even though he's been reduced to training pigs, Durov has never wavered for a moment from this positive behavioral animal training theory. In fact, he believes that if humans employed his family's theory—not only when they interacted with animals but also with each other—then they would all enjoy a more peaceful and more enlightened society.

As he starts back to his wagon, he squints. He sees a cloud of dust coming toward him. Wolfgang sits ramrod straight on his mare, cantering toward the circus compound. Recalling how clean everything is here in Germany, Durov walks swiftly toward Wolfgang to head him off. He doesn't want Wolfgang to immediately spot the pigpen.

"Good day, Sergeant Major."

Wolfgang brings his horse to a halt. "Whoa, Elsa. There now."

As he comes alongside the horse, Durov notices that Wolfgang has fitted his high, over-the-knee boots with spurs. Durov cringes at the thought of spurring a horse to make it behave. His father never used spurs; he would gently lay the reins on one side or the other of a horse's neck to get him to respond, then reward each positive movement. Durov breathes deeply as he tries to keep his anger in check. The circus needs this man to give permission for them to perform. Durov can't antagonize him for any reason.

And even if Wolfgang approves, he might charge a prohibitively hefty head tax.

"Nice horse you have there, Wolfgang."

"Elsa." He pulls up sharply on the reins, forcing the bit deep into her mouth.

Durov is enraged at this bit of cruelty, but holds back. He is quite puzzled to see that Wolfgang is actually extremely effusive in complimenting his horse.

He pats her mane as he says, in his high-pitched, thin voice, "My pride and joy, ain't you, my Elsa?"

Durov carefully watches the spurs to see if Wolfgang is going to use them, and he's immensely relieved that only a slight lift in the reins seems enough to still the horse. She neighs and snorts and stands completely quiet, not even swishing her tail.

Wolfgang smiles broadly under his wide, handlebar mustache. He brings his tall and gangly frame to sit up even straighter in his highly polished leather saddle. "She's my übertier (my super animal). Been with me five years now. A performing Lipizzaner."

Durov is pained to notice that the horse is sway-backed and not especially high-bred. He hesitates to bring it up, but can't resist. "Pardon me, but I thought performing Lipizzaners were only stallions, not mares, and especially not…ah," he doesn't want to mention the swayback, "ah…dappled mares."

Although Wolfgang continues to maintain a frozen smile, the tips of his intricately curled mustache flop down. "Well, yes…technically you're right. She don't have the pure Spanish bloodline, but I tamed her just the same. See here." Wolfgang clicks his teeth and squeezes his thighs. Elsa starts a sidestep, lifting her hooves high and crossing one over the other. "Dressage. Fine as you'll see in the Royal Spanish Riding School in Vienna."

It seems to Durov that the mare actually enjoys her performance. When

Wolfgang clicks again, she stops, whinnies, and assumes her totally still stance.

Reaching out his hand to stoke the horse's head, Durov hesitates, then asks Wolfgang's permission: "May I?"

Wolfgang nods, and Durov gently grabs her harness, patting her slender forehead. Her ears swivel and prick in Durov's direction, and he smiles to hear her nickering softly, a sign of affection. The famous Lipizzaners are bred to strict Aryan standards, with specific ratios of the length of the brow to its width at certain points along their heads. Durov is amazed, and even a bit saddened, that Wolfgang would have gone to all that trouble to train her, since this horse most certainly does not meet the criteria of an Aryan purebred. Elsa snorts and lifts her head, as if to reassure him that even though she doesn't have pure blood, she can perform like the best of them. Durov immediately feels a bond with this animal, which is apparently reciprocated—as he pets her some more, she sighs, drawing in a deep, satisfied breath and letting it out slowly and audibly through her fluttering mouth.

"Seems she likes you," Wolfgang says, with slight annoyance in his voice. He dismounts, standing a foot taller than Durov, who stands at just about the horse's back. Wolfgang strokes her mane, hard. She turns and snorts, curling her upper lip and exposing the pink of her gums. She seems to be smiling at Wolfgang, although Durov has the distinct impression of a trace of fear in the animal's soft brown eyes.

Wolfgang continues, with condescension in his voice, "You got a way with horses. What is it you do in the circus?"

Durov hesitates to tell Wolfgang he trains pigs, especially as they are standing next to a horse, the type of animal he's loved all his life. Petting even an old and broken down horse such as Elsa infuses Durov with a longing he's tried to suppress for more years than he cares to admit.

"I...ah...take care of the animals. Train them as well."

"Good thing to tame animals. Must be made to obey and—"

Durov snaps, "I didn't say I tame them; I said I train them. There's a big difference."

Wolfgang's watery blue eyes bulge, and his jaw jerks back at Durov's abrupt tone. Elsa senses his anger and whinnies. Wolfgang pats her harder to quiet her. "Stay, girl." He turns to Durov. "You suggesting I don't know how to treat my animals?" Elsa rears up. Wolfgang grabs her harness and sharply yanks her back down.

"*Prekrati eto* (stop that)." Durov can't help himself. "She should be comforted when she's startled, not wrenched into submission."

"*Nein!* That's nonsense. You ain't never been to war with a sturdy mount under you. These animals is just dumb creatures who exist at the mercy of us—their masters. Every moment of their lives is meant to do what you order."

Durov clenches and unclenches his fists. He knows the circus has to curry favor with Wolfgang, so he grits his teeth, his weathered face turning purple with controlled rage. "Of course, you know your horse better than any other man could."

Wolfgang's thin voice becomes more robust with his apparent success in winning the argument. He says, "*Ja, ja.* Glad you see it that way." He straightens his uniform. "Direct me to Madame Natasha's wagon, *bitte*. I have business to conduct."

Fighting to control both his anger and his pride, Durov forces himself to bow to Wolfgang as courteously as possible. "*Bezuslovno* (certainly). Would you like me to water Elsa? Maybe rub her down for you?"

Wolfgang, clearly pleased he's got the upper hand, reaches into his pocket for some sweets for Elsa. She settles down and slobbers them into her mouth. "*Danke.* Kind'a you."

Durov directs Wolfgang to Natasha's wagon, then leads Elsa off. As they go, he pats her flank, immensely happy to have a horse in hand...any horse.

CHAPTER TWENTY

ANNA GAILY EMERGES from Natasha's wagon clutching the ringmaster costume to mend. Now that she has permission to do her own act, Anna joyously twirls down the wagon steps. She practices a *ronde de jambe* twist of her leg and then leaps to the bottom step. The costume goes flying and lands on the ground. She giggles as she bends to fetch it. As she rises, she bumps into Wolfgang, who has doubled over his tall, bony form, in order to assist her.

Anna's pure white skin turns deep burgundy. "Oh my. Excuse me." Her large, dark eyes enlarge even more, as they travel over his gigantically tall, albeit skinny, frame that is covered with gold braid and glittering medals. She whips the fabric behind her and sinks into her deepest and most graceful curtsy.

Wolfgang swishes off his helmet and bows in return. "*Fräulein, verzeihen sie meine Klumpen.*"

She stares blankly.

He repeats, smiling weakly, "*Meine Klumpen...*" Then he seems to understand that she doesn't understand and switches to Russian: "*Prosti menyait* (forgive me). I was only trying to assist you to recover your...ah..."

She brings the fabric around to the front and gently cushions it in her hands. "*Spasibo* (thank you). Ah, I have it now. Ah, no harm done." Anna can hardly speak, so dazzled is she by his gentlemanly manners and his shining helmet…but mostly by all that gold braid all over his chest. *Natasha was right: they're just dripping with gold!* "No, certainly, I'm the one to excuse…" she hesitates, searching for the proper way to address this impressive and most likely wealthy gentleman. *He must be some kind of general. And I'm sure generals are gentlemen, aren't they?*

"Not at all, *Wenig Stutfohlen.*"

Anna is horrified, "*Shtup hole in* (what did you say)?"

"*Nein, nyet,* not *shtup—Stutfohlen.* What I said was that you were a little filly—*malen'kaya loshadka* (little) *Stutfohlen* (little filly)."

"Oh, I'm sorry. I misunderstood."

Wolfgang exhales sharply as he shifts his helmet in his gloved hands, posing as if sitting for the portrait of a victorious warrior. "I'm here on official business."

Anna turns back toward Natasha's wagon. "You must want to see Madame Natasha, the owner of the circus."

"Clever girl!" Wolfgang guffaws, falling out of the pose and all over himself. "How did you guess?"

Anna blushes again, marveling that such an important and wealthy man is attempting to impress an insignificant girl like her. Anna modestly brushes back her lustrous black hair and smiles weakly. "Just a lucky guess, I suppose, Herr…ah?"

"You may address me as—" But before he can get his name out, Wolfgang smartly clicks his heels. Still in his spurs, however, he stabs himself, then tries to ignore his pain by hopping around and smiling at her, as if he were on parade.

Anna is terribly flattered. She isn't exactly sure how to flirt—she's never had the occasion because her father and brother have kept her so sheltered—so she swishes herself around, pouring it on thick. "What brings you to see us?"

Wolfgang sidles up to her. "*Ya lyublyu tsirk* (I just love the circus)."

"Oh really? So do I, you know." She sways her hips. "All the glamour, the sequins—" She parades herself in a little circle.

Wolfgang starts to sweat. "You know, we are trained to spot fillies of exceptional breeding. Who can produce exceptional...ahem..." He rolls his eyes. "*Nachwuchs.*"

"Now see here."

"*Nachwuchs*—you know, *otprysk* (offspring)."

Anna shakes her head, not sure this is a compliment. Then, deciding to take it that way, nods and says, "Oh really?"

"I would say, you're just about the best *Zuchtstock* (breeding stock) I've seen in a month of Sundays."

"*Spasibo.*" Anna curtsies. She's never been complimented so highly by any man. She titters and blushes and moves her slender leg in a high kick back and forth in the grass, in what she assumes is a seductive manner.

Wolfgang checks to see they're alone, then leans way, way down to whisper, "So if I was to ah...*Frage nach*—"

She jumps back. "Look here. I'm a good girl."

"Of course you are. What I mean was to ask for your hand in marriage. *Prosi ruku o brake.* To whom would I speak?"

A deep blush flares over Anna's heart-shaped face. She can hardly blurt out the words. "Well, well, I...ah...I suppose it would be my brother Ivan Ivanovich. He's the one who really runs our act now."

"Ivan, did you say?" Wolfgang raises his eyebrows.

"You might have met him with Madame Natasha this morning...in town?"

"Oh yeah. Kinda flighty fella. Likes to 'float around,' if you know what I mean."

Anna frowns at this slight to her brother. "He's a trapeze artist, if that's what you mean."

"Yeah, that fella. So I'd see him?"

"I suppose so." Anna can't believe her good fortune. She twitters and smiles and twitters some more. "The subject hasn't really come up before."

"Well now, my luck, ain't it?" Wolfgang chews on a corner of his handlebar mustache, then bends down to kiss Anna.

Just then, they are interrupted by Boris, who comes tripping by—quite literally tripping over his long robe. He nods as he passes Anna and Wolfgang, does a double take seeing Wolfgang and Anna about to kiss, and makes an abrupt turnaround.

Wolfgang frowns, obviously annoyed at Boris's intrusion. In his thin, reedy voice, he asks Anna, "And just who might this be, *Fräulein*?"

"This is our Boris. His father was a magician, but he's more of a clown now. Boris, aren't we fortunate to be visited by such a distinguished—" she whispers aside to him, "*and wealthy*—gentleman?"

Boris grabs her arm to take her aside. "Anna, my dear girl, I think Anatoly wants to speak with you about the—"

"Oh, he can wait." She breaks away from Boris. Desperate to hold Wolfgang's attention, Anna resumes her flirting. "This general here was telling me how much he likes the circus, weren't you?"

"Why…yes. I just need to *Frage nach in Heirat*."

Boris interjects, "We don't do that sort of thing around here—at least not in public."

Wolfgang bellows, "Oh…very funny…*nyet*…what I meant to say was I got to finish a few formalities with your Madame Natasha and then get with this filly's *Bruder*."

Boris pulls his pint-sized frame up to its full height, which just about reaches Wolfgang's belt buckle. "We don't brood either. We're clowns. We make people laugh."

Biting her nail, Anna watches Wolfgang slap his knee and laugh exaggeratedly, obviously for Boris's benefit.

Anna purses her lips, thrilled when Wolfgang suddenly bends aside to whisper so only she can hear: "I'm looking forward to seeing your act tonight, little filly. After the performance, maybe we can—"

Boris swishes his cape between them, breaking them up. "That would be nice. But, your generalship, we have a strict curfew here." He tugs at Anna to come with him. "I'm sure Anatoly would love to help you with your rigging *now*, my dear Anna."

Wolfgang coyly says, "Anna, a real nice name to go with a real—"

Boris rushes forward, his nose reaching just up to the scabbard that houses Wolfgang's sabre. His deep voice involuntarily rises an octave as he says, "You are so kind to notice, but we really must run along now to prepare for tonight. I'm sure you and Madame Natasha will sort everything out."

Anna is crestfallen. *Oh no! My one big chance and Boris is ruining it for me!*

As he tugs Anna along, Boris's tenaciousness is finally too much for her. She gives in, flashes Wolfgang a big smile, and stamps her tiny foot at Boris, as she reluctantly allows herself to be led away.

CHAPTER TWENTY-ONE

NATASHA'S HEART POUNDS as she hears thudding up her wagon steps, accompanied by a jangling noise she can't quite place until she realizes it must be Wolfgang's spurs. *That oaf! If he stomps in here wearing those damned things, he'll tear up my rug.* She looks around and, seeing her desk a blizzard of papers, she frantically shoves them into every available drawer and cabinet. She squares her broad shoulders, puts on a smile that would melt a glacier, and flings the door open just as Wolfgang, helmet under one arm, is about to knock.

Natasha swiftly moves outside and greets him on the top step, which forms a small landing at the entrance to her wagon. "Good day, Sergeant Major. My, your uniform is as grand as ever. And look, are those spurs you're wearing?" Wolfgang stupidly looks straight down, then has to curve his tall frame around to check that he's wearing the spurs on the rear of his boots. As he turns in the small platform space, his sabre twists around, nearly stabbing Natasha, but she jumps aside just in time.

Determined to get him to remove his spurs and not tear up her rug, she raises her deep voice in as high a lilting pitch as she can muster. "I'd love to see them close up. I've never seen such elaborate and...and...spurious things on any man's highly polished, and in fact, gleaming—your boots are absolutely gleaming, aren't they?—boots." Before Wolfgang can get a word out, Natasha continues her rapid pace, "Would you mind letting me see them? I mean, I don't want to impose, but I'd surely love to examine such wondrous, carved, gleaming things for myself."

She takes his arm and ushers him just inside the wagon. He has to bend considerably to get into the door, and even inside, being several inches taller than Nikolai was, he still can't quite straighten up. She guides him to a chair right next to the door, takes his helmet, places it on a small table, and motions for him to sit. "There…please be comfortable as you remove those spurs—so I can admire them up close."

Wolfgang seems hypnotized by her patter. Obviously used to following orders, he complies with a combination of pride and puzzlement. He offers her the spurs, and she grabs a handkerchief to hold them high. "You must be a very diligent soldier to keep these polished to such a magnificent finish." She rests them on the nearby table. And before he can put them back on, she says, "Let's keep them here, so they can gleam in the afternoon sunshine while we talk, shall we?" She decides to press her luck. "Maybe removing that long sword will make you more comfortable?"

His pale blue eyes flash, and his thin voice becomes gruff, as he quickly retorts, "I never take off my sabre when I'm on duty."

Natasha regroups, terrified to make him angry. "Oh, of course not. Silly me. Would you like some tea?"

He softens toward her and grins sheepishly, his gaunt cheeks reddening. "Madam, we soldiers, we don't drink on duty." Looking about, however, and finding no one else present, he says, "But if you was to have a draught of beer, shall we say?"

"Oh…beer…of course," she says. His eyes widen. "Sorry, no." His eyes narrow. "I haven't had time to procure any supplies in town. I came directly back here after our meeting. I knew you'd be waiting to examine the papers for the circus people so you could rapidly approve us all and be on your way." She shakes her head up and down. "*Da?*"

He shakes his head back and forth. "*Nyet.* I mean, not so fast, Madame. You shouldn't want me to slack in my duties, just 'cause I been smitten by that little filly coming out of your wagon just now."

Natasha looks puzzled. "Filly? We actually don't have any horses in the circus right now. That's kind of a long story, and you'll have to ask Durov, but—"

"Not a horse. A young lady. And quite the lady she is with her long black mane. Little scrawny, but nothing can't be fixed real soon. She'll be living with me in my barracks. We don't have no heat…" He smiles lasciviously. "But I'll keep her warm, I will. And nothing a little hard work scrubbing the barracks and lots of potatoes and sauerkraut won't fix."

"I'm sorry, I don't follow. Are you talking about Anna Tatianna?"

"Anna, that's it. Pretty name for a pretty filly. I'm gonna be the proudest bridegroom you folks ever seen." He starts to hum what sounds to Natasha like a German drinking song. "Now where are them papers?"

Natasha's olive skin drains of color. She can't believe her ears. Anna and Wolfgang? There must be some mistake. But surely it can wait until the paperwork is finished and the circus gets permission to perform. *We can't displease Wolfgang, or he'll run us out of town.*

"Of course, let me show them to you. Nice tune, by the way."

"Wagner. He sure did get that Master Race thing just right. Heard a' him?"

Natasha gulps. "Master Race? Seems I have." She offers him a wad of papers. He jerks back in disbelief at the mess. She quickly smooths out the papers for him to examine.

Humming away, he looks through them. "No degenerates here?" Natasha shakes her head no. "No sexual deviants?" Another no. "How about any religious troublemakers?"

"Troublemakers?"

"We're all Christians here. We don't like no one preaching different."

Natasha thinks back to Boris's sermon for Nikolai. "Believe me, there is no one in this circus likely to preach anything—ah, I mean, anything different than what you're accustomed to hearing."

Wolfgang nods his satisfaction. He whistles the crescendo to the "Love Potion" aria from *Tristan and Isolde,* as he paws through the rest of the papers. Then he hands the papers back to Natasha. "I think that just about covers it." He pulls out a scroll, motions for a pen. Natasha rummages through the desk, more objects flying, until she finds an inkwell and a quill. He signs with a flourish. "Your permit to perform for three nights. And seeing as we're gonna be family, no head tax." Natasha breathes a huge sigh of relief. Wolfgang adds, "Now I got to get back to the barracks to tell the men my good fortune."

"Ah, thank you for your approval—and for the break on the head tax."

Wolfgang rises, his head butting against the ceiling as he automatically clicks his heels. As he turns toward the door, his sabre knocks over some teacups on the bureau. The teacups fall, to Natasha's great relief, unbroken onto the rug.

"Sorry, Madame."

Gritting her teeth, she says, "Think nothing of it, Sergeant Major."

As he reaches the door, he bends down to pick up his helmet and spurs. Gazing fondly at the spurs, he says, "Taming is real important to horses—and to women. These can do quite a bit of damage to an animal"—his lips curl maliciously—"or a woman that don't want to be tamed proper."

Natasha's dark eyes round into spheres of sheer terror. "I'm sure they can." She shivers, imagining poor Anna at the mercy of this horrible creature. She resolves to find a way out for her *devushka* Anna. As she searches for an excuse, she forces herself to be pleasant, for the sake of the profitability of the circus. "Ah... now before you go, there's just one more, teensy thing. It's about Anna." *What can possibly be some plausible excuse why the girl can't marry this monster?* "Well...ah...you see...she's...already betrothed."

Wolfgang's gaunt face falls in on itself. "As in, she's already pledged to be married?"

"I suppose that's what betrothed means."

Wolfgang paces about, knocking things over. "She didn't say nothing about that. Why that little—"

"Oh, you mustn't blame her. She doesn't really...I mean...she didn't know about it when she spoke to you. I'm sure this is just a terrible misunderstanding."

"How could she not know?"

"Please, a moment and I'll explain." *How could she not know? Good question. How could she not know? Oh, I've got it.* "Her brother Ivan—"

"That swishy fella?"

"Yes, well, Ivan came to me—it was just last night after we made camp, it was. And he told me that someone here, in this very circus, had asked for her hand in marriage. To be married right away. Tonight, even. After the performance. As I'm the head of the circus, of course, he was doing me the honor of asking my permission. We're a family, we are."

"The kaiser don't cater to people in the same family marrying—"

"Oh, no, nothing like that, I assure you. Someone from an entirely different family who is employed here in our circus family, if you know what I mean."

"No, I don't."

"Never mind about that circus family rot. It's just what people say so they feel more...ah...more together."

"I hear all you say, but if it's all the same to you, I'd like to meet this fella. Talk to him tonight." Wolfgang swishes his sabre menacingly. "Men can usually be persuaded to do what's best for them and their...ah...circus family."

Natasha follows the glint of the sabre with terror in her eyes. She clasps her large hands against her ample bosom, in a kind of prayer. "I'm afraid everyone is really busy preparing for tonight's performance. Now that people know you've given your permission, you wouldn't want us to be a flop, would you? That wouldn't look good for you, now would it?"

Wolfgang scratches his head. "I guess not. And I suppose you could say there is honor to uphold here—being that the kaiser and the tsar are cousins." He sits to fix the spurs to his boots. "Rest assured, I will be back tonight to see for myself what this is all about. And I aim to bring all my dragoons with me to make sure everything's on the up and up." He looks back and forth at Natasha who is pacing back and forth in the small wagon. "She sure would make me proud. Give me ten children I bet." He spins the spurs before he attaches them. "Just so you know, I don't give up easy, Madame."

Natasha mutters under her breath. "An admirable trait, Sergeant Major." *By St. Michael, I don't give up either. I must find Anna right away and sort this out.*

Wolfgang springs from the chair, once again hitting his head on the ceiling. Natasha winces sympathetically for his benefit. He picks up his helmet, nods, and bows. Her heart pounds almost out of her ample chest, as she opens the door and watches him, spurs jangling, lope down the wagon steps.

CHAPTER TWENTY-TWO

THE AFTERNOON SUN is bright in the cloudless Prussian-blue sky. Durov and Sasha are in the pig corral practicing the new *Ich will den Helm* helmet trick. Durov is anxious to finalize everything—just as soon as he can get hold of a helmet. He hasn't felt this energized since he took his family's colt to train in the field, all those years ago. The helmet act will be his salvation, the redemption of the honor of his family he's craved all these years. He chuckles to think he will be the sensation of the circus and the children will be absolutely delighted. More than that, everyone will know how expertly the Durovs train their animals—without harming them in any way. *We will revolutionize how people treat animals all over Europe!*

He dances a little jig, his thick body surprisingly light and balletic, as he prides himself on how wonderful it is to have the gift of imagination. That's what the circus inspires. And the gift of artistic freedom to create something unique and worthy of applause—and respect. Finally, Natasha is certain to admire him too. Maybe she'll even come to care about him...

Well, at least he'll be making her money.

As he watches from behind the fence, Boris shields his eyes from the piercing sunlight. Durov boasts what an expert animal trainer he is, as he makes sure to tell Boris the details of his methodical technique. After she performs exactly as he asks, he says, "Now all I need is a helmet."

"Oh, I almost forgot." Boris reaches deep into a pocket in his robe and brings forth an actual, real German helmet.

Durov is ecstatic. "How did you get this?"

"I could tell you I materialized it, but really, I lifted it from some soldiers marching by. I had to offer them copious amounts of vodka. Apparently they're only used to drinking beer—which, you know, has a much lesser alcoholic content."

"Yes, yes. Tell me, how did you get the helmet?"

Boris waves his hands about, with his magician's flourish. "Patience. I'm coming to that. As they slept off the vodka, I secreted one of their helmets into my father's magic box." Boris gleefully rubs his hands together, then spreads them wide in a theatrical fanfare. "When their superior officer came by and saw them sleeping, he yelled at them. They awoke with a start, searched for the helmet, but had to scramble back to their barracks without it."

"A very clever disappearing act, Boris. I owe you some vodka."

"Copious amounts."

Durov reverently takes the helmet and starts to train his dear Sasha. She dutifully steps on the helmet with her hoof and flips it up onto her head. Durov feels so proud he could kiss her. In fact, he does just that, each time she flawlessly executes the maneuver. It's a bit tricky because of the pointed top; but she manages it with the proper spin, so it lands correctly between her ears every time. "That's it, my intelligent piggala. Wait till they see you tonight!"

Boris applauds, admiring not only Sasha's gifted performance, but also his helmet's contribution to Durov's new act.

Just then, Anatoly rushes to the corral fence, wads of fabric spilling over in his hands. His blonde curls fly about as he screeches to a halt. "Durov, this is just so c-complicated. I don't know how I can f-finish it in time."

Durov bends down and hugs Sasha. Then he calmly walks over to his brother and hugs him too. "Anatoly, calm down. The helmet may be the key to the act, but the uniform you're sewing is very important too."

"There's so much braid and m-medals and iron crosses and—"

Boris jumps in: "We know you can do it."

"But everyone will k-know if it's not true to life," Anatoly moans.

Durov pats his brother on the shoulder. "Now, now. The costume doesn't have to be true to life in every respect. People will get the idea."

"Of course they will, Anatoly. Don't fret. But... speaking of true to life—" Boris flashes a cherubic smile, reaches into another pocket, and brings forth some papers rolled up in a scroll. "See here, I'm about to make a bunch of posters for your act tonight. I've drawn one as a sample."

"Let me see." Durov grabs the scroll and unwinds it to reveal a circus poster featuring him, the helmet, and Sasha dressed up as the kaiser— complete with his military uniform with rings and rings of gleaming gold braid. Durov is ecstatic. Despite his bulk, he lifts himself off the ground in a kind of balletic leap—or as close to it as he's ever likely to get. "This is fantastic, Boris." He slaps Boris on the back. "You've got to make several more. We'll get the four dwarf brothers to stand on each other's shoulders and nail them up, high enough so these tall, blonde townsfolk can read them. You've really outdone yourself."

Anatoly collapses on the ground. "And you've outdone me too. Look at the d-detail you've put into that uniform."

Durov grins, nods, and gaily walks around, holding up the poster and striking exactly the same pose Boris has drawn.

Anatoly moans. "It's so v-very a-accurate."

Boris knits his brows and strokes his goatee. "What's wrong with that?"

Anatoly sobs. "It's f-far more a-accurate than my c-costume."

As Durov realizes the full extent of Anatoly's distress, he feels a special, deep affection for his brother. He hates to put him under any kind of pressure, as he knows he's a gentle soul compared with the hard-bitten fellow Durov has had to become after their family tragedy. He sits Anatoly down and wraps his arm around his slender, heaving shoulders. "That's all right, my dear brother. Just do the best you can."

Boris's voice is deep and comforting as he kneels beside the brothers and spreads the poster out before them. "Anatoly, all people need is the illusion to make it seem real. They fill in the details for themselves." Anatoly looks uncertain, so Boris continues. "Take it from me, my father was an expert illusionist. That's the secret of being a great magician—or a great performer of any kind." Anatoly still looks puzzled, so Boris continues, "Half of every performance is believing in what you're doing. My father used to say that anyone can perform a trick, but if you bring the audience in with you, weave a dramatic story for them, they'll believe in you and your act."

"I think I see w-what you're saying," Anatoly says through a waterfall of tears.

Boris snatches the poster away, trying to be as patient as possible. "Please don't sob onto the poster; the colors will run. I'd like it to be as accurate as possible, so I can make copies."

At the mention of accuracy, Anatoly wails, burying his face in Durov's shoulder.

As Durov comforts Anatoly, he studies the poster. It will be so wonderful for Boris to make lots of copies for the four dwarf brothers to distribute all around town. Suddenly, Durov's struck with a horrible thought. "Boris, I'm not so sure you can put these posters up all around town."

"Why ever not?"

"What if Wolfgang or any of the other dragoons sees them? Do you think they might be offended?"

"Why would they be offended? See how the kaiser's uniform is rendered with such meticulous care? How we are honoring his magnificence?"

"Boris, the uniform is on a pig."

"She's a handsome pig. Well, maybe a pretty pig, as pigs go."

"But she's still a pig."

Anatoly adds optimistically, "A very t-talented pig. Boris, have we ever t-told you how smart our little ones—"

Boris rolls his eyes. "Many, many, many times."

Durov's voice is kind and patient. "Anatoly, that's not the point. Boris, and everyone else for that matter, knows they're smart—especially when we train them as expertly as we do. I'm just concerned that Wolfgang's not going to take what we're doing as a compliment."

Boris turns the poster upside down and around, then winces. "I guess it's not really a compliment, is it?"

"No, but we've got to convince him it is."

"Maybe if I perfect it a bit more…"

"*Da*. You run along and do that, Boris."

"I will make it great." Boris stands, moving the poster this way and that in the sun. He sticks his thumb up to measure the drawing. Durov turns and notices Wolfgang jangling by, presumably on his way to find his horse. Durov stands Anatoly up and takes him gently but firmly by the shoulders. "Anatoly, I think you should go now. Just do your best on the costume, my dear brother. Let me figure out how to handle Wolfgang." Anatoly brushes back his thick, wavy blonde hair, stiffens his upper lip, gathers the fabric, and slinks off.

Durov quickly walks over to Sasha in the corral, takes the helmet, and hides it behind a post. He then turns his attention to Wolfgang, who looks somewhat dejected—he hopes it's not because negotiations with Natasha have broken down.

"How did things go with Madame Natasha?"

Wolfgang's face crumbles into a mass of deep ruts.

"Are you looking for Elsa? I hope things went well with—"

Wolfgang stiffens and adjusts his uniform. "Yes, everything's set. I just had a misunderstanding with a little filly, but no matter. I'm going to straighten everything out tonight, when I return with my dragoons." His voice menacing, he says, "She'll see the light. I know she will because I can be very persuasive. Me and my dragoons can be right persuasive, if you know what I mean."

Durov has no idea what Wolfgang is talking about, as they don't have any horses in the circus. He's about to ask for a clarification when Wolfgang looks around and clenches his fists. His lip starts to quiver like a child launching into a temper tantrum. "Where's my Elsa? I need my Elsa now."

Wolfgang sobs and hangs his head just over Boris—who has, much to Durov's horror, not gone off to make changes in the poster, but instead plopped himself on the ground in front of the corral. Durov gasps, shocked that Boris hasn't had the sense to retire to his wagon with the poster. Boris is so engrossed in copying that he hasn't noticed Wolfgang approach. As Wolfgang cries and stands above Boris, one of Wolfgang's tears falls onto the poster.

Boris looks from side to side and holds up his hand. "It is raining?" Then he twists around to look above him. At that moment, Wolfgang spies the poster and rubs his watery blue—and by now, misty—eyes to get a better look.

Wolfgang bellows, "What in our emperor's name is that?"

Boris says, "This? I'm just perfecting it. Durov thought it was very good. Do you like it?"

Durov holds his breath. Wolfgang will almost certainly take offense at ridiculing the kaiser. He might just shut the circus down. Durov leans over the poster and frantically tries to hush Boris. "Oh, I didn't say that, Boris. Why don't you give it another try, in your wagon."

Boris, so intent on his handiwork, hasn't fully comprehended the gravity of the situation. Admiring the poster, he says to Durov, "But I thought you liked it. You just asked me to perfect it, didn't you?"

Wolfgang rapidly blinks, trying to clear his vision. Durov sweats profusely, speaking through gritted teeth: "What I said was that your artwork always seems best when you complete things *in your wagon*. Why don't you roll this up right now and take it—"

"Is that what I think it is?" booms Wolfgang, full force on top of Boris—who, flattened by the reverberation, lands on top of the poster. Wolfgang bends his lanky frame like a praying mantis and shoves Boris aside—sending him rolling—to reveal the poster in its full glory. He squints to get a better look. "Is that a…a *schwein*?"

Durov winces, nods feebly, and takes a step back from Wolfgang.

Wolfgang's words come in a torrent: "Am I looking at what I'm seeing? Could it be possible? No, certainly it ain't possible. But yes, I think it is…is that a *schwein* in a uniform?"

Durov takes two steps back.

"A *schwein* in the uniform of our beloved kaiser?"

Boris proudly stands and brushes himself off. "Why, thank you. How nice it's all so clear."

Wolfgang quakes in anger, his spurs jangling. "Seems right clear to me," he says as he grabs the poster in his large, bony hand. He stomps over to Durov and peers down at him, pointing at the poster. "Does it seem right clear to you? Is that you in the poster?"

Boris interjects, "Of course, that's him. I thought you said it was clear—"

Wolfgang wheels sharply around. Towering above Boris, he bellows down at him: "Did I ask you?"

Boris opens his mouth to respond but, finally sizing up the situation, rapidly shuts his mouth. He zooms down into his robe, shaping himself into a cone. A faint "no" can be heard from within. Boris's hand comes up and out of the robe to grab the poster, but Wolfgang keeps a tight hold. The hand shrugs and disappears down into the robe—which, with Boris inside, smoothly glides away. Durov is left staring directly into Wolfgang's gold-braided chest.

In an instant, Durov's whole world hurtles past him. He can't afford to jeopardize the entire circus, but he doesn't want to give up his fabulous new act—he hasn't felt this good about an act in all the years he's been training pigs. Still, it's a bittersweet moment for him. He can't dazzle the crowd like his father did with the majesty of their horses and his glamorous mother riding atop their prized stallion. But at least he can show the world his prowess in animal training with his beloved Sasha.

Durov squares his square shoulders. "Sergeant Major, I realize it might seem a bit strange to you. But rest assured, this act pays the highest compliment to your extraordinarily well-groomed kaiser. Please realize we are taking all this trouble to recreate, in the utmost, meticulous detail—well, in as much detail as we can, given what meager materials we have at our current disposal and given how arduous a journey it was for us over the mountains—"

"You think having my beloved emperor in your act is a compliment?"

"Of course. Our circus is quite democratic. We play to all groups from the highest born to the lowliest workers. But our highest calling is for the children—to inspire them to develop their imaginations, rehearse, and perfect a craft." Durov nods vigorously, asserting himself in the hopes of convincing Wolfgang. "Not only that, but we bring laughter and joy into their little lives. That's what we live for." Wolfgang looks skeptical, so Durov redoubles his efforts. "The children will think of your glorious kaiser when they see his uniform. You want to keep the presence of your most magnificent emperor foremost in their minds at all times, don't you?"

"Ah...well...of course. But, wait a minute. It ain't gonna be the kaiser they'll be seeing, it'll be"—he turns around toward the pigpen—"those filthy, dumb creatures. I don't see how anyone in their right mind could think they might resemble—"

"Excuse me, did you happen to say filthy and dumb?"

"That's what I said."

Durov seethes but manages to smile, seeing an opportunity to smooth things over. "Well really, I'm sure you aren't aware, and I'm confident that once I tell you, this whole misunderstanding will be cleared up. Pigs, you see, are very clean animals. They only roll in the mud to cool and scratch themselves, not to make themselves dirty. And when they scratch themselves, they're actually cleaning themselves...in a manner of speaking." Wolfgang looks puzzled, so Durov continues, "And, as far as being dumb, it's actually quite the opposite. A pig is the most intelligent of all the animals you can train. Even—and I really hate to admit this—but a pig is even more intelligent than a horse. And I've always loved horses, don't get me wrong. In fact, my family used to train horses—"

Wolfgang digs his spurs into the grassy field. "Why you degenerate gypsy. There ain't no more majestic a animal than a horse." Wolfgang's beady blue eyes squint down into thin slits.

Durov starts back, "Of course, horses are majestic. I know how majestic...stately even"—Durov continues—"regal...grandiose...magnificent...splendid..." With each adjective, Wolfgang's eyes open back up, just a bit, until they are as wide and round as beer mugs. Durov concludes, "Horses are all these things, because as I was saying, we used to train them."

Wolfgang growls. "The likes of you? Tame horses?"

"I didn't say tame; I said train. You can never tame such a beast. Each one has its own personality. You train them to act in concert with your wishes. Not as master and servant, but as colleague and colleague, as it were."

Wolfgang sputters incoherently as Durov continues. "Well, to be sure, it was primarily my father who trained the horses. Follow me and I'll show you."

Durov leads the incredulous Wolfgang to the side of Natasha's wagon and shows him the faint painting of his parents' act. Wolfgang looks intently at the wagon, then back at the man before him. Durov smiles bashfully. "Note the family resemblance. My parents were remarkable. But of course, that was a long time ago."

"I can see that. Look here. Just because you come from horse breeder stock, I'm going to give you a break."

Thank goodness, I knew I could convince him. Durov nods expectantly. Then, suddenly, Wolfgang tears up the poster and stomps it into the ground, shredding it with his spurs. Durov looks on, horrified, as Wolfgang viciously slashes the poster with his sabre, sending the shredded pieces flying.

Wolfgang growls through clenched teeth, "I'm going to forget I ever saw this blasphemous piece of *schwein* manure."

Durov stands perfectly still—shocked, appalled, fuming—as he watches it snow scattered pieces of poster in the bright afternoon sun.

Wolfgang flashes a defiant smile, his upper lip curling under his broad, corkscrew-curled mustache. "Now that we settled all that, where's my Elsa?"

Durov balls his hands into fists, tightly opening and shutting them as he breathes deeply. He must resist his almost irresistible urge to punch Wolfgang on his thin nose that sits in the middle of his weasel-like face. *Calm yourself. There'll be other acts and other times. Don't be an idiot. You can't allow your pride to jeopardize the entire circus—once again.* Durov bites his tongue, swallows his pride, and leads Wolfgang to his horse.

CHAPTER TWENTY-THREE

NATASHA PACES THE length of her wagon, which isn't very long at all, waiting for the unnerving jangling of Wolfgang's spurs to fade. She hyperventilates, horrified that this martinet of a soldier, this giant scarecrow, this brutal bean pole, actually intends to lay claim to her dear little Anna. Nikolai had mostly been too drunk to consummate much of anything—which had, in truth, been quite a relief to Natasha. So she's come to think of Anna as the only daughter she might ever have. She wants only the best for the girl—even if Anna chooses to leave the circus and have a family of her own. Natasha isn't thrilled at the prospect—she would lose an important member of a lucrative act—but she takes pride in her selflessness. She shudders and crosses herself. She thinks about Anna having to live with Wolfgang in his unheated barracks and being forced into a life of servitude, broken only by brief respites to have a child. She must find her right away, so they can figure out how to get out of the terrible lie she told Wolfgang—that Anna is betrothed and to be married that very evening.

Natasha listens at the door, then decides she's waited long enough for Wolfgang to depart. She hefts down the steps of her wagon to look for

Anna, relieved to find Wolfgang nowhere in sight. Meanwhile, Anatoly rushes by, clutching his heap of fabric.

"Anatoly, have you seen Anna?"

"N-no, Madame Natasha. P-pardon me. I've got to sew this c-costume for our new act tonight."

"Oh, that's right. I hear you're going to bring in the crowds. Off you go." She thanks St. Michael that she won't have to worry about ticket sales and can concentrate on saving her dear Anna.

Natasha starts toward the Zubov Trapeze Family's practice tent, when she's nearly run over by what looks to be a conical-shaped apparition on top of two rapidly moving feet. "You there, watch where you're going."

Boris sticks the top of his head through the top of his robe. "Is he gone?"

"Who?"

Boris takes his deep baritone voice up two octaves: "Wolfgang. Oh, Madame Natasha. *Eto Uzhasno.*"

"Yes, I know it's terrible. *Moya bednaya devushka.* My poor Anna. What's to be done?" Natasha feels a sense of impending doom—a mother seeing her beloved daughter given to an oaf even worse than Nikolai, if such a thing were possible.

Boris jumps up to his full, diminutive height. Puzzled, he strokes his goatee. "Madame Natasha...Anna? What are you talking about?"

Natasha gestures wildly. "Wolfgang thinks he's going to marry her. But I told him she was already pledged to be married—and tonight—after the performance." She gasps, catching her breath. "Still, he didn't take it too well. He's coming back with his dragoons to woo Anna one last time after the performance. He—and his dragoons—can be quite persuasive."

Boris gulps. "Tonight? After the performance? Quite persuasive?"

Natasha strides back and forth, wringing her large hands. "That's what I said. Are you deaf as well as...never mind—"

Boris also strides back and forth, opposite Natasha; so much shorter, he takes two steps to every one of hers. He also wrings his hands, although they are significantly smaller and more delicately expressive. "She can't possibly marry that…that…Philistine who has no appreciation of fine art—"

Natasha rolls her eyes. "That's the least of Wolfgang's faults."

Boris declares, in his deepest, most resolved, Shakespearean voice, "We will have to find someone to marry her, that is all."

Just then, Anatoly calls from his wagon: "Boris, can you help me lay out all this braid. It keeps getting tangled up."

Boris calls back, "I'll be right there, Anatoly."

Boris and Natasha simultaneously look at each other. "ANATOLY!"

Boris adds with enthusiasm, "He's in love with her anyway."

"Yes, but—" Natasha's face falls. "Where will we get a Russian Orthodox priest in Germany to marry them tonight?"

Boris thinks a moment, then reaches into his robe and pulls out a round, flat object. He flicks it against his leg and it expands to his black magician's top hat. He folds the brim inward so it looks like the stovepipe-style black hat worn by Russian Orthodox priests. "My *Kalimavkion*." He reaches into another pocket and pulls out a long black shawl, which he drapes around his shoulders. Finally, he digs way down in his coat and retrieves a heavy cross on a metal chain that he whips around his neck. He makes the sign of a Russian Orthodox blessing. "Bless you, my dear."

"Boris, you can't marry them." Natasha violently shakes her head. Her long chestnut braid flies back and forth, hitting Boris in the face multiple times.

Boris winces, rubs his cheek, and snickers. "Wolfgang doesn't know that. It'll work for tonight. They can have a proper ceremony when we get back to Russia."

"It's not what I would have wanted for her, but any port. Boris, go tell Anatoly." As Boris turns to leave, she corrects herself: "I mean, tell Anatoly, but don't tell him." Puzzled, Boris wheels around for further instruction. Exasperated, Natasha says, "Just tell him to go to Anna's wagon in an hour." Boris nods and starts off again. Natasha says, "But don't tell him why." Boris wheels back around. She nods. "Well, go on." In a final burst of frustration, Boris rushes out.

Crossing herself, Natasha feels resurrected from the dead. She can hardly believe they've figured a way out. Not ideal, but better than seeing Anna married to that monster. She heads toward Anna's wagon. "Now where's my Anna?"

Natasha passes by Anna's family's tent. Ivan and his father, Sergey, are practicing. Ivan is doing handstands into flips while Sergey spots him and adjusts his trajectory. She hesitates for a moment to admire Ivan's form, then catches herself, looks around, and not seeing Anna, continues to the girl's wagon. She pounds frantically on the door. "Anna, are you in there?"

CHAPTER TWENTY-FOUR

ANNA HEARS FURIOUS knocking on her wagon door and looks out to see Madame Natasha's face fill the small side window. *How nice! She's heard about my good fortune with the general and has come to wish me well.* Anna twitters, giggling and bursting with happiness as she helps the older woman into her wagon. Natasha collapses onto the trundle bed and, as usual, sends all the neatly assembled pillows flying.

"I'm so glad you came, Madame Natasha."

Natasha holds her side and gasps, "*Devushka*, my dear Annala, I must save you from a horrible fate."

"Oh, that's no longer necessary. Wait till I tell you about the fine and wealthy general I just met." Anna can hardly form the words to tell Natasha of her good fortune. "You were right. People here are dripping with gold. This tall...oh, he's oh so tall. I could hardly see his face, but I think he must be very handsome. And oh so distinguished with his sabre and his spurs—"

"Anna—"

"And all his medals—"Anna pirouettes around her wagon.

"*Devushka*...stop...listen to me." Natasha thrusts herself up from the sofa, grabs Anna's tiny hand, and presses it deep into her ample breast. "Anna, I'm sorry to be the one to tell you, but he's not what you think."

Anna peers up, trying to read Natasha's distraught expression. "He's not already married, is he?" The color drains from her face as a slow feeling of dread comes over Anna. She weakly allows Natasha to take both her hands and kiss them. Then Anna steps back, exploding, "I knew it was too good to be true. I'm too skinny, aren't I? And a circus performer to boot. My brother's right: no respectable man would want me."

"Oh, he wants you all right. But you don't want him."

"Of course I want him. Maybe you didn't see him, but he's just like you said: he's dripping with gold—"

"That's not real gold. It's only a uniform and they all have the same kind of fancy dress. The generals down to their privates...ah...down to the privates in their army."

"I don't understand." Anna's hot tears well up.

"The kaiser, he was born with his left arm severely damaged." Natasha gasps. "He's always tried to hide it by holding things in his left hand when he's photographed."

Anna, afraid Natasha will collapse, gets her some water.

Natasha gulps it down and continues, "Not only does the kaiser wear his own elaborately designed uniforms, but also he has them made for his whole army. On top of that, he's preparing for war. So he dresses up all the soldiers to make them feel very important. To pump them up, so they'll want to fight."

"Who are they going to fight?"

"The French...maybe the Russians...anyone around. What does it matter? These Germans just love to fight."

"What's this got to do with Wolfgang?"

Natasha pulls Anna to sit next to her on the sofa and puts her arms around her. "Wolfgang isn't a general, he's only a sergeant-major."

Anna shakes her head, utterly confused and clinging to the slimmest hope possible. "That sounds pretty good."

"It's not good. He doesn't have any money. And he lives in rough and unheated barracks, where you'd have to live as well. Keep it clean and—"

Anna opens her mouth to speak, but no sound comes out. She feels her world collapsing. She catches her breath and stammers, "I w-wouldn't have a h-home of my o-own?"

"I'm sorry to be the one to tell you. But it's best you know the truth." Natasha squeezes Anna tight. "While there's still time to get out of this terrible, horrible, impossible situation."

Anna narrows her dark eyes, takes a deep breath, then sobs. "I don't want to get out of any *situation*. I want a gentleman and a home and—" She weeps into Natasha's breast, and Natasha kisses the top of her head as she runs her fingers through the girl's long raven-black hair.

"There, there. I know this is distressing, but we have to act right away."

Anna sniffles. "What can we possibly do? This is all so dreadful. I led him on." She crosses herself. "I all but promised I'd marry him—and tonight."

Natasha winces and turns her head away. "Well—"

Anna knows that look. "Madame, what have you done?"

"Well, I kind of…Well, I guess I…" She blurts out, "Well I had no choice but to tell him you were already promised to someone and that you'd be married tonight."

Anna feels the blood draining from her. "*Kak*????"

"That's why we have to find someone to marry you before he returns."

Anna draws back, in a state of total shock. "But who?"

Natasha rushes to the window, pulls the curtains shut, whips around to Anna, and whispers conspiratorially, "Well, Boris and—"

"I can't possibly marry Boris. He's much too old. And anyway, Lottie wants to marry him."

"Of course you can't marry Boris. But he and I were discussing the fact that there's someone in our little circus who's been in love with you for quite some time."

Scratching her head, Anna is puzzled. "Who?"

"Well, he's really very honest. And some say attractive, in his own blonde, curly-headed way."

"I can't imagine."

Natasha takes a big breath and lets it out, "Anatoly."

The girl feels enormous relief as her eyes widen and she giggles. "Oh, now I know you're joking. You've been teasing me all along. What a relief!"

Natasha clears her throat, and in her deepest, most somber voice, says, "I'm afraid I'm not joking."

Anna stands frozen. All her hopes, her fantasies, her visions of living an elegant life spin before her and crash without a net. In an instant, the life she's longed for is gone. The breath rushes from her as she doubles over in pain and holds her stomach. She whispers, "This can't be. Please, Madame Natasha, please tell me this isn't happening to me."

"I'm so sorry, my dear. But Anatoly will be good to you. See how good he is to all his...well...never mind. He's a good man." Natasha offers Anna a handkerchief to wipe her tears and blow her nose. "Now straighten yourself up, my dear. Anatoly will be here soon, so it's up to you to get him to marry you."

"But who will marry us here in Prussia?"

"I've got that covered...well...sort of. Just trust me. If you don't get Anatoly to agree to marry you, then that hideous, odious, horrible dragoon will either claim you as his bride or run us out of town." Natasha hugs Anna tightly. "Think of it as your greatest performance ever."

Anna gasps as she tries to lift the fog from her brain and the lead weight from her heart. She quickly surveys her options. And as she begins to catch her breath, she starts to accept Natasha's solution as the only feasible way out, for the circus and for her. But she feels compelled to ask, one last time, "There's no other way?"

Natasha nods solemnly. "I wouldn't lie to you, my darling Anna."

Anna manages a weak reply, "No, I'm sure you wouldn't."

"That's the spirit, my girl. Think of it this way: You're going to walk on the high wire and dazzle Anatoly. I know you can do it."

"Dazzle him?"

"My darling girl, he's already blinded by his love for you. Just leave Wolfgang to Boris and me."

"Dazzle Anatoly?" Anna takes a deep, resigned breath and mutters, "Dazzle him. Dazzle him." Her heart-shaped face breaks into an enormous smile. "I can do dazzle."

CHAPTER TWENTY-FIVE

DUROV FEELS HIS knees buckling as he watches Wolfgang ride away on his unfortunate, swaybacked mare. He is awash with emotions: contempt for that officious man who holds sway over the circus, fury at the untenable situation their little circus is in, and grief over being denied the artistic freedom to perform his amazing new act and restore honor to his family. He tramps over to the corral and collapses next to Sasha. He leans over her, scratches her head, and begins to weep.

For years, he's felt like a second-class citizen in the circus. He clings to Sasha's fat, warm body. With her large, saucer-like nostrils in her splendid turned-up snout, her mouth appears to be in a perpetual, optimistic smile. Much as he's come to love Sasha and the other pigs, he's never wanted to acknowledge how humiliating it's been to step down from training horses to training pigs. He's grateful that his mother, after her rape by the Cossacks, didn't live long enough to see his disgrace. What happened to his father, because of him, was also horrible. As their family no longer had an act in the circus, his father was obliged to become a laborer, preparing the wagons, tents, and riggings for touring. Durov knew his father was only going through the motions in a despondent trance. Without his beloved wife to give him comfort, his heart soon gave out. Durov has accepted complete responsibility for both their deaths. As penance, he took it upon himself to care for his younger brother, for the performing animals, and for the livestock that travel with the circus as a source of food.

That's when Durov realized how smart and trainable pigs were. He secretly kept a piglet hidden after it was weaned. He trained it. Successful, he trained some more and put together an act. When he showed it to Nikolai, Nikolai disparaged Durov mercilessly, even though he roared with laughter at the antics Durov put the pigs through. Nikolai reluctantly agreed that Durov's pig act was good for business—the children loved how the pigs could count, recognize playing cards, waddle through trick doors, trundle up ladders, and scoot down miniature slides.

Now Durov's tears fall onto Sasha's head as she perks up her pink, hairy ears and grunts in commiseration. "Oh, my dear Sasha, I'm sorry." His struggle with Wolfgang has made him realize he's always played it safe and kept the act on a basic level. He's never wanted to advance to the limelight, perhaps as a punishment for his past transgressions. He's come to think of himself as unable to be successful in the world of the circus— which, in Russian society, is actually held in high regard and in some respects valued as highly as the opera or the ballet.

Since coming up with the *Ich will den Helm* act, Durov has discovered his old spark, aroused by the pure joy of presenting something entirely new and unique. It might even allow him to realize a small fraction of his family's former glory. Had they not lost everything, his parents might have lived their dream to perform in one of the imperial state circuses, set up in their own, dedicated buildings in St. Petersburg or Moscow, with full-scale equestrian branches and sophisticated schools for acrobats and trapeze artists. If his father's expertise in training animals had been recognized, the family might have been able to publicize their refined, positive behavioral training methods. That would have impacted trainers and prevented countless brutalities from being inflicted on animals throughout Russia and even Europe.

But most of all, Durov bemoans the fact that his family could have settled down under the auspices of the tsar, stopped touring, and had a home—something his dear mother desperately wanted, especially since she knew that riding horses was something she would only be able to physically do for so long. Although his family dined at the first table in the canteen, she longed for lace tablecloths, fine silver, and a proper school for Durov, even as he was learning the family equestrian business. As for Anatoly, she wanted him to do something "better" than the circus. She wanted him to go into an honorable trade, especially as the boy had such a sunny disposition and used to be so well spoken.

Durov's chest heaves with despair as he recalls that Anatoly never stuttered as a little boy. When the Cossacks overran their camp, Durov had screamed for Anatoly to hide, but he's always wondered if Anatoly actually witnessed his mother's brutal rape, as Durov and his father were forced to do. Perhaps that was why, after that, Anatoly never got his words out properly. And it was all Durov's fault.

Durov weeps openly as he relives his family's ruinous decline. *All because I had to show them how good I was at training our little colt.* Sasha snorts softly, gently nudging him with her snout. Durov knows that animals, especially pigs, can be even more empathetic than some humans, and he's grateful that Sasha's so caring and supportive. They sit together for a while until Durov's grief is penetrated by a soft tapping sound.

Boris has returned to the corral. He taps his magic wand against his leg and talks to it. "Come on then. You can do it." Boris stops short when he sees Durov in a heap next to Sasha. He blurts out, "What's all this blubbering about?"

Durov, embarrassed to be discovered draped over his pig bawling, quickly rises and brushes himself off. "Boris! Shouldn't you be practicing your magician's act for tonight? Going from clown to magician is a big deal." Though Durov wants the best for Boris, he feels a twinge of jealousy that tonight Madame Natasha has given Boris permission to realize his dream of becoming a magician, while Durov will have to wait for his chance at fame. Graciously, he says, "You'll be a hit tonight, Boris. Have you talked to the dwarf brothers about the changes in the act?"

"They're only too happy to have one less in that damned, crowded cart."

"I thought that was what makes it so funny."

"Well, I'm getting too old to be squashed every night by all four of them. They won't admit it, but I know they relish flopping harder and harder on top of me. Besides, my unicycle is really worn down. No matter how much grease I apply to the wheel, it doesn't spin freely. And when it jams up, I can't control my juggling bats and balls."

"I've seen you taking them in the face, but I thought that was part of the act. Well, anyway, I'm happy for you. Somebody's got to make a splash to entertain the crowds."

Boris bashes the wand against the corral fence. "I hope so, but I can't get this damn thing to work." Suddenly, he looks askance at Durov. Puzzled, he says, "I thought you were going to be the biggest attraction tonight with your new act."

"It's all off now."

"I am truly sorry to hear that, my friend. Wolfgang didn't seem to care too much for the poster. Do you think he'd think more highly of your act if he saw you perform it in person?"

Durov closes his eyes, visualizing the crowds laughing and applauding Sasha dressed up as the kaiser. He swallows another sob. "I'm afraid that would just make it worse."

"What are you going to do?"

Durov feels himself sinking back down into his lowly position in the circus. Resigned to continuing to serve out his penance, he says, "We'll just have to do the ladders and doors act. I hope that, without time to rehearse, the little ones don't confuse the ladders with the doors. Sasha can still count and do her sums. Anatoly packed away our giant abacus, but I'm sure we can find it. And she has a great memory—almost as good as Zoya's."

"That elephant never forgot I once accidentally hit her with my magic wand. She grabbed it in her trunk and flung it half a kilometer."

"Maybe that's why it doesn't work." Durov can't resist a smile. "Why don't you give it back to her and let her fling it again?"

"Very funny. But really, I am sorry about your act. It took a full bottle of that rot gut vodka to get those dragoons drunk and lift that helmet for you."

"I'm sorry too. But Sasha can adjust back to her old act tonight." He turns to her, wiping away his tears as he revels in her intelligence and his expert training. "Can't you, my little piggala?" Durov pets Sasha and then manages to choke back another flood of tears as he heads for the gate. "I've got to find Anatoly and tell him he doesn't have to sew that costume after all."

Boris blurts out, "Oh, I just spoke to him and he's on his way—" He steps in front of Durov, blocking him at the gate. "I mean to say...ah...perhaps you should practice with your"—big scowl—"your little pigs. After all, it's been some time since you performed. We've crossed the mountains, and after all that thin air, they might need a...ah...a breather—I mean a refresher."

Durov glances thoughtfully at Boris. "You're probably right. All the more reason I need to find Anatoly right away."

Boris's cherubic face reddens. He shuts his eyes tightly, then opens them wide, as if he can't believe what he's about to say. "I could help you rehearse with your...ah...your pigs. That way, you won't have to disturb Anatoly. I mean, he's been under a lot of pressure lately and—"

"You're right. I should find him and—"

"I really think you should rehearse. See here—" Boris waves his wand back and forth. "Abracadabra."

Durov's anger at the situation rises to the surface as he snaps at Boris: "You don't have to do tricks with your wand at this very moment."

"I'm not doing tricks. Abracadabra. That's the name of my wand." He flicks up the wand. "Abracadabra, up…up…up." He smiles weakly at Durov.

Durov rolls his eyes. "*Prosti* (sorry)."

"Think nothing of it. Now back to your pig act. Do you need me to keep time for them to march in? Or maybe I could tap out the signals for the card trick. Amazing how Sasha draws an inside straight every time. I know Anatoly signals from behind the curtain, but I've seen it so often I could—"

"Boris, is there something wrong?"

Boris stamps his foot. "Two taps for each correct card, is it? Something wrong? Why would there be anything wrong with Anatoly? He's a fine young fellow. You've done a remarkable job raising him. A good man, fit to make any woman a good husband—oh I mean…a fit man…he's so fit…in such good shape…you're lucky to have him in the act."

Durov scrunches up his weathered face and shakes his head at Boris's erratic behavior. Then, deciding to ignore him, he steps outside the gate. As he turns to fasten it, he sighs, "Yes, I am lucky he's—"

Boris stammers, "Of, of course, you should really…really find Madame Natasha and let her know you're not going to perform the helmet trick."

Durov feels a terrible sinking in his gut. "I hate to tell her. She wants a big act to draw the crowds." He lets out a heavy, despondent breath. "I suppose it must be done."

"Sooner than later. You'd best get it over with."

Durov fastens the corral gate and bends down, fondly clapping Boris on the shoulder. "You're a good friend, Boris. In moments like these, I really appreciate how close our circus family is."

Boris swishes his wand. "You'd be surprised how much closer it's about to get."

Durov gives him a puzzled look.

CHAPTER TWENTY-SIX

IN A FRENZY, Anna straightens up her wagon and does her best to ignore an impending sense of doom. She frantically wipes at the tears she's cried all over her silk pillows. She picks up the last pillow, a square bolster of red- and cream-colored silk, and holds it to her tiny breasts. She can still smell her mother's perfume, which triggers searing memories of how loving she was. She'd always told Anna to stand tall and hold her chin up, even as her father and brother made fun of how petite and scrawny she was. Thinking back to her mother flying through the air in her glamorous sequined costume, Anna has to admit she's always loved the trapeze. *Soaring...turning...I right myself and sing with my body, making waves through the air...the freedom of flying...for one split second, no one controls you!*

Anna throws down the pillow, furious at how her father and brother have made life in their act completely untenable. They've made her want to escape—to be a fine lady so her mother would see they hadn't succeeded in beating her down after all. Anna sniffles as she pushes aside the plank of wood covering her mother's precious porcelain tub. She desperately needs a soak to feel safe. To wash away her salt tears and summon her courage. To slide down and luxuriously lull her long, beautiful neck from side to side, comforted by the water in the bath as she is when the rain patters on the roof and washes away her sorrow and fear. A bath will make her brave enough to accept that she has no other choice but to try to convince Anatoly to marry her—and fast.

Although she worries there might not be enough time before he arrives, she heats the water in the samovar and pours it into the tub. She twists her long hair up into a knot on the top of her head and, trembling, lowers herself into the warmth. She sighs deeply as she leans back. The rim of the tub is cold on her neck, so she takes a sponge and squeezes, dripping water along the full length of her neck. She revels in the calm safety of the warm, clean water. This is where the memories of her mother are most vivid, and she dreams of soaring high and defying gravity—a winged creature aloft, the crowds gasping at her swan-like beauty, just as they did for her mother.

A soft knock on the wagon door. *Nyet! Anatoly! So soon?* Anna bolts out of the tub, quickly dries, and throws on her dressing gown, annoyed at herself that she failed to allow more time to primp. As she ties her robe, she catches a glimpse of her slightly disheveled self in the glass. She smiles coyly. *Not having time to dress properly might not be such a bad thing if you want to get a man to propose.*

She opens the wagon door, feigning surprise. "Anatoly! *Dobro pozha- lovat!* How lovely to see you."

Anatoly, seeing her in her robe, hurriedly spins and turns his back to her. His hands fly over his eyes, and he says, in a muffled sputter, "I'm s-sorry, Anna T-Tatianna. I did not m-mean to d-disturb you."

Anna takes him by his shoulders and gently turns him to face her. "You haven't disturbed me. I'm glad you came." She pats her topknot twist of hair and replaces several errant strands.

"You are? I mean, I-I'm glad to be here. B-Boris said you wanted to see me." Flustered, Anatoly looks around the wagon for something to distract him. He picks up a series of items—her hairbrush, the soap, a scarf—his

184

pale skin turning deeper shades of red with every item. Boyishly grinning, he asks, "W-what did you want to see me about? I really must get back to s-sewing a very important costume for tonight. You see, Durov and Sasha—she's our pig—"

"You and your brother are well respected in the circus."

"Our f-family used to be—"

"In fact, I hear you're the best animal trainers around."

"But we're not f-first in the circus p-parade, like you. And your f-father and b-brother."

At the mention of her family, Anna feels a rush of rebellion. *I'm going to choose my husband, not them.* She studies the young man before her, who shyly shuffles his feet. She's never really looked closely at him, and she's pleased to find a sweet, handsome face topped by a mop of amazingly curly hair, spun gold as if he were some kind of prince. *Don't be silly: this is strictly business. And only in an extreme emergency would I ever consider marrying a pig trainer.* She takes a deep breath. *This qualifies as an extreme emergency.*

"But you're both fine men. And actually"—she takes a lock of his shoulder-length hair and twists it around her finger—"quite handsome men. I wonder why you never married."

"Durov, m-married? No, he's very s-satisfied with his p-pigs. Oh—I mean...making up new acts. They're quite c-complex you know, with all the little l-ladders and the chutes. You don't want a pig to miss c-coming down the—"

Anna turns away and rolls her eyes. She musters her courage and turns back. "*Nyet*, I mean, why have *you* never married, Anatoly?"

He gulps. "Me? Well, t-there's so m-much to do, p-putting out the s-slop and—"

"I should have thought you'd have a girl, by now."

His voice rises an octave. "Have a *devushka* (a girl)? Y-you m-mean...couple with a...I've seen the a-animals doing it of c-course, but I've never—"

"That didn't come out right." Anna says sweetly, through gritted teeth. She realizes she hasn't much time and comes close. "Anatoly, you're so tall...and such hands...strong but fine." She takes his hand, leads him toward the tub. "I think of your hands often, when I bathe." He gulps, resisting, but she gently drags him along. "My arms get strained, you know, from the ropes on the trapeze. I've often thought of you, rubbing my shoulders, taking the strain away—" She cranes her long neck this way and that, in poses she imagines are seductive.

"Anna, I s-shouldn't be here." He starts to shake. "What if your f-father, or Ivan—"

"I promise, they're all busy checking the rigging for tonig—"

Anatoly's boyish face brightens. "Rigging...d-didn't you want me to set up the r-rigging for your solo tonight? Is that why Boris said I should come?"

Anna musters all her feminine wiles, given how inexperienced she is. She shakes her head seductively, causing her long black hair to fall out of her topknot. She swishes toward Anatoly. "That's so thoughtful of you, but right now, I really need you to rub my shoulders." Anna sits on the side of the tub, back to him, and lowers her robe, at first just an inch. She shuts her eyes, holds her breath, and lowers her robe a little more—this time enough to bare her shoulders.

She turns slightly to catch his eye and is touched to see light beads of sweat on his pale forehead. Finally, he shakes his hands out to relax them and obliges her by gently rubbing her shoulders.

"Like t-that?"

"Mmmm. Maybe a little harder." Anna is pleased that, while Anatoly is clearly terrified at first, he seems to be getting into it.

He rubs for a while, then relaxes, then adopts a rhythm. "Anna, w-while we're being honest, I just want you to know that I've...well...I've wanted to do this...well not this exactly, but s-something very similar—"

Anna is strangely moved by his touch. She leans back into him and whispers over her shoulder, "I think I know."

Anatoly continues to rub her shoulders, although Anna is concerned that he's showing no signs of going any further and certainly not proposing. She must get even bolder. "Anatoly, you know what I've also dreamed? I've dreamed you'd take this sponge, squeeze it up here"—she hands him the sponge and directs him to her throat—"and let the water flow down onto my—"

He jumps up, propelling the sponge into midair. He watches as it lands, soapy, on the rug. Then he bends to pick it up, trying to blow-dry the water from the rug. He carefully places the sponge on the rim of the tub. "I'm s-sorry, Anna T-Tatianna I-Ivanova. I really must go now. My b-brother— worse still, your b-brother, worse still, your f-father—"

Anna leaps from the side of the tub, pulling her robe tight around her. She frantically rushes to the door to stop him. "Anatoly. Don't you realize I'm asking you to marry me?"

Stopping short, he lowers his chin and gnaws on his lip. "You...you are?" He looks stunned, cautious, suspicious, and finally, disbelieving.

She presses against him, whispering, "Yes, you silly goose."

Anatoly hesitates, obviously trying to think of something to say. "G-geese aren't very smart. Not like pigs, you know."

Anna bites her tongue to avoid screaming in frustration. "Anatoly, this is serious."

He steps back and studies her, searching her large black eyes and then her entire heart-shaped face. Finally, he smiles. "Yes, Anna. I understand now."

Relieved that Anatoly finally seems to get the message, Anna leans in to kiss him.

He pulls back. "But we have to do it the right way. I must...really I must ask your father for your hand." He thinks again, winces. "Do I have to?"

"No, no. Madame Natasha says she'll take care of everything with my father and Ivan. We can even be married tonight—it'll be more like an informal, maybe even a kind of civil ceremony. Madame Natasha says we'll have to wait for a religious ceremony until we get back to Russia."

"Of course, I'd want to do everything in the most honorable way."

Anna, touched by his gallantry and his refusal to take advantage of her, needs to seal the deal. She softly kisses him. This time, however, she's stunned to feel a warmth wash over her, as if she were immersed in her bath. It's a warmth she hasn't felt since her mother died. Her mind races. She's yearned for this same secure feeling, and now she's amazed to find it in Anatoly's embrace. Deep down, she knows her determination to marry a gentleman has more to do with defying her family—to get out from under them—than to get away from the circus, which she also knows is in her blood. And she realizes, if she marries Anatoly, he can help her with the rigging, and Madame Natasha will let her have her own act. *I won't have to leave the circus, and I'll soar through the air like I've always dreamed.* She kisses Anatoly, now with complete sincerity.

Anatoly kisses her back, at first softly, then with gentle but greater firmness. He brushes aside her thick tresses and nudges her neck, whispering, "Are you sure?"

"Yes. I'm sure."

He takes her hand, firmly leads her back to the tub, and sits her down on the rim.

She twists her neck up toward him and smiles as he picks up the sponge.

CHAPTER TWENTY-SEVEN

D UROV'S STEPS, NO longer balletic, grow heavier and heavier as he approaches Natasha's wagon. The laughter in his eyes is thoroughly extinguished. He's completely defeated by Wolfgang and furious at having to give up the only thing that's excited him in ages—performing a new and absolutely incredible act. He hates to let Natasha down. He knows all too well how financially strapped the circus is and how important it is to her to bring in the crowds. Even more important, however, is that he's begun to find Natasha increasingly attractive. Now that she's free of Nikolai, he's allowed himself to fully appreciate her. He admires her and is proud that she speaks her mind. He finds her sharp tongue more defensive than hurtful—a kind of mask he sees right through, a mask that hides her deep-rooted insecurity. She's also won him over because she's been exceedingly good to everyone in the circus. She has never played the queen, despite her wealthy background and her status as the circus owner's wife.

As he gets within sight of her wagon, he hesitates. *Don't be so stupid, Durov. What could she see in you? Especially now you've knuckled under to that bastard dragoon.*

Boris walks with Durov, still trying to get his wand, Abracadabra, to produce sparks.

Durov turns to him, his voice melancholy: "Boris, I don't know how to break the bad news to Natasha."

Natasha flings open her wagon door and plunges down the stairs, her deep voice like sharp bits of gravel. "What bad news?"

Like greased lightning, Boris scoots around Natasha to the other side of her wagon. Shaking, he peers between the steps as he involuntarily raps his wand against the wooden wheels. Sparks fly into his hand. "Ouch. Not now, Abracadabra."

Natasha looks around, puzzled.

Durov suppresses his laughter at Boris's antics, takes a breath, and solemnly approaches. "Madame—"

Sweetly, she says, "Durov, please call me Natasha." Then, her tone turns urgent as she says, "Quickly, tell me about your new act and how much money we're going to make. I don't have to tell you, the future of our circus rests entirely on your shoulders."

Durov looks down, searching for a crevice to open up and swallow him whole. "My dear Madame Nat—"

She says, smiling coyly, "I told you, call me Natasha."

"Yes, well, Natasha. I'm sorry, but Wolfgang and I had some words after he left you."

"What's that awful man done now?"

Boris bounds out from behind the wagon. "We feel exactly that way about him don't we, Durov?"

"What are you two getting at?"

Durov says, "I think you'd better sit down."

Reluctantly, Natasha takes a seat on the bottom step of her wagon.

Durov starts off, gently, "You know, that act we were going to do—"

"Yes, yes, the new act. Your pig and the kaiser. Hysterically funny."

Boris jumps in, "It was. If you thought it was funny when Durov's pig pushed the baby carriage with all the piglets inside, you should have seen that pulchritudinous porcine Sasha—that is her name right?—you should have seen how she flipped the helmet up onto her head—"

"Just tell me what happened."

Durov hesitates, then blurts out, "I tried to convince Wolfgang that the children would see their glorious kaiser's elaborate military uniform in all its glorious detail. That they would have him foremost in their minds."

Natasha interjects, "What's wrong with that?"

Boris says, "He made sure to tell Wolfgang that the uniform would be splendidly displayed—"

"Yes?"

"But Wolfgang said the kaiser would take offense if the uniform was displayed on a pig."

Natasha jumps up. "Can't the kaiser take a joke?"

Boris says, "Seems the kaiser can't take a joke."

Natasha plops back down, utterly deflated.

Durov continues, "Wolfgang threatened to destroy the circus if I performed."

Natasha hangs her head in her hands. "No new act? No crowds? No money?"

"I'm afraid not, Natasha."

She quips, "Call me, Madame Natasha."

Ivan comes along, swishing his cape. "Like my new cape? Karanska made it for me just now...for our grand opening tonight. Isn't it grand?"

Natasha moans, "Our opening's not going to be so grand." Ivan twirls around, ignoring her. As he spins by, she shouts, "Durov's not going to perform his new act tonight. Wolfgang says it offends the kaiser. So we won't have the crowds we were expecting."

Coming to an abrupt halt, Ivan says, "Not perform?" He zeros in on Durov. "I never took you for a coward."

Durov rubs his square jaw, feeling like he's been slugged by the very man who wants to take Natasha for himself. "Look here, Ivan. We can't risk having them destroy the entire circus over a single act."

Ivan sticks his handsome chin out. "Look here, Durov. We can't risk not doing your act. Everyone—apparently—thinks it's funny. But more important, we need the money." He turns and smiles seductively at Natasha. "Don't we, Natasha?"

Reddening, Durov argues, "Yes...but—"

"But nothing. Didn't anyone ever hear of artistic freedom? It's the principle of the thing." Ivan sallies up to Natasha. "Don't you agree, Natasha?"

Durov sharply sucks in his breath, feeling a torrent of rage at Ivan's goading. He desperately wants to do his act, but he doesn't want to destroy the circus in the process.

Natasha thinks a moment, then says, "Ivan's got a point."

Boris adds, "The kaiser doesn't believe in artistic freedom, or freedom of speech, or any kind of freedom. The tsar certainly doesn't, and they're in the same family. These monarchs stick together."

Ivan raises his voice, "We might as well destroy the circus ourselves, as to allow them to censor us that way."

Durov is certain that Ivan doesn't believe a word he's saying—he's only trying to curry favor with Natasha and maybe get Durov arrested and out of the way. It's one thing to jeopardize himself to do his own act, but everyone will suffer if Wolfgang orders the dragoons to destroy the circus. On the other hand, who is Wolfgang to tell him what he can and can't do? And how dare Ivan throw such a topic as artistic freedom up to him in front of Natasha—the woman he's coming to...he thinks he's falling in...he's liking more and more?

Squarely setting his square shoulders, Durov says, "Natasha, you're right. If we change our act for him, where will it end?" Durov mimics Wolfgang, pacing back and forth like a martinet: "Durov, you can't drink your tea with a sugar cube in your mouth. You must put the sugar cube in your cup. And Durov, you can't make love to your wife in that position.

Of course I don't have a wife, but if I did—" He realizes what he's said, blushes, then quickly adds, "I mean, he's not going to make me dance around like a trained bear."

Natasha says with admiration, "That's right, Durov. He can't tell us what we can and can't do."

Boris jumps in. "But he thinks he can. Even more important, his dragoons think he can." Everyone nods, and they all start pacing back and forth, trying to think of a way out. Finally, Boris waves his wand. "I have it. The perfect solution! If Wolfgang can't see Durov's act, then he can't order the dragoons to tear the circus apart."

Natasha asks, "If Durov performs, how can we prevent Wolfgang from seeing his act?"

Boris is triumphant. "My father's magic box!"

Everyone looks bewildered.

Boris explains, "Look here, we send the four dwarf brothers to spread the word in town—very quietly and under cover, so it doesn't get back to Wolfgang. But the townsfolk will come in droves."

Natasha adds, skeptically, "*Da? Da?*"

Boris rubs his neat goatee, encouraged. "Wolfgang says he loves the circus, doesn't he? So we invite him to see things up close—on a seat up front—right on top of my father's magic box."

"I don't know…" Durov shakes his head in disbelief.

Undeterred, Boris continues, "Just before Durov's act, I ask Wolfgang to stand up for an even better view, then I open the box and…Presto— that's the name of my father's magic box. Presto opens up and swallows Wolfgang whole. Until after Durov's act. Then we let him out. We thank him for taking part in the most amazing magic trick, which everybody has just witnessed and wildly applauded. We say we're sorry he didn't see it because his part of the trick took place inside the box. We assure him that he's the star of the show. And he's none the wiser."

Natasha sneers, "Wolfgang has never been what I would call 'the wiser.'"

Durov looks down suspiciously at the small man with the wand. Then he breaks into uproarious laughter. *What a relief! A way out for him and the circus!* He takes Natasha into his arms and spins her around, while Ivan watches, his mouth agape.

Ivan scoffs, flashing his aerialist's cape as he leaves. "You all go ahead and talk this nonsense. I'm going to prepare for my act tonight."

With his eyes laughing once again, Durov watches Ivan go. He turns to Natasha, ecstatic. "*Eto zamechatel'no*! Madame Natasha."

"Yes, it's wonderful, isn't it? Call me Natasha, Durov. Call me Natasha."

CHAPTER TWENTY-EIGHT

ANNA'S PORCELAIN SKIN is flush with the heat of being cherished by Anatoly. Together, they sit on the rim of the tub. She has lowered her robe, just past her shoulders. She allows him to drip the warm water from her bath down her long neck. For the first time, she truly feels like the lovely swan she's always dreamed of being. While they're both too shy to go any further, she's actually very glad of that. He's clearly not going to take advantage of her in her desperate situation. She revels in his warmth, as he takes the sponge and rubs her neck and shoulders while looking away to preserve her modesty.

"Mmmm. That feels wonderful, Anatoly."

Encouraged, he caresses a stray strand of her voluminous black hair. "I-I guess you have to tie all this up when you perform." He swallows hard. "It's s-so beautiful...when it flows free like this."

She leans in, offering him encouragement.

He lifts her arm and slides the sponge along it, whispering, "We were taught to value...to cherish all the animals we are blessed to know. I don't mean animals, but...you know what I mean." He takes a towel and helps her up, drying off her shoulders and helping her pull her robe tight.

Anna feels a strange tingling, something entirely new. "That's wonderful, Anatoly. Where did you learn to do that?"

He smiles shyly. "Well, Demetri and the little pigs like to be cuddled, you know."

"I didn't, but that's good to know...I guess."

Anatoly kisses her on the lips, murmuring, "I could do this all day."

His stutter has all but vanished. She feels an immensely gratifying sense of her own attractiveness as a woman—that she could have such an effect on any man, even a pig trainer. She nudges him. "So could I..." Then all of a sudden, she breaks away. "Oh! No, I couldn't. We've got to get ready for tonight."

"Oh, I've got to f-finish sewing S-Sasha's new c-costume."

"And I need help with the rigging for my solo. Madame Natasha promised I could go on tonight."

"Anna, if you don't m-mind me saying...you are going to be a star...well, I mean, more than you already are. I'm going to be there to give you a b-boost, so you can climb onto your platform. Make sure you're s-safe. Rigging-wise, I mean."

This is the happiest day Anna has known since her mother died. She gives him a big hug. "Now run along and fix that costume. I'll get dressed and meet you at Madame Natasha's wagon, so we can see what she has in mind for us to be married."

He smiles sheepishly and turns to leave her wagon, giving her one last loving glance before quietly closing the door behind him.

Anna twirls with happiness, joyously sending the pillows flying.

⁓⁕⁓

Excited to tell Natasha how things have gone with Anatoly, Anna quickly dresses and runs to find her. It's getting late in the afternoon, and the sideshow acts are milling about and setting up. She passes them, her hair flying as she smiles and waves. They wave back and cheer, obviously happy to finally be performing again.

She gaily dances down the midway, watching Bronzy test out his mallet and strongman rig. She giggles when the four dwarf brothers crash into one another as they warm up on their unicycles. And she smiles at the bearded and fat ladies as they primp in front of the wagon they share, shoving each other out of the way to look in their full-length glass. She laughs as she ducks, narrowly missing a whoosh of fire, as the fire-eater tests the strength of his blaze.

Anna discovers Boris in the circus tent with Natasha, Durov, and Lottie. Natasha hugs Anna. And Durov embraces Anna, lifting her gently off the ground and saying, "Anatoly just now told me the good news. I couldn't be happier to welcome you to the family, my dear."

Anna is deliriously happy to be surrounded by her new circus family, who are infinitely more supportive of her than her own family.

She stands wide-eyed as Boris explains the workings of Presto, his father's magic box. He has positioned it down front, next to the first row of benches. He opens the lid, they all peer inside, and he bends over to demonstrate. "So Presto has this false bottom, which is usually the escape route. When someone goes into the box, that's how they exit the box." With a theatrical flourish, Boris adds, "I'm going to remove the false bottom for tonight, so Wolfgang can't get out. That's where we'll keep him until after Durov's act."

Lottie leans over the side of the box. "That's quite clever, Boris. Can I borrow this sometime?"

"I'm sorry, my father wouldn't approve. He never cared to mix the psychic with the earthly craft of sleight-of-hand. He was an old school magician, you see."

Lottie flicks her shawl alluringly. "But you're quite inventive...and intuitive. Not old school at all."

Preening, Boris eyes her. "I suppose intuitive isn't exactly psychic—"

"Just, shall we say, enlightened." Lottie leans closer to him whispering, "Your father couldn't object to that, could he?"

"Enlightened? No, I'm sure not." He leans even closer to her. "I'd be happy to discuss it further."

Anna giggles. She's touched at how Lottie continues to pursue Boris and pleased to see Boris finally returning her overtures.

Natasha turns to Boris and Lottie and clears her throat. "If you two don't mind, we've got a performance."

Lottie says, "Oh yes, Madame Natasha. I've got to set up too." She trails her shawl seductively and winks at Boris as she leaves. "I'm looking forward to collaborating with you, Boris."

Boris grins and rubs his goatee as he watches her go. Then, noticing the others grinning at him, he clears his throat and says to them in his deep, commanding voice, "Finally, as we agreed, after the circus is over, I will 'perform' the marriage ceremony for Anna and Anatoly."

After experiencing a sense of calm that everything is under control, Anna feels like her brother has just dropped her ten meters. She stamps her foot. "Boris? Boris can't marry us."

Natasha wraps her arm around the girl. "Shhh…Wolfgang doesn't know that. I promise we'll have a proper ceremony as soon as we get back to Russia."

"Don't worry," Durov adds. "We'll sort all this out properly—and honorably, I assure you—when we get home."

Anna hesitates and looks between Natasha and Durov, who nod encouragingly. She's wanted to become part of a loving family for so long, and it's hard to absorb all that's happened so quickly. Would she have found Anatoly a suitable match if she hadn't been pressured into it by that horrible flap with Wolfgang? Must she give up her dreams of having a home and a wealthy husband? Yet, if she can realize another dream—to have an act of her own and to revel in the thrill of defying gravity—surely that will make up for the other. She thinks back to Anatoly's loving touch and feels a boundless warmth. And, encircled by the tenderness of Natasha and Durov, she feels confident they will make it all work out.

Ivan rushes in, screaming at Anna, "What have you done, *Ty malen'kaya suchka?*"

Natasha shouts at him, "Don't you dare call her that."

Despite Natasha's intervention, Anna immediately feels reduced to a fearful child. She attempts to muster the courage to stand up to him, timidly saying in a tiny voice, "You bully. You don't scare me." But as Ivan continues to scream, she bursts into tears.

Durov steps between Ivan and Anna. "See here, Ivan Ivanovich, you may not have wanted me in your family, but that's the way things are now. You've got to think of the good of the circus and your sister. You can't stand by and allow a brute like Wolfgang to marry her."

Ivan continues to protest, but Durov backs him away from Anna. "Have I made myself clear?"

Still sobbing, Anna is grateful that Natasha grabs her away from her brother.

Natasha growls, "Ivan, you'd better not threaten Anna again."

Ivan swallows hard and reluctantly nods. Anna can hardly believe that her new family has made Ivan back down.

Durov says, "It's settled then. I'm going to get ready for our big night."

Anna watches Durov go, ecstatic to have not only Anatoly rooting for her, but also Durov protecting her. Maybe they are only pig trainers, but everyone's always looked up to them. And now she's proud to be in their family.

Boris, still preening over his magic box, Presto, chucks Anna lovingly under her chin. "It will be all right, my dear. I promise."

Ivan, having held back until Durov left, sidles up to Anna. She assumes he wants to make amends. Instead, he takes her arm, pinches it hard, whispering, "You may think this is finished but—"

Boris jumps in: "Ivan, what do you think you're doing? Didn't you just hear Durov—" Boris gives Ivan a sharp push to stop him from further assaulting Anna. Ivan goes careening into the magic box, and the lid slams shut. Pounding and muffled screams are heard from within. Boris gasps, "That wasn't supposed to happen."

At first, Anna is horrified, but then she starts to giggle. Natasha also laughs, deeply and gruffly. Boris laughs out loud. Pretty soon, they're all howling, completely drowning out Ivan's shouts from inside the box.

Natasha tries to catch her breath. "All right, Boris. All right. We've had our laugh. Get him out."

Boris waves his wand over the box with a flourish. "Abracadabra...open Presto." The box remains locked shut. Boris tries again. "Open sesame." He smiles weakly, tries a couple of times more, and then sits on top of the box and surreptitiously pounds on the side. "Open up, damn it." Pounding is returned from inside.

Anna abruptly stops laughing. "Boris, what are we going to do? We need Ivan for our act."

Natasha turns to Anna and quickly adds, "That settles it. Now you definitely get to do your solo."

Anna breaks into a big smile. "Oh, thank you, Madame Natasha!" She twirls. "I'll be flying like a swan..."

Boris and Natasha enjoy her for a moment, then look at each other, cross themselves, and simultaneously blurt out, "Wolfgang! By St. Basil, what about Wolfgang?"

Anna abruptly stops spinning. Natasha grabs Boris by the shoulders, lifting him off the ground, his feet kicking wildly in the air. "Boris, *bezmozglyy* (you idiot)! Where are you going to hide Wolfgang while Durov performs?"

"I-I don't know. Put me down, and I'll figure something out."

Natasha drops him. "You'd better."

"What if I can't?" Boris winces.

"By St. Basil, then don't tell Durov," barks Natasha.

More pounding and screaming are heard from inside the box. Anna thinks how much her brother deserves this. She's going to be able to do her solo without fearing him. She just hopes that Anatoly and his brother won't pay too high a price for this snafu. If Boris can't get Ivan out of the box, Anna prays that Wolfgang will be somewhere upwind when the brothers Durov perform with their pigs.

CHAPTER TWENTY-NINE

DUROV IS A large and bulky man, but this evening, he's dancing like a ballerina. It's a fortuitous sign that the late afternoon weather is fine and clear, with fluffy white clouds wisping across a pure, azure sky. Good weather is always an inducement for potential customers to stroll over from town to see what's going on. And if Federoya the monkey-grinder is on his toes, these strollers will be swiftly converted into paying customers. Lottie's brother Bronzy, the strongman, works with the other laborers to secure the last of the spikes that hold up the "main" tent. Durov personally sees that the benches inside are arranged nice and straight. "Germans like everything in neat rows," he cheerfully reminds the crew.

The excitement is palpable, and even Zoya, the elephant, trumpets in anticipation, although not exactly in time with the three-piece band warming up. The musicians typically set up first outside the tent, to direct the patrons to the sideshows. And when the performance is about to start, they scurry inside the tent, to play for the circus parade and the show itself.

Although Durov is ebullient, he can't stop worrying that something will go wrong. He nervously checks over his pantaloons and his bright crimson, long-sleeved shirt. He wants to show off his family's precious heirloom sash in the best manner possible, so he nervously ties and unties it around his waist. It is woven in the distinctive pattern of his family's colors—a rainbow of reds, yellows, purples, and greens—all the colors of the circus. Tears well up as he recalls the first time, as a child, he saw his father don this sash. It represents all that his father held sacred about the circus, and now he feels that his salvation rests upon his ability to redeem himself tonight.

Anatoly scurries in. "I think everything's set." He spies the sash. "Oh, f-father would be proud to see you wearing our colors again."

"I'm not so sure about that," Durov says, solemnly.

"But you—and we—have done the best we could, haven't we?"

Durov clutches Anatoly and brings him to his chest, stifling a sob. "We tried. That's all I know."

In Durov's strong embrace, Anatoly can hardly get the words out: "And now, with our new act, we'll be famous, won't we?" He steps back, his soft blonde eyebrows arched together in hopefulness.

"Famous. Yes." Durov gravely whispers, "One way or another."

Durov is, in fact, laced through with utter terror, his throat closing up with emotion—sorrow over their horrific past and elation over what could be their illustrious future. He grabs Anatoly, kisses him on both cheeks, and pushes him away. He doesn't want Anatoly to see his tears. His voice raspy, he barely gets out what he wants to say to Anatoly: "Run along and tend to the little ones now."

Anatoly gulps down a sob of his own, places his hand reverently on their family's sash around Durov's waist, and then hurries away.

As Durov watches his brother race off, he begins to pace, waiting for the signal to start the circus parade. He decides there's time to check on Natasha. He knocks gently on her wagon. She opens, and to his great relief, she's dressed in a much better fitting ringmaster's costume.

He looks around the wagon and is astonished to see she's finished transforming Nikolai's pigsty into a warm and bright home. This must mean she's going to stay with the circus after they get back to Russia. Maybe they can put their wagons together...but no...he mustn't get ahead of himself. Still, she makes a very handsome woman, and he finds a lump in his throat as well as a warm urge of desire spreading below his sash.

He notices, however, that Natasha seems agitated. "Durov, there's so much going on...ah...but I'm glad you came. How do I look?"

She turns around, somewhat awkwardly modeling for him. He admires her fine, full figure, especially her generous hips—always a sign of good livestock-breeding potential. He moistens his lips. "You look wonderful, Natasha. Anna got that costume to fit you in...ah...I mean...in all the right...ah...correct places." He's tempted to brush back ringlets of her thick chestnut hair, now coiffed loose around her braid; but he resists, as he finds the ringlets quite fetching the way they are.

She crosses herself. "Thank St. Basil." She coils up her plait and dons the ringmaster's top hat—which no longer slides down, but fits perfectly across her broad forehead. She jauntily taps the top of her top hat. "We're all set. I mean, I'm all set. At least I think we...ah....are all set."

"Is there something wrong?"

"First performance jitters. I hope everything's going to come out of the box all right. I mean, I hope—oh, just tell me again the order I announce the acts for the circus parade."

"First, you give the signal for the band to move inside the tent. Then, Bronzy and Lottie bring everyone inside."

"Everyone who's paid, that is." Natasha rubs her hands together. "We're sold out, did you know? Those four dwarf brothers managed to secretly circulate enough of Boris's posters to bring in the crowds."

"Wonderful, isn't it? Then after everyone is seated on the benches—"

"They're nice and straight, aren't they? These Germans like their—"

"Yes, they're straight. I saw to it myself."

Natasha grabs a sheet of paper from her desk. "Good. I've written down the order for the circus parade. It's the same to announce as each act goes on?"

"Except that you've got to give Zoya time—"

"Who's Zoya?"

"The elephant. She doesn't like to be crowded by the trick dogs."

"Oh yes, I remember Nikolai telling me one of those little dogs got too close and yapped at her foot."

"She wouldn't hurt a mouse, but elephants have feet that are shaped such that they actually walk on tiptoe. We were terrified she'd lose her balance, put her weight down, and inadvertently crush the dog."

"I heard she whipped her trunk around, picked the dog up, and tossed him five meters."

"Fortunately, he landed in the trapeze net, although he kept bouncing higher and higher until his trainer, Boulkari, rescued him." Durov shakes his head. "That dog was never the same."

"What do you mean?"

"Afterward, he always made a beeline for that net. Seems he loved bouncing, so Boulkari finally got him his own trampoline and put it in their act."

"Got it." Natasha writes a note on her paper. "Pack dogs away from pachyderm."

Durov is in his element. The woman he loves is writing down his very words. She's depending on him for everything to run smoothly. His eyes sparkle, and his thick chest swells. He revels in the knowledge that she needs his calm and steady advice. He hasn't felt this confident and in charge since the disaster with the Cossacks. Still, something torments him. The memory of their sabres flashing, cutting...

He knits his brows, trying to clear the fog of his terrible memories.

"Durov, is something wrong?"

"Just thinking about something that happened long ago. I'm glad we don't have to worry about Wolfgang and his dragoons."

Natasha hesitates, then blurts out, "Yes, of course not. Boris has it all in hand."

"I'd never forgive myself if something terrible happened."

Natasha winces, crossing herself. "Neither would I, Durov. Neither would I."

Durov smiles lovingly at her, gives her a swift bear hug, and heads back to his pigs.

Natasha excitedly strides through the backstage area in her ringmaster's costume and her top hat, which she taps with her baton as a sign of respect for the performers and crew. They applaud her and bow, giving her courage. She heads straight to the main tent and Boris's father's magic box. She calls for Boris to give her a status report. He rushes out from backstage, dressed not in his clown outfit but, for the first time, in his father's magician's costume.

She screams, "Ivan's still in there, but you managed to change into your costume?"

Boris's head is swathed in a crimson silk turban with a graceful peacock plume sticking out. "Do you like my turban? Lottie loaned me one of her feathers—for good luck."

Natasha shudders as she feels the ire of Wolfgang and his dragoons bearing down on them. "You'd better work your magic on that box. Get Ivan out and Wolfgang in, or I'll—"

"Yes, yes. I promise." He jumps on top of the box, and to his surprise, a small trapdoor pops out on the side. He bends down to look through it.

Ivan's eye is large and bloodshot. His voice is a muffled torrent: "You get me out of here this instant, *bezmozglyy*!"

Natasha leans over Boris to hear. "What's he saying?"

"He says he's quite comfortable in there, so don't worry about him."

"I'm not worried about him, you numbskull. I'm worried about Wolfgang. He'll be here any minute. Where are you going to hide him if Ivan's still in the box?"

"I don't suppose there's room for two inside. My mother used to wait in there to leap out and have my father saw her in half. Did I ever tell you that's why I turned out so short? Anyway, she had room in there for her knitting as she waited and—"

"You moron. You're not supposed to have both of them in there. You're supposed to get Ivan *out* and Wolfgang *in*. And Ivan needs to have enough time to warm up before his trapeze act."

More muffled shouts from Ivan inside the box: "My feet are a mess of cramps."

Natasha yells, "What did he say?"

"He says his muscles are ramping up."

"Good thing." She pounds on the box. The tip of Ivan's toe, in his slipper, sticks out of the tiny window. "That's right, Ivan. You keep warming up in there. Boris will get you out soon enough."

<hr />

Anna is shaking with a terrible bout of stage fright. She's fashioned a new costume from remnants in her mother's trunk. Her father never let her wear sequins like her mother wore; he always told her she was too young and chaste. But Anna thinks it's because he was insanely jealous of how beautiful her mother looked wearing them—and of how all the men in the circus were completely in love with her. Now Anna's cut down the bosom in the front of her costume to make her neck look even longer and more swan-like. She's sewn her mother's sequins all over. She's added a bright red sash around her petite waist and a red ribbon in the braided coils of her luxurious black hair, which she's wreathed around her head.

Anna trembles as she dons her trapeze cape for the circus parade. She wraps the cape around and secures it with a pin, so the sequins underneath won't show to alert Ivan and her father of her new act. Despite a wave of nausea brought on by nerves, she's never been more excited. She races backstage to get in line for the parade, and she sees Natasha in her ringmaster's costume. She's thrilled she's been able to please Natasha by finally getting her costume to fit. Just then, another paralyzing bout of queasiness overcomes her, but this time it's not stage fright.

Natasha rushes to her. "Are you ill?"

"Oh, Madame Natasha. I thought I was so happy about Anatoly. But I just realized I don't want to trade having my family boss me around only to have my husband boss me around."

"I can't see that being a problem with Anatoly."

"He's really quite gentle, but in some ways, he knows his mind too."

"That can be a benefit, in the right balance. Of course, I don't know from personal experience. But, my dear, you just have to learn how to do what you want to do, even when your husband thinks you're doing what he wants you to do."

Her heart in her throat, Anna looks up at Natasha and weakly asks, "How do you do that?"

"I don't know. But I'm sure you'll figure it out. Now let me see your new costume."

Anna proudly undoes her cape and twirls around.

"Lovely, my girl. Now run along and get ready."

Fastening her cape back up, Anna joyously skips off.

⌒⟶⊶⊙⊷⟵⌒

Natasha paces behind the rear flap of the circus tent, forcing herself to observe the time-honored tradition not to appear in costume before the show starts. She can hardly help herself, as she gleefully watches the horde of customers arrive. The patrons are starched and neatly pressed.

Apple-cheeked women and girls wearing long blonde plaits are accompanied by ruddy-faced men sporting neatly trimmed handlebar mustaches. Natasha notices that the children are infinitely better behaved than children in Russia. She marvels that everyone queues up in a neat line to buy their tickets, in stark contrast to all the shoving and pushing that goes on back home.

Federoya's organ-grinder act is in full swing. Watching it, she thinks it's odd that some people choose dogs who look just like them. For example, a tall, thin, gray-haired lady will choose a lean, gray wolfhound. A short puffy girl will gravitate toward a French poodle. Well, Natasha muses, Federoya's pet monkey—a spindly, brown, feisty thing—is precisely the animal equivalent of his master. They even have the same hand gestures. The monkey stops grinding long enough to hand each patron a ticket after Federoya takes their money. He tosses the monkey a peanut every time he sells a ticket, and the monkey shells it and pops it into his mouth with one paw, continuing to grind with the other. Natasha has heard the organ grinder's excruciatingly cheerful tune hundreds of times, and she's frequently made fun of its annoyingly simple rhythm. But this evening, from her hiding place backstage, Natasha gaily hums along, quietly applauding each ticket sold.

CHAPTER THIRTY

THE CIRCUS PARADE is about to begin when Natasha feels a jolt of terror as she sees Wolfgang and a dozen dragoons arrive. They are dressed in their most elaborate tunics, crisscrossed with highly buffed leather straps. Their chests are draped with reams of gold braid. A blinding mix of medals dangles from every chest. Natasha watches with considerable amusement as they strut and preen before the tall and short, and the wide and narrow sideshow mirrors. How ironic that they hold the fate of her circus in their gloved hands, while they laugh like children and elbow each other, making fun of their deformed images in the mirrors.

Natasha quietly steps along the back of the midway, so as not to be seen by Wolfgang and the dragoons. She spies Bronzy, the strongman, who is trying to convince Wolfgang to try his luck swinging the mallet to ring the bell at the top of the pole. Natasha ducks behind a tent flap and crosses herself. She hopes Wolfgang will make a solid hit and ring the bell, which will raise his spirits and maybe put him in a good enough mood not to do anything too destructive. She nods vigorously, signaling from afar for Bronzy to make sure he rings the bell while distracting Wolfgang. In fact, Bronzy outdoes himself, ringing the bell not only for Wolfgang but for all the dragoons who try their hands. The top of the pole sounds like a church bell, as it rings continuously and loudly. In Russia, the priests ring the bell to deflect evil spirits—Natasha crosses herself and fervently prays that today's bell ringing will serve the same purpose.

She strains to see how Boris is making out in his attempts to get Ivan out of the magic box. From her hiding place behind the tent, she can see the edge of the box, directly down front, in a position of honor. Boris is perched on top, doing sleight-of-hand card tricks for a group of well-scrubbed children, under the skeptical but increasingly softening eyes of their Teutonic parents. *Please God, let Boris have done his part.* Beads of perspiration appear on her upper lip as the little band sounds a flourish, signaling it's time for the circus parade—and after that, the start of the performance. Finally, it's up to her to give the hallowed signal. *Ladies and gentlemen and children of all ages...*

Natasha wipes away the sweat on her face and gathers her courage. She feels a tap on the top of her top hat. Turning, she is relieved to see Durov, who smiles broadly. Feeling giddy, she says, "This could be the biggest night ever. Wait until I step out into the center ring."

"Natasha, we only have one ring."

"Of course." Her cheeks burn. She so very much wants to succeed in order to repudiate her family, make them ashamed that they disowned her. "Wait till my family reads about our triumph in the papers back in Moscow. I might even be able to appear in society again."

"That would be wonderful."

Suddenly, her smile fades to a dark frown. She's come to care very much about Durov. He's not what she might have dreamt about—a pig trainer and all—but he's a strong, honest, and caring man. She truly doesn't want any physical harm to come to him. "Durov, are you sure this is worth the risk? We could pull up stakes and head back, right now."

He speaks slowly, distinctly: "If we lose all our money this summer, we won't be able to feed the animals over the winter."

"Feeding the people or the animals. *Oy*, what a choice." She pauses, then adds, tongue in cheek, "How many pigs in Sasha's last litter?"

Durov's square face reddens. "You wouldn't."

"A joke."

Durov snickers. "Very funny. We could use you in the act. How are you at climbing little ladders?"

Natasha affectionately cuffs his arm. She enjoys this easy banter and begins to imagine them as a couple—joking about troubling things, laughing, and facing life together. She can't resist one last joke. "Durov, I admire you. You'll be remembered in all of Russia for your valiant sacrifice."

"Sacrifice?" He gulps. "I will?"

Then, catching her humor, he smiles, shakes his head, and gives her a reassuring hug—which, she's thrilled to note, lasts a long time. In fact, the hug lasts so long that the band has to reprise their opening flourish three times. She gathers herself together. The mischievous twinkle in Durov's eyes is all Natasha sees as she steps out into their one and only ring.

⚜

Durov's nagging fears are somewhat calmed as the circus parade goes off without a hitch. Well, not entirely without a hitch: the trampoline-loving trick dog gets a bit too rambunctious doing his circles and runs into Lyudmila, the dancing bear. But it turns out all right as the bear and the dog, on their hind legs, take a quick spin around, miraculously in perfect waltz time, before their trainers manage to separate them. Thinking this is part of the show, the audience applauds wildly—even the group of dragoons sitting next to Wolfgang, who sits where Boris had been, on top of the magic box. Durov thinks, *What a great idea Boris had—to push Wolfgang into the box right before my act. What a relief!*

After the parade, as the performance starts, Durov goes to get Sasha. He leads her on a soft leather leash studded with sequins that he's fashioned just for her. He brings her to the backstage dressing area, next to his old leather trunk that's covered with faded travel stickers. He sits her down and opens the trunk, kissing the icon within and then pulling out the costume Anatoly has lovingly sewn for her. He smooths it out, then suddenly gasps as he notices streaks of light from the opening in the tent flaps falling directly onto the bosom of the costume—turning it bright scarlet, like splotches of blood. He shudders, crosses himself, and murmurs a prayer, imploring St. Gregory to ensure no disaster befalls them this evening.

Sasha looks up at him with her soft brown eyes and wiggles her corkscrew tail.

Durov chuckles as it occurs to him that she is actually calming him down. "Yes, my little piggala. Thank you. You're anxious to wear your new costume, aren't you?" She grunts and nudges his knee as Durov starts to dress her.

Anatoly comes to check on them. Durov hugs his dear brother and kisses him on both cheeks. Anatoly has the other piglets on leashes, and he brims with pride, motioning to the royal family costumes he's whipped together for them. Durov thinks that tonight's success might at least somewhat compensate Anatoly for all the pain Durov caused their family.

Durov finishes dressing Sasha and is delighted to see her in the full military uniform of the kaiser, down to its elaborate coils of gold braid. He slips her a slice of apple he keeps in his pocket to reward the pigs for doing their tricks. "You look marvelous, *moya devushka*, Sasha."

Anatoly holds up his hands in warning. "Don't give her too many treats. I don't want her bursting her seams. I haven't had time to reinforce them."

"And what a costume it is, my dear Anatoly! You've outdone yourself. And look at the little ones."

Demetri, Petrova, Gregory, Anton, and the other little pigs are dressed as various members of the kaiser's royal family—his cousin Nicholas II, the Tsar of Russia, his grandmother Queen Victoria of England, his cousin Christina the Queen of Sweden, and so on. Durov puffs out his chest, feeling a deep sense of pride and love for his porcine family. He dances around each one, petting them in turn. "The people in the audience will burst their seams when they see them sitting at the royal trough, eating their way through Europe."

CHAPTER THIRTY-ONE

Backstage, Anna warms up in a corner of the tent. Since Ivan didn't show up for the circus parade, her father Sergey marches over to her. He grabs her arm and bellows, "Where's that brother of yours? It's bad luck to miss the opening parade."

Anna snatchs the side of her cape to hold it closed; he can't see her new sequined costume underneath. She trembles as he glares at her, his thick chest and powerful arms bulging under the folds of his own trapeze cape.

"He'd better say a prayer to St. Basil for forgiveness. You know how superstitious I am."

"I'm sure he will, Papa Sergey." She crosses herself. "And to be certain, I'll kiss the icon and say an extra prayer to the Virgin."

Sergey has barely left to warm up in the practice tent, when Anatoly scurries by. When he sees her, he stops and breaks into a huge smile. She opens her cape to reveal her costume.

Anatoly's eyes pop. "Oh, my Anna. You look...ah...incredible."

She rushes to him and he opens his arms. The two kiss...and kiss...and kiss. She finally breaks apart. "Be careful of my sequins! I didn't have time to sew them on as securely as I would have liked."

He shyly runs a hand through his mop of curly blonde hair. "I know what you mean."

Anna's delicate white skin turns a deep crimson as she thinks how happy she is. Absent-mindedly, she rubs her arm where Ivan pinched her earlier in the evening and her father grabbed her just now. A nasty bluish bruise is raising.

Anatoly carefully takes her arm and lovingly rubs it. "No one will ever mistreat you, when you ar-are my wife." He kisses her arm...and keeps kissing it...right up to her shoulder. She giggles as she lets him plant a last, solid kiss on her lips. Then she tenderly pushes him back.

"Is everything all ready for my act? Did you know that Natasha's putting me on right after your act?" Anna joyously levitates. "Then I'll have time to catch my breath before my father, Ivan, and I go on for the finale. They'll have to let me wear my sequins because there won't be time for me to change."

"I've tied your rigging off across the ring. They won't know about it until after you're climbing up to the platform." He hesitates, then adds, "I'm also putting up the net. Just in case."

"You don't have to do that."

He is gentle but very firm. "Yes, I do, Anna."

"All I'm going to do is climb, then twirl and do my dance on the rope with the balance bar. When I'm done with that, I'll store the bar on the platform and put my foot in the loop." She enjoys showing off to him as she spins and lifts her leg high over her head. He gulps. She adds, "I won't be transferring to another rope, so there's no need for a net."

Anatoly firmly says, "Anna, I won't hear of you doing it without a net. That's all there is to say."

Taken aback at Anatoly's commanding manner, she pauses, wondering if he might be too bossy. Then he hugs her, whispering, "I'm not trying to control you, like your father and Ivan. I love you. I just don't want anything to happen to you."

Anna freezes, in a state of utter confusion. For years, she hasn't had anyone who deeply cared for her, yet she wants to be in charge of her own act.

Anatoly watches her intently, then adds, "If you insist, I'll leave the net down."

She pauses a moment, then nudges him and steals another kiss. "No, you're absolutely right, Anatoly." She shudders to recall how her mother died when her father refused to put up the net that night. "Of course it's better to be safe. I'm being silly." Anna looks into Anatoly's loving eyes as she shakes off the sorrow of the past. She smiles broadly. "It's almost time. We've got to go."

He gives her a final, long, deep kiss, which makes her dizzy. Anna feels her heart bursting through her sequins.

Natasha's large palms are sweating as she finishes announcing the trick dogs. Leaving the ring, she's horrified to see Wolfgang still sitting on top of Boris's father's magic box. *Why isn't Wolfgang inside that damned box like Boris promised?* She diverts from her usual path out of the ring to pass by Wolfgang on her way backstage.

Her ordinarily deep voice is thin and squeaky with high anxiety, although she manages an overly gracious smile. "Are you and your men enjoying the circus, Sergeant Major?"

He hops off the box, clicks his heels, and bows to her. His sabre rattles against the side of the box. Natasha hears a soft moan from within. Surreptitiously, she kicks the box twice to see if Ivan's still inside. Two soft knocks from within indicate that he is. She groans.

Natasha searches for a way out of this mess. In a panic, she sidles close to Wolfgang and unleashes a rapid-fire patter: "Well, I know you love the circus, but really, don't you think you've seen enough? The rest is mostly the same kind of thing as in circuses all over. Besides, it's more for the children, don't you agree? You and your men wouldn't want to be thought of as children in front of all the townspeople, would you?"

Annoyed, Wolfgang turns to her. "Listen, Madame Natasha. I just try to enjoy myself now and not remember this afternoon with the little filly. But you should know that the matter ain't finished. I never take no for an answer, and my dragoons are gonna back me up."

"Of course they will, but really, that won't be necessary. I'm sure you can appreciate what a terrible misunderstanding this has been."

"I ain't so sure about that. By the way, where is the lucky man?"

"Oh, he's backstage...ah...somewhere."

"You got a Russian Orthodox priest to marry them on such short notice?"

"Ah...yes...matter of fact, we did." Natasha waves to Boris. He immediately dons his priest's collar and garb. He quickly removes his silk turban, substituting his stovepipe clerical-looking hat, fastens on his long, fake, bushy, black beard, throws the iron cross around his neck, and darts over. He blesses anyone and everyone in his path, including one of the trick dogs that has strayed from the act currently in progress in the ring. Having to stand on tip-toes to reach the adults, he concentrates on the children. "Bless you my child...bless you my child."

Looking down at the children in his path, he doesn't see Wolfgang and runs right into his sabre. He shrieks, "Oh my God!" Wolfgang looks at him, askance. Boris deepens his already deep voice another two octaves and says, "Oh my God, my God who blesses us all." He scampers past Wolfgang and across the front of the audience, blessing the crowd and the rest of the dogs as he disappears backstage.

Natasha winces. "Don't mind him. He's just warming up for the ceremony."

Wolfgang laces his fingers through his highly curled moustache and sniffs disagreeably. "We'll see about that." He then turns away from her and back to the performance.

Her panic rises almost uncontrollably. She makes another effort to get Wolfgang to leave, but he's only halfheartedly listening to her as he intently watches the dog on the trampoline. He says to his comrades, "Isn't that little fellow amazing? See how he summersaults!" Wolfgang jumps up and down, clapping his hands. He nods to his men who immediately follow his lead, jump up and down, and clap.

Exasperated, Natasha gives up on Wolfgang and looks for Boris. Finally locating him backstage, careful not to disturb the act in progress, she frantically motions to the box and then to Wolfgang. Boris motions back, wildly shaking his head and throwing up his hands in total exasperation. Wolfgang glances over, looking at her sideways, obviously wondering why she's flailing her hands about. Groaning, she smiles weakly and makes a flourish as if she's leading the band. Then she tips her top hat to him. Having exhausted all alternatives, she's horrified that there is clearly no way she can get Wolfgang to leave. The very next act is Durov's. She has no choice but to find Durov and stop him from performing his helmet trick.

CHAPTER THIRTY-TWO

DUROV SNEAKS AN anxious look at what's going on in the ring. The four dwarf brothers have just lugged out their shiny black cannon and are stuffing Vasha into it. He pretends to wail and cry and flails his arms about. The dragoons seem especially gleeful at the idea of shooting a dwarf out of a cannon, and they clap and stomp their feet expectantly.

Despite his own anxiety, Durov laughs out loud as Pasha, Masha, and Max wheel the cannon around. They pretend to aim it at various audience members, while Vasha cries crocodile tears. Finally, they position it in front of the trapeze net and ignite the fuse. They stick their fingers into their ears and wait... nothing happens. Vasha in the cannon looks down, breathes a huge sigh of relief, and then... *boom*! He flies into the net and gets stuck, head down. He violently kicks his feet while the other dwarf brothers race around, pantomiming their wailing and crying. Finally, Pasha, Masha, and Max jump up into the net. They pull exaggeratedly at Vasha's legs and waist, and with the greatest effort, manage to free him. They all summersault out of the net and bow to wild applause. Durov is pleased that the dragoons are especially delighted.

He hears the trick dog music that indicates he's next. He alternates between frenzied impatience, a feeling of joyful pride of accomplishment, and a sense of impending doom. He kneels down, adjusts Sasha's leash, and pets her tenderly. She grunts and gently tugs at her leash. "Yes, I know. I want to go on just as much as you do. We'll have our chance very soon, my dear little piggala."

Durov draws in a long breath, infused with soft particles of sawdust that dance in the air. He rallies, knowing that every act falls within the sacred tradition of the circus he was raised to respect. It gives him courage to know that every animal is a gift from God and should be treated as such. He resolves that no matter what befalls them, he will continue to treat all the living creatures around him—his brother, Natasha, Anna, and all the pigs—with honor. And he will keep up the traditions of the circus—as his father instilled them in him—with every fiber of his being.

Anatoly gathers the little ones together, trying to keep them calm. He, too, is giddy with excitement. "They know s-something important is a-about to happen."

Durov folds his brother into his burly arms. "This is the most important day of our lives. Thank you, my brother, for all your hard work. Our father might not have been ecstatic about us having a pig act, but he would have been proud to see us make important use of his ideas on training animals. We'll be a beacon to all circuses everywhere."

Just then, Natasha, disheveled, dashes over to them. She breaks up their embrace.

"Natasha, are you all right?"

"Damn Boris, and damn that damn magic box."

Durov takes her hand in his free hand, keeping a tight hold on Sasha's leash as the pig pulls back and grunts. Durov says, "We're about to go on. What's wrong, Natasha?"

She grabs Durov by his shoulders. "Get your pigs out of their costumes right away. You can't perform the kaiser's helmet act tonight."

The pigs start to snort. Durov is alarmed, as he sees they're becoming increasingly disturbed. "Natasha, you're getting them upset."

"They're going to be more than upset if Wolfgang sees them. Ham for the kaiser's eggs."

Durov gasps. "I thought that right before we go on, Boris was going to make Wolfgang disappear into his father's magic box."

"That was the plan. But it's not working out. Trust me, Wolfgang is front and center. And Boris can't get to him to budge."

Durov goes into a panic. The trick dog music is coming to an end. If he acts fast, he and Anatoly can cut away the costumes and improvise something. He knows his pigs are smart and they'll catch on. What to do…the trick where they read from the wooden books, turning the "pages" with their snouts? What about doing their sums? Anatoly can get in position to signal them for the correct amounts—oh, wait, Anatoly hasn't gotten his figures right lately. Or maybe—

Something stops him. He desperately wants to make Natasha proud. He wants to save the circus and have her love and marry him. He also wants to honor his father by telling the whole world about their sophisticated, behavioral animal training methods. All the whipping, all the beating, all the cruelty perpetrated on animals could come to a swift end. People could realize it's better to use psychology than the whip. If he allows Wolfgang and his dragoons to put a stop to him, it will demean his life's work, his entire family's craft, and in fact, their very existence. *He can't muzzle me like a trick bear!*

Resolute that he is not going to be cowed by the kaiser and his dragoons, Durov makes one last try to convince Natasha. "But the helmet trick will bring the house down."

"That's what I'm afraid of."

Durov looks Natasha in the eye and says, "I'm sorry, Natasha. They just can't silence me."

Stunned, Natasha stands mute. Durov turns to see Anatoly, who is extremely alarmed and on the verge of tears. Durov takes a deep breath and claps Anatoly on the back. "We're going on, Anatoly. You must finish getting Demetri, Petrova, and the little ones ready."

The music swells at the end of the dog act. Natasha screams, "Durov, you can't."

The audience cheers and breaks into wild applause while the dogs yelp in appreciation. Durov readies Sasha and says a silent prayer. It's just the four clowning dwarfs, juggling on their unicycles to warm up the audience, and then it's Sasha and their pig act.

CHAPTER THIRTY-THREE

A S RINGMASTER, NATASHA has dutifully memorized the order of the acts. First, the dwarf brothers shoot one of them—she can never tell them apart—from a cannon. Then the trick dogs dance on their hind legs—and hopefully none of them takes a piss on a customer. Then the dwarf brothers come back on, juggling bats and balls on their unicycles, to warm up the audience for Durov's act. She stands frozen, her mouth so dry she can't speak. She knows that when the dwarfs are done, they'll usher Durov and Anatoly into the ring with the little pigs in tow, followed by the mother pig, Sasha. Natasha needs to announce Durov's act, but she can't move; she opens her mouth, but no sound emerges.

Years ago, her father took her swimming in the frigid Baltic Sea. When she dove underwater, it was so cold that she stopped breathing. Everything seemed to happen in slow motion, without sound—until they came and rescued her. That's what it feels like now, as Durov heralds the Royal Family Dinner Tableau, with the pigs in their various costumes. Cold feelings of dread creep into her and latch onto her spine, like poisonous jellyfish. Anatoly drags out miniature benches for the pigs to sit on. The pigs eat from a shallow, wooden trough. Natasha clamps her hand over her eyes, then compulsively peeks through her fingers.

"It's dinnertime for the royal family!" Durov announces. With a flourish, he motions to the little pig, Demetri, and says, "Here we have Tsar Nicholas II."

The crowd murmurs and applauds the pig dressed as the tsar.

Natasha feels momentary relief. *The Germans never did like the Russians.*

"And here we have Queen Victoria." More applause. *They hate the English even more.*

Natasha forces herself to glance over at Wolfgang and the dragoons. Although Wolfgang twitches a bit apprehensively in his seat on top of the box, he seems to be appreciating the joke…so far.

Natasha crosses herself and says a prayer as she watches Durov, in his light step, dance off stage. He quickly returns, and with a great theatrical flourish, he ushers in Sasha dressed as Kaiser Wilhelm II. Natasha gasps as she looks over to see the tips of Wolfgang's enormous handlebar mustache swiftly curl up and down…up and down…up and down.

In the middle of the ring, with great fanfare and musical accompaniment from the little circus band, Durov introduces Sasha. Natasha has to admit that the pig does look amazing in all that gold braid. She sees Anatoly signal for the other pigs to stop eating at the trough and oink their tribute to the kaiser. She thinks she hears the crowd roar, but it still sounds like she's underwater—everything filtered and muffled.

She holds her breath as she watches Wolfgang slowly levitate, lifting the whole of his gangly frame. The other dragoons don't appear to notice him, as they seem glued to the ring and what's going on inside.

Although Natasha's eyes are riveted to Wolfgang, she can't resist sneaking a peak to see the trick Durov has so proudly perfected. He leads Sasha around so everyone can admire her costume. Then, he places a helmet on the ground before her. Throwing his voice loudly and clearly for the entire crowd to hear, he makes it seem as if Sasha is speaking the words: "*Ich will den Helm.* What did you say? *Ich will den Helm* (I want the helmet)."

Sasha uses her hoof to send the helmet flying into the air. It's spinning up...up...and...it lands squarely between her ears! Screeches of laughter explode as the audience gets the joke: 'I want the helmet' also means 'I am Wilhelm'...the kaiser. Even through the haze of her terror, Natasha hears deafening applause for Durov and his pig.

But then she turns back to Wolfgang, who has risen to his feet, his sabre drawn. "*Du schmutziges Schwein* (you filthy pig). In the name of our glorious kaiser, ruler of all Prussia, I arrest Durov and his pig."

The other dragoons, momentarily confused, quickly jump up and follow Wolfgang's lead. Wolfgang bellows like a wounded ox, "Get those *schwein*. Shred those obscene costumes. Skewer the filthy beasts."

⁓⋅⊰⊱⋅⁓

As Sasha successfully executes the trick, Durov's heart beats wildly with pride. Vindicated at last. Joyous, he experiences the triumph of his life. He's sure of winning Natasha's love and restoring his family's honor. He's certain of his place in the annals of animal training history. Just then, all hell breaks loose.

He whirls around, deafened by the roaring of the crowd. It must be because of his triumphant act, but the noise seems more than that. He strains to find out what's going on. All of a sudden, he spies Wolfgang insanely charging full speed at him. Instinctively, he moves in front of Anatoly to protect him.

Durov watches helplessly as the screaming people in the audience rush from the benches across the ring toward the one entrance to the tent. In their panic, people run smack into the little pigs. In their own terror, the little pigs frantically scurry about, squealing horrifically. Audience members trip every which way over the pigs; a terrifying profusion of neatly dressed blonde men, women, and children go flying without a net.

Knocked off balance, Durov falls to the ground. Sawdust whirls all around, obscuring him in the riotous, trampling crowd.

229

Natasha hears Wolfgang yelling and yelling. "The costumes! The *schwein*! In the name of the kaiser, cut them to ribbons!"

Anna, who has been waiting in the wings, ready to go on right after Durov, rushes to Natasha. "What's happening? Where's Anatoly?"

Grasping her stomach in pain, Natasha manages a coarse whisper: "I saw him a moment ago. Durov was trying to protect Anatoly. But then he got knocked down, and I lost sight of them both in the sawdust."

Anna sobs and buries her head in Natasha's ample breast. The dragoons charge the pigs, sabres glinting fiercely in the early evening light that slants in from the side flaps of the tent. The unbearable squealing cuts Natasha to the quick. She watches shredded costumes fly. She hears the screams of townswomen desperately trying to drag their howling children to safety. Several dragoons head backstage, overturn old and battered trunks, rip off performers' costumes, and slash the costumes to shreds. Yelping wildly, the trick dogs attack the dragoons, who kick and cut at them.

Even as she flinches at the horrific scene swirling about her, Natasha manages to tightly grasp Anna's hands. She brings them both down onto their knees and bends to cover the girl with her body. Natasha slams her eyes shut, crosses herself, and prays it will all be over soon.

Durov is living the nightmare that has plagued him for years, invaded his peace, and threatened to destroy his sanity. At last, he is triumphant, as his act receives a standing ovation and he commands the full admiration of a wildly enthusiastic crowd. But then, everything crashes down around him. Even through the fog of his worst dreams coming true, Durov is absolutely stunned at the destruction—the speed at which Wolfgang and his horde of dragoons attack and destroy.

The dragoons draw their sabres and swing their arms around and around in circles, as if on horseback. Just like the Cossacks, they circle and gear up for the slash—a thrust that comes diagonally and downward, like lightning. Durov's first instinct is to block Anatoly from their blades. But he has hold of Sasha's leash, and he trips over it and goes down on his knees into the sawdust. At least he's got hold of her, he thinks, then a Prussian blade slices through her strap. He's thrown back on his rear, and then he's trampled by the terrified German townsfolk racing for the exit. He feels a man's boot on his cheek, a woman's heeled shoe on his shoulder, and a rash of pattering children climbing straight up his back. He struggles, in vain, to rise to his feet.

Particles from the sawdust create a windstorm, completely blocking his vision. He looks directly above him through the dust and spies Wolfgang's sabre, its ornately carved hilt flashing. He thinks—in this slow motion moment of time, where everything is suspended because it is too terrible for his mind to absorb—how odd it is that the hilt of the Prussian sword is so elaborate compared with the very stark, utilitarian Cossack sabre. Still, it appears every bit as deadly, especially when wielded with the same vicious, irrational hatred. In a daze, he wonders how any soldier can get so angry at any animal—but especially at a pig, whose mouth is perpetually upturned in a gentle smile.

Through the dusty skirmish, Durov begins to comprehend something quite disturbing. It seems that he's screaming, "Anatoly, Sasha," but he can't actually hear anything. Slowly, the gruesome screeching of animals, women, and children penetrates, even as the blur around him swivels out of control. Suddenly, he's at the top of the circus tent, looking down at the melee from above. He hears a deafening crack. It's the main tent pole breaking in two! But no, through the sawdust, the pole appears to be entirely intact. He seems to be screaming again: "Sasha... Run... Oh God. No... Sashaaaaaaa." What was that cracking noise, if it wasn't the main tent pole?

As Durov slips into unconsciousness, he realizes it was his head.

CHAPTER THIRTY-FOUR

THE GLOOMY SHADOWS slowly brighten and illuminate the darkest corners of Durov's mind. Barely conscious, he struggles to open an eye. His vision clears sufficiently to reveal, through the dim, early evening light of a high window that's covered with bars, that he's in a prison cell. There is a pallet of filthy straw, a rickety wooden table with a candle, a single chair, and an empty tin bowl and spoon. He recoils at the smell of something foul—a metal trough along the rear stone wall of the cell. *Oh, look. That's where I piss.* He notices that the trough is set at an angle with a small opening into the next cell. *Oh, I get it. I piss here, and it runs downhill to the next guy. And he pisses, and it runs down to the next guy. Clever. Ha! I'd hate to be the guy in the last cell!* He laughs a big, broad laugh that sends sharp stabbing pains through him.

As Durov gains more of his mental faculties, he attempts to lift his head. He encounters what seems to be a sharp iron rod inserted into his neck. No, the rod isn't in his neck, it's around his neck. And it's tied to a rope that has hog-tied his hands and feet together behind his back. He grits his teeth and moans. *Never did like that expression...hog-tied.*

A bolt of pain sears through him as the fog of memory finally lifts.

Sasha...oh, my Sasha! He last recalls a flash of steel, glinting above his dear Sasha's head. He remembers Wolfgang stepping on her corkscrew tail and slicing at her military costume. Reams of gold braid catapulted into the air, mixing with the silver bands of a dozen sabres, swishing into rainbows of fabric.

He rocks back and forth on his stomach, kicking his legs out and trying to loosen his bonds. He grunts and sobs and groans. Exhausted, he whimpers: *It was only an act. We didn't mean any offense. Well, maybe we meant a little offense, but surely not enough for them to demolish our little circus.*

Durov's mind drifts. He sees Sasha, rolling in the mud to cool herself. *Ich will den Helm...I just had to do it, didn't I?* His eyelids flutter as he visualizes the unspeakable scene. Will I ever see my brother again? Natasha? She was just beginning to care for me. No, that can't be true. What would she want with a pig trainer? Someone who caused this ghastly calamity through his own stubborn pride? Still, when he thinks about her, he manages a smile and a twinkle in his eye. *We'd have had sturdy children, wouldn't we?* But then he sucks in a deep breath and bangs his forehead on the concrete floor. *What am I talking about? Now it's only Anatoly to carry on the Durov name.*

He opens his eyes to the heavens. *Dear Sasha. There you are, up there, squealing in your field of dreams. Here I am, down here, crying in the cell of my nightmares.*

Durov is abruptly pulled out of his reverie as he hears the familiar jangling of spurs. He turns to see Wolfgang approach the bars of his cell. Wolfgang's hair is disheveled, the gold braid on his tunic is frayed, and the breast of his coat is blotched a dark crimson. Durov sees him take out a huge ring of keys and, after inserting two that don't work, manages a third one successfully. The door comes clanking open.

Durov twists frantically as he tries to look Wolfgang in the eye, which is not easy from his trussed position on the concrete floor. He shouts, "Are my people all right? My brother? Natasha? Sasha?"

Wolfgang calmly looks down, a smug and triumphant smile spreading under his large handlebar mustache. "Please don't yell. It makes the other prisoners hard of hearing."

As he listens to Wolfgang's squeaky but calm voice, Durov feels a lump like hot coal sitting at the bottom of his stomach.

Wolfgang continues, "I generally try to take care of my prisoners. I hate filling out all that paperwork when they die."

Durov swallows his pride, knowing precisely who has the upper hand. "I'm sorry. I just want to know if you've…well…if they're still alive. My brother? Natasha? Sasha?"

Wolfgang seems genuinely offended. "We don't kill defenseless degenerates like your circus people." He takes his sabre out and twirls it in circles above him. "What do you take us for?" After two complete turns, he holds the sabre midair. "Who's Sasha?"

Durov hesitates for a moment. Then, wincing, he adds in a voice barely above a whisper, "My pig."

"Your goddamned *schwein*? That filthy beast, what caused all the trouble?"

"Well, yes. When you put it that way."

"I dun know. But we skewered his costume right good."

"Her costume. Sasha is a her."

"Whatever you say." Wolfgang brings the sabre diagonally down. Durov smashes his eyes shut, bracing for the fatal blow. He hears a whistle. Then he realizes that Wolfgang has sliced through the rope that trusses him, splaying his arms and legs out onto the floor. Durov, now resting on his stomach, breathes deeply and rapidly, finally catches his breath, rolls to his side, and crosses himself. He thanks the saints he's still alive as he watches Wolfgang sheath his sabre.

"That ringmaster lady wasn't no worse for the wear, when she stopped screamin' that is. And that little filly, sweet little thing, got off all right too. Still not sure about her marrying someone else, and you can bet I intend to pursue it right after we clear this mess up with you. Anyway, can't say as I know what happened to all those screeching critters, though."

Durov awkwardly maneuvers his bulky frame to a seated position on the cold stone floor and looks up defiantly. "Why would you stoop so low as to attack defenseless circus animals?"

Wolfgang shakes his head. He lights the candle on the table, pulls over the chair, and sits down with a tired huff. "Let's get something straight. The kaiser, he ain't happy about your ham-handed *schwein* act. But because the tsar is his cousin, he don't want no interracial trouble." He adds with a sneer, "Especially since cousin Nicky's had so much trouble of his own recently. Word is to keep this whole ugly affair quiet. And it's my solemn duty to carry out the ugliest wishes of our emperor."

"That's a relief."

Wolfgang bends down and looks menacingly into Durov's face. "Otherwise, you'd have all been dragged out and horsewhipped by now."

Durov shudders, quickly adding, "We wouldn't want to offend the tsar, would we?"

Wolfgang quips, "Ever see a man tied for the lash? Some chew right through the bits we put in their mouths."

"Hungry are they?"

Wolfgang looks confused.

"Just a thought. Anyway, thanks for the candle, it was getting dark in here."

Wolfgang stands. "It's going to get a lot darker for you—you're lookin' at two years in this place, if you don't apologize and make it big and public."

"Two years? Apologize? For what?"

"Are you as dumb as your pig?"

"Pigs are actually very smar—"

"Stop that! You got to say how you lied about our glorious Emperor Kaiser

236

Wilhelm—by making a foolish costume and teaching a filthy *schwein* an obscene trick that mimicked our glorious Emperor Kaiser Wilhelm."

Each time Wolfgang invokes the name of the glorious kaiser, he vigorously salutes into the empty air. Durov stifles a snicker.

"It wasn't obscene. And I didn't lie to anyone. The Durov family never lies—especially not to the children. Besides, didn't you see how everyone was laughing?"

"We did happen to notice." Wolfgang pulls an inkwell and quill pen from his breast pocket, which he neatly places on the table. He pulls a parchment scroll from another pocket and waves the scroll in Durov's face. "See this? It's a declaration you got to sign. Or you'll be spendin' two years right here in this very cell." He throws the scroll onto the floor. "Read it and think long and hard, pig tamer."

"Pig trainer—not pig tamer."

Wolfgang snorts and marches out of the cell. He fiddles with the keys and manages to lock the cell door on only the second try. Durov hears Wolfgang's spurs jangling down the stone corridor. He wants more than anything to tackle Wolfgang and bring him to his pompous, boney knees. But the dragoon is out of reach, so Durov scrambles over to the scroll and tries to read it in the dimming light. He slumps, waves of guilt crashing over him, as the shock and horror of Sasha's death finally sinks in. *Sasha…my dear piggala…please forgive me. Up there, you know there will be air and light and all the colors of the circus. Down here, there's nothing but the truth. It is without light and color, but it is here all the same.* Durov holds his head in his hands and weeps without restraint.

CHAPTER THIRTY-FIVE

NATASHA, HER FACE streaked with makeup and tears, stumbles slowly in a daze through the main tent, backstage, and midway sideshow booths. The weight on her heart presses heavier and heavier. She surveys the rubble of what's left of the circus and tries to give comfort, as best she can, to the performers and stagehands. Everyone is covered with dust and blackened smoke. Some apply salve and wrap minor wounds. As the dragoons, looking for the pigs, stomped up the stairs of various wagons out back, one tipped over a lantern and set fire to the canteen. Smelling the food cooking, the circus people rushed there, put the fire out, and plopped down—too tired and demoralized even to eat.

Anguished, Natasha surveys piles and piles of shredded costumes and overturned trunks of make-up and props, their contents ripped and scattered. Although extremely grateful that no one was actually killed, she feels despondent. Overcome, she crumbles onto a pile of shredded costumes. Her trembling hands twist all that remains of her ringmaster's top hat—an empty brim. *Who'd have thought they'd riot over a pig? And did they have to skewer every single costume in the whole bloody place?*

She feels dreadful about Durov—how Ivan had egged him on, and how she'd wanted him to perform to save her from financial ruin (and maybe even penal servitude). But she certainly never wanted him to be harmed—or the circus destroyed. She did try to stop him, didn't she? Of course she did. But he was too proud, wasn't he? It's not her fault he was so stubborn—or is it? She never really cared for those little beasts, but the way he tried to protect that big one—Sasha, was it? *He is a man of principle. I'll say that for him.* She crosses herself and laments that now he's in prison and only St. Basil knows for how long. Once again, Natasha feels completely alone. She sobs into the shredded pile of costumes, picking a rag up to blow her nose.

Anna staggers by in shock, unsteady and awash in her own tears. Her hair, which had been neatly coiled for her high wire act, is now a mess of flyaway strands. And her sequined costume is blackened with soot and hanging by a precarious few threads. She modestly hikes it up, sobbing. "Madame, wasn't it horrible? How could they do so much damage in so little time? I'd heard Germans were efficient, but really—" Taking care to keep her costume in place, Anna gingerly climbs up on the pile next to Natasha, sobbing some more. "Anatoly tried to rouse Durov, but he was out cold."

Natasha envelopes the girl with her arm. "I hate to imagine him waking up in a German prison. All over a pig act."

The strongman, Bronzy, and his sister Lottie, lurch up and collapse at the base of the pile of costumes. Devastated, Bronzy bellows through his tears, "Madame Natasha, I grabbed my dumbbells and swung them around and around. I tried to stop them, but they struck with such speed."

Lottie sniffles. "I sent my séance props flying. My spoons, my forks, and even my knives—although they aren't very sharp." She wipes away a tear with one of her shawls. "I concentrated as best I could, to fling them at the soldiers. But they were racing around so fast, chasing after the pigs, and changing direction all the time. I couldn't land a blow."

The four dwarf brothers, in their ripped clown costumes, straggle in as well. Pasha carries a broken wheel from his unicycle, while Masha carries a broken seat from his. But Vasha is smiling as he produces a split bat. "I was juggling my bats and my balls when they attacked. See how I managed to split this one?"

Pasha grabs the bat to examine it. "It's split right down the middle."

"How did you do that?" Max asks.

"Wonderful!" Masha says. "Who did you hit?"

Vasha grins sheepishly. "Well, I actually didn't hit any of them. The dragoons were swinging their sabres so wildly I couldn't get close. But I did throw all three of my bats, and one of them landed on the top of a helmet."

"So you did get a dragoon?" Max offers.

Vasha winces. "Actually, it was Sasha's helmet."

"Oh, too bad," Masha quips.

"Better luck next time," Pasha adds.

"Next time?" Vasha says. "I don't think so."

Natasha shakes her head in sympathy; she feels truly sorry for all the earnest and dedicated circus people. She tries to comfort them: "It wouldn't have mattered. No one could have stopped them. I'm just glad no one was hurt."

"It's a miracle everyone seems to be more or less in one piece," Bronzy says.

Natasha is just beginning to feel some semblance of relief when Anatoly limps in, covered with mud. "It's t-terrible! Did you see how t-they attacked the l-little ones? All those s-soldiers in their shining b-boots, running every which way, s-slashing at them." He turns to Anna, his lips quivering. She holds her arms out for him, then quickly boosts her costume up. She motions for him to climb onto the pile of costumes. He scrambles up and rushes into her embrace.

"How cowardly do you have to be to skewer pigs?" Natasha scowls.

Anatoly wails. Anna rubs his back and throws Natasha a nasty look.

Natasha hastily adds, trying to muster sympathy for the pigs, "Sorry, Anatoly."

Anna turns to Anatoly and softly asks, "How many did they get?"

He lowers his eyes and whispers, "They got every s-single one. The Queen Victoria v-velvet costume, the Duke of Wales's red t-turncoat, the tsar's b-black tunic, the—"

"I mean, how many of the little pigs—Demetri, Petrova...you know?"

"Oh, the s-soldiers were much too slow to get any of the pigs. Luckily, I had put a slight coat of g-grease under their c-costumes to make them easier to s-slide off and on. In all the excitement, I managed to s-slip them out of their costumes. The dragoons slashed all the fabric to bits"— he smiles weakly—"but they couldn't c-catch any of the little ones." His boyish smile broadens. "Greased l-lightning, don't you know."

Natasha lets out a huge sigh, completely surprised at how relieved she is to hear the little pigs are safe.

Anna claps her delicate hands and smiles. "That's marvelous." She pauses, then tentatively asks, "But what about Sasha?"

At that, Anatoly collapses in tears. "I lost t-track of her. It was horrible. All that s-slashing. Six of them surrounded her. All I saw was their boots." He wails. "Durov's n-never going to g-get over it."

Anna whispers, "We're so sorry, aren't we, Madame Natasha?"

Natasha, sincerely moved by Anatoly's grief, says, "I never thought I'd be upset about a pig. But believe me, Anatoly, I am."

Bronzy, Lottie, and the four dwarf brothers sniffle and murmur their condolences.

Anatoly chokes up as he produces a long, rainbow-colored swath of fabric. "Before he fell, Durov took t-this off and threw it to me. Our family's sash. He w-wouldn't have given it up lightly. It's the s-symbol of our family's circus tradition—although there's not m-much left of that now."

Natasha tears up, moved by Anatoly's description of the honor of the Durov family, as symbolized by the sash. She is about to commiserate further when Boris arrives. He wears his father's spotless magician's cloak— not a hair out of place under Lottie's borrowed, purple silk turban with its outsized feather plume perfectly intact.

Boris calls up to Anatoly sitting next to Natasha and Anna on the pile of shredded costumes, "I'm so sorry, my good man."

Astonished, Natasha is also furious to see Boris pristine and in one piece. She jumps down from the pile and yells at him, "Boris, where have you been? And why do you look so...so...unscathed?"

"Looks belie the trauma I, too, have suffered. I've had my own cross to bear."

Lottie hurries to Boris. "I'm so glad you're safe. Oh, and my turban too." She straightens the feather on top.

Ivan charges in, shouting at Boris, "You miserable son-of-a Cossack."

Boris smirks at Ivan. "Now that we've shared what we've shared, I would have thought you'd have been more...ah...civil."

Ivan shrieks, "Civil?" He goes for Boris's throat, but Natasha steps between.

Natasha screams, "Stop it you two. Tell me what happened."

Boris proudly swishes his robe. "If you calm down and give me a minute, I will tell you." He strokes his goatee and clears his throat, so his deep Shakespearean voice will carry. "I was convinced that if I wore my father's robe, and if I truly concentrated, I could discover the secret to Presto— my father's magic box." He swishes his robe in a graceful arc. "At first I was gentle—and graceful I might...add. But when the dragoons charged, I swung the robe—fast—over the box. I heard a click and realized something sewn into one of the sleeves passed over some sort of secret mechanism in the box...and Presto!—that's the name of my father's box, did I tell you? Anyway...Presto! The box opened up!"

Natasha looks down at Boris and says, through gritted teeth, "So why didn't you get Ivan out and put Wolfgang in?"

Ivan growls, "Yes, Boris. Do tell."

Boris winces. "Well, I was going to get Ivan out, but the dragoons had drawn their sabres and were so menacing that...I...well...I didn't want Ivan to get run through."

Natasha shrieks, "You mean you didn't want *you* to get run through."

"That too." Boris sinks down, disappearing into his robe. The turban gets stuck in the cone-shaped opening, so Boris reaches up and plucks the plume and then the turban down into the robe.

Ivan shouts into the cone, "So you jumped in on top of me, and the box locked shut again?"

The robe shakes violently.

"That's why your robe and Lottie's turban are so spotless," Natasha adds, exasperated.

The diminutive Lottie, her shawls askew, gently walks over to Boris's cone-shaped robe. Natasha is touched by her sympathetic manner; Lottie kneels down, pushes his cloak aside, and looks the small man directly in the eye. "But you figured out the trick to the magic box, didn't you?"

Boris struggles up and peeks around. "Yes, but by that time it was too late. I'm really sorry, everyone. It was too late to get Wolfgang in the box, so I jumped in to keep me—and Ivan—safe."

Natasha says, "Then when the screaming and panic were over, you unlocked the box and came out."

Boris hangs his head. He reaches down into his robe and hands the turban to Lottie. "Thank you for loaning this to me." He reaches deeper inside and pulls out the feather plume. "Oh, and this too. It would have been a nice touch to my act, if I ever could have been a real magician."

Boris contritely turns to leave, but Natasha bars his way. The circus should probably pack up and limp back to Russia as soon as possible, but she feels compelled to do everything in her power to save Durov. "Not so fast. We need you to finally perform a real magician's act. To visit Durov in jail and slip him the hacksaw you've hidden in your cloak."

"But I haven't hidden a hacksaw—oh, I see what you're saying. But prison?" Boris's teeth chatter. "I've never been inside a prison. Only magic boxes. And that was claustrophobic enough."

Ivan quips, "Tell me about it. Especially if you're caught underneath a clown who's trying to be a magician."

Natasha jumps in, "Ivan, leave your personal proclivities out of this." She turns to Boris. "You're our only hope of getting Durov out of jail."

Lottie, Bronzy, Anna, and Anatoly enthusiastically shake their heads in agreement.

Ivan holds up his hand. "Natasha, I disagree. We should return home immediately before there's any more trouble."

Anatoly scoots down from his perch atop the pile of costumes, followed by Anna, who manages to keep her ripped costume modestly in place. Anatoly raises his voice, not exactly a shout, but the closest Natasha's ever heard him.

"You don't mean we sh-sh-should l-leave my br-br-brother to rot in j-j-jail?"

Natasha looks between the soft-spoken and gentle Anatoly and the handsome scoundrel Ivan, who is the same kind of womanizer Nikolai was. She sees Bronzy, Lottie, and Anna nervously waiting for her decision as the owner of what remains of the circus. She feels her stomach lurching as that familiar feeling of vulnerability invades her every pore—she is alone again, now that Durov's in jail and they have no way of knowing what his fate will be. She must decide what to do, not just for her own sake—she really wants to save Durov—but for the sake of their entire little circus.

Durov isn't used to being alone. When you're in the circus, there's always someone around practicing their act, stagehands needing help to pack or unpack, a pig to train, a ladder to mend, or a costume to let out because a piglet grew too fast. But now in his cell, he's increasingly anxious that there's no one to help...or laugh with.

He goes to the bars, leans out, and calls down the stone corridor. "Anyone home?"

A variety of snickers, whistles, or outright guffaws comes back from the other prisoners. *I guess they aren't in a talkative mood.* Dejected, he shuffles over to the chair next to the table and picks up the scroll, then, in disgust, lets it fall. He turns, hearing a twitter in the corner. He holds perfectly still, trying to figure out where the noise is coming from. He rattles the scroll again, and the twitter starts again. His animal trainer instincts kick in, as he slowly gets up and gently jiggles the scroll, stepping toward the corner where the twittering appears to be coming from.

One step, rattle the scroll, a twitter. Another step, rattle the scroll, a twitter. As he reaches the corner, he looks down to see three mice, with soft brown, twinkling eyes, standing on their hind legs.

Immediately, Durov is flooded with a great sense of relief that he's not alone. He crinkles up his weathered face and laughs, very gently and quietly. "Little ones, don't be afraid."

They scamper through a crack in the stone. He kneels down and tries to see where they've gone.

⁓⚜⁓

Anna shrieks as Ivan grabs her hand and pulls her away from her dear Anatoly, even as she struggles to keep her torn costume in place. She feels helpless at the hands of her brutish brother and prays that Natasha will intercede on her behalf.

Anatoly takes a step toward Ivan, but Ivan motions for him to stop, yelling, "You aren't officially my brother-in-law yet. So you aren't family. I'm the one who has to act in the best interests of my family and the circus."

Anna's hopes and newfound happiness—at what a wonderful life she's going to have with Anatoly—are dashed. She struggles to free herself from Ivan's grip.

Anatoly looks around, hesitates, takes a deep breath, and stomps right up to confront Ivan.

Ivan pulls Anna away from him, railing at her, "You were only going to marry him to keep from having to marry Wolfgang. Don't tell me you actually care about this pig trainer."

Horrified that Ivan has guessed her original intent, Anna shouts, "*Ostanovit'yego.* Stop it, Ivan. Let me go."

"You're an aerialist. We're first in the circus parade." Ivan sneers at her.

Anna musters all her courage. "Ivan, don't you dare say anything more."

Ivan smirks. "Annala, my dear little sister, I know you. You're not going to lower yourself to a pig trainer. You're much too ambitious."

Anatoly looks quizzically between Anna and Ivan, and then it slowly dawns on him what Ivan is talking about. He is crestfallen.

Anna can't bear to see Anatoly hurt. She turns to her brother. "Ivan, you are a horrid monster."

He retorts, "You know you can't have a real act without me and our father."

Although Natasha, Boris, and Lottie voice their objections, Anna has the sinking feeling that her brother could be right. She looks at Anatoly's sweet face and thinks back to the way he caressed her in her bath. She's longed for that kind of love, but she also realizes how much she wants to fly. To be cheered by the crowds as they look up to her on the trapeze. Even an act of her own on the high wire can't replace her first love—the trapeze.

Natasha interjects, "Ivan, this isn't the time. We've got to stick together."

Anna thinks again of Anatoly's loving hands on her shoulders and how he gently poured water down her neck. How he urged her to use a net but agreed to set her rigging anyway. How principled he is without being overbearing and controlling. How she could feel safe with him for the rest of her life. And then it comes to her—she wants this kind of love more than anything else, maybe even more than flying. She chews her lip, gathers her strength, and pulls away from her brother. "Ivan, you're wrong. I love him. I know it's hard for someone as egotistical and selfish as you to believe, but it's true."

Ivan opens his mouth to yell at Anna, but before he can utter a word,

Natasha steps between brother and sister and stares Ivan down. Turning tail, he quips, "You'll be sorry my little Anna. Natasha. You'll all be sorry."

The wind goes out of her and Anna's knees buckle. Natasha catches her, and Anatoly rushes to put his arm around her and lead her to a bench. Sitting beside her, he stares intently at her. He hesitates, looks puzzled, then speaks softly, "It's true? Really, Anna? W-what you said before?"

Anna feels her heart melting for this curly-headed, sweetest of fellows. "That I love you? Of course, you silly goose."

Anatoly sighs. "Now geese. They're not very bright, and they're quite difficult to train. You have to shout over all that honking—"

Giggling, Anna flings her arms out to hug him, then quickly sees to her costume before it can fall. "Anatoly, now I know you're just teasing me, just kiddin—"

"Kids? Baby goats? Now they're really—"

She plants a big kiss on him.

Natasha jumps in, "You two, that's enough of that...for now. We've got to figure out what to do. We're not leaving without Durov. And Boris, you're going to use all your magician's skills to get him out."

Boris gulps. "Madame Natasha, forgive me for mentioning this, but I'm not so sure that's going to be possible."

Boris turns to slink away, but Lottie throws one of her scarves around him and reels him back. "I can help you, Boris. With your intuitive powers and my psychic powers, I'm sure we can combine the forces of the unearthly and the earthly to do it."

Anna feels a rush of optimism, until Natasha adds, "And Anatoly, you're going to help Boris and Lottie spring Durov."

Seized by fear for Anatoly's safety, Anna has an overwhelming urge just to run away with him. But Durov welcomed her to their family, didn't he? He lifted her up in a joyous bear hug. She sighs deeply. There's no other way—they must rescue Durov, and it's up to her to give Anatoly courage.

She whispers to him, "I know you can do it. You're much more capable than you think."

Anatoly blinks. "I am?" He lovingly looks at Anna, takes a deep breath, and declares, "I am." He stands and wraps the Durov family sash around his waist. "While Durov's in prison, I'm the head of this family." He gulps. "But we'd better get him out as soon as possible."

Anna leaps up and plants another kiss on Anatoly, holding his chin in one hand and what remains of her ripped costume in the other.

CHAPTER THIRTY-SIX

D UROV ANXIOUSLY PACES his cell, rolling and unrolling the scroll. He holds it up toward the small barred window, desperately trying to make out the writing. But the sun has nearly set, taking with it most of the light.

How dare Wolfgang order him to apologize for besmirching the kaiser with his pig act? Durov bristles at having to express regret for something he considers his highest achievement in artistic expression. After all, isn't artistic inspiration the stuff of all civilized culture? Isn't having the opportunity to let your imagination run free and land on a subject—even a politically charged subject—something to be valued in society? Especially if it provokes a collective and true response—in this case applause by the patrons of the circus? And doesn't this response affirm the underlying art and validate the artist in the most crucial way? *Who am I kidding? It was just a pig act.* Durov feels the lump in his stomach sagging him down, as he strains to read the Teutonic writing on the scroll.

After a while, Durov gives up, puts the scroll down on the table, and on hands and knees, slowly crawls to the corner of the cell looking for the mice. "Where are you, little ones?"

As they approach the garrison, Natasha can't stop shaking. It is laid out before her—a high brick wall forming a square, with a tower in the far corner. Of course, it's only natural that the place would be fortified, but there are so many, many, many soldiers. Sentries march back and forth in front of the gate; they are dressed in fine tunics with sabres at their sides, and they shoulder rifles that are fitted with bayonets. When they reach the end of their route, they transfer their rifles to the other shoulder, whip smartly around, stomp and click their heels, and then start back in the other direction. Guards are also stationed at the small watchtower next to the entry gate. Natasha squints to see into the compound itself. She feels her blood draining as she spots dozens of soldiers milling about, polishing cannon and stacking supplies.

Natasha screws up her courage to proceed, bravely leading their little party consisting of Anatoly, Anna, and Lottie. In his long magician's cloak, Boris trails farther and farther behind.

Natasha fumes that Boris keeps tripping over the hem of his robe, now heavily weighted. She twists around and angrily whispers to Lottie, "Tell Boris to keep up. We need to be let in all at once, or this isn't going to work."

Lottie falls back to encourage Boris, who says, through gritted teeth, "This damned hacksaw is so much heavier than I thought." But to mollify Natasha, he starts to double time, even as he clanks with every step.

As Natasha and their little band approach the sentries marching outside the gate, she's surprised, and quite pleased, to see them stop and stand at attention. They allow her party to go right up to the sentry box. A German guard, as tall and thin as Wolfgang, slips open the sentry-box window and cocks one eyebrow under a shiny helmet with the same golden top-like protrusion on its dome. Like the dragoons who wrecked the circus, every single one here in the garrison has precisely the same, broad, handlebar mustache as Wolfgang—also waxed into tight curls at the end. Despite her dread, and the apprehension she's built up regarding their mission, Natasha has to laugh at the thought of a whole fortress full of exact replicas of Wolfgang.

The sentry clears his throat and cocks his other eyebrow as if to ask why she is there.

Adopting her most respectful and serious tone, Natasha says, "We are here to visit…" She turns to Anatoly, "*Oy, bozhe moy*, what's Durov's full name?"

Anatoly stammers, "V-Vladimir Leonidovich D-Durov."

"We are here to visit—"

"I heard him," the guard barks, slamming the window in Natasha's face.

After a moment, the side door of the sentry box whisks open, and the guard appears and salutes while clicking his heels. He sneers, "I will escort you to Sergeant Major Wolfgang, who will decide if and when you can visit the prisoner."

As they walk along the dank stone corridor, lit by a series of flaming torches, Natasha is confronted by a series of putrid smells—although she can't tell whether they're from the rancid pallets of straw on the stone floors in the cells or from the prisoners themselves. She fights an almost overwhelming urge to turn and run back into the clear air.

She glances behind her and is touched to see Anatoly comforting Anna, and Lottie comforting Boris. Would that Durov were free right now to comfort her in this terrifying place. Hearing Boris's cloak clanking along the floor, she whispers, "Keep that quiet, will you?"

Wolfgang appears at the end of the corridor and walks briskly toward them. "Well, now, Madame Natasha. I'm glad you came. I see you brought reinforcements."

He eyes Anna lasciviously. She cowers behind Anatoly, who bravely steps forward. "Y-yes, S-Sergeant M-M-Major W-W-W-Wolfgang. We are h-here to see my-my-my b-brother."

Wolfgang walks around Anatoly to get a better view of Anna. "And you brought the little filly, I see."

Natasha's ferocious motherly instincts kick in. "I'm sorry that you and your troops didn't stay for the marriage ceremony last night. I'd like to introduce you to Anna's new husband, Anatoly." Anna pats Anatoly's hand to reinforce their new marital status.

Wolfgang draws his bean pole frame up even taller and suspiciously eyes Anatoly and Anna, who lean into one another and smile as if portraying a newly wedded couple.

Boris moves behind them and puts his arms around the happy couple, which causes his cloak to clatter.

Wolfgang jerks his head back and forth in the narrow corridor, his large Adam's apple bobbing up and down. "What was that?"

Lottie swiftly pulls the hem of Boris's cloak up and under one of her shawls. "Oh, nothing your Sergent Majorship. Just a special bodice I'm wearing to keep...ah...my modesty forbids me from describing anything further." She wraps an outer shawl around her. "I'm sure you understand."

Wolfgang leans way down, pinching his watery blue eyes nearly shut to examine Lottie and Boris. He barks, "No, I ain't so sure I understand." He zeros in on Boris, who starts to shake uncontrollably. This causes the hacksaw to shred the hem of his cloak and fall in pieces to the stone floor. The racket reverberates throughout the prison. Boris starts to disappear down into his robe, but Wolfgang grabs him, lifts him up, and shakes him. More metal parts clatter.

Natasha wants, more than anything else in the world, to take Boris's robe, swish it around them all, make them disappear, then reappear safe and sound back home in Mother Russia. She offers the only excuse she can think of, in such short order: "Oh, Boris...you didn't say you'd brought Wolfgang a present. How nice." She turns to Wolfgang and smiles weakly. "I'm sure Boris thought you could use some finely crafted pieces of metal...well blades of...I mean a sawtoothed metal fabricated—"

"Enough!" Wolfgang releases Boris from his talons, bends down, and collects the pieces of the hacksaw in his large hands, nicking one of his fingers in the process. He sucks the blood from his finger as he leans down, nose to nose with Boris.

Boris gulps, trying to be helpful. "Better put some vodka on that. You don't want it to get infected."

Wolfgang snarls, "I'll show you. When I'm done havin' my men give you fifty lashes, you can pour your own vodka over your own back—or what you got left of it." Wolfgang smiles sadistically, while Boris whimpers like a wounded animal.

Natasha is startled to see Anatoly take a deep breath and step up. He rapidly puts together the pieces of the hacksaw and demonstrates it. "See h-here, this is excellent w-worksmanship. D-don't you think you could keep the hacksaw and leave our friend B-Boris here alone? F-fair trade?" He saws the blade in the air, back and forth in front of Wolfgang. Then he picks up a torch from the wall, extinguishes the flame, and deftly begins sawing through. "Wouldn't this come in h-handy in your b-barracks?"

Natasha admires Anatoly's quick thinking and silently prays Wolfgang will be sufficiently persuaded to make the deal. She is heartened when he picks up the saw and starts to work on the torch himself, chuckling at how smoothly it cuts through the iron.

"Not bad. Our German blades are almost always better than anything around, but I got to say, you got an inventive contraption here." Wolfgang snickers. "Oh, all right. You can have this little man back."

Boris, who has been sweating bullets, nearly collapses with relief. Lottie props him up.

Wolfgang adds, "And you can visit your Durov fellow, but make it quick. I've been meaning to build Elsa a new hitching post, and I'm gonna try this fine saw out." He takes the hacksaw and, whistling "Ode to Joy," turns to leave. He calls back over his shoulder, "Down the corridor, next to the last cell on the left."

Natasha's relief is palpable. Anna gives Anatoly a quick kiss, and Lottie mops Boris's sweat-covered brow, leading him along. They arrive at Durov's cell, and much to Natasha's relief, they find him healthy and in one piece.

CHAPTER THIRTY-SEVEN

A S HE HEARS Natasha and the others approach, Durov plunges into a state of panic. He wants to hide, but there's nowhere to go. He knows he let everyone down because he was pigheaded enough to insist on performing, even though he'd discovered at the last minute that they hadn't gotten Wolfgang into Boris's magic box. Natasha may be stubborn sometimes, but she was absolutely right to insist he not go on. And how can he face Anatoly? *Just as my dear brother was about to find true happiness, I've destroyed all his hopes—like I destroyed our entire family.*

Suddenly, Anatoly is there, in front of the bars of his cell, with tears staining his cheeks and his mass of curly hair completely disheveled. "Durov, are y-you all r-right?"

Durov rushes to him, hugging him between the bars. "Anatoly, can you ever forgive me?"

Anna maneuvers under Anatoly to hug Durov, and then Natasha piles on, extending her long arms and large hands around both Anna and Anatoly to embrace Durov as well. Durov is overwhelmed by their collective love and support, which only makes him feel worse. He breaks away and starts to pace the short length of his cell, in order to squelch a torrent of sobs he's too embarrassed to let loose in front of them.

"I really don't deserve this kindness from all of you. I wouldn't blame any of you if you just returned home and let me starve in here."

Anatoly says, "How could we do that?"

Anna jumps in: "Of course we couldn't. We brought you some black bread and cheese."

She motions to Boris, who shyly steps over, digs into a pocket in his cloak, and comes out with some flowers. Natasha rolls her eyes. Boris smiles weakly, hands the flowers to Lottie, then digs again, finally coming up with a package of brown wrapping paper.

Lottie hands the package to Durov. "Anna found this in what was left of the canteen."

Durov is sure he doesn't deserve such kindness since they probably have very little to eat themselves. He hesitates, then gratefully takes the food and puts it on the table. He turns back to them, hardly bearing to ask, "Wreckage? Was anyone hurt? How bad is the damage?"

Natasha crosses herself. "No one was killed, thank St. Michael."

Anatoly winces. "Seems they were after the costumes and only certain animals, like our little ones."

Durov's throat constricts with such dread that he can't get out a sound to ask any more. Anatoly finally offers, "Miraculously, none of them was harmed except for…S-Sasha." Fighting back tears, Durov shuts his eyes tight and leans into Anatoly, who cradles him through the bars. Durov feels immense relief from Anatoly's caress, but is immediately over-whelmed by the humiliation of his failure. As he starts to break away, he notices Anatoly is wearing their family's sash.

"This is good, Anatoly. You're the head of the family now, with a good woman at your side." He finally gives into his feelings and tears cascade down his broad cheeks. "It's only you now to carry on the Durov name."

Natasha gently breaks in: "Well, I for one, am not giving up. Durov, did Wolfgang tell you anything about a trial?"

Durov collects himself, trying to focus on what Wolfgang told him about the scroll. His recollections are quite muddled because of the shock he's been through. But he manages to go to the table and motion to the scroll next to the inkwell and quill pen. "Wolfgang gave me this scroll to sign. Said because the tsar and the kaiser were cousins, he didn't want an incident. If I sign, I can go home. If not, I spend two years in this cell."

Natasha motions for him to bring the scroll over, then quickly reaches through the bars and swipes it. "Why haven't you signed it already?" She starts to unroll it to read it, but the light is too dim. She hands it to Boris. "Take it over to the torch there and read it, so we can get Durov out of here and return home."

Anatoly's face brightens. "So Anna and I can be married proper."

"And I can have my own act on the high wire," adds Anna.

Boris says, "And I can be a magician in our new circus at home—can't I, Madame Natasha?"

"We'll see about that, but yes... why not. Now what does the scroll say?"

Boris reads by the light of the torch. "It says: 'The Kaiser, in his most magnanimous and generous way, has decided to pardon the Pig Tamer Durov—'"

"How many times must I tell them, I'm not a pig tamer, I'm a pig train—"

Natasha barks, "What does it matter, Durov? What else does it say, Boris?"

Boris reads: "'And that in keeping with the finest circus traditions which the people of the German state of Prussia believe in—'"

Greatly relieved, Durov says, "That doesn't sound so bad. I could put the Durov family name to that. Go on, Boris."

Boris reads ahead, gulps, shows it to Lottie, and says, "Why give them the satisfaction of reading any more, why not just sign it and let's get out of here."

Lottie hesitates, then quickly adds, "That sounds like a very, very good idea. Durov, there's not much more—"

Durov eyes them suspiciously. "Read the rest."

Boris sighs, then reads some more, "'I offer The Kaiser and the German people my sincerest apologies—that's quite nice, actually." Boris looks up hopefully. But Durov points to the scroll, so he keeps reading. "'My sincerest apologies for lying to the people about the glorious Emperor Wilhelm, who has only the good of his people at heart—'"

Durov jumps in: "I told Wolfgang it wasn't a lie to do my act. In fact, Anatoly's costume was quite faithfully rendered, don't you think?"

Natasha says, "But it wouldn't kill you to say it was a lie, since the pig really wasn't the kaiser."

Durov considers this. Then, desperately wanting this whole catastrophe to come to an end, he says, "I suppose not. All right, I'll sign." They all nod vigorously. Durov nods too, but adds, "Just for the sake of accuracy, read the rest, Boris." They all groan.

Boris hums down the page and, with an exaggeratedly mock casual tone, says, "Looks like just boilerplate to me."

He shows it to Lottie, who nods frantically. "Boilerplate, that's all."

"Read it," Durov insists.

Boris sharply exhales, then reads, "'That I have defiled all that is good and honorable about the circus, which I would see if I were more than just a lying bastard pig tamer.'" Boris looks up and winces. "Well, I don't think the term bastard is meant literally, just a figure of speech—"

Durov explodes: "He has no right to make me grovel. To drag my family's reputation through the mud. If you want a blacksmith, you know who's the best. If you want animal trainers, you come to the Durovs. I'm an honest performer. We don't take money from people if we can't give them a good show."

Natasha's tone, restrained at first, becomes increasingly angry. "No one's saying we didn't give them their money's worth. In fact it was quite a show."

Durov staggers under the full weight of these vicious attacks on his honor and his family's unique animal training abilities. It feels like someone has stabbed him in the chest. He whips around to Boris. "Everyone says we're the best at training animals. True magicians with our animals. How can I let them ruin that?"

Boris says, "People will still remember you and your brother."

"For defiling all that's good and honorable about the circus?"

Natasha jumps in. "What do you care what the kaiser wants to tell his people? We can go home and perform there."

Durov tries to clear his mind long enough to weigh the myriad of arguments racing through his head. How much is he just being stubborn, and how much is he honoring a principle worth going to jail for? He looks around to see them all nodding their heads expectantly, silently praying he will sign. Everyone he loves most in the world—now that Sasha's gone. Halfheartedly, he says, "Maybe you're right." Durov hears a huge sigh of relief from the other side of the bars.

Boris adds, "Of course Natasha's right. Let's go back to Russia, and let the German people worry about how repressive the kaiser is."

Durov grudgingly takes the scroll and goes to the table, about to sign with the quill pen and ink Wolfgang has left for that purpose. But something nags at him. He turns to them and says, "But the children...if I sign this, they'll put it in all the newspapers. That I lied to them. That I'm only a bastard pig trainer."

Boris mutters, "Well, technically it says pig tamer, but"—Natasha elbows him—"nevermind."

Durov continues to ponder, reasoning out loud: "They come and laugh at how clever we are. I feel like I protect the children, like I do my animals. They trust me in the same way. To train an animal, you've got to be consistent. If you do one thing one day and another the next, they never know and they never trust. Animals become bitter and vicious that way. So do people. This would be like saying, 'I didn't mean to make you laugh, little children. Ha-ha. I took you in. You trusted me and I fooled you.' That's cruel." He rolls up the scroll. "You might as well beat them as to tell them it was all a lie."

Natasha shouts, "Look, Durov, you call me stubborn. What do you think you're being right now? Can you give up your life with all of us for a few words on a piece of paper?"

Terrible flashes of all his past failures race before Durov's eyes, and he desperately wants to wave them away with the stroke of this quill pen. But he sighs deeply and shakes his head. "My dear ones, I can't sign."

Natasha pleads, "We need you to help rebuild the circus. Durov, I can't do it alone. I'm tired of being alone."

Durov can't bear to see the woman he loves so distraught. But he simply can't bring himself to sign. "Anatoly understands, don't you? If I sign this, he can get anybody to sign a lie about anything he wants. That will give him power over people's minds and thoughts. Over their honor even. Where will it end?"

Natasha sobs uncontrollably. Durov is stricken. He goes to the bars and tries to put his arms around her. Anna cries too, and Anatoly embraces her. Lottie hugs Boris, who looks on with a sad, "I told you so" expression.

Durov straightens himself up, wiping away his tears. "Anatoly, it's up to you to help Natasha get our circus family back to Russia. You are much more capable than you know. Look on the bright side—two years isn't so long. Be sure to get married by a real priest, and if your first child is a girl, name her Sasha."

CHAPTER THIRTY-EIGHT

DUROV CRANES HIS neck through the bars to watch his visitors leave. He sniffles and wipes his nose with his sleeve, muttering to himself, "Two years isn't such a long time. When I get out, we'll have an anniversary celebration for Anatoly and Anna, and I'll drink myself under the table. Maybe she'll have her first child by then. And another on the way. That would be cause for celebration indeed."

He tramps heavily over to the table—his light, balletic step has vanished into the dank of the prison cell. He has just a spark of hope that Natasha will wait for him, then immediately banishes that thought. Too unrealistic. Too much to expect. *She'll probably always be mad at me for not signing that lying confession. I wouldn't blame her.* She shouldn't turn to Ivan in her loneliness. He's as much a womanizer as Nikolai, and she would be horribly humiliated by him too. Surely she's stronger now than she was when she was seduced by that oaf. Since then, she's negotiated with Wolfgang, taken on the role of ringmaster, and done a very fine job. What a woman!

Visualizing her in Nikolai's costume and top hat, he chuckles. Didn't she make the most of it! And wouldn't they have made a good pair, running the circus together—with the same kind of mutual respect his parents showed each other. They depended on each other's strengths to make more of their lives together than they would have separately. He slumps, his normally twinkling eyes blinking sorrow. All that's gone now. He stifles a sob, exhausted from fear and anguish. He tries to take comfort that, at least, Anatoly found a good woman he loves. His brother will surely stand up to Ivan and protect Anna, just like he protected all the little ones.

But, thinking about Sasha, Durov is finally overcome. He sinks down onto the chair next to the table. He tries to avoid another crying jag by looking around. Then he spots the brown paper package. *Good old Boris, smuggling bread and cheese for me. Took more courage than I imagined him capable of.* He hopes Lottie will get Boris to marry her, so they, too, can make a life richer together than apart. He smiles as he thinks of them figuring out a joint act—merging her psychic powers with his traditional sleight-of-hand magician's expertise. Fingering the package of food, Durov glances around to make sure the guards aren't looking and unwraps the brown paper. He has a thought and rips the paper into small squares, which he brings to the trough along the rear of the cell, where the prisoners' excrement flows. *Paper for the toilet. What an unexpected luxury!*

Durov returns to the table and breaks the cheese into small bits. He purses his lips and whistles, calling into the corners of the cell, "Where is my darling Vladimir?" He bends down, searching, then gets a small piece of cheese. "Vladimir? Mikhail? Gregory? Where are you? I have some black bread and cheese for you. It's very precious, and I'm not sure if we'll get any more. Come, my little mice."

He crawls on all fours toward the corner. "For your first trick, you'll learn to stand upright." Durov rips a small corner from the crimson, long-sleeved shirt of his costume. "Then, we work our way up to giving you all tiny red flags to carry and march in unison. When we get back to Russia, that should make the tsar stand up and take note." Durov whistles softly, makes kissing noises as he inches toward the corner of the cell. "We'll be famous! Vladimir? Mikhail? Gregory? My little ones…we have two years to perfect our act."

As they leave the prison and walk back toward what's left of the circus, Anna voraciously chews a fingernail. Her heart breaks to see Anatoly's normally bright and smiling face furrowed with grief. Natasha follows, angrily talking to herself, while Boris and Lottie bring up the rear of their morose little parade. Anna strains to fully comprehend how bad it is. In the distance, through the darkness, she cringes to see the sagging main tent and several wagons turned over. Smoke lingers in the crisp evening air.

Anna turns to Anatoly. "I'm so very sorry that Durov feels he's got to stay here in Germany to uphold your family's honor."

"It's your honor too now, Anna. Since you will be my w-wife as soon as we get home. That is, if you still w-want to marry me."

"Of course I do. And you're right about the Durov family being my family too. I didn't mean to suggest otherwise." She whispers, "It's only that Madame Natasha's so furious, and I think she thinks he's being pigheaded—you should pardon the expression."

"Well, he p-probably is. But if you knew my brother as I do, you'd u-understand how he feels about honor and..." His voice trails off. He manages a weak smile, gingerly takes her delicate hand in both of his, and kisses it. "Anyway, I suppose I can manage. He's always told me I could do more than I ever th-thought."

As they get closer to the circus camp, rage tightens Anna's face. "I wish I had someone so supportive in my life. Ivan never wants me to excel because I might show him up."

Gently stroking her arm where Ivan bruised it, Anatoly says, "P-pardon me for saying this, as he's your brother and all, but that means he really doesn't l-love you. Otherwise, he'd want you to shine in any way you can, just like my brother wants me to."

Anna is terribly confused—happy to think how much the brothers love each other, but saddened to have been totally bereft of that kind of love from her own family after her mother died. She bursts into tears. "I'm sorry, Anatoly. I really can't bear to think of him in that terrible prison for two years."

Anatoly breaks down as well. Natasha catches up to them and envelopes them in her arms. "There, there, my children, I know it's really hard to think about going back to Russia without him. But I'm sure he'll be resourceful enough to survive and come back to us."

Lottie whispers to Boris, "I knew this wasn't going to turn out well. Remember, I had a premonition?"

Boris mumbles, "I suppose we should have listened to your psychic advice when we had the chance. My sleight-of-hand trick hiding the hacksaw didn't work very well, did it? And I almost didn't make it out of there alive—fifty lashes—horrible to think of it." Boris's knees wobble. "I've never been so frightened in all my life—even when my father tried to teach me to swallow a sword and it got stuck in my…well…never mind." He gulps. "I'm sorry I let everyone down."

"Don't be discouraged, Boris," Lottie coos soothingly. "You were under a lot of pressure in there, and Anatoly's hacksaw might not have been the best way to get Durov out of there anyway. Perhaps we need something more subtle."

"You have a better suggestion?"

As Anna listens to Boris and Lottie, she bites the inside of her lip to stifle a moan. She really doesn't want to start off her marriage to Anatoly under such a cloud of anguish. And, not that she doesn't think Anatoly is perfectly competent, but she would prefer—as everyone else in the circus would—to have Durov lead them back over the mountains. With desperation in her voice, she turns to Lottie. "Can you think of any other way? We'll try anything."

"Anything except going back into that dreadful place," Boris interjects.

Anna cringes as Natasha explodes: "How else do you think we can get him out?"

"We can risk going back in there," Anatoly says, "but we can't get him out if he doesn't want to come."

Natasha strides back and forth, thinking out loud: "So we have to make him want to come out. How can we do that?"

They pace around the sagging canvas tent, the turned-over benches, and the piles of shredded costumes. Finally, Natasha says, "Lottie, can you do one of your psychic things? How about putting yourself in his place and imagining what could motivate him to voluntarily agree to sign that declaration?"

Boris says sarcastically, "Yes, Lottie. Maybe you can dematerialize him, make him disappear in his cell, transport him into the ether, and we can collect him out here."

"Disappear, you say?" Lottie retorts. "What if he doesn't disappear into thin air, but after he signs his name, maybe his signature disappears?" She adds, sardonically, "Could you arrange that, with your sleight-of-hand, Boris?"

They start pacing again. Anna prays to the Virgin that they come up with something.

Boris paces, then stops, huffing in his deep, precisely articulated voice, "No need to be sarcastic, Lottie. I realize I failed you all just now, but...wait a minute...his signature would just disappear. Disappear...disappear..."

They stop short to listen to Boris. He swishes his magician's robe. "That's it!" Scurrying around him, they listen intently as he exclaims triumphantly, "That's it, don't you see? It's as plain as the nose on a clown's face."

Natasha leans down, nose to nose with Boris. "What is?"

Boris clears his throat, strokes his goatee, and smiles broadly, knowingly. "Disappearing ink."

Anna has a moment of pure, joyful hope. "Disappearing ink! Of course!" She pauses, confused. "What is that?"

Meanwhile, Lottie hugs Boris. "Of course, Boris. You're brilliant."

"But what is it?" Anatoly says.

Boris is jubilant. "It's the kind of ink you use to write. When you first write with it, it looks like it's real. Except hours later, it completely fades and there's nothing left."

Anatoly scratches his mop of curly hair. "But where does it go?"

"It just vanishes into thin air."

"It'll be like he never signed in the first place," Natasha says with glee.

Hugs and kisses all around. Claps on Boris's back, as they cheer him.

But after they've had their initial celebration, Anna's feeling of joyous, cautious optimism fizzles. Weakly, she says, "What if they come after us when they discover there's no signature? We can't move the wagons and the animals fast enough to outrun them."

That stumps them, until Anatoly comes up with a thought of his own, which Anna finds a rare but welcome development. Anatoly says, "I don't think Wolfgang will follow us. Remember…he said the tsar and the kaiser don't want—"

Natasha fills in the rest: "An international incident."

Anna isn't so sure, but she doesn't want to throw cold water on Anatoly's idea. Perhaps it's just wishful thinking, but it's the wishful thinking of the man she loves. "All right. Let's say it works, how are we going to pull it off?"

Lottie jumps in, "That's the easy part. Don't you remember the inkwell Wolfgang put on the table in Durov's cell? And the quill pen he left for Durov to sign?"

Natasha is ecstatic. "Yes, yes. I have an inkwell just like that on my desk in my wagon. All we have to do is fill my inkwell with Boris's disappearing ink, smuggle it in, get it to that table, and smuggle the old inkwell out. Durov can sign without Wolfgang any the wiser."

Tears of joy well up in Anna's eyes. "We can leave for Russia."

Anatoly gets it now. "And after we're gone—"

"Presto vanisho, no signaturo." Boris brims with pride, and Anna claps her hands in celebration.

Boris continues, "Wonderful, wonderful. I know a potion to make up a bottle of disappearing ink. But who's going to get the new inkwell into the cell and smuggle the old one out?"

Everyone turns slowly to look intently at Boris, who starts to shake. Anna's joyous mood crashes like a lead balloon.

CHAPTER THIRTY-NINE

B Y THE TIME they return from the prison, it's pitch black. So Natasha asks the crew to bring gaslight lanterns into what's left of the main tent—and to clear away the rubble. She desperately wants Boris to succeed in conjuring up the disappearing ink, as it's clearly their last chance to save Durov. Despite how angry she is that he wouldn't sign, Natasha admires Durov's integrity and how, at all costs, he insists on maintaining his family's honor. *That could be my family too. Wouldn't I want him to uphold our honor?* But then she chastises herself for getting ahead of things and tries to focus on the task at hand.

Natasha watches expectantly as Boris manages to get his father's magic box open again. He searches along the inside and extracts several snuffboxes of powders, some small vials of liquids, and a number of flasks. Her strong hands tremble as she and Lottie help him set these items out along a bench, while the four dwarf brothers install themselves as a cheering section perched on the top bench—the only other bench left intact.

Boris mixes powders and liquids in various combinations, testing each mixture as he goes along.

"We know you can do this," says Pasha.

Masha says, "Of course we do."

"We always knew you'd be more than a clown," adds Vasha.

Max quips, "What's wrong with being a clown?"

Pasha says, "Nothing's wrong with being a clown,"

"But isn't it better," Masha adds, "to be a magician who can conjure up anything he wants?"

Vasha says, "Boris, how about conjuring up some tasty goulash?"

"And some beets," Max licks his lips. "Everyone's hungry, and there's hardly anything left in the burnt-out canteen."

Suddenly, an ominous bubbling emanates from Boris's flask. Billows of nasty black smoke curl up and through its narrow neck. The flask shakes precipitously and explodes, sending pieces of glass flying and cutting Boris's hand.

"What in God's name is happening, Boris?" Natasha screeches.

Lottie ducks behind the bench and covers her head with one of her shawls. "Good heavens, Boris. Perhaps you should mix a little less of each. Try it out first."

Boris holds his wounded hand and, in a wounded tone, says, "Maybe I'm not as psychic as you are. I'm just trying to find the formula as fast as I can."

Lottie peaks from under her shawl, slowly rises, and tenderly wraps one of her scarves around Boris's hand. "Of course we know you're doing your best. But we want you in one piece."

"You do?" Boris asks shyly, as they look at each other lovingly.

Natasha can hardly contain her anxiety. "All right, you two. There's work to be done."

"Yes," says Pasha.

Masha asks, "Can we help?"

"Let us help you with the powder," adds Vasha.

"We're good at throwing powder around and into the audience—sometimes in place of water in the pail, but not always." Max grins weakly.

Boris seethes, "So it was you who left that water in the pail that I threw at that bosomy lady back in—"

"Never mind, Boris," Natasha breaks in. "Get to the ink, will you."

Before Boris can mix anymore, the four dwarf brothers scamper down from the top bench and grab flasks and powders and vials of liquids.

Boris yells, "*Nyet...nyet*! You'll get them all mixed up."

Pasha says, "Isn't that the idea?"

"Of course it is," adds Masha.

The dwarf brothers juggle the flasks and the powders and the vials of liquids. Suddenly, the dark liquid in one of the flasks disappears.

"Did you see that?" asks Vasha.

"By St. Basil," Pasha adds, "the liquid was there one minute, and then it wasn't."

"Well, there you have it," says Masha.

Max declares, "Disappearing ink!"

Natasha is incredulous, but delighted. That moron magician Boris and those crazy dwarf brothers have inadvertently conjured up the formula. These circus people certainly are odd, but they do have heart, and they clearly only want the best for Durov. And she has to admit she does as well, despite his stubborn refusal to sign.

"What have you got there?" She grabs the flask and holds it straight out, praying it won't explode.

"Let me see that," Boris says. He grabs the flask and whips it back onto the bench. Lottie pulls out a feather, they dip it into the liquid, and Boris starts to write on a ripped up poster. "What shall we say?" Boris asks.

Lottie snickers, "Let's write a note to the kaiser asking for his forgiveness."

Natasha laughs—these circus people certainly do have a sense of humor. "That's a great idea," she says.

Boris writes and writes and writes, turning the poster over, writing sideways and around the edges in a circle.

"You're not Tolstoy," Natasha barks. "We just need to know the ink will disappear."

Smiling weakly, Boris stops writing. Lottie holds up the poster, and they all stand reading it, twisting their heads around and moving from front to back to follow Boris's circular scribbling.

"Nice words," says Pasha.

Masha adds, "Very eloquent."

"Poetic too," offers Vasha.

"Tolstoy couldn't have written it better," says Max.

As they stand reading—and watching—and reading—and watching—they shuffle nervously.

"How long will it take?" quips Natasha, frustrated.

Boris strokes his goatee thoughtfully, then shakes his head. "Who knows?"

CHAPTER FORTY

IN THE MISTY dawn, on the morning after the destruction of the circus, Anna kneels next to Anatoly on a pile of straw in the pig corral. Smoke lingers from the burned canteen tent and the wagon that overturned and caught fire in the melee. Anna struggles to help Anatoly nurse Sasha's five orphaned piglets, who are squealing pathetically. She swallows hard, fighting against her despair, as she works with him to gently nudge their teeny mouths onto the fingers of a glove he's filled with warm milk and pricked to open small nursing holes. Anna giggles as one of the piglets latches onto her finger and starts sucking. She glances over at Anatoly, admiring how he pets them. He softly murmurs encouragement as he coaxes them to suck and paw at the glove with their miniature hooves. She can't imagine how he knows to do this, but she's sure it means he'll make a wonderful father.

Suddenly, Anna sits back on her heels, shuddering. Will she make a good mother? Could she possibly have the patience to deal with a little, helpless creature, crying hysterically and looking to her to meet all its earthly needs? A searing ache rises in her gut. She longs to be comforted herself, rather than to be the one doing the comforting. A moment of panic—she's certain she's not ready to have children anytime soon, or maybe not anytime. And just when she has within her grasp the promise of her own high-wire attraction—with her own beautiful sequined costumes. Would she have to give it all up to have a child? Being as slim as she is, she experiences another terrifying thought—the dangers of childbirth. She flinches, scrunching up her heart-shaped face as she looks, in horror, at Sasha's motherless piglets.

"They're just little pigs," Anatoly teases softly. "Not some kind of monsters." He makes sweet kissing noises as he gently re-inserts a gloved finger into a piglet's mouth. Just then, Anna is startled to see something hit him like a lightning bolt—he sits straight up, raises his head to the heavens, and starts to wail, drowning out all the piglets' squeals. "They need their mother. Poor Sasha…poor, poor…"

Anna lets him cry a moment, then cradles him. He leans into her embrace, then wraps his arms around the piglets and cradles them too, as if they were human quintuplets. Anna looks at him—having such a kind and sensitive man isn't such a bad thing after all. And, strangely, the act of offering her love to comfort him actually makes her feel loved by him—a dynamic quite alien to her but deliciously surprising.

Ivan walks briskly by, his arms full of costumes and rigging to pack up for the trip back to Russia. He stops short when he sees Anna and Anatoly slumped together in the animal corral. "Look at the happy couple. I knew it wouldn't be long before Anna Tatianna, my dear sister, you'd be rolling in the mud with your new family."

Livid, Anna jumps up, races across the corral, and pummels Ivan. He laughs and grabs both her delicate hands in one of his and twists her around. "Still gnawing your finger nails? Can't satisfy your anxiety any other way—even though you're married now?" She tries to break away, but he holds her fast. "Wait a minute, now I come to think of it, Anna Tatianna, you still haven't told me how you and Anatoly managed to be wed last night. I didn't see any Russian Orthodox priests wandering around. You know it wouldn't be legal if you were married by a German priest." He gives her arm another sharp pull. "Explain to me how it all happened."

Seething, Anatoly swiftly but carefully lays the piglets down onto the straw and props them up to continue feeding. Then he rushes over to free Anna. "You l-let her g-go."

But Ivan holds on. "You and who else is going to make me? I'm still her brother, and unless you're lawfully married, she's still under my control."

Feeling her world caving in, Anna desperately stomps on her brother's foot, causing him to release her. He shoves her against Anatoly, who holds her away.

Natasha rushes up to them, screaming at Ivan, "What's going on? This is no time to fight. We've got to pack up the circus, make one last trip to the prison to spring Durov, and head back to Russia."

Seething, Ivan says, "I thought that son of a pig was too pigheaded to sign. I heard he's going to rot in jail for two years."

Anatoly lunges for Ivan, but Natasha steps between.

Out of Anatoly's reach, Ivan smiles wryly and takes Natasha's arm. "Of course, I can take charge of getting the circus back home, if you will permit me."

Natasha jerks away, shouting, "I will permit nothing of the sort. We can manage without your interference. Get out of my sight…go and pack up."

Anna is delighted to see Natasha put Ivan in his place, once again. But a horrific sinking feeling washes over her as Ivan says, "I'll go for now. But I'm sure this so-called marriage is a sham. If she's compromised herself, I'll be stuck with her forever—no man will want to marry her." He pivots on his heel, calling back over his shoulder, "Except perhaps Wolfgang."

Distraught, Anna feels weak as a kitten. While Anatoly comforts her, Natasha yells after Ivan, "How could you wish Wolfgang on your very own sister?"

Ivan's faint voice returns, "I can always get another aerialist for the trapeze. And if Wolfgang won't let us go back to Russia without marrying her, well then—"

Anna whispers to Anatoly, "He wouldn't dare...would he?" Anatoly hugs her, but she can't help feeling a dread like she's never known. She is sinking, feeling faint...

CHAPTER FORTY-ONE

As Anna collapses onto the straw, all of Natasha's motherly love for her comes rushing to the fore. As she and Anatoly tend to her, the piglets run over and nudge her. Natasha's stomach turns as she shoos them away.

But Anatoly stops her. "They just want to comfort her. Pigs are very intuitive—sometimes even more than people…and especially more than Ivan."

Natasha moves aside to let Anatoly minister to Anna. Feeling extremely vulnerable herself, she wishes Durov were here to fight Ivan and save Anna. Anatoly bends over Anna, rubs her forehead, and kisses her cheeks. She opens her eyes and looks up at Anatoly, who smiles his love and encouragement down upon her.

Natasha is touched so profoundly that she goes weak in the knees and collapses down next to them. She is astonished how, in the midst of their horrific situation, this young couple can be so loving. It's a sense of true love she's longed for but, until she met Durov, found utterly elusive. Natasha sits for a moment, wallowing with the piglets, then looks around, snaps to, and decides she's not going to be defeated in a pigpen in a field in Germany. It's up to her not only to get Durov to agree to sign with the disappearing ink, but also to keep Anna away from Wolfgang. She attempts to gather her wits and find the strength to figure it all out, but that, too, eludes her and she crumbles back down onto the straw.

Boris, Lottie, and Lottie's brother Bronzy, come along, lugging mounds of trash toward the fire heap and organizing things to pack up. As Natasha looks up at them from the straw, she feels a rush of gratitude. She's relieved to see the bear-like Bronzy helping to get the circus on its way—huffing as he carries four times what either the diminutive Boris or the even smaller Lottie can manage.

Then it strikes her: somehow they're going to have to get Ivan out of commission and prevent Wolfgang from pursuing Anna; and Bronzy and Lottie are just the people to do it. Of course, they can't use the magic box again, because Ivan, despite being obtuse and self-centered, would immediately figure it out. But Boris is also going to have to be enlisted because he holds the greatest sway over Lottie. And while Natasha hasn't figured it out yet, she knows that Lottie and Bronzy hold the key to thwarting Ivan while she's busy springing Durov.

She decides to work on Boris to get on Lottie's good side. In her most solicitous, deepest, and melodious tones, Natasha starts to flatter Boris: "You're such a genius. A real magician, I'd say...now that you got that disappearing ink to disappear."

Boris articulates, in his precisely articulate voice, "Why thank you, Madame Natasha. I am truly gratified you noticed."

"Of course. How could I not notice what a brilliant magician you are."

"Really?"

"Certainly. When we get back to Mother Russia, I'll be happy to sponsor you as a full-fledged magician in our new circus."

Boris twitters his gratitude. "How thoughtful of you, Madame. I am happy to make my contribution. To have Durov sign with my new invention." He reaches into his robe, producing the inkwell from Natasha's wagon. "I am eternally grateful you promised to smuggle my disappearing ink into the prison without me. I couldn't possibly go anywhere near that dreadful place again. The very thought of Wolfgang gives me the psychological shivers, no offense, Lottie."

"Of course, of course," Natasha says. "We're all set to return to Russia, and we might have just enough to salvage from this rubble to start rehearsing a new circus—with your new magician's act—except for one teensy, itsy-bitsy problem."

Boris, Lottie, and Bronzy look at her, puzzled.

Natasha takes a deep breath and launches into the plan she's making up on the spot.

CHAPTER FORTY-TWO

THE PERFORMERS AND the crew work to get the wagons ready for their journey back to Russia. Meanwhile, Natasha fervently hopes that this morning, the circus will have its last and most auspicious performance in Germany. She gathers together a not-very-impressive assortment of circus acts: the four dwarf brothers with the cannon they use in their act, Boulkari with his trick dog and the net the dog loves to bounce in, Lottie with all her draping lavender shawls and plumed and turbaned finery, strongman Bronzy with his "ring the bell" mallet and bell—as well as two tall poles he carries like matchsticks, one under each arm—and finally, Anatoly with his crisscrossed and draped trapeze rigging.

Although Natasha's ringmaster's costume is tattered beyond recognition, she improvises with a variety of remnants that Anna has quickly, and quite miraculously, sewn to fit her—more or less. As promised, she leaves Boris at the camp, asking him to care for Anna, just in case Wolfgang slips back looking for the girl. She sincerely appreciates how enthusiastically Boris agreed—especially after she threatened to make sure he'd never perform as a magician anywhere in Russia. But she is, after all, indebted to the little man for pulling out all the stops to sweet-talk Lottie into accompanying her today.

As their little parade comes within sight of the fortress and the prison within, Natasha sees Ivan marching purposefully ahead. She scurries forward to catch up with him before he can summon Wolfgang to tell him Anna isn't actually married. She calls to him, "Ivan...how nice...I mean, isn't it nice we've all got the same idea?"

Ivan puffs up his well-muscled chest and looks at her askance. "What idea is that, Natasha?"

"To leave Germany right after your grand public relations triumph."

"My what?"

Natasha holds her breath and proceeds. "Why, your final, amazing, impressive act in front of the vast, extensive, and appreciative audience in the fortress up ahead."

Ivan sneers. "How am I going to manage any kind of act? The circus is in ruins."

She motions behind her. "Ah, but you see, if we can't bring the audience to the circus, we can bring the circus to the audience. You've heard of performing before the troops? Entertainers showing the public's appreciation for the unwavering service of the soldiers?"

"Frankly, I've never heard of such a thing."

"It's becoming all the rage. Especially before an army attacks a...ah...any country nearby. It'll be in all the papers: how the talented Russian circus performers—and especially the magnificent Ivan Ivanovich Zubov, trapeze artist—entertained the kaiser's troops to improve their...ah...morale."

"I thought their morale quite high already—they took great pleasure in destroying our circus last night."

"But they didn't get to see the best part. Your amazing, incredible, phenomenal last act—the climax, as it were." She plows forward. *How can I keep from gagging as I flatter this egotistical fop?* Natasha blushes seductively, then continues, "The climax of the entire circus. Imagine being deprived of that. You are so clever, Ivan."

"I am? Well of course, everyone says so." He hesitates, then adds, "How do you mean?"

"The notoriety of staging a performance outside their fortress will bring accolades throughout Germany and beyond. When the German women hear about it, they will swoon at your silky, slippered feet."

Ivan turns back to study the motley circus crew with their assorted, and considerably abbreviated, equipment. "I can't perform with any of that."

"But Bronzy's brought two poles, and Anatoly can put up your platform and rigging. Boulkari's even brought the net his trick dog loves to bounce in and—"

"A net would detract from the magnificence of my act."

"Of course, just a thought. But you would be missing out on all the notoriety."

"Well, if I did agree to perform, I don't see a ladder to climb up to my platform."

"Glad you brought that up. See there—" Natasha points to the cannon the four dwarf brothers struggle mightily to drag along.

Ivan cracks his knuckles and shakes his head. "So?"

She grins. "You know how, in their act, Pasha, Masha, and Max shoot Vasha out of the cannon, high up and into the net? How about they shoot you up and you land, with your usual grace, on your platform? What an amazing—actually explosive—feat to start your act!" *By St. Basil, I hope he buys this!* Natasha motions to the ramparts of the fortress. "Can't you see the troops lining up all along the walls, applauding wildly for you? We've even invited the press from town. They're all going to be there to watch—and report in incredible, excruciating detail—on your amazing, oh-so-muscular and graceful—did I say graceful?—prowess."

Natasha tries to quell the pounding in her chest as she and Lottie race through the prison corridor, listening with delight to the laughter and excited applause from atop the ramparts outside. Snickering, she recalls how Bronzy positioned the two poles and Anatoly fastened the platform and the rigging aloft. Meanwhile, Ivan strutted on the field in front of the walls, bowing to the soldiers, while Pasha, Masha, Vasha, and Max wheeled the cannon around and around after him. Ivan even jumped up and did a series of lewd acrobatics on top of the cannon, making broad, seductive movements, crassly playing to the German soldiers, who made obscene gestures and hooted and hollered for more.

Now, as they approach Durov's cell, Natasha's heart stops when she sees Wolfgang's gangly frame slouched in a chair just outside. He's snoring thunderously, the tip of his sabre rattling rhythmically on the stone floor with each deafening exhalation.

As they gingerly approach, Natasha can just make out that Wolfgang is talking in his sleep. "Elsa, my loyal horse. My Elsa...no...not jealous of...new filly...Anna." He snorts, bears his teeth, and whinnies. Entirely in his deep sleep, he straightens up and appears to be taking the reins, laying them sharply on both sides of what he's riding. "Anna...yes...my Anna...will learn."

In outraged disbelief, Natasha whispers, "The monster."

Uproarious laughter from outside makes its way down into the stone corridor. Natasha flinches, fearing the applause will turn into a massive liability, should it awaken Wolfgang before they can switch the inkwell. She prays that Wolfgang's inkwell still sits on the table in Durov's cell.

Natasha murmurs to Lottie, "Where is Boris's inkwell?"

Lottie uncovers layer after layer of scarves and shawls, producing a

286

small object wrapped in yet another scarf. "I wrapped it tightly, so nothing would spill."

Natasha, trying to tamp down her rising panic, whispers, "How are we going to get past Wolfgang?"

Lottie taps her temple, signaling that she has an idea. She hands Natasha the inkwell, plucks the plume from her turban, closes her eyes tightly, and swishes it across her forehead, mumbling, "Elsa...not Anna...Elsa...not Anna." She tiptoes to Wolfgang, takes a deep breath, and swishes the feather across—and just inches from—his forehead.

Holding her breath, Natasha keenly watches as Lottie keenly watches Wolfgang's face. His mustache curls up, then down, then up again, as he nibbles his lower lip, muttering, "Elsa...not Anna..."

Lottie beams and looks over at Natasha, who grins, pleased that Lottie's psychic transfer of thought appears to be working. Suddenly, Wolfgang snorts and whinnies in his sleep. Lottie is so startled that she lets the feather fly. Just before Wolfgang is about to settle back down to continue sleeping, the feather lands sideways on the waxed and tightly curled tips of his mustache, where it begins to ride up and down with his resumed snoring. The two women stare as one: Natasha, tall, angular, and broad and Lottie, petite, gossamer, and soft. They follow the feather on its journey...up and down...up and down.

Natasha must act immediately to substitute the inkwell while Wolfgang slumbers, but she's too terrified to budge, lest she create a movement of air that would dislodge the feather and awaken Wolfgang.

A soft voice comes from within the cell. "Who's out there?" Durov emerges from the bleak shadows. The morning sun has not yet penetrated the small, high window, so he blinks, trying to adjust to the light of the torch in the corridor.

Durov is disheveled, his hair unkempt, and his circus clothes ragged, even scruffier than when they'd left him last evening. Natasha is over-whelmed by sympathy. He's aged a year in only one night. She's furious at him for being so impossibly stubborn, but that quickly dissipates as he visibly brightens when he sees her.

Natasha touches her finger to her lips so he won't call out. Then she softly moves to him. She cautiously inserts her hand in between the bars.

"What's this? You brought me some more black bread and chee—"

"Something much better." She hands him the inkwell wrapped in Lottie's scarf. "Take this and trade it for Wolfgang's inkwell on the table. Quickly—before he wakes." She turns to Lottie. "Can you keep him asleep a few minutes more?"

Sweating profusely, Lottie stares intently and breathes in time with Wolfgang.

Natasha shudders as laughter and cheers penetrate from the ramparts above.

Durov looks upward. "What's that?"

Natasha smirks. "Ivan's performance of a lifetime. You know the cannon the four dwarf brothers use in their act?"

"I certainly do. Every show, I have to help Max get the right mixture of powder, so Pasha and Masha don't knock Vasha senseless. Too much and Vasha flies well beyond the net. Too little and he lands on his head, just in front of the net. Tricky business, especially with Boulkari's trick dog yapping, always trying to bounce into the net."

"For once, it doesn't matter how well you taught Max. They're about to get Ivan into that cannon. He thinks they're going to shoot him up onto a platform Bronzy's rigged to perform for the troops."

"Why would he want to perform for the troops? Their morale already seems pretty high—"

"Never mind."

"But Ivan's much too big to fit," Durov continues thoughtfully. "You've got to be small like a dwarf—have some space around you to launch properly."

Natasha bounces gently on her heels, delighted how clever she is.

"They're not actually going to shoot him out. They're just going to let him climb in and get stuck."

"That won't be very entertaining."

Smothering a groan, Natasha looks over at Lottie and Wolfgang. "How's he doing?"

Lottie, not wanting to move her head away from Wolfgang's rhythm, waves her hand to reassure Natasha.

Natasha continues, "Ivan knows Anna and Anatoly aren't married. He's going to give up Anna to Wolfgang, so they'll let us leave."

"Why that son of a—" Enraged, Durov starts to shake the bars, but Natasha quickly stops him.

"Quiet, please. We don't have much time. Listen…you've got to substitute this inkwell and give me that one from the table, before Wolfgang wakes up. Then you can feel free to sign the proclamation and we can leave."

Natasha's pride wells up. She's had a horror of prisons, ever since she moved into Nikolai's disgustingly filthy, prison-like wagon. Nikolai humiliated her at every turn. But she's pleased with herself to have overcome all that. She's the one who figured out how to save Durov, save Anna, and save their little circus. Her father never would have approved of her consorting with all these madcap people—or of her falling in love with a pig trainer. But in the world she inhabits now, she's about to realize the greatest possible success. This is more important than walking down the grand staircase at the Winter Palace in St. Petersburg in an ill-fitting ball gown, flanked by men her father had to bribe to escort her. What she's doing at this moment—on her own and by her own wits—is what's most important in her life now. Supporting this brilliant, creative man with revolutionary views that will change the method of training animals in the whole of Russia—and even throughout Europe. Perhaps even bring about a fundamental, behavioral change in how men treat women—as long as the women keep their husbands' vodka carefully hidden away.

Durov weighs the new inkwell in his hand and sighs heavily. "I'm sorry, Natasha. You've gone to so much trouble for me, but I've already told you why I can't sign."

With unshakeable confidence, which renders her totally unstoppable, Natasha says, "Oh, but with this ink, you can sign. Trust me."

CHAPTER FORTY-THREE

D UROV IS IMPRESSED and deeply moved by Natasha's courage, especially with Wolfgang slumped not a meter away, albeit snoring loudly.
If the dragoon were to awaken and discover her plot, she'd find herself in
an adjoining cell, and neither of them would ever get back home. Natasha
is whispering something that seems to be extremely important, although
he barely hears her—he's marveling at the risk she's taking and how
deeply she must care in order to come up with such a dangerous and outrageously inventive plan. Still, how long will the ink remain visible? Will
the Germans let them cross the mountains, once they discover the trick?
Or, as Natasha vehemently argues, will they be all too happy to bid them
good riddance and avoid a family rift between the kaiser and the tsar?

In his gut, Durov knows that Natasha must leave this very minute
and take with her the poor pint-sized Lottie—glued as she is to watching
a feather that has somehow miraculously settled horizontally across
Wolfgang's handlebar mustache. Odd, how it floats up and down with his
impressive, thunderous snores.

Natasha breaks in: "Durov, did you hear me? Take this inkwell, and
exchange it for the one on the table."

Emboldened by Natasha's urgency, he decides that if this woman loves him that much, for once, he's going to allow himself to be the one who is protected. Perhaps his penance is finally over. Maybe, for all the good deeds he's done to raise his brother and help the circus folk all these years, he deserves a bit of happiness. Since his arrest, his feet have felt impossibly leaden as he's paced his small cell. But now, he tiptoes softly, in his familiar balletic fashion, lifting his bulky frame nearly off the stone floor as he virtually dances to the table to make the switch. As he starts back with Wolfgang's inkwell from the table, the dragoon sneezes—sending Lottie flying backward and landing on the stone floor in a puddle of scarves and shawls, her turban askew atop her head.

Durov stands stock still, praying Wolfgang won't awaken. He watches in horror as the feather, knocked upward by the sneeze, wafts slowly downward, floating in curlicues and threatening to land bulls-eye, nub down, in Wolfgang's recurrently gaping mouth. Natasha rushes over to try to blow the feather away, while Durov strains to see. *It's going to be all my fault if she gets caught.*

Lottie rapidly collects herself, and Durov anxiously watches as she and Natasha play a kind of terrible badminton with their sharp breaths, trying to move the feather away from Wolfgang. More applause and laughter from outside permeates the stone corridor. Durov is certain this will be the last straw, and sure enough, Wolfgang wakes with a watery-blue, bleary-eyed stammer. He looks directly upward at two pairs of ladies' breasts heaving and sighing above him.

Wolfgang appears to be transfixed as, for the moment, he doesn't move. Then he lets out a ferocious bellow and pushes his arms upward, sending Lottie and Natasha aloft, subsequently landing hard on either side of him. Durov quickly hides Wolfgang's inkwell behind his back. Natasha motions to Lottie to follow her lead as they both crawl in circles in front of Wolfgang's highly polished boots.

Natasha jerks her head toward Lottie and, for Wolfgang's benefit, moans, "They must be around here, somewhere."

Durov watches the women in admiration, thinking how maybe the dwarf brothers should accept women into their clown act, seeing as they can be most entertaining crawling about like that. Lottie creeps closer to the cell. While Natasha diverts Wolfgang's attention by lifting up one boot and then the other to look underneath, Lottie flings her hand up for Durov to deposit Wolfgang's inkwell, which she promptly stashes under one of her shawls.

Wolfgang allows his boots to be moved twice. Then he stomps up from his chair, nearly crushing Natasha's hand. He roars, as much as possible, in his high-pitched, warbled voice: "What is the meaning of this? I thought you people was on your way back to Russia."

Durov takes a deep breath, as he feels he must do something to contribute to the ruse. "They were, Sergeant Major. But Natasha here is so fond of horses, aren't you, Madame? That she had to bring Elsa one last present, didn't you, Madame?" Playing along, Natasha shakes her head, while Durov reaches into his pocket for some leftover slices of apple meant to reward Sasha for performing her helmet trick. As he hands them to Wolfgang, Durov chokes up, visualizing his dearly departed pig.

Natasha finishes his thought. "There they are! *Da...Da...* I was looking for them. We really wanted to give Elsa a parting gift, on behalf of our little circus."

Wolfgang looks askance at them. "I don't know what you think you're doing here—"

"Oh, please. You know how much our circus folk love our animals," Natasha says, as Durov thrusts the slices of apple into Wolfgang's bony hands.

"And Elsa became adopted as one of our circus family, with her marvelous ability to perform, given all the taming you did," Durov adds, choking back bile rising in his throat at having to flatter Wolfgang by using the term *taming.*

Wolfgang shuffles his feet, looking downright grateful. "Right nice a' you folks. No hard feelings?"

Natasha jumps in: "Hard feelings? Us?" She looks directly at Durov, as she adds, "In fact, I think Durov wants to make amends and sign your proclamation after all, don't you?"

Durov stares intently at Natasha, admiring all she's done for him. But he hesitates, as he thoughtfully surveys Wolfgang. There's one last thing that must be done before he feels justified in gaining his freedom. "Well, I'm considering it, but—"

"But what?" Natasha squawks.

Durov calmly continues, "Wolfgang, I realize it means a great deal to you to avoid having Russia embarrass Germany. I understand you found our act offensive, although we didn't mean any disrespect—well, maybe we meant a little disrespect, but only in the way of good fun that is traditional in all circuses. And I know how much you love the circus."

Wolfgang bashfully swings his glossy boot back and forth. "You got that right."

Encouraged, Durov gears himself up, trying to avoid making eye contact with Natasha, who is swearing under her breath.

Durov adds, "Just so you understand, when we make fun of someone, it's only because we think highly enough of that person to do so. Otherwise, we wouldn't bother."

Wolfgang scratches his head. "I ain't so sure there's much difference."

"Oh, but there is. So I'm going to ask you to understand one more thing before I agree to sign."

Durov sees Natasha, beside herself, wringing her hands.

Wolfgang looks suspicious, but nods for Durov to continue.

"When we say we have a circus family, we mean just that. And just like you'd go to any length to protect the kaiser, who is the head of your family, so to speak, we feel obliged to show the same loyalty to protect all the members of our family. Including our little trapeze girl, Anna Tatianna."

Durov waits for a response from Wolfgang, who seems to be having trouble absorbing what he's saying. Since Wolfgang hasn't immediately exploded, it must be a good sign. Durov gingerly proceeds, "So if you will agree to let us all go back to Russia, including the happy couple, so to speak, I will sign."

Out of the corner of his eye, Durov sees a look of admiration spread across Natasha's face. Lottie takes the end of her topmost shawl to wipe her moist eyes. This nearly causes Wolfgang's inkwell to clatter to the stones, but she grabs it just in time.

Wolfgang chews his upper lip, gathering a swath of his mustache into his mouth. "That little filly was right pretty." He leans way down and says, under his breath, "But truth be told, a bit scrawny for my kind a' life."

Durov eagerly takes up the thought: "I'm sorry to say you're absolutely, positively, completely correct. She's a delicate little creature and probably wouldn't have done you as proud as...as...your Elsa."

Wolfgang stares at the slices of apple in his hands and starts to blubber. "You people really are good to your animals. That goes a long way in my book. I'm right sorry we couldn't a' met under better circumstances."

Durov is sincerely inclined to agree with Wolfgang—better circumstances would have been vastly preferred. He breathes a huge sigh of relief that Natasha's plan is working, and that it appears they will all be going home—all but his dear, departed Sasha.

CHAPTER FORTY-FOUR

STEEP MOUNTAINS LOOM ahead under a crystalline sky. Anna proudly sits in the front carriage of her circus wagon next to Anatoly. Her prized porcelain tub is secured within, and Anatoly has hitched the Durov wagon, with the cage for the little pigs, in tandem behind. To spread the load of the wagons and the cage, Anatoly has rigged a double harness for his own mule as well as Anna's mule, Daisy. But Daisy, seeming to sense the forthcoming effort, pulls up for a rest.

"Here, Anatoly, would you please take these dandelions for her?" Anna hands him a bunch from her basket.

Anatoly flashes her a big, boyish grin. "What a nice treat!" He playfully mocks eating a dandelion. "I always taste our animals' food first, to make sure it's safe and nutritious."

Anna feels an unfamiliar peace as she watches Anatoly jump down, stroke, and feed both mules. She's amazed that any man could be so solicitous of his animals—creatures Ivan only disparaged and abused. She looks back along the caravan to the wagon Ivan smugly drives, with their father sitting stoically next to him.

She giggles and asks Anatoly to tell her again what happened at the fortress when they were rescuing Durov.

Anatoly strokes the mules and grins. "You want to hear it again?

Anna vigorously nods. "I could listen to what happened to Ivan a thousand times and still want to hear it again."

Anatoly jumps back onto the buggy next to Anna—she leans against him, visualizing and giggling.

Anatoly says, "Well the dwarf brothers paraded Ivan around the parade grounds, stuck in the dwarfs' cannon. He was howling."

Anna pantomimes Ivan howling. She snorts and laughs.

Anatoly continues, "And the more the soldiers applauded, the more he screamed. Until Durov, Natasha, and Lottie made it out of the prison. When they were clear, Bronzy, in his strongman costume, marched forward and worked with all four dwarfs as they comically strained...and tugged...and pushed...and pulled to lift Ivan up and free him."

Anna flushes with delight remembering, after they were back in camp, how the dwarf brothers pleaded with Ivan to add his cannon performance to their act. Bronzy earnestly promised to rescue him every night. But Ivan, aghast at the outrageous insult, turned heel in his slippers and stomped off to pack for the trip home.

"And you, my dear Anna, are free from Wolfgang. Thanks to Durov's pigheaded stubbornness, holding out for one last thing before he signed."

Anatoly gets Daisy and his own mule moving again. *It's amazing,* she thinks, *how he can cajole such stubborn beasts into working together. Perhaps it will be the same with our children. Together, we will gently but firmly reason with them—that was how it was with mother. And we won't simply discipline them in the service of some parental sense of power and ego. Who knows,* she muses, *it might be possible to overcome years of all that horrible conditioning by Papa Sergey and Ivan. I might be able to allow myself to love and be loved in a real family of my own— not just in my daydreams.*

Anna looks up ahead at Durov, who confidently steers Natasha's wagon at the head of the caravan. She's delighted that he's acquired a newfound pride, which she can hear in their easy banter—Durov's sure voice and Natasha's deep, thoughtful responses. They seem to be arguing as much as discussing, although doing both without recrimination—something foreign to her that she'll have to get used to in her new family. She couldn't be more grateful to Natasha, whom she's come to deeply love as a second mother. Natasha could have left her to Wolfgang, in the service of the circus, but she put herself at grave risk to save Anna from a brutal fate.

Scanning the horizon behind, Anna prays that Wolfgang and the dragoons aren't following. Natasha said they wanted to be rid of the circus, and Anna truly hopes that's the case. She's wanted happiness for so long, and she can hardly believe she's finally found it in the most unlikely place—with a pig trainer, not a gentleman. Well, in some ways he's more of a gentle man than she could have hoped for.

She looks out to see the early summer fields, a rich ochre about to burst with green, everywhere sprouting new growth. Russia will not be so fertile just yet, but she knows it will be verdant quite soon. Then the wheat fields will go on forever. In any case, it will be home, and they can rest and rebuild.

She giggles to hear Boris's deep, articulate voice booming from the wagon behind, as he lectures Lottie on the magician's craft. Anna leans out to see Lottie nodding thoughtfully, as if putting Boris under one of her psychic spells. She knows Lottie wants to work with Boris to achieve something of mutual benefit, not just to influence him for the sake of her own self-esteem. Like Durov and Natasha, Boris and Lottie have plenty of arguments built into their discussions. But Anna is excited to think how they will work together to advance Boris's act, while Lottie will still have her own fortune-telling sideshow. Just as Anna will be happy to help Anatoly with the little ones, while he helps her develop her high-wire expertise—each providing support to the other without competition or jealousy. It's so different from how she grew up. It will take some getting used to. Anna knows she has a tendency to be a bit petulant, even selfish, but that's because she's had to fight for every inch. If she agrees to remain in her family's trapeze act, she's certain that Durov, Natasha, and Anatoly will ensure that it will be with the understanding that she can have her own high-wire feature. With Anatoly as her husband, and Natasha and Durov as surrogate parents, she settles back into the easy, rhythmic jostling of the wagon, with a deep sense of joyous optimism.

Natasha is grateful that Durov took charge of organizing the animals for the caravan while she worked with Bronzy and the other circus people to salvage what they could and load the wagons. She chuckles, thinking back to how Ivan was stuck midway into the four dwarf brothers' cannon as they paraded him around the field in front of the fortress. The soldiers roared at what they thought was part of the act, and the more hysterically Ivan ranted, the more they guffawed. Even so, she thinks back to the time after Nikolai's death when Ivan was the crafty one, making all those plays for her as he did. *Oy, so handsome…oy, such a duplicitous opportunist.*

Natasha glances over to see Durov's sure command. She admires the grace of his movements despite his bulk—it's as if he's orchestrating the mules into a new act. She likes Durov's assured competence and willingness to help others get their jobs done—versus Ivan's self-centered narcissism. Part of her bemoans not being able to merge the positive traits of both—the competent and loving Durov with the handsome and solicitous Ivan—into some idealized man. But she sees no point in wishing for the impossible. She's firmly ensconced in her new life with Durov—a man with whom she feels entirely comfortable. She's sure he'll respect her, work with her, and not boss her around like Nikolai did and Ivan tried to do.

Still, it's hard for her to let her guard down entirely. But she supposes that's only natural and it'll just take time. She's confident that Wolfgang will accept the signature and file the scroll away. Even if he ever realizes the signature has disappeared, she's certain he won't raise a stink—not only would it be very bad for him personally to have "lost" a signature on an official scroll, but he clearly doesn't want any further international trouble. She looks forward to crossing the mountains, and she eases back, contentedly bracing against the bouncing of the carriage.

As they clatter along the road, despite their seemingly easy banter, Natasha senses that Durov still mourns the loss of Sasha. She thinks it a bit daft to put so much of yourself into an animal, and a pig at that, but she's come to see the little ones more clearly through his eyes. Smart, loyal, clever at figuring things out—even if it means they rummage with their little pink snouts through her personal belongings looking for trinkets to chew on. *At least he's taught them not to slobber.* And she must confess, she's actually happy that the pigs no longer scurry frantically away from her like they once did.

"They're accepting you, Natasha," Durov happily remarked as she helped load them up.

Durov was clearly astonished at how affectionate the pigs were becoming to her and pleased she was meeting them at least halfway. That's fine with her, as long as Durov doesn't try to bring them all into her wagon for high tea—a new tableau he's decided to put into his act. She can't exactly say she's jealous of what Durov had with Sasha, but she recalls how unabashed he was with her. There's a part of her that wishes he'd curl up and play with her as he did with…that's silly…she's only getting to know him. She knows they'll face enough adversity getting home to test them, and hopefully develop their feelings for each other—perhaps maturing them into a deepening love.

Despite the cloudless blue sky and the bright early summer sunlight, it's beginning to get chilly along the road. After they raced back from the prison, they were only able to get away midmorning. And although the sun is still high in the west behind them, it will be dark soon. She knows they must get as deep into the forest as possible before stopping—just in case Wolfgang decides to follow them after all. She'd watched Durov sign and blow on the scroll to dry the ink, fervently praying that the very act of blowing would not accelerate the disappearance of the writing.

Natasha was proud of how Durov negotiated that last bit to secure Anna's freedom before he agreed to sign. They all took Wolfgang's unexpected positive reaction as a signal that he'd be happy to be rid of them—and would therefore overlook the small matter of having Durov's signature vanish. Maybe Wolfgang will even laugh about it—he said he loves the circus. Anyway, they need to make as much time as possible, so Natasha volunteers to take the reins and allow Durov some sleep. He was so exhausted after his night in prison, poor man.

She looks ahead and feels exhilarated to be returning to Mother Russia. Over the fast approaching mountains, the steep ridge before them brightens orange in the refraction of the setting sun. Durov drifts in and out of sleep. *Thank St. Gregory he doesn't snore like Nikolai. But,* Natasha sadly notes, *it's not exactly a peaceful sleep, with his uneasy mutterings.*

⁓◦༺◦⁓

Drifting in and out of sleep, Durov is barely conscious of his head bouncing up and down with the wagon as they proceed into the forest. As he dreams, images of the prison float about his mind. He snorts, as he doesn't much care for the filth. But what he really hates is the lack of light—the terrible thought of living in that dark cell, without all the colors of the circus for two long years, makes him fear for his sanity. He nods his head, dreaming of how proud he is that Anatoly understands why he can't sign, and of how he's even prouder that Natasha got Boris to figure out how he could.

In his sleep, Durov smiles to himself thinking, "Fine woman, that

302

Natasha." Then he snorts again as he recalls how stubborn she is...but he's glad she's so stubborn. She really must care about him to have risked so much. He dreams of leading them all back to Russia, crossing the mountains with their caravan floating effortlessly on clouds. Looking down from his cloud, he sees the dragoons led by Wolfgang, galloping toward them. Just as they are about to overtake them, however, the circus takes flight on the wind. The animals are terrified, but the four dwarfs gleefully circle the clouds with their cannon, lighting the fuse and propelling Ivan into the sunset. As his dream progresses, Durov scrunches down in the wagon, comforting himself as details of his new life form in his subconscious: *With a woman like Natasha, we will rebuild the circus, I don't need to keep to the shadows anymore, like I was living in a prison of my own making, and I deserve the chance to perfect my theories of animal training and to show Russia and the world what can be accomplished with patience and kindness.*

As he starts to lift himself out of his dream and toward his awakening, he formulates in his mind how their circus will attain its true place in society. Although he isn't yet awake enough to articulate it, his vision flashes in front of him: *Our little circus will once again bring together entertainers of every shape and size from every region of Russia and maybe even beyond—something truly democratic in a country struggling mightily under the yoke of the tsars. It isn't just the performers who are so acceptably diverse; we do our best for the serious amusement of our patrons, who are themselves drawn from all walks of life, sitting together under the big tent—well, maybe it's not so big. What a confluence of mutual respect and goodwill we'll have—the proudest of Russian circus traditions!*

He sinks back down into his dreams and imagines how his gentle brother will marry that sweet girl. Although she's very petite, she's strong with determination, and she means so much to Natasha. He chortles to himself in his sleep. *And Ivan...he looked so ridiculous jammed into that cannon. That reminds me, I've got to readjust Max's powder mixture before Pasha and Masha shoot Vasha out again, or there'll only be three dwarf brothers. How those soldiers laughed. Soldiers...oh no...soldiers...dragoons with their sabres....Oh, God. No...run Sasha. Run...run...SASHA!*

———❦———

Natasha nudges Durov to wake him. "Durov, you're talking in your sleep."

As he continues to mutter, Natasha hears squealing, and shakes her head, sure she's hearing things. But no, there is squealing, coming from somewhere.

Natasha's certain she's losing her mind. But then she looks down to the side of the road. A flash of pink. Streams of gold braid trailing in the dirt. No...surely a chicken...or a dog...pink in the setting sun, not pink as in...pig? A ripped German military tunic flutters in the wind. Is that a pig trying to cross the road? Running around the wagon wheels?

Natasha pulls up on the reins, stops the mules, and rubs her eyes in disbelief. Sasha, still wearing the shreds of her Kaiser Wilhelm costume, gleefully squeals and prances back and forth in front of the wagon.

Durov starts and wakes, his eyes blinking wildly. "*Oy*...I was having such a dream. I heard Sasha squealing." He starts to sob. "It was horrible." He looks over at Natasha. "I never should have gone on. It was all my pride and—"

"Durov, stop. Listen to me. That squealing you heard—look down, in front of the wagon."

———❦———

Durov struggles to awaken fully from the kaleidoscope of his dreams. After floating on clouds and enjoying the admiration of the Russian people

304

for his new methods of training animals, he recalls sweating and shaking as he relived the horror of the dragoons destroying the circus and slashing everything around them. He vaguely hears Natasha's voice, but it's a long distance away and under water. He forces his consciousness to breach the surface of the water, and he gulps in a deep breath of sharp mountain air.

As he comes to his senses and breaks through his dream state, he hears Natasha insist that he look down, in front of the wagon. She seems to be saying something, over and over. "Look down, in front of the wagon."

He leans forward, just as the sun catches a shred of bright gold braid still clinging to a large, round, pink body with a corkscrew tail. Durov gasps, "I must be seeing things...is that...by St. Gregory...it is."

His heart leaping, Durov leaps down from the wagon. His bulky frame seems to float over to Sasha. As he reaches her, he slides down into the gravel road to hug her. *Da, da, moya devushka.* She roots her snout into his chin and licks him all over his face, as he laughs and takes her head in his hands. He looks up and shouts to the caravan, "Come, see who's here!"

Anatoly hears the joyous commotion. He gives Anna the reins, jumps down, and races to join Durov. Even Boris clambers down from his wagon to applaud the return of the prodigal pig.

The little circus band gathers around Durov and Sasha, clapping and shouting. "It's a sign. She's alive. What a smart pig. Durov's never been happier. We can all go home now. By St. Gregory, it's a miracle."

Durov sits in the road next to Sasha and grins broadly as he acknowledges their applause. Sasha stops licking Durov's face long enough to snort and bow to the crowd. His eyes twinkling, Durov chortles as he hugs his pig.

THE END

ACKNOWLEDGMENTS

I AM INDEBTED to the late Russian-American Nobel Laureate Wassily Wassilyevich Leontief for personally giving me the idea to look into the life of the Russian circus performer Vladimir Leonidovich Durov. As an act of civil disobedience in Germany in 1907, Durov trained his pig to mimic the war-mongering Kaiser Wilhelm II and was arrested. Professor Leontief was a lover of ballet and theatre. As we were discussing my interest in writing a piece for the theatre dealing with censorship and freedom of expression, he told me of Durov's brand of anti-militaristic satire, described in Joel Schechter's non-fiction book, *Durov's Pig: Clowns, Politics and Theatre.* (Note: Schechter's book contains some hilarious photos of Durov and his pig that can also be found at: http://www.circopedia.org/Vladimir_Durov.) This single incident provided the springboard for me to create my entirely fictional world of circus characters.

Professor Leontief's interest in freedom of expression was long-standing. During his early years in the USSR, he sided with campaigners for academic autonomy and freedom of speech and was detained several times by the Cheka, the precursor to the KGB. In 1925, he was allowed to leave the USSR and he emigrated to the U.S. There he more fully developed his input-output theory of economics, which was used by the Allied forces during World War II to identify ball bearings as the target for bombings designed to most effectively cripple the Nazi war effort. Professor Leontief generously gave his time to those of us interested in perpetuating not only his economic theories, but also his ideals of freedom of expression. I am forever grateful to him.

Others I must thank during my long journey from economist to playwright to novelist include: Cassandra Medley and Chris Ceraso at Ensemble Studio Theatre in NYC who schooled me in dramatic structure and character development; Michael deBlois, Jean Fallow, and Elisabeth Welch who were instrumental in mounting the production of the play some years ago at the Church Street Theatre in Washington D.C.; early readers of the novel who provided important feedback including Andrew Tank, Peter Firestein, Skip and Betsy Lefler, Regis Donovan; and others who lent their expertise and support including John Stanmeyer, Catherine K. Contopoulos, Katie and Michael Newman, Gillien Goll, Karen Carhart, Christa Dowling, Miriam Prieto, Karen O'Donnell, June Kelly, and Palma Fleck.

There never would have been a novel version of this story had it not been for Diane O'Connell, her *Write To Sell Your Book* methods, her editorial acumen, and her writer's retreats at the Kemble Inn in Lenox, Massachusetts. Her unfailingly positive but rigorous approach helped me expand my earlier play, and in brainstorming sessions, she helped work through some plot twists that, I hope, contribute to the overall madcap conclusion of the novel. I also need to thank the production team at Station Square Media, including: cover and interior designer Steven Plummer, copyeditor Linda H. Dolan, proofreader Cristina Schreil, and post-production manager Janet Spencer King.

Finally, I wish to thank my husband, Howard Greenhalgh for painting the fanciful portrait of Sasha the pig in the Kaiser's helmet. Howard endured innumerable hours of character and plotting discussions and read too many drafts to count—all with an abundance of love and support.

ABOUT THE AUTHOR

CAROLYN KAY BRANCATO fuses her extensive research background with her lifelong involvement in theatre to create unique and lifelike characters in compelling historical settings.

She has written two nonfiction investment books, *Getting Listed on Wall Street* and *Institutional Investors and Corporate Governance*, published by Business One Irwin.

Carolyn has been a director, choreographer, and playwright. Her plays have been mounted at such venues as Steppenwolf in Chicago and the John Houseman Theatre in NYC, as well as at the Church Street Theatre in DC. She created the play *Censored* to celebrate the First Amendment – bringing to life banned books, art and other cultural institutions that have been repressed in the United States.

Carolyn lives in the Berkshires with her husband. This is her debut novel.

Made in the USA
Las Vegas, NV
06 June 2022

49864396R00184